more than LIES

they're locked between love and hate

A MORE THAN STANDALONE, BOOK ONE

N. E. HENDERSON

DEDICATION

For Charisse.
Thank you for getting me to the end.

PROLOGUE
SHAWN

"Shane," I call out as I run out my bedroom door, hauling butt down the stairs to find my brother. He is the coolest person I know, and I want to be just like him when I grow up. He's eleven years old, but he always tells people he is six years older than I am. He's not. I'm five, and my birthday falls the month before his does, so he really is only five years older than me.

"Shane!" I shout a little louder as I land on the next to the last step. Steadying myself, I leap to the bottom. "Yesss! I made it," I squeal when I realize I have finally jumped down without landing on my butt. This calls for another jump off the ground as I throw my fist high into the air.

Dang, where's Dad when I need to show off my moves?

Once all my excitement settles down, I remember why I ran down to the living room in the first place. My brother!

Eyeing the room, my brown eyes land on the picture sitting on the end table next to the couch. It displays the face of a pretty woman with blonde hair and dark blue eyes. She looks happy in the photo. Mom says this was her best friend since diapers—or something like that. My mom gets sad when she stares at that picture. I don't know why she keeps it around if it *"hurts her heart,"* as she says it does. I've never met the lady. I don't know why I haven't if she and my mom are such good friends.

I turn my head, looking away from the picture. Shane's not in here, so I head into the kitchen, where I find my mom pulling stuff out of the refrigerator. She's always in the kitchen—at least when she isn't at work being a doctor—or so it seems. I'm not complaining, though, because she makes the yummiest things in here. And by yummy, I mean YUM-MEE.

"Hey, baby," she says with a broad smile, turning around to speak to me. She's wearing her pink apron with lots of flowers over her dress. This has to be a good sign.

"I'm *not* a baby, Mom." I mean, really, I'm five. I'm not a darn baby anymore, but she doesn't seem to get that, even though I tell her every day—a bunch of times a day, in fact. And she claims I have a one-track mind and can't remember what I've been told from day to day. Pretty sure it's the other way around, lady. Not that I'm going to tell her that. No freakin' way! I'd get the back of my head smacked in a heartbeat, and that stuff is not fun. Not that it hurts, because it doesn't, but it's embarrassing as heck, and she always does it in front of my friends or my brother and his friends.

"Sweetheart, you will always be my baby for forever and ever. You know that, right?" Her voice is like an angel. When she's baking, Mom is usually singing and going on and on about how this is her only time to relax and enjoy peace and quiet. *Whatever that means.* My mom is a confusing person for sure, but then, so is my grandma. I'm so glad I'm a boy.

"Where's my brother?" I ask, purposely ignoring her question. I will not be a baby forever. I'm a big boy who does big boy things, just like Shane. I peer up at her and wait. She's smiling as she closes the fridge.

There's a ton of stuff laid out on our countertop, so I know she's about to bake something that I'm going to love. The *"baby"* calling will be forgiven. I so love this lady because she knows the way to my heart. Through chocolate!

"Out back. I think Shane's . . ." I stop listening once she's told me what I want to know.

I bolt for the sliding glass door that leads to our big backyard. Our backyard rocks! We have a big wooden swing set with two slides and a sandbox underneath. Not to mention a ginormous pool. I'm not allowed near the pool unless Mom or Dad is outside. Plus, there's a gate with a lock, and I'm not tall enough to climb over it yet.

Swimming is my favorite thing to do. Too bad summer is not year-round. I'd be in that sucker right now if it were. I mean, why do we need winter? Cold weather stinks. It's freakin' cold. Well, maybe winter's okay for that one day a year when Santa visits but other than that, it should be summer all the time.

Walking down the steps leading into the yard, I see my brother walking out of the gate toward the front yard. I pick up my pace and follow him.

"Shane, wait for me!" I call out.

He stops and turns to look in my direction as I run toward him. I see another boy walking up behind my brother. I've only seen him one other time. Shane told me his name is Trent, and he moved in a few blocks from our house not too long ago.

"Whaaat do you wannnt?" my brother drags out as he crosses his arms across his chest. "I'm busy, Shawn." He's been giving me this same speech for a month now, and it's as annoying as the first time I heard it. He's been busy ever since he met that Trent kid. Now, my brother never has time to build Legos or play with me in the backyard. He used to love swinging on the giant tire swing with me while Dad pushed us or jumping on our trampoline like monkeys.

He's always gone with the new kid or closed inside his bedroom playing the guitar he got for Christmas. And I don't like either.

"I want to show you what I drew. It's so coo—"

"I'll check it out later. I'm going to hang out with Trent." He turns away from me.

"Hey, so what do you want to do today?" Shane asks Trent, ignoring me.

I don't hear Trent's response to my brother because something small and purple catches my attention. It's standing behind Shane's new friend. The purple thing is moving. The deep, dark color reminds me of Donatello from the Teenage Mutant Ninja Turtles. Donny is no Raphael, but he's still a Ninja Turtle, so he's cool in my book.

When the purple thing slides from behind Trent, I see it's a girl. She stares back at me and smiles like she's shy or something. The thought occurs to me that she's a very pretty girl.

Whoa, dude . . . stop right there. Wrong! Girls are not pretty. They're girls, and that purple I saw was her dress—a gross, yucky dress. Again, thank you, Jesus, that I'm a boy.

I walk closer, standing next to my brother so I can get a better look at this non-pretty girl. She has long, wavy blonde hair that comes down to the middle of her back, and her eyes are really dark. At first glance I think they're black, my favorite color, but after looking a little harder I see they are the darkest shade of blue I've ever seen. Her eyes kind of remind me of the sky when it's really dark outside. They're big, round, dark blue globes staring back at me.

So *not* pretty.

"She can stay here with Shawn."

I pause my train of thought about non-pretty girls and glance up to my brother's face. Who can stay with me? Her? I wonder if she likes to play Legos. Do girls like Legos? Hmmm . . . I never thought about that before. I don't have any friends who are girls. Does she want to be my friend? She looks about my age. What do girls do for fun? I draw and do a whole lot of other cool things.

"Nah, dude, Taralynn comes with me. You want me to go down to the creek, my little sister comes too."

"Taral . . ." Uhhh, I don't need this now. Come on, dude, just say it. *Taralynn.* I can say it in my head. Why can't I say it out loud?

"Taral . . ." It still doesn't come out right. She's still smiling at me, though, but then goes back to hiding shyly behind her brother. Stupid "L" sounds. I'll just call her Tara. It's safer to stick with Tara. No need to look stupid in front of this girl or my brother, for that matter.

"Can I come too?" I ask, with a little bit of hope in my voice. If Tara's going, I should be able to go too, right? My brother looks down at me, and I can already tell before he speaks that he's going to say no. I used to be his best friend. Now it seems he never wants me around, and I don't know why.

"Stay here. I won't be gone long." And with that he leaves me standing alone in the yard. When Tara doesn't follow her big brother, he tugs on her hand to pull her along. I see her smile fall from her face, and soon they are all out of my sight.

What makes her so special?

Why does she get to go, and I don't?

She's just a girl, a stupid girl, in a stupid purple dress.

And my brother ends up being gone all day, not returning until it's time for dinner.

Stupid Tara with a stupid name I can't even say.

CHAPTER ONE
TARALYNN

17 YEARS LATER

"What's one word that best describes you? Don't think about it. Just say the first thing that pops into your head."

Is he for real?

I want to roll my eyes. Instead, I smile and force my eyes to widen as I bring the glass of pinot grigio I'm clutching to my lips, attempting to buy myself more time to answer his annoying question. The cool liquid slides down my throat in a smooth swallow. I hate it. I'm not a wine girl. I'm a beer and tequila girl. This crap sucks, and I'll never acquire a taste for it.

Oh yeah, his question. Hmmm, let me think.

"Honest," I respond, making my voice sound soft and sweet.

Liar!

I don't intend on telling this joke of a date the truth. He would cringe. I am many things, but honest is not one of them. Lies spill out of my mouth quicker and smoother than the truth ever has. Most of the time, I don't realize I've told a fib until it's already been said. I've been lying and keeping secrets since before I learned how to write my name. It's the only way to survive in my family. At least for me, that is.

"What about you?" I ask, turning his question around on him. I don't care what his answer is. I'm bored. I lost interest in him half an hour ago. There goes another lie. I was never interested in him. He should have kept his mouth shut, and then maybe I would have suggested sex in lieu of dinner.

Okay, not really. After all, that would certainly get back to my parents, and the last thing I need them to think is their daughter is a whore. I'm not a whore.

That is not a lie. Though maybe in some people's eyes, I might be considered one. I'm sure if my mother knew I had casual sex every now and again, I would be the worst daughter in the history of all daughters. I would be an actual embarrassment to her instead of the one she runs her mouth about me being.

I'm a twenty-one-year-old college senior; of course I'm going to have a little sex here and there. Sorry, but I don't see that being so much of a big deal—or even a sin. There are plenty of *real* bad people in this world to count as actual sinners: murders, pedophiles —those sickos.

Tonight, unfortunately, I will not be engaging in casual sex. Tonight, I plan on being the good little girl everyone thinks I am. The girl everyone expects me to be. I have a sudden urge to puke. That goody-two-shoes role damn near everyone I know puts me in is exhausting.

Everyone except Jared, and maybe Mase, expects certain things from me. I've become more open and honest with Mason over the last year than I ever have before. I'm not so sure my best friend, Matt, even knows the real me anymore. Our relationship has changed—for the worse, and it bothers the ever living heck out of me.

"Well, I can't say honest. You've already stolen that one. Let me think." He taps his index finger against his lips as I glance up to meet his blue-gray eyes. How long before this is over? "Athletic."

I give him a once-over again. Well, as much as I can. The lower half of his body is blocked by the tabletop. I guess his and my idea of athletic are totally different. I doubt there is much fat on his body—if any—so he's scrawny. I don't do scrawny. I mean, he'd do for a Tuesday night romp in the sack, but that's all it would be. And if I'm honest with myself, which is rare, I'm not into quickies. Quickies suck, and don't get me off.

My idea of athletic is a tall, muscular man with abs so cut they will make you lose count adding how many packs he's sporting. Calf muscles so defined you'll trip over your own feet as you walk behind him. And arms, God, his damn arms are so big, just the thought of those beasts wrapped around you will have you drooling. Tattoos—what woman doesn't like an inked man? Shoot, just thinking about my ideal muscular man has me all hot and bothered. Not to mention wet. Yep, wet, and there is zero I can do about it. Mr. Wannabe Lawyer guy here isn't going to cut it tonight —or any night.

Really, I'm not a whore. I promise.

"Hello," I peer up at a set of fingers snapping rapidly in front of my face.

That is not annoying at all.

"Did I lose you, Tara?"

"It's Taralynn," I say with a bit more bite than I usually do when people decide they have a right to shorten my name. "And I'm sorry," I follow, trying to be as apologetic as I can in my I'm-so-bored-please-stab-me-in-the-head-with-a-dart state of mind.

"What? No one has ever nicknamed you Tara?"

"Sure they have, but my name isn't Tara. It's Taralynn. It's Taralynn on my driver's license. It's Taralynn on my birth certificate. It's Taralynn on my social security card. It—"

"I get it," he rudely interrupts me. "You don't like being called Tara. So, I guess it's my turn to apologize to you. I'm sorry, Taralynn." He says my name in a patronizing way that makes me want to ram the heel of my shoe into his balls. I wonder what mommy dearest would say if I did something like that?

"It's fine." It's not, but whatever. No one calls me Tara. Well, no one except the one person who can't stand me. "It's a common mistake."

That's the problem with having a double first name. People take it upon themselves to shorten it. It's not that I don't like it; in reality, I'd prefer it. I mean, whose bright idea was it to give their children two first names? A stupid person, obviously. In other words, my parents.

"So, I was saying before you spaced out, your mother tells me you're in school at Ole Miss. What are you studying? I graduated from there two years ago."

Of course he did. Did he really think University of Mississippi Alumni Jacob Evans, prestigious lawyer to the rich, would sanction his daughter going on a date with someone who graduated from State or even Southern Miss? Hell no. Effin' snob. Don't even bring up a junior college graduate, and certainly not a man without a degree.

"English." I'm certain I can predict the next thing he'll say to me. You would be surprised how many people hear you're going for a degree in English and automatically assume you want to be a teacher. I am certainly not teacher material. It takes a certain person to do that job. I, for one, do not possess the skill to teach another person.

"A teacher? You plan to teach?" He perks up, his eyes honing in on me.

Told ya!

Schmuck.

"Not at all." I snort out a laugh. "I'm a writer, actually. My mother didn't mention it?"

"No, she did not," he tells me, taken aback. Literally, he leans

back in his chair as if he wasn't expecting this to be my choice of
career. Or attempt at a career. It's more of a dream at the moment.
It doesn't surprise me, what he's confirmed about my mother,
that is. Katherine Evans is the epitome of a southern lady—or
what she thinks a southern lady should be and act like.

"I'm sure it was an oversight." It wasn't. A daughter who's a
wannabe romance novelist doesn't fit into her proper little world.
In fact, it's embarrassing to her. She has been vocal about that
since I was in high school. Sharing my hopes and dreams with my
parents was a big mistake on my part.

"Fiction or non-fiction? I personally love non-fiction. Give me
an autobiography, and I'll be thoroughly entertained for hours."
Loser. Okay, I shouldn't be so judgmental. Just because
autobiographies, biographies, tell-all books, and the like aren't my
cup of tea doesn't mean they are crap. They are just crap to me. I
couldn't care less about some political figure that was in office fifty
years ago. I don't give two craps about the lives of the latest
washed-up celebrity.

"Fiction. I write romantic stories." I lean forward, grabbing the
large wine glass next to the plate of food I polished off twenty
minutes ago, downing the remains. When will our waiter bring the
darn check so we can leave? Please, God, have mercy on me
already.

"Oh." Shocker . . . not. Like everyone, he's thinking smut. Not
that that isn't accurate. It's just not the whole picture. I say
romance book, and people think sex book. Just because there is sex
in a book doesn't make it a sex book. That is just plain rude. It's
romance, people—in as many different shapes and forms as the
human body.

About the same time as Princeton, I mean Preston, is trying to
find something to say, my phone chimes telling me I have an
incoming text message.

I quickly retrieve it from the table, welcoming the distraction.
When I see it's my brother, Trent, my face lights up like Christmas. He

always has that effect on me. Trent is the only person I'm related to that I actually like and get along with. He gets me, always has, even when no one else did. And being the big brother he is, Trent always shows up when I need him the most. Just like now, even if it's via text message.

Trent: Hey you. What's up?

Me: Boredom, clad in a cheap suit from TJ Maxx thinking he's a big shot. You?

Trent: Judgmental for someone whose favorite store is Target.

Me: Touché.

Trent: Mom said you were on a date. Figured I'd see if you needed an excuse to leave. Ky's on her way home and should be heading through Oxford in the next few minutes.

Me: It's practically over; just waiting on the check. Is she stopping or heading straight to Tupelo?

Trent: Tupelo, unless you need her.

Me: I'm ok, just ready to get out of here.

Trent: Still coming down in a few weeks?

Me: Of course, I'm ready to party in Jack-town.

Trent: You seem to think there's shit to do down here. I assure you, there is not.

Me: Whatever . . . it's where you are. That's all that matters.

Trent: Awww . . . my little sister misses me. Shucks, I'm touched.

Me: Shut it, butthead.

Trent: Get home safe. TTYL Sis.

Me: K, love you!!

Trent: Love you more, brat.

That isn't possible.

I place my cell phone back on the black linen tablecloth before looking up to see a set of eyes masking a shade of irritation. When our eyes meet, he casts his to the side, glancing out into the restaurant.

What the fudge is his problem? I am not about to apologize for having a quick conversation with my brother. With Trent in his second year of residency at the medical center in Jackson, I don't get much time with him. I'll take what I can get when I can get it. My brother comes first to me, and I don't see that changing any time soon—not for this bloke anyway. Bloke . . . ha, I love that word. I crack myself up. Why couldn't I have been born British? They have the coolest slang words.

He speaks, bringing me out of my inner thoughts. "I paid the check while you were on the phone."

Yep, that's the source of his sour attitude. He tips his wine glass back, polishing off the rest of his drink. I don't respond. I don't care to. He stands, so I stand too, and we make our exit from the restaurant.

The ride home is quiet, which is more than okay with me. I have zero in common with this guy except for our parents' economic and social status. Okay, maybe I shouldn't go that far. I mean, it's not like I know his parents. Maybe they aren't snobby douchebags, but . . . let's be real. They probably are.

Within ten minutes we arrive at my house. I say *my* house, but in reality, I just live there. For the past three and half years, I've called it mine, but it's Shawn's house. Actually, it's his grandparents', but they retired and moved to Florida close to fifteen years ago. They kept the house because they had hoped their only two grandchildren would attend the University. They almost got their wish. Their eldest, Shane, did, along with my brother. Those two had been friends since childhood and shared the house about six years ago. Shawn, the younger grandchild and current "owner," only attended for the first semester of our freshman year. He decided college wasn't for him, but evidently the house is since he still lives here.

We have two other roommates, Mason and Matt. Matt and I have been best friends since ninth grade. Shawn and Mase . . . well, they've been thicker than thieves since we were little kids. Mason's family moved into our neighborhood about a year after my family did when I was five years old.

"Nice house," Preston comments as he shuts off the engine. I'd have to agree with him. The place is pretty stellar, especially for a group of college kids living here rent-free. It's a four-bedroom, three-bath house, and being the only female, I somehow lucked into getting the master bedroom. I'm still not sure why Shawn let me have it, but I'm not complaining and certainly not going to rock the boat to inquire.

There's a nice size backyard with a pool and an amazing kitchen on the backside of the house. I love to cook. Next to reading, it's one of my favorite things to do. It's relaxing and a great way for me to unwind. In all honesty, it's probably the reason Shawn allowed me to live here. His mom taught me everything I know about cooking. I'm not a jealous person—at least I don't think I am—but when it comes to Shawn and Shane's parents, I'm a little envious. They are nothing short of amazing.

Lucky bastards.

"It is," I finally agree after unbuckling my seat belt. He does the same, and I'm guessing he's expecting me to invite him in. There is a party going on inside, after all. It's a Friday night, and at a little past ten, this place is just getting started. There's always a party happening on the weekends at the house. I'd be rude not to invite him in. Hell, maybe he might find a girl better suited for him than me. There is someone for everyone, or so Mrs. Braden, Shawn's mom, is always telling me. I'm just not convinced that person exists for me. Well, at least not the one I want.

If you can't have the one you want, then what's the point?

"Want to come inside?" I'm surprised to find myself actually not annoyed by this idea. I'm sure this guy isn't as bad as I have imagined. So what if his parents are friends with mine? Does that mean he's self-centered like they are? No, of course not. I'm being unfair to the guy. I should at least give him a chance, right?

But this isn't the first time my mother has swindled me into going out with a guy.

As I'm thinking, he responds, "Sure." I look him over once more before opening the car door and climbing out of his yellow Corvette.

Wonder if he realizes the yellow screams, "Look at me, I'm a douche"? Probably not. I'm guessing that thought never entered his head.

I silently laugh to myself.

Reality is, I'm simply not attracted to him. If I was, I wouldn't be making fun of his car in my head. I doubt the thought of douchery would've even popped up. Fact is, no amount of spending additional time with this guy will change that. Now I'm regretting the invite. Oh, well, too late. As I round the car, he's hanging back, waiting for me to lead the way, so I do just that. The moment he places his palm on the small of my back, my body stiffens. I speed up slightly, trying to give him a hint that I don't like him touching me. To my dismay, he does the same and places his hand back in the same spot.

Take a hint, dude.

As I open the front door, we're greeted with a blast of loud music. A smile graces my face as we walk over the threshold. I love music, especially loud, screaming, obnoxious melodies. I'm a rock-n-roll and metal with a side of country and a dash of Harry Connick Jr. kind of girl. My mood is already tipping up for the better as I step out of the way to allow Preston to enter.

After I close the door, I kick off my purple heels that match my dress, leaving them by the entranceway.

"Remove your shoes," I order. Preston gives me a questioning glance, but complies.

"There are always a ton of people coming and going around here," I explain. "The house belongs to one of my roommate's grandparents. The first time a party was thrown here, the floors had to be redone the following week. Do you know how much it costs to have someone sand and re-polish the floors in a house that's all wood?" I don't give him a chance for a response. "A lot." And it was. That was almost a decade ago when Shane and Trent lived here, but still. I don't even want to imagine what it would cost today.

I lead Preston down the hallway, bypassing the living room to my right, and head straight toward the kitchen. The smell of grease and cheese infiltrates my nose before my eyes land on the array of pizza boxes everywhere.

This is going to be a fun clean-up for me tomorrow. Ugh.

"Want something to drink?" I toss over my shoulder as I enter the kitchen, walking to the junk desk where I plug my iPhone into the charger. As I pivot, heads look our way. Mason has his arm thrown over a petite redhead I've never seen before. It's not unusual. He's got a different bedmate every week. I halfheartedly smile as my man-whore of a roommate gives me a knowing shrug. Matt has his girlfriend, Amanda, tucked in front of him. He nods my way while Amanda scrunches up her nose. It's a failed battle on Matt's part. His girlfriend and I will never be friends, but since he is my BFF, I'll make nice with her even when she's being a catty bitch —which is often.

I turn my attention back to my guest, awaiting his reply. "Drink?" I ask again, with a touch of annoyance at having to repeat myself. His head is slow to turn. I glance around him, noting that he's caught the attention of one of Amanda's friends she brought for the weekend from Mississippi State.

"Yes, please. A glass of white wine would be good." Is it appropriate to roll your eyes in front of your date? Nope, I don't think it is. I go for a sympathetic smile.

"We don't have win—"

"I have Sauvignon Blanc," Amanda interrupts as she presses off Matt's chest. "You want?"

"Absolutely, thank you."

Well, isn't he just so well freakin' mannered.

"Aren't you going to introduce all of us to your new friend, Taralynn?" Amanda pins me with a stare as she pulls the refrigerator door open, grabbing the bottle with one hand and closing it with the other. She successfully plays the nice card when she wants to impress someone.

"Everyone, this is Preston," I reply in an even tone. "Preston, everyone."

Am I being rude? Probably, but it's not like he'll be around after tonight. I did the one-date thing to make my mother happy. There's zero potential for a relationship with him, so I don't feel the need to tell him everyone's name. Heck, I'm not even sure who everyone is. Sure, many of these people are over most weekends, but they aren't exactly my friends. I socialize with them a little, but I don't know them as well as Matt and Mason do. I know the ones that live in our neighborhood or frequent the local pub I work at, but the others? No clue. I'm sure most go to Ole Miss like Matt, Mason, and me, but it's a big campus, and I'm too busy for much of a social life beyond hanging with my roommates.

"Taralynn!" Amanda's voice scolding, and I want to roll my eyes. "That just won't do." She precedes to hand Preston a glass of golden liquid, then starts rattling off the names of everyone hanging in the kitchen. When she's done doing that, she grasps his elbow and hauls him off toward the living room, where I'm sure she's introducing him to more people. It's no surprise when her friend Cassie—another snobby bitch I don't like—tags along.

"Good date?" I swing my head in Matt's direction. His question doesn't require a response. Even without the steely glare I give him, he knows full well I didn't want to go on the stupid date, nor is Preston my type. "That won't go over well with the evil queen, you know."

By evil queen, he's referring to my mother. I coined the name for her after watching Snow White when I was ten because really, that's how I see my mother. She hates me, and nothing I ever do will please her. I'm damned if I do and damned if I don't. And believe me, I've tried. It's taken a lot of years to finally come to this realization. I wish I knew why my own mother dislikes me so much. If I knew what I did, maybe I could fix it.

"I don't care. I went. It's done, and there is no need to do it again."

I pull open the refrigerator, grabbing a Corona for myself. After slamming the door closed, I pop the cap off with a bottle opener and toss it on the counter before taking a swig. Now *this* is what I've needed all night. It's so much better than that wine junk I had to endure at dinner. It needs a lime, but after glancing around the counter and not seeing any lying out, I turn my attention back to my friend.

"Lie to someone else, why dontcha." He's right. As much as I hate it and hate myself for caring, I do. I care way too much what my parents think of me. I know full well I'll never measure up to the daughter they want me to be, but I'm just tired of trying so hard. I see no point anymore. They don't give a crap about what I want or what makes me happy. They never have.

Walking over to stand next to Matt, I bump his hip with mine, confirming he's right, but not verbally acknowledging it. The way his light ash brown hair is sticking up in all different directions makes him look like he just crawled out of bed. It does that when he's in dire need of a trim. He's only three inches taller than me at five feet, eleven inches tall, and he's lean. He looks like an effin' Ken doll without the blond hair.

"So," I tip my beer to my lips before continuing. "Trent wants us to come down in a couple of weeks. Kylie is throwing a Halloween pool party at their house in Jackson. Y'all game?"

"Yeah, but how does that make sense?" Mase chimes in. "Costumes, makeup, and water don't go hand-in-hand."

"I don't think it's so much about the Halloween part. That's just her excuse to throw a pool party. I think she misses this." I gesture around the room, indicating the house that's getting in full swing.

Kylie, my brother's girlfriend and the love of his life, is a social butterfly. She loves people. All people. She will strike up a conversation with anyone, and by the time she's done with you she knows everything about you, your family, and your friends. I love her, but we are complete opposites.

"So we don't have to dress up, then?" Matt asks, sounding relieved. He isn't into Halloween. He won't admit it to anyone, but I know it freaks him out. He can't watch the movie *IT*. Clowns are the devil in his mind. That thought makes me snicker, causing him to bump my hip—but unlike my friendly bump, this had a punch behind it. He knows I know, but neither of us verbalizes it.

"Don't think so."

I take another sip as I see Amanda and Preston re-entering the kitchen with Cassie trotting behind. Amanda sees the lack of distance between her boyfriend and me and directs a nasty scowl my way. I down the remains of my beer, and then I walk over to stand against the countertop where all the liquor is lined up next to the refrigerator. If I'm going to deal with her crap tonight and have Preston here too, I need something stronger. I pour a shot of tequila and down it. Most people do tequila with salt and lime, but not me. I like the awful burn it leaves, and without the lime it lingers longer. Yes, I'm an odd one.

I turn around, catching sight of Shawn, my third roommate, as he enters the kitchen. It's unusual for him to be home this early on a Friday night. He's usually stumbling in after the house winds down and when he's three sheets to the wind. He surveys the room, eyeing me, and then gives Preston a once-over. In that short span of time, he's already sized up my date and doesn't like him. It's no surprise. On the rare times I do go on a date, Shawn has always found something wrong with them. He's not shy about voicing his comments either. I don't know what his problem is. He bangs every Barbie doll that shows him her thong.

He heads my way, so I turn away from him and around, facing the bottle of tequila and shot glass as Shawn pulls the refrigerator door open. If I had to guess, he's retrieving a Corona of his own. I fill the glass again and quickly down the shot. If he's going to be in my presence for the night, I need all the mellowing I can muster. Shawn makes me nervous. He always has. He probably always will. And the bastard freakin' knows it.

When I turn back around, I see I was right. Shawn is tilting a Corona back and takes a long drink as he looks at me.

I look away, because, well, I have to. It's hard to look at him and not ogle. Shawn's six-foot-two stature towers just above my five-feet-eight-inches. I'm not tiny by any means, but neither is Shawn. Where I'm a little fluffy, he's cut. I've seen Shawn plenty of times in next to nothing. His thighs are massive and drool worthy. The entire length of his left arm and most of his muscular back are embellished with tattoos. At the moment, he's clad in a black T-shirt with the logo of the tattoo studio he works at, Southern Ink, displayed on the front, and loose-fitting blue jeans that don't look that loose on him.

I might be attempting not to ogle, but every female in this room, except the redhead attached to Mason's hip, isn't making the same attempts. I roll my eyes. Shawn gets this type of attention often—too often.

"Who are you?" Shawn demands, looking at Preston and eyeing him from head to toe. Shawn's not much of a social person; well, he is, to a degree. He was always one of the popular kids in high school, but he doesn't seek people out or shoot the shit. He does, however, make a point to know everyone who enters the house. Shawn is in charge of making sure it stays intact and that no one gets hurt while they are here. Ultimately, what he says goes. He'll kick someone out without a thought if he thinks they're being stupid or might be untrustworthy.

"Oh, that's Preston," Amanda pipes up even though she wasn't the one being spoken to. "He's Taralynn's date." The bitch sounds smug, and I have no idea why. When is Matt going to wake up and see the hideous behind the facade? Probably never. Why? Because men think with their cocks, and Matt is no different. He's been dating Amanda since high school. I didn't get it then, and I don't get it now.

Shawn comes to perch against the section of the counter I'm leaning against. His hip presses against mine. He wraps his inked-covered arm around my shoulders, pulling me into his side. I have no choice but to wrap my arm around his lower back while the palm on my other hand rests over the material covering his abdomen to steady myself. I'm not foreign to Shawn's body. I've known him practically my whole life. There have been plenty of times that I've touched him or he's touched me. All innocent, of course. He's the only person who knows where to tickle me and loves to remind me of that fact as often as possible. But this touch . . . has great potential to be anything but innocent.

I glance up to meet his stare, finding Shawn's eyebrows turned inward. His creamy brown eyes have golden flecks sparkling throughout the shade tonight. That only happens when he gets pissed off. So what's his deal now? I've often wondered and even fantasized if that same intensity increases when he's turned on too.

"Date, huh?" His tone bites into me. I can only nod my confirmation. Being pressed against him this way is as much torture for my body as it is for my brain. Shawn makes me feel and want things no other man ever has. It's not like I want to feel this way about him. Especially since I'll never end up in his bed. He's made that clear multiple times. Always when I'm drunk, when I have the courage to tell him I want him. Every time, he rejects me. He shuts me down. You would think I'd stop trying by now. No matter how big of an A-hole he is to me, I continue to be drawn to him.

Let me tell you. It sucks big donkey balls.

He looks back in Preston's direction, eyeing him as if contemplating what to say. I'm not sure why. I don't believe for a second that Shawn gives two craps who I go out with. The only thing I figure is maybe he doesn't like the vibe Preston is giving off and wants him out of his grandparents' house.

His eyes turn to me, his lips forming a snarl as he leans down to my ear. "You planning on taking Princeton over there upstairs for some boring-ass missionary tonight, Tara? I mean, as a writer of romance and someone who reads trashy books, can't you show the guy a better time than that?"

It takes me a few seconds for what spilled out of his mouth to register. The heat rises in my face instantly, but my brain can't fathom it. He didn't just say that to me! But he did. I shouldn't be surprised, but I am, because Shawn rarely makes his nasty comments where others can hear them. They've always been for my ears only. Apparently not tonight, though. Without looking around, I can tell from the sharp gasps and Amanda's snickering that everyone heard what he said.

"No, I didn't think so," Shawn mutters with a smirk.

I can't stomach their looks, so I bolt from the kitchen. I don't care that I'm being rude to Preston and leaving him to fend for himself. I didn't like the guy anyway. It's not like I wanted a second date. I didn't even want to go on this one. He can tell my mother whatever he wants.

Shawn is an effin' jerk and a half.

CHAPTER TWO

SHAWN

As my bare feet stomp down each wooden step, the pounding inside my skull intensifies. Why did I take those shots at the bar, followed by whatever it was I poured down my throat when I got home last night? I knew I had to be up at the ass crack of dawn. I don't think I've seen daylight this early in the morning since I was in high school. I hated it then too.

I round the bottom of the staircase and then head toward the kitchen. Pausing, I do a double take as I notice bodies sprawled out on every surface of the living room. Shaking my head from side to side, I attempt to wake up a little more, but I only end up intensifying the throbbing pain in my head.

What in the hell?

Entering the kitchen, I take in the dirty dishes, pizza boxes, empty beer bottles, and spilled booze everywhere. Never in my life have I seen a bigger mess. Granted, I'm never up this early, and by the time I do rise, everything is spick-and-span the way it should be, thanks to my clean freak roommate.

I'm not oblivious to everything Tara does around here. My other roommates and I are spoiled by Tara's efforts, and I like it that way. She cleans and cooks—and does both well. So I'm a bit taken aback by the current disastrous state of my kitchen. This is not like Taralynn Evans at all.

"Mornin'," I mumble in Mason's direction as I head to the coffee pot. He's sitting off to my right at the small circular dining table, reading a car magazine and sipping a cup of joe.

After opening the cabinet directly above the Keurig and not finding one damn coffee mug, I peer into the sink and then every granite surface surrounding the area. How on earth is every dish in the house dirty, and where the hell is Tara? I close the cabinet door and pull open the dishwasher. Damn. It's empty. I have no choice; I have to wash my own cup if I plan on drinking something.

I shouldn't be irritated, but I am. I don't recall ever washing a dish in my life. And the smell in this place is making my weak stomach roll as I quickly wash a mug. If it weren't for the faint aroma of Folgers lingering from Mason's brew masking some of the God-awful smell, I probably would have hurled the moment I walked in.

"Since when do you get up before ten?" Mason asks. Once I place the K-Cup in the machine and then press the start button to make myself a much-needed cup of coffee, I glance over in his direction.

"Since I have to make up for the two days I was out sick last week." The stomach bug my three roommates and I came down with a week ago was no joke. Put my ass in bed for two solid days. Not that I can complain too much. It got my mom to come cook us dinner once the four of us could stomach food again. And I tell you this, there is nothin' like Momma's cookin'. Well, that's not exactly true. Tara comes in at a close second, but she isn't my mom. I may be a momma's boy, but you'll never get me to verbalize that shit. No way. No how. Not happening.

"Couldn't you just reschedule your appointments for another day?" Mason is my best friend. Has been since he, his parents, and two older sisters moved to my old neighborhood back in Tupelo when I was six years old. We have been partners in crime since the first day we met. He's the fun one. Laid back and doesn't take anything too serious. He's currently in his last year of college and still doesn't have a job because his parents pay for everything he's ever wanted. I'm not jealous. I simply wasn't raised that way. I dropped out of college after one semester and started working full-time here in Oxford.

I'm a tattoo artist.

Throughout high school, I apprenticed under a guy in my hometown. I've always loved art, and it's probably the only thing I've ever been any good at. College wasn't for me. I already knew that back in high school, but my mom begged me to give it a try. I can't tell that woman no, so I gave it a shot. Like I said, it wasn't for me. Looking back, I realize I probably should have stuck it through since I'm considering buying the shop where I work.

"Sure, I could've moved them to a different slot. And most I did because they're regular customers that don't have any problem waiting for me. A few people were impatient, so I decided to go in a few hours early today, all next week and next Saturday too." I take my freshly made coffee from the machine to add a tablespoon of sugar before taking my first sip. Hopefully the caffeine will fight off my headache before I need to get to work. I'm opening the studio in an hour, but I still need a shower before I leave. "Besides, I also had to take off the Saturday after Halloween because of your sister's stupid party."

"If it's so stupid, why are you going?" He tosses the magazine he had been reading across the table. Even the small surface of the kitchen table is littered with mess. Not that Mason cares. He doesn't clean up around here, either.

"Because I need to get out of this town. I'd rather be going to Georgia, but Jackson will have to do." Thanksgiving can't come soon enough. I'm itching to get on my four-wheeler and do some riding. Some people like to vacation at the beach, others love the mountains or even a touristy town. My crew and I like to get dirty.

"We'll be there soon enough, man. Hell, we spent damn near

a week there during the Labor Day holiday last month." True, but I'd ride every weekend if I could. It's a hobby I'll never tire of. If I didn't love my job so much, I'd probably be jealous of Brian Fisher from Fisher's ATV World. That man has one cool ass job.

I finish the remains of my coffee, then start another round. It seems to be helping my head, so why stop? After another cup brews, I turn back around and brace my back against the only non-disgusting counter surface I can locate. I change the subject. "So where's Tara? It's not like her to let this type of disaster go on." Yeah, disaster is the right word for the disarray that is my house right now.

He doesn't answer my question, but a scowl streaks across his face for a moment before he huffs out a breath. "Don't you think you were a little rough on her last night?"

What is he talking about it? What have I done this time?

I think about it for a minute, recalling anything I did or might have said to Miss Sensitive when I got home last night. "You're going to need to elaborate. I didn't do or say anything unusual to her that I can think of." Sure, I was messing with her about the joke of a man she went on a date with, but that's what I do. I give Tara a hard time. I always have, and I probably always will. Besides, that douche isn't worth her time. I'm not stupid; I know the date was a setup and made mandatory by Tara's mother. Tara does everything to make that bitch happy yet never succeeds. I don't understand why she still tries.

"Dude, come on. You embarrassed the hell out of her." Mason lifts the lid of a pizza box that's piled on top of more pizza boxes on the table. Taking a piece out, he shoves the hearty slice into his mouth. That is disgusting. Not leftover pizza, but pizza that's been sitting out for at least twelve hours.

"Man, I barely remember driving my drunk ass home last night." Usually I'm not that dumb, but last night I wasn't thinking with a clear head. I had to get out of the bar before I made the mistake of fucking the one chick I'll never touch with a ten-foot pole ever again.

"Bro, you waltzed in here,"—Mason gestures around the kitchen with his hands—"sized up her date, and proceeded to ask Taralynn if she and 'Princeton' planned on going upstairs for some good ole boring-ass missionary. And that's an exact quote. I don't even think the guy's name is Princeton." I cringe momentarily, wondering how Mason knows I said that to her. Yeah, I remember saying it, but I whispered it in her ear. Tara tells Mason a lot, so maybe she told him later on, but then I remember she stalked off to her bedroom, leaving her date to fend for himself. That was not very Tara-like.

"What, did she come crying to you about it?" Tara and I aren't exactly friends, but we aren't enemies either. Our brothers, Shane and Trent, are best friends, so Tara's been a part of my life for a long time. We went to the same school and graduated together. In all honesty, Tara is the only reason I graduated at all. It's weird, really. She was always a part of my little group in some way. Maybe because Matt—my other roommate and Tara's best friend—is good friends with Mason. And I'm pretty sure my parents love Tara more than her own folks do. I lucked out in the parent category, whereas Tara did not.

"That would be a negative. I heard the question loud and clear. Pretty sure people in the other room heard you over the music. You're a dick, dude."

Shit. I'm going to have to make that up to her if I plan on eating decent food tomorrow night. Like I mentioned, Tara is a damn good cook. She cooks two big meals a week, and the leftovers sustain us for the rest of the week.

"Dude, I was fucking with her. I didn't mean it." Mason doesn't reply as the sound of the front door slamming shut catches our attention. Seconds later, a disheveled Tara walks in. My eyes immediately take in the same purple dress she was wearing last night. Her blonde hair, which normally reminds me of honeysuckles in the spring, is a mess. Taralynn Evans doesn't do messy.

I turn away from her to grab my coffee and shove a spoonful of sugar in it. I know she didn't leave with the douche-prick she brought home last night. I seem to remember he left with one of Amanda's friends about an hour after Tara went to bed. At least I thought she went to bed. So where on earth did she go? I take a deep breath, pulling oxygen into my lungs, and then force my irritation out along with the air.

Why am I even bothered by the thought of her sleeping elsewhere?

I turn back around only to have my fresh cup of coffee removed from my hand. "I need this more than you." Tara glares at me as she and my coffee walk off toward the fridge.

She pours creamer into the mug while I stand there stunned. Mason laughs.

"Piss off, Mase." Tara turns her glare away from me as she takes a sip of coffee and leans against the granite island countertop. "Ouch," she draws up, removing her ass from where it was touching. Mason laughs harder. I'm eyeing them both, wondering what the joke is.

"What's wrong with your ass, Taralynn?" His question is laced with the amusement only Mason Morgan finds at other people's physical pain. I won't lie, though, I'm also interested in her answer.

"Leave me alone, Mason. I'm going to bed. I'm tired."

Tara starts to walk off, but before she exits, Mason chimes in again. "Stop. I have a serious question." She turns around. "Really." He's smiling, which tells me he's not serious. Mason is never serious. He's messing with her too, yet I'm the only one that ever gets faulted for it. Her eyebrows push up. She's waiting for him to continue. "Does Jared use his hand or a belt when he spanks that ass?"

What. The. Fuck.

I cut my eyes to Mason and then back to Tara. She huffs out air through her mouth, then walks out without a reply.

I did not hear that correctly. There is no way in hell Tara is dating Jared.

"My bet is on his hand. Jared's always been a hands-on type of guy. Wouldn't you agree, Shawn?" My head rolls back over in his direction. He's smirking, and I want to punch him in the mouth.

"Are you telling me Tara is seeing that piece of goddamn shit?"

"I wouldn't say 'seeing,' but I guess it all depends on how you define that term. Hooking up on occasion? Yes. Dating? Certainly not. After all, Taralynn is, and has always been, hopelessly in love with your stupid ass." That last sentence came out flat, his carefree and playful tone gone.

So that scene was for my benefit. Yes, I'm fully aware of the way Tara feels about me. I'm not blind, nor have I ever been. Tara wears her feelings and heart out in the open for everyone to see. Does that mean I'm going to let her make the mistake of sleeping with me? No. I'm a selfish bastard, sure, but I'm not heartless. The sweetness that is the essence of Taralynn Evans couldn't handle me.

Without acknowledging Mason as he chants, "Spank that ass . . . spank that ass . . . ." I leave, stalking off upstairs to take a scalding hot shower. There's a pair of long tan legs that I need to forget about seeing this morning because the same pair nearly killed me last night. And the only way to forget is to replace it with another image.

Every dress she owns should be burned.

Today was brutal.

The longest day of my life!

I'm never missing another day of work. I don't care if I have the mother lovin' flu. I barely had a chance to scarf down a bite to eat the entire day. One of my appointments ran much longer than I anticipated, pushing every other appointment that followed back two hours. Had my mind been clear and focused, I would have realized before I started working on the chick that she didn't possess the endurance needed for the tattoo process.

I have one rule. If I think the person is unsure, can't handle the process, or isn't ready, then I will not tattoo them. I don't care if they've waited seven weeks just to have me do a piece on their body. I won't be someone's regret, ever. A tattoo is a commitment for life. You need to be damn sure it's something you plan on sporting when you're ninety.

The girl from earlier today, my two o'clock appointment, not only wasn't ready, but her pain tolerance was lower than low. I've inked a ton of pansies before, but today took the cake. Had my mind not been clouded with a certain blonde that's been a thorn in my side since I was five years old, then I would have realized this before I was 10 percent into the outline. The start of a good tattoo is much worse than a finished, colossally fucked up one. I had no choice but to make the girl continue on. Pretty sure she hates me more than the devil himself after today.

So here I am, walking into Level at a quarter to eleven on a Saturday night to drown out the visions of what I'll never have. The same ones I've tried for years to rid myself of but never succeeded. I could kick Mason's ass for putting images of Tara and Jared in my head. What the hell is wrong with her? Him? For fuck's sake. Doesn't she remember how mean he was to her in high school?

No, of course she doesn't. Why? Because he talked shit behind her back, and I dealt with him without Tara's knowledge of anything.

Senior year, he told all his friends—I was one of his friends back then—he slept with Tara. I knew it wasn't true the moment the lie left his lips. I could always tell when the dick-face was lying.

But that didn't stop me from losing my shit and getting in a fight with him.

Our friendship came to an end that day.

He's a douchebag, and she deserves better. I'm not saying I deserve her, because I don't. She deserves better than me as well. The only thing I've ever—or will ever—offer a woman is a quick and meaningless screw. I'm fine with that fact, and it works for me.

I walk up to the bar. There are no available seats, but I'm still able to catch the attention of one of the bartenders. I yell over the crowd and live band, telling the guy I'd like a Corona. While I'm waiting on my beer to arrive, a brunette sitting on the stool in front of me turns and flashes her pearly whites up at me. She's attractive. The woman is dressed like a slut, but definitely not bad to look at. Most importantly, she's the opposite of the conservative little twat I'm trying to remove from my head.

Yes, she'll do all right.

"Hello, darlin'." I flash my own seductive smile down at her. It hooks women on the line every time. Not that I need to. I know I'm quite nice to look at. I take good care of my body. Sure, I drink a lot, but I also work my ass off in the gym five days a week to keep in top shape. I have ink covering my left shoulder all the way down to my wrist. On my inner forearm is an image of a beautiful woman. The art is done in all black, except for her dress, which is a deep purple. The masterpiece covering the majority of my back is a work in progress that will be completed within a few months. I guess I would describe it along the lines of a Jackson Pollock painting. The design is my own and not near as busy as one of his paintings. Each line is made to look like someone took a paintbrush and started slinging colors in all different directions on the surface of my back. Currently the only colors I have completed are black and red, but I plan on having my buddy and boss, Adam Manning, finish the design with a dark blue and a little purple.

"I'm Misty Lawrence." Damn, even her voice is the opposite. Tara breathes out a melody of sweet musical sounds every time she opens her pretty little mouth. This bitch sounds like she's speaking through her nose. With enough alcohol, though, I'll be able to drown out that sound.

"Well, Misty, it's a pleasure to meet you." I reach past her, sliding against her arm as I reach for my beer. I don't take my eyes away from hers as I lift the bottle to my lips, tip it back, and swallow.

"Don't I get a name?" She cocks her head to the side and lifts an eyebrow.

"Shawn." It's a simple reply and all she needs to know. I glance down to her right hand, noticing the stamp indicating she's at least twenty-one. This is an eighteen-and-up club, and although eighteen is technically legal, I don't sleep with teenagers. The hand stamp means she's fair game.

"Sexy name on a sexy guy." Her dark brown eyes glide slowly down my torso before rising and meeting mine again. This is too easy. I could take her to one of the bathrooms and be done with her within minutes and onto the next chick, but before I can make the suggestion, a body bumps into me from behind, followed by a strong arm wrapping around my shoulders.

"Hey, bro, who is this sweet little thing?" I roll my head to see Mason making the same suggestive eye motions Misty was throwing me a few moments ago. When I look back in her direction, the corners of her lips have lifted high. She likes the attention. And hell, it's been a good long while since Mason and I have tag-teamed a girl. This could be fun. More fun than the five-minute fuck I had planned on giving her.

"Misty, this is Mason." Now, where to take this party? The bathroom is still an option. My house is not. I don't fuck in my bed. It's for me and me alone. Bitches don't make it that far.

"You, sweet thing, are real cute." He scoots closer toward her. "Why don't you let me in on the fun too?" Good, he and I are on the same page. We usually are. Mason doesn't care for anything long-term either. Unlike me, though, he doesn't mind a bedmate from time to time, as long as they remember up front that it's only for one night.

Mason leans in closer to her ear and whispers something out of earshot.

"I'm down," she singsongs.

"Hey!" The sound of Tara's voice draws my attention away from the brunette to her. "Where's my beer?" I glance over at her, glaring at Mason with her arm crossed tightly in front of her chest. Her chest that is very much on display and very much un-Tara-like. Had I not clearly heard her voice, I might have done a double take.

"Sorry, I got a little sidetracked." Mason laughs and smiles back at Misty. Tara glances at her, then rolls her eyes, seeing exactly what distracted him. When I take in her appearance from head to toe, I see no reason she should be giving Misty an eye roll when she herself is under-dressed. Tara's honeysuckle blonde waves are hanging loosely below her shoulders. She's wearing a strapless, extremely short black dress that is snug around every curve. And in those black heels, Tara is standing damn near my own six-foot, two-inch height.

Fuck, I'm pretty sure I'm getting hard just from looking at her. If there was any blood left in my head, I'd have adjusted my crotch by now.

"You suck, Mason," she huffs and brushes past him to the bar. The bartender hurries over, ogling her tits while asking her what he can get her to drink. She blushes once she realizes his focus is on her ample cleavage rather than her face. She may be dressed that way, but Tara is anything but confident. She has been socially awkward since we were kids and is extremely shy. It takes her a while to warm up to people. Once she does, though, her timid personality vanishes.

"So are we doing this, or not?" Mason's voice booms over the noise.

"Oh, we're doing this. See ya, Tara." I place my empty beer bottle on top of the bar and grabbed the brunette by her wrist, pulling her off her stool and out of the bar without looking behind me. It's going to be damn near impossible to drown out the sight of Tara's body in that dress. Doesn't mean I'm not going to try. "Where's your place, Misty?"

"How about we go to yours?"

"How about we not." Before I can finish telling her why we are going to her place and not ours, Mason chimes in.

"Sweet thing, tonight is about having a fun time, but that's all it is, and it'll only happen once. Are you okay with that?" Mason stops her, making her turn to face him as he waits for an answer.

"I can handle that."

"Good. Now, like my friend asked, where's your place?" He drapes his arm across her shoulders, pulling her closer to him as she relays her address to me, which isn't far from here at all. We all pile into my truck and head to her apartment. After a five-minute drive, we arrive and enter a small one-bedroom apartment, from what I can tell upon my first glance around the living room.

Small hands come up around me from behind before Misty comes around to my front. She moves her hands up to my shoulders and then goes to stand onto her tiptoes to lean in for a kiss on my lips. That's not going to happen. I grasp the brown hair at her nape, halting Misty an inch before she reaches my mouth. "I got something you can kiss, but it's not my mouth, darlin'."

Mason pulls her into him and away from me. "Yeah, well, I got lips that need to meet hers before her mouth lands on your dick, brother." He falls down onto her couch, bringing her with him, where he immediately seeks out her lips. This is where Mason and I differ. He loves foreplay, and lots of it. I only want the end result. The faster I get there, the better it is for me.

"Where's your alcohol?" I ask as I head toward what looks to be a small kitchen. When I enter the small space, it is in fact tiny. The room is a galley layout you would find in your typical apartment.

"Liquor is in the . . . oh, God," she gasps loudly. "Cabinet above the stove. Beer—oh yes, ahhh . . . just like that." Another gasp follows as I open the refrigerator door and locate a Michelob Ultra. Not my usual, but it'll do. ". . . in the fridge." I'm already guzzling the cold liquid when she finally gets the words out. Mason can have his playtime while I sit back and wait. Foreplay is for romantics. I'm only interested in blowing my load.

I finish the beer and then grab another and an extra for Mason. "Hey, Misty, what would you like to drink?" I can be nice and bring her something too.

"Wine, please." Her tone is breathy. Mason seems to be working her over nicely. If I had to guess, I would bet his fingers are knuckle-deep inside her pussy right at this moment. I set our beers down on the counter and search for a wine glass. Once I've found one, I grab the bottle of white wine I saw in the refrigerator and pour her a generous amount. No need to keep refilling. Might as well use the whole glass. Once I'm done, I grab our drinks and head back into the living room.

Sure enough, when I round the couch, Mason has her on top of him, dress pulled down. Her modest tits are exposed, and the hem of her dress is bunched at her waist. Her panties are on the floor, and Mason is pumping two fingers in and out of her. "You like that, don't you, girl?" Mason's voice has taken on a deeper tone.

I pass Mason his beer. He grasps it with his free hand, pulling it to his mouth and tipping the glass bottle back, downing the contents without losing his pace inside Misty. My right hand goes up to her head, where I rest it on the back of her scalp for a moment as I take a sip of my beer.

Watching the scene in front of me, my dick begins to thicken. Yes, I get turned on watching other people fuck. It's hot; I'm not going to lie. Even though my friend is only fucking this chick with his fingers, it's still turning me the hell on.

I fist my fingers around the brown locks, tightening my grip until I have a snug hold on her. I tug, pulling her head back little by little as I bend forward, lowering my body and bringing my mouth to her jawline. My mouth parts, and I run my lips up the length of her neck and across to her earlobe, taking it between my teeth, biting down briefly before pulling myself away from her.

"Oh, God, that feels . . . ohhh God . . . good."

Mason continues his assault on her pussy with his fingers. The slippery sound tells me she's dripping wet. And that brings a smile to my face, but not for the reason you're guessing. My reasons are purely selfish and simple, really. No man wants to fuck a dry snatch.

Mason raises his back off the couch, lifting up to take a tit into his mouth. We've done this a time or two together, so I take the other into my mouth, sucking lightly.

"I'm going to come." *That's the point, doll.*

Her body tenses, so I adjust my grip on her and suck a little harder.

"Ahhhh, ohhh my God . . . yes. Yes!"

When her cries die out, our mouths pop off her nipples at the same time. I right my body upward. Misty now has her palms planted on Mason's chest, and she's trying to catch her breath—or that's what it looks like she's doing.

Mason is lying back against the arm of the couch again, drinking his beer.

"Darlin'," I whisper next to her ear. "I'm ready to get this show on the road. And tonight, I plan on fucking your ass while my friend partakes in your dirty little cunt."

"Oh, yes, please." A smile spreads across her face, and her eyes light up like a Christmas tree.

"Have you ever been fucked in the ass?" Not that I care, because there is a first time for everything, but I like to know what I'm dealing with.

"Yes." Good. I don't particularly care to walk someone through the process of how to get my dick inside.

"And do you like getting taken there?"

"Yes."

"Then point me in the direction to find your lube."

"Bedroom," she huffs out. "Down the hall." Her arm lifts away from Mason, pointing straight in front of her. "Bed side table drawer."

"Darlin'," I purr out as I walk off.

"Yes?" she asks on a yelp, and I know Mason has begun playing with her clit.

"Don't come again while I'm gone. If I return and my buddy tells me you did, I'll end this party before it starts. You feel me?"

"Uh-huh."

Good little bitch.

As I make my way into her bedroom, I pop the button on my blue jeans and slide the zipper down. The restriction is getting painful. Turning my head I scan her bedroom, spotting the only bedside table in the room.

Opening the drawer, I see more fun things than just a plastic container of KY. This girl has a kinky streak. There are furry handcuffs, what looks to be a cheap flogger that'll tear apart after one use by anyone that knows what they're doing, and several short strips of silky material, which I'm sure are supposed to be used as restraints. I mumble a small laugh as I take one piece of material out of the drawer, stuffing it in my back pocket before swiping the lube and closing the drawer.

Making my way back down the hall, I see her straining to hold back. She's biting down on her bottom lip like it's going to save her from drowning.

As I enter the living room, I retrieve my wallet from my back pocket to remove a condom. Once I have it out, I stuff my wallet back in its place and tear open the wrapper. Tossing the foil pack to the ground, I push my jeans down and roll the latex over my junk. When I reach my playmates, I grasp Misty's hair in my hand once again. You could say I have a thing for pulling a woman's hair. I like the control I feel when I do it.

"You ready for this?" Mason already has his pants kicked off at the other end of the couch with a condom covering his own junk positioned under her pussy, ready for me to give the word.

"Fuck, yes." And with that, my fist tightens while I place my palm on her bare shoulder. Without warning, I shove her down onto Mason's dick. "Oh, my fucking God," she says on a scream. I smile as Mason grits his teeth. He was expecting it, but it's always the same reaction with him.

"Lean forward, darlin'," I demand as I lightly push her head to lean her closer to Mason.

After shucking my pants and kicking them off, I position one leg onto the couch next to Mason's leg, settling in directly behind Misty. Grabbing my dick in my hand, I pour a generous amount of lube on me. After dropping the small plastic bottle to the floor, I position my cock against her tight opening and move my eyes to meet Mason's, telling him I'm ready. He backs a few inches out of Misty without coming completely out.

"Hey, Misty?" I call out to her as I reach into my pocket to retrieve the smooth material, bringing it up next to my head and shaking my hand to show Mason. He grins.

"Yeah," she breathes.

"Cross your hands behind your neck, wrists together."

"Why?" My jaw locks and I punch forward, forcing myself inside about two inches, causing her to yelp. I had intended on being gentle until her intrusive question fell out of her lips.

This is our game, and the bitch needs to understand she is just a participant.

"Because I said so." It's a bark, and I shove inside another inch. Her arms immediately comply, going up and locking together behind her neck. With my palm, I smack her ass cheek before looping the material around her wrists. Once secured the way I want them so she can't easily pull loose, I move my hands lower, cupping her hips and pressing forward gently until I'm buried deep inside her hot ass. "That's much better, isn't it?"

"Sure, but how am I supposed to balance myself?" Her muscles tighten, squeezing my cock.

"You're not. We got you, babe," Mason drawls after draining the contents of his beer and dropping the glass bottle to the carpeted floor. "Just relax and let us fuck you into oblivion." She complies, her muscles loosening a fraction from around me.

Mason nods, and I pull myself backward as he flexes his hips upward, invading her cunt.

"Oh, God . . . fuck me, oh God."

"We are, sweetness." Mason chuckles as he eases back down to the couch. I press forward, meeting her back as I take myself as far as I'll go. "How do we feel?"

"A-fucking-mazing." After another few seconds of sliding in and out of both of her entrances, we find a rhythm and start pumping. Her ass is tight, and feels so good. I won't last long. Not that I care, but I have to hold back long enough.

"Oh, my God." Misty squeals, telling me Mason has applied his thumb to her clit. I grit my teeth to gain my control, but this chick's ass is so tight. She needs to hurry the hell up.

"I'm going to come, oh . . ." Thank fuck, because the pressure in my balls is becoming too much. I look to Mason so we can get our timing accurate and blow this girl's mind. He nods, once.

"Sweetness, how close?" he asks with a tight expression. I can feel her muscles contracting when I press back in.

Pulling back out slowly, I mouth, "On three." I slowly press in one last time. "One." Misty can't hear me, and luckily, the concentration on giving Mason the cue has allowed me to regain control over my body. "Two."

"Now, I'm . . . oh shi . . ."

"Three." With as much force as I can muster, I ram my cock into her at the same time Mason forces himself back into her pussy. Misty lets out a bloodcurdling scream that pierces my ears, but I shake it off.

If I didn't know it was an explosive orgasm that ripped through her, I would have thought we hurt her. But when her body falls limp against mine with a whimper escaping her lips, I know she's more than fine.

Pulling out, I look at Mason, who gives me the go-ahead. That's all I needed, and I start pounding in and out of her. Mason is doing the same. "It's too . . . oh, God." Neither of us gives her an ounce of mercy. She'll come again and be feeling blissful in the end. The pressure builds at a rapid pace inside me. My body thrusts on its own accord. This is the release I need. These are the moments I look forward to. When everything I feel inside me stills. In and out, my pursuit of release continues.

A roar tears from my lips upon spilling myself into the condom as a long, drawn-out moan from Misty seeps into my ears. Just as quickly as the buildup started, it's gone. I've gotten what I wanted. I'm satisfied—for now, at least.

Pulling out of her, I remove myself from the couch and walk to the bathroom to discard the used protection and to clean off my dick.

When I finish, I walk back out to retrieve my jeans. Once I have them pulled over my hips, button fastened, I go in search of another beer.

I can hear the pants coming from Misty's bedroom. Mason has her back there, and the door is wide open. I'll let him have his fun. I'm spent and ready to crash out. If I know Mason, he'll be another hour with her, so I might as well drink up or get some shuteye before I have to drive us home.

The latter is probably best since I will not drive drunk again. I'm still pissed off at myself for doing it last night. What the hell was I thinking?

CHAPTER THREE

TARALYNN

P ulling in one long breath through my nose, the awful scent of stale cigarette smoke invades my nostrils all the way down into my lungs. My eyes snap open, and I want to hurl, or maybe cough up said lungs. Either way, it's time to get out of here. My shower and comfy bed are calling my name.

I try to untangle Jared's limbs from my body, but since I'm lying on my stomach with his heavy frame practically on top of me, it's not an easy task. Soft and gentle movements will never get him off me, so I do the only thing I can, given my circumstances. Planting my palms onto the mattress, I push my body off the bed. With the combination of that and jerking my shoulder backward, he stirs.

Unfortunately, I'm not quick enough, and he encases my midsection with his arm. Perfect. Just perfect. "Babe, stop moving. Go back to sleep."

"Let me up, please. I'm going home."

Please don't make this a big deal, I chant silently in my head, but I know he will. It's my fault. Two nights within the same week—let alone consecutive nights—are a big NO with Jared. He wants more; I don't. Doing this to him only makes things between us worse.

He releases me, and I feel him rise up onto his elbows from behind me. I'm quick this time, though. I hop my naked self out of his bed and then search the floor for my dress. I know it's here somewhere . . . Jared isn't exactly the cleanest person I know, and with the lights off, my task is more difficult.

"It's three-thirty in the fucking morning, Taralynn." Isn't he full of the obvious? His alarm clock was staring me in the face when I opened my eyes. I know what time it is. That doesn't change the fact that I'm ready to go home. Home, so I can breathe normal air.

The sound of sheets rustling signals Jared's movement on the bed. Seconds later, there's the click of the lamp, and soft light filters through the room. I instantly see my black panties, but when I bend to swipe them off the floor, Jared's palm connects with my butt. I yelp from the quick bolt of pain. I should have expected that. He loves my ass. I have no idea why, but it becomes his obsession when we're together.

"Was that necessary?"

"Always. Don't leave." He leans back against the wooden slats of the headboard. The smooth satin cloth that held my wrists in place a few hours ago while he drove his cock into me is still looped through the center of the headboard. Jared likes to play rough, which is a huge turn-on for me and keeps me coming back for more.

"I'm not staying." I never stay, and he should be used to it by now. Last night was an exception because I was hurt and mad. And by the time Jared and I finished wringing every ounce of pleasure out of each other, I was exhausted and accidentally fell asleep.

"Why not?" Reaching over to the nightstand, he retrieves a half-empty pack of cigarettes and his lighter. My nose scrunches up as I push myself into gear. The sooner I'm dressed, the sooner I'm out of his room that's about to smell more like an ashtray than it does now.

"Don't do this." I slip my legs into the silk material of my Victoria's Secret underwear, pulling them over my thighs until they meet my core. I strap on my bra and continue, "It's just sex. It's always been just sex, and you told me you could deal with that arrangement."

I bend once more to pick up my dress, but this time my butt is facing away from him. My ass does not need any more attention tonight. I don't know what he used on me earlier, but eventually he replaced his hand with a flexible material. Perhaps a belt; I'm uncertain since I never asked. I was too lost in the painful yet amazingly pleasurable sensation.

Does that make me a screwed-up person? Maybe. Hell, do not let my mother find out. She would light my butt on fire. Literally.

"I handle our arrangement just fine, baby. Doesn't mean I don't want more of you." After my dress is in place, I look at him. He's disappointed. He's always disappointed when I leave like this. "Look, if you're determined, let me throw some clothes on, and I'll take you."

"I don't think so. You're still drunk."

"And you're not?"

"I didn't say that. I live a half mile from here. It's no biggie. I can walk and be there in ten minutes." I don't give him a chance to think it over. I bolt from his room without so much as a goodbye kiss.

Once I'm down the stairs, I almost run into a large body on my way to the front door.

"Whoa, T." I look up to see Cole, Jared's best friend. Hair so blond it's almost white, baby blue eyes, and a crooked grin greet me. Cole reminds me of Mason. They're both the easy going, go-with-the-flow type.

Cole dubbed me "T" when I met him during the first week of our freshman year of college. He and Jared had also met that week and quickly fell into a tight friendship.

I roll my eyes at his use of the nickname. Not that it does any good. It's never mattered that I've explained to him numerous times that my name is Taralynn. "Where are you off to so late in the night?"

"Home, and it's early in the morning."

"If you say so, but I didn't see your car outside. Jared taking you?"

"No, he's probably back to sleep by now. I'm just going to walk."

"I don't think so. Throw something on to cover your arms. I'll take you. Meet me outside." With that, he pivots and is out the door, not allowing me to protest. Cole really is one of the nice ones, and like Mason, could easily snag a great woman—if they ever outgrow their too-much-fun ways. I follow, grabbing Jared's long-sleeved flannel shirt off the coat rack as I exit. Cole's Harley is right out front, next to Jared's. Like Jared, his only means of transportation is a motorcycle.

Unlike a lot of girls, I'm not scared to get on with him. Cole and Jared have both been riding motorbikes since they were in high school. From everything I've witnessed, they are relatively safe drivers. "Here, put on the helmet." Cole snags Jared's helmet off his nearby bike, holding it out for me to take. I do, securing it in place while he settles his long legs over his motorcycle and cranks it to life. Their neighbors have to hate them. The machine sounds like a beast.

I mimic his moves, swinging my leg over and hoisting myself up, making sure I don't touch my bare leg to the scorching hot exhaust pipe. Once my hands are secured on his hips, I give him the go-ahead to leave. He doesn't, though, and I see the slight chuckle he makes as his shoulders jump up and down.

Cole grabs my wrists, wrapping them around his waist, and I roll my eyes yet again. Not that he can see, of course, or would even care. His cool palms slide up my thighs and yank me forward. My chest meets his back. "Now that's more like it."

Cole doesn't have any romantic or sexual feelings for me. He's just doing this to mess with me. He loves taking advantage of moments when he can get a rise out of me. I've just learned over time to not give him the satisfaction. So, I wiggle as far against him as I possibly can and squeeze him tighter around his abdomen.

The bike shoots forward, beginning our short ride. Like I said, I don't live that far. The mid-October morning air is way too cold on my skin. I didn't like it when I rode home with Jared from the club, and I don't like it now.

A few seconds before I know Cole will arrive at my house, he leans the bike to the left, accelerating as he does, to pass a vehicle. Why it's necessary, I haven't a clue—because as soon as he pulls back into the lane, he turns into the cul-de-sac Shawn's house is on. He parks on the street but doesn't cut the engine. There is no need to since he won't be coming inside. Cole isn't exactly friends with my roommates, especially Shawn. Shawn and Jared are enemies, which makes him and Cole enemies too.

Shawn and Jared were tight until our senior year of high school. They had a falling out and have acted like mortal enemies ever since.

I hop off, and while I'm removing the helmet, Shawn's truck pulls into the drive. Cole waves, and now it makes sense. He did that for Shawn's benefit. Allowing him to see me on the back of his bike, I'm sure of it. Asshole.

"Thanks for the lift."

"Anytime, T. See ya later." He takes off, and I turn to walk up the driveway.

Mason comes stumbling out of the passenger side of Shawn's truck. Without looking at me, he walks to the house. The poor drunk probably doesn't have a clue I'm behind him. Seconds later, Shawn rounds his truck. His hard eyes land on mine, but I don't care. I walk past him without a word, following Mason.

Once inside the door, Mason turns left to make his way down the hall toward his bedroom. Once he's gone, I kick off my heels and move forward toward the kitchen in search of alcohol. The buzz I had kicking when I fell asleep is gone, and I want it back.

Looking to my right as I pass the entryway to the living room, I see young people scattered about and passed out. Typical.

Once in the kitchen, I go to the counter by the fridge where all the liquor is lined up and grab the open bottle of tequila. Pouring a double shot into a tumbler sitting on the countertop, I toss it back, swallowing it in one burning gulp. I used to love this feeling, but not so much anymore.

Going so long without needs ever getting satisfied eventually turns into frustration on a catastrophic level. Sure, I could go upstairs and pleasure myself until I come, but satisfaction won't follow. It never has. I want more than what I'm capable of handling by myself.

Jared's great, but he isn't what I want. Even drunk, my head realizes what my heart desires most.

I hear Shawn enter the kitchen behind me, but I don't turn to acknowledge his presence. Seeing him only makes it worse. Instead, I pour another double shot of liquid fire.

"Why the fuck was that prick bringing you home?"

After Mason made it known yesterday morning that I'm sleeping with Jared, you'd think Shawn would know the answer to that question. He probably does. He just wants me to verbalize it. I'm not going to.

"Leave it, Shawn." I twist around and pin him with a stare. I toss the tequila back, but this time my eyes widen. Ok, maybe my buzz wasn't so much gone like I originally thought.

Wow. That was stout.

"How much have you had to drink?"

"Enough that I should be in bed." What's with the twenty questions? More importantly, why does he even care? From what I saw earlier tonight, Shawn and Mason left with the brunette trash from Level. I don't have to guess what they left to go do, and I certainly don't want to imagine it.

"So, let me get this straight. You got onto the back of Cole's bike, drunk? Are you fucking crazy, Tara?" He doesn't wait for a reply. "Or do you have a death wish?"

"Neither! Are you done now?" His palm smacks the side of the refrigerator before turning away from me and disappearing down the hall. Moments later, I hear the door to the bathroom down the hall slams.

I turn back around, pour yet another double shot, and down it. I'm going to pay for this when I wake up, and it's going to be so much worse than yesterday morning's hangover. Screw it. If I'm going to do it in the first place, might as well do it right.

"You know, it's only a matter of time before Holly has him back in her grasp. You don't stand a chance with Shawn; you never have." Cassie's catty, bitch-ass voice assaults my ears. I guess she must have been in the living room and heard us.

Sometimes she's worse than Amanda. I put up with Mandy's shit because she's dating my best friend, but it'll be a cold day in hell before I deal with her friend's crap. Without giving it a bit of thought, I turn and leap forward. She needs a good butt kicking. I'm not a fighter. I know I can take her if I tried, but I don't actively seek out confrontations. My mother would flip her lid, so I do what's necessary to avoid that at all costs.

Before I reach her, a set of massive arms grabs me around the waist, pulling me backward until I'm against his hard chest. "Get. Out. Of. My. House." Shawn bites each word out through clenched teeth. I know they aren't directed at me. Even if I weren't looking at her shocked expression, I'd know they were aimed at Cassie Winston.

"What?"

"I don't think he stuttered, Barbie." Okay, Barbie is usually held for Holly, the queen bitch herself, but I had to. Sue me if you don't like it. I don't usually act like this, but I've had my fair share of alcohol tonight.

"You won't disrespect her or anyone else that lives here. Last time I checked, you don't live here . . . so leave." His words are still a bark. Shawn can come off quite scary at times. Frankly, Cassie looks like she's about to pee her pants. Inside, I'm loving it. This is so much better than me punching her. "Or I could let Tara go, but I don't think you want me to. Trust me, she will crush you."

I will? Hell, I don't know if I will or not. But I'm willing to find out. I've never hit another person in my life. I'm bigger than Cassie in every way, sure, but I'm not going there.

The snootiness crosses her face again. It's the same one my mother wears around me. She should have been my mother's kid. I'm certain she and my mother would get along much better than my mother and I do. "Yes, she would."

Oh, that bitch went there. Yes, I have issues with my weight. I'm not overweight, I don't think, but I'm not skinny by any means, and it doesn't matter how much I work out. I'm never going to be a small size. I love to cook, and I love to eat the food I cook. It's just not in the cards for me. Doesn't mean I like it, but she doesn't have the right to throw it in my face, especially with Shawn standing right here.

I try to jump forward, but Shawn's hold on me tightens. "Leave! Now." Another bark, only this time his voice is deeper. It's a warning.

"Whatever." She turns, walking through the kitchen and exiting the house as quickly as her feet will move.

Once the door clicks closed, he releases me, and as he steps backward, the warm flannel shirt I'm wearing, Jared's shirt, is pulled off my body. I turn, facing Shawn. What the heck is that about?

"Go take a shower!" My jaw drops at his order. Seconds after, he rips the shirt down the middle, making two unwearable pieces.

What the flyin' . . .

The material is discarded, landing in a pool on the tile floor.

I plant my hands on my hips in a defiant gesture. He's not about to order me around. I might take that crap from my parents, but I won't from anyone else. "Excuse me?"

Shawn wastes no time. He springs forward in an instant, making me step backward until my back collides with the wall. He continues to close in on me, placing his palms on the flat surface of the wall next to my face and leaning in. "You smell like him, and I don't fucking like it."

Well, tough shit.

"Because you smelling like a cheap whore is so much better," I lash back. I don't waste my time, either. I place my palms on his chest and push as hard as I can. It might not have come across as a shove because his body didn't move away from mine as much as I intended it to. "Piss off, Shawn."

With those last words, I leave the kitchen, taking myself up the stairs to my bedroom for a shower—not because Shawn ordered me to, but because I do, in fact, stink.

If I wasn't as drunk as I am right now, I might have stopped to analyze what just happened between us, but I don't. I'm going to struggle enough just getting out of my clothes to shower tonight, or this morning, or whatever the hell time of the day this is.

He is a mother-effin' jerk!

CHAPTER FOUR

SHAWN

A short, loud chiming sound rings through my ears.

I hate that sound. That sound tells me that, once again, my drunk ass forgot to flip the silent switch on my cell phone before falling into bed at whatever time I managed to get home this morning.

Another piercing chime rings out, and this time I groan.

I reach out and grab a spare pillow, covering my head with it. The pillow that should be under my head is undoubtedly somewhere on the floor. For as long as I can remember, I've always woken up lying on my stomach with my face buried into the mattress. Today is no different.

A third chime rings out seconds after the last, immediately followed by two more before I jut out my hand, blindly feeling for my cell phone on the nightstand. Around the eighth chime, I finally locate the source of disruption. Without looking, I flip the switch to silent and drop the phone.

It's not like I don't know who's texting me.

Buzzing. Loud motherfucking buzzing agitates my eardrums.

Assholes.

The person who invented text messaging should be punched in the dick.

The person who invented group texting capabilities should be shot in the aforementioned dick.

More annoying buzzing. Silent switch, my ass. The vibrating is nearly as annoying as the chime.

I flip over onto my back and snatch my phone off the table, giving in to the relentless messaging.

Bingo.

It's my roommates, a.k.a., my friends. Well, maybe that's a stretch. I mean, sure, Mason and I are best friends and have been since first grade. Matt, on the other hand, is more Mason's friend than mine. I like the guy all right; I've known him since junior high when he moved to Tupelo from California. That, I still don't understand. People move out of Mississippi. No one moves to this shit hole of boredom, especially from somewhere like California. But he and I never really clicked.

Opening the text message, I scroll up to the top, reading through what these shits think is important enough to wake me over.

Tara: I'm at the store. Do y'all need anything?

Mason: Condoms

Tara: I'm serious, asswipe!

Mason: So am I. Can't go blowing my shit into any cunt. Bitches be nasty.

Matt: Hope you covered your shit with that ho from last night.

Mason: Don't be calling my chicks hoes.

Matt: Ok, skank then.

Mason: Fuck you. That bitch was hot.

Matt: I'll pass, man. I'm satisfied with my permanent pussy.

Me: New fuckin' roommates. That's what I want.

Mason: Yeah, with big tits. They can room with me.

Tara: Um . . . Mase? What size? There's a lot to choose from.

Matt: They probably don't have a small enough size to fit his pencil dick.

Tara: Brand?

Me: He's fucking with you, Tara. Jeez.

Mason: Sorry, I couldn't resist. lol

It's funny, and I want to laugh, but the pounding inside my head won't allow it. For someone as smart as she is, she doesn't catch on to the obvious.

After tossing my phone onto the crumpled sheets, I roll out of bed to go locate something to take the pain away. As I exit my room, I see the door to the bathroom and hear the awful noise of the latest pop music coming from behind it. That tells me Matt's little girlfriend must be in there.

I think back, recalling she was here when I got home last night. I also recall the snooty little bitch being just that—a bitch—to Tara. I don't care if Amanda is her best friend's girlfriend; I wouldn't take that shit from her or her annoying friend Cassie. They continually make digs and snide comments to Tara, and I'm over it. Tara is the nice one, the one that doesn't start shit, the one that keeps the peace. She stays non-confrontational for Matt.

Fuck that shit.

With thoughts of Tara distracting me from my task of finding something to curb my hangover, my eyes land on her bedroom door. If she's shopping, that probably means she's at Target. If that's the case, Tara won't be home for at least another hour since the nearest Target is over seventy miles away in Horn Lake.

I enter her room, which is always clean and smells the best in the house. That's not to say the rest of the house stinks, because it doesn't. The plus of having a neat-freak roommate is that the house is always clean too. Hell, I don't remember the last time I made my bed or even washed my own clothes. Come to think of it, I don't think I've ever done a load of laundry in my life.

I turn on the faucet inside the shower to hot, knowing I'll be damned if I wait on Matt's girl to get done. I locate some generic pain reliever in the medicine cabinet, toss the pills into my mouth, and then down a glass of tap water.

After about ten minutes of standing under the scalding water, the pain in my head starts to ease up just as the water cools. I'm sure I have our extra houseguest to thank for that. This circumstance is actually normal, which is why Tara keeps a variety of our soaps and shampoos stocked in her bathroom. Without wasting another minute, I quickly soap up from head to toe, rinse, and shut the water off.

After wrapping a towel around my waist, I pick up my discarded boxers and head back to my room. As I walk past the hall bathroom, the door opens, and Amanda comes barreling into me.

"Oh, shit," she stammers as I steady her with one hand while keeping a firm grip on my towel and dirty laundry with the other. Her breath hitches when she looks up to see me, and her face flushes. "I—I'm so sorry, Shawn."

"Don't you have class during the week?" I see this bitch enough on the weekends. If Matt wants a full-time, live-in girlfriend, then maybe his ass needs to move somewhere else. It's not happening in my house.

"Usually, yes, but Holly and I went to a concert last night, so I skipped. I'm heading back once I get dressed." She steps away from me as I sidestep her to head to my room.

"Whatever," I mumble, but turn back to face Amanda. "Cassie isn't welcome here any longer. You got me?"

"What? Why not?" She doesn't give me a chance to answer her. "Cassie is always nice to you, Shawn. If it weren't for Holly being in love with you, she would have tried to get with you herself. She likes you but doesn't want to cause a rift between her and Holly. I don't understand." One hand clutches her towel, and the other is parked on her left hip, classic bitch style.

"Then understand this: I've had all I'm willing to stand of Cassie disrespecting Tara." I move in closer to her. Using my height as intimidation, I continue. "That will go for you too, if you continue making snide little comments to her. Don't think for a second that I won't eighty-six your ass just because my roommate continues to blow his load in your pussy."

"Why . . . I mean . . . what?" she stammers, along shaking her head. I don't understand what she isn't grasping here. I was perfectly clear. "I don't get it, Shawn." Her voice has turned hard, and her eyebrows are drawn together. "You can't stand that goodie-two-shoes any more than I can. I don't get why my boyfriend remains friends with her."

The pain inside my head had been mellowing up until this point.

What I don't understand is why her boyfriend keeps her around in the first place. There is not one thing likable about the woman standing in front of me right now.

I step even closer, bending down so I'm mere inches from her face.

"Do not ever assume you know what I think, who I like or dislike, or anything else, for that matter. Tara would not live here if I didn't like her. If you understand anything, understand this: the only reason I allow you in my house is that you happen to be dating her best friend. Ya feel me, Amanda?"

Her mouth is hanging open, but even the most dimwitted person on earth would have understood that, so I feel my point has been made.

I'm done with this stupid bitch. She has taken up far too much of my morning. I turn on my heel and walk the short distance to my bedroom.

Once I'm behind closed doors and inside the room, I finish toweling off and throw on clean boxers, gym shorts, and a T-shirt. I exercise every weekday morning before showing up for work. One of the perks of my job as a tattoo artist is my hours aren't the typical eight to five. Starting my day at noon—I'll never complain. I love what I do, and I get paid damn good money to do it.

I walk out of my room without doing my hair. There's no point since I'll be showering again in two hours. Yeah, it may be a little weird that I shower before and after a workout, but it's not like I'm in any condition to clean up when I get home from a night pounding drinks back at a bar followed by the few minutes inside whatever random chick that decided to give me a piece inside or outside of said bar.

If I could, I'd wash their stink off me before crawling into my bed, but in most cases, I'm lucky to make it to my room, let alone into my bed and underneath my covers. A shower is definitely out of the question, skank or not.

I walk into the kitchen to see Matt eating from a bowl at the table and Mason standing in front of the coffee maker. I'm not a huge eater before a workout, but I need more than cereal and coffee.

I grab the tall carton of egg whites, shredded mozzarella cheese, and a container of mixed fruit from the fridge. I make my breakfast and join my roommate at the table. Shoveling a forkful of food in my mouth, I level my gaze toward Mason.

"You ready to finish up your ink?"

"Absolutely. I'll be seeing you once I get out of my last class, around one this afternoon." He takes a drink of his coffee as Amanda walks into the kitchen. She heads over to Matt.

"I'm out of here, babe. See you this weekend." She kisses the side of his head, and he nods. I don't get these two. It's easy to see he's not that into her anymore, so why does he keep her around? It can't be for her personality, because she is severely lacking in that department.

I'm happy to see her go and direct my attention back to Mason.

"Yours is the easiest one I'm doing today." Once I finish shading red into all the flowers, he'll be complete. "Cosmo is coming in today, and then he'll be back on Friday for me to finish up. He's getting a piece done on his forearm."

I met Cosmo my senior year of high school when I started

apprenticing at a local tattoo shop in my hometown of Tupelo. At the age of forty-nine, Cosmo became my first solo tat, and I got to pop his tattoo cherry. He's come back for seven more since then. Everyone says when you start getting tattooed that it becomes an addiction, and I think that holds true for a lot of folks.

"That old man is cool as shit," Mason remarked. "It's been a while since I've seen him. I think I'll shoot him a text and see if he wants to grab a beer later this afternoon."

Cosmo took a liking to Mason and me back in the day. He's often said he's come to see us both as the sons he never had.

"You should do that. I wish I could join, but I have a full schedule until 6:30, so there's no way I'll be able to."

It sucks, but I'll get to catch up with him for an hour or so while I'm working on the outline of his ink.

"Dude." I turn to glare at Matt. "I don't roll that way." I know he isn't that into his girl, and I doubt she even gives good head. Bitch is too worried about her own self to care about someone else. But jeez.

"Huh?" he questions through a mouthful of cereal.

"Stop rubbing your foot against my leg." I push at him with my leg.

"I'm not." He's looking at me like I'm stupid.

"Seriously, what the hell?" Seconds after pushing him away, he's back to doing it again.

"I'm not touching you," says the motherfucker that's about to get kicked. "Beast is under the table."

"Excuse me?" What is this jackass talking about? Who the fuck is Beast?

"Beast," he repeats. I look at him this time like he's the stupid one. Pretty sure he is. "The cat."

"We don't have a cat." I scoot my chair backward and look down. Sure enough, a big fat fluffy furball is rolling around between my feet. "Why the fuck is this thing in my house?"

I hear plastic bags rustling and turn to see Tara walking into the kitchen carrying multiple grocery bags. I guess she wasn't at Target after all, but I don't care about that. I'm concerned with the feline in my kitchen—the one that certainly does not belong in here or in my house at all for that matter.

I look back at my roommate.

"Don't look at me. Ask Tara. She's the one that started feeding the stray."

I bend down and pick Beast up. Why am I even calling this animal by name?

"Want to explain?" I raise my eyebrows at Tara, but she doesn't seem to care.

"Explain what?" I wait. "All I did was feed a hungry critter. He sleeps with Mason." Her eyes are peering into mine a little too innocently, but I turn, facing Mason.

"Hey, get off my ass. That fluffy bastard is warm." He takes offense. "You all can fuck off." He walks in my direction, coffee in his right hand. "Give me my fuckin' cat."

He takes the furry little shit and walks off.

So now we've gained a cat.

What the hell is next around here?

As I PULL into my driveway, parking my F-150 beside Tara's BMW, I shut off the ignition and relax into the driver's seat. Today wasn't bad by any means. Bad or good, I'll always tell you the same. I love my job. I even like some of the guys I work with. A few don't have the talent it takes to make it in the tattoo world, but that doesn't mean they aren't good people, because they're great. They're simply not meant to be tattoo artists.

It's not my place to tell them that, though. It's Adam's. He's my boss and the owner of the studio. Adam is easily one of the best artists I've ever come across. Some of the shit he can do with a tattoo machine is bad fucking ass. I may design every bit of art I have on my body, but Adam is the guy that inks it into my skin.

Being a talented tattoo artist doesn't equal being a good businessman, however. To be fair, I can't say he isn't good at the business end because I've never seen his finances. The shop is always booked out, lights on, and well stocked with supplies. It's the management part that I have issues with.

Adam is everyone's friend. I've never run a business, but logic and common sense dictate that you can be friendly with your staff, but it's a bad idea to be friends. I'm sure it works for some people, probably even in the tattoo world, but not in our studio. At least not where my boss is concerned. He can't fire anyone, let alone dish out constructive criticism. Trust me, there needs to be a lot of critiquing happening at Southern Ink.

I've witnessed the man hire a guy based on the dude's personality alone, taking his word on his talent rather than seeing his portfolio. I doubt some of the fucks at the studio know what a portfolio is, much less have one.

I'm hoping to change this in the next few months. I've been on Adam's ass for nearly a year trying to get him to sell me the business. Three years ago, I would have never considered the idea of running a business. I'm still not so sure I know what I'm getting myself into, but I can't sit back and allow a place I love go down the drain. That's exactly where I see it heading if things around the studio don't change.

Adam finally agreed today. I'm not sure what changed his mind, but whatever it was, I'm glad.

I'm waiting for him to give me a price and speak to his lawyer about what needs to happen to get the ball rolling. The sooner the title changes, the sooner I can start making the changes I feel are necessary for Southern Ink to grow and improve. Removing the dead weight, placing a guy who has potential under an apprenticeship, and finding exceptional talent is where I plan to start.

I remove my keys and open the truck door, sliding out and taking a deep breath.

Home.

I don't know what it is about this place that I love so much. Perhaps because I spent a lot of time here as a kid when I would come stay with my grandparents on the occasional weekend or holiday. This house, this city, here feels right. It's another reason I need to get the studio on track. If I can't, then I can't stay working there. I take pride in what I do, and I want to work in an establishment that takes the same pride in the work its staff puts out.

It's Wednesday night, my favorite night of the week because it's family dinner night with my roommates. What makes it so special? Well, you'd know if you ever had the pleasure of eating a meal prepared by Tara. The woman can cook, and good too.

As a kid, Tara spent a lot of time at my house because her brother was always over. My mother took a liking to Tara early on, from what I remember. My mom taught Tara a lot of what she knows. They have a bond over food, and I get to reap the benefits.

I used to think no one would ever surpass my mom's cooking, but then I became roommates with Tara three years ago. I'll never admit to that, though.

I remove my boots, kicking them off and shoving them against the wall with my foot. Then I pivot and make my way through the living room. The TV is playing what I'm assuming is a college football game that either Mason or Matt recorded on the DVR the previous weekend. I don't look to see what teams are playing. Frankly, I don't give a shit. Sports aren't my thing. I played in middle school and high school because my friends did, but I never enjoyed it.

Mason is asleep, lying face down on the couch. A few hours ago, I finally finished the shading on his tattoo. It was about a year ago when Mason decided he wanted a tattoo. He told me he wanted something bold and powerful with an Asian theme. His mother is from Korea, so he grew up with a lot of Asian influence in his home. He's never been to Korea, but he wanted a badass tat that represented his heritage. What I designed is my best work to date.

The tattoo covers his back and ends down his left leg. A blue-green skull sits in the center, with a wicked snake looped from the top of his right shoulder and ending on the outer side of his left thigh. The Asian theme comes into play with the vibrant colors and flowers spaced around, popping off his flesh.

It's cool as shit, and I almost wish it was on me. This is a piece that I'm most proud of. It's taken a little over a year to complete because of his schedule, but it turned out awesome.

Matt is passed out in the recliner next to the couch. I guess the game wasn't that happening if they couldn't remain awake through it.

I pass through, making my way toward the noise coming from the kitchen. As I near the door, the smell of seafood penetrates my nose. I smile big. I'd know that smell anywhere.

Cioppino!

It's my favorite meal. It's a seafood soup of flavorful goodness.

I lean against the doorframe and take in the view in front of me. I only have seconds before she realizes I'm here. Tara's blonde hair is pulled back into a messy bun. She's wearing a loose black T-shirt and white shorts, standing in front of the stove. Once my eyes land on her thighs, I can't see anything else.

Shit.

You'd think I'd be used to it by now. I've known her practically my whole life. We grew up together. Tara is so embedded into my own family that the guest bedroom inside my parents' home was designated hers years ago. My grandparents only use it maybe once or twice a year when visiting. Any other time it's Tara's, and I'm pretty certain she even has clothes and toiletries at my parents' home, the same as Shane and I do.

My mind begins to wander, and I have to force myself to stop imagining something that will never happen.

But God, the image of those beautiful legs wrapped around me is . . . something I need to stop thinking about.

Pushing myself off the doorframe, I walk closer in her direction until I'm standing directly behind her. She doesn't know I'm here yet, so when she steps back, stepping into me, she practically jumps out of her skin and screams.

"Freak!" She huffs a large breath of air out of her lungs as she turns to look at me. "You suck."

"Will you say 'fuck' for me, just once?" Tara rarely cusses. When she does, it's because she's either thoroughly pissed or extremely excited. And I find it to be really cute. "Please. It's just a four-letter word."

She quickly turns her head, but not before I see the pink in her cheeks from the blush I've caused.

Success.

"Go away. I'm trying to finish dinner."

"I know. I could smell it from the other room. It's divine. What did I do to earn my favorite meal?"

"What makes you think I cooked this for you?" Tara points to the tall stainless steel pot on the stove before eyeing me. "It happens to be my favorite meal as well. Just as chocolate cake is my favorite dessert." She lifts her index finger to point to the table.

Holy smokes, tonight is going to be wonderful, and I am going to fall into my bed a fat and happy man. I'll definitely need to spend extra time at the gym tomorrow.

"Shit, people, others are trying to sleep in this place." We turn to see Matt walking into the kitchen. He goes directly to the refrigerator and pulls out a clear bottle of golden beer.

"Grab me one of those, would ya?" I call out before he slams the door closed. Tonight couldn't get more perfect. Beer and a great meal will surely only relax me further.

"When do we eat? I'm starving." Matt directs his question to Tara as he hands me a beer.

"Never, if you come in here with that attitude." She turns back to the stove and stirs in what looks to be shrimp. That signals we are minutes away from dinner, so I head over to the sink to wash my hands.

"It was just a fucking question, Taralynn." He sighs in frustration. I don't know why, but he and Tara have been off for some time now. "Can you please let whatever's crawled up your ass lately out?"

I'm not getting into the middle of their shit, so I towel dry my hands and open my beer. The first sip is always the best. It's cold, refreshing, and smooth as it flows into my mouth and down my throat.

Her back is to Matt, but I can clearly see her profile. Tara's jaw locks, but she just looks forward without saying a word.

"Go get Mason up, would ya?" I look toward Matt. "She's almost done, so we'll be eating in a few."

He nods before tipping his glass bottle up and taking a sip, then walks toward the living room.

"Drama going on in BFF-land?" I lean against the countertop in front of the sink, waiting for her reply.

"Hell if I know," she breathes. "You'd have to ask him that question."

Tara grabs an oven mitt from the drawer next to the stove and puts it on to pull the freshly baked French bread from the oven.

We definitely have it made around here.

"Will you grab the bowls while I slice and butter the bread?" She turns to face me after getting the bread knife out of the knife block.

"Well, I'm not going to say no while you're holding that thing," I joke as I push off, twisting to my right to get the bowls as requested. Once I have four in my hand I place them on the counter next to the stove. I go ahead and grab four spoons from the silverware drawer, as well, and place them next to the bowls.

Mason and Matt walk into the kitchen. Mason rubs his palm over his short hair and then down his face to wake up.

"How is your back feeling?" I ask him. He looks in my direction and then heads to the fridge.

"Nothing more than a dull ache. I downed two packs of powdered aspirin when I got home." He retrieves a beer of his own, twists the cap off and tips it up to his lips.

"Shit, dude, that's over sixteen hundred milligrams." I laugh out. Damn, the pain isn't that bad—fucking pansy ass little bitch. Normally I'd call him on that shit, but I'm not in the mood. I want an easy rest of the night. I want to enjoy a delicious meal and kick back with my friends.

"Exactly, which is why I'm not hurting."

"Let's eat, guys," Tara calls out. I'm first in line. You don't have to tell me twice.

I scoop a hearty amount of seafood goodness into my bowl and grab a piece of hot bread before walking over to the table. My friends do the same. Tara is always the last to fix her plate and the last one of us to sit down to eat.

As soon as her ass hits the cushioned seat of the chair, I raise my spoon to my lips, anticipating the deliciousness about to slide down my throat. Before I taste victory, I feel a swift kick in the shin.

"Motherfucker." I turn to look at Tara staring at me. She rolls her eyes.

"Mase, you're up for grace this week." She looks back in my direction, cutting her sapphire eyes at me while shaking her head.

Don't women know not to come between a man and his dinner?

I set my spoon down on the table, lace my fingers together in front of me, and bow my head.

"Thank ya, Jesus. Now, let's dig in." Mason laughs at his short but sweet praise. Now don't go taking that as an insult to the Lord.

We are all God-loving people. We may not show up to church often, but we love and respect the guy.

The first spoonful of my soup is always the best. Sometimes I wonder how I stay in such good shape when I have Tara as a roommate. The woman can cook, and she feeds us well.

I don't make it to my second spoon because the ringing of the doorbell interrupts us. Irritation is automatic.

My house is full of life except for Sunday through Wednesday —which are off limits to almost everyone. This is a known fact. Wednesdays especially because we have designated it family night, and by family, I mean the four individuals that live in this house. Are they my family? No, they aren't in the traditional way, but we all grew up together. Mason is damn near as close to a brother to me as my own brother, Shane.

Tara grits her teeth at the interruption. This is actually her rule. She doesn't ask for much, but when we all moved in, she suggested family dinner night with no interruptions or outsiders. I liked the idea. After a year of enjoying those evenings, we added a Sunday night dinner as well.

Her chair skids backward. Tara rises and walks off to answer the front door.

"Hey," I call out. "Unless the motherfucker is related to one of us, kick the bastard in the dick." I go back to spooning more cioppino into my mouth. Next I tear off a piece of bread with my teeth and chew.

Moments later, I hear a shrill voice that I had never planned to hear again.

I look up to see the bitch I screwed last Saturday night outside of Level. What the fuck is this shit?

"Hey, you," she coos. "You're a hard man to track down." The blonde with choppy short hair comes to stand in front of me. I place my spoon down and stare at her. This shit is stalker fucking crazy. I knew that night I was making a mistake. I saw crazy in her eyes the moment our eyes met, yet still I decided to shove my dick into her. I should have known this would come back to bite me in the ass. I've only made the mistake of fucking crazy one other time. That was high school. I can blame that shit on stupidity and a dick I didn't know how to control. I got nothing now.

I catch Tara out of the corner of my eye. She's glaring daggers at the back of the chick's head. If I remember correctly, her name is Addison.

Tara has a jealous streak. That's one of the reasons I'd never bring another girl home. It's not like I'd want to anyway. Always fuck a bitch at their place or any place that isn't your own. That's my motto. Don't bring them home, then there's no reason for them to show up because they don't know where you live.

"Can I help you?" I finally say. Mason and Matt both lean back into their seat, watching this scene play out. They know me well. They know I don't want anything to do with a chick after I've screwed her. Even the women I fuck know this. I make it perfectly clear so this type of thing never happens.

I push my chair back and turn sideways to await her answer.

"I wanted to see you. We had a great time the other night and you forgot to give me your number, silly." She smiles. It's a forced but a hopeful smile.

"I didn't forget a damn thing." That's harsh, I know, but she doesn't need to misinterpret me this time. "Sweetheart, I fucked you. I fucked you outside a nightclub at that. Now, I don't fuck any pussy I don't want to fuck, but understand this. I've never met a pussy I'd want to fuck twice."

Her mouth drops. She's silent for a time. Pretty certain I've shocked the little thing.

The sound of a door slamming enters one ear and goes out the other. I don't think too hard on it. I have a female in front of me to deal with and to get out of my house. She has successfully ruined dinner. If I know Tara, she's going to hold that against me for a few days.

"I . . . but we . . . what . . ." She can't finish a sentence, so I decide to help her out.

"Look, I'm not trying to be mean, honey, but I don't even remember your name." That's a lie, but she doesn't need to know that. Why give her hope? There is no hope whatsoever here. "It was just sex. I made that perfectly clear. I don't know where you got other ideas, but for me, sex is just sex."

"But—"

I don't give her a chance to plead her case. I mean, this is already getting ridiculous. I almost feel sorry for this girl.

"There are no 'buts'. Now please get out of my house."

Again, her jaw drops. I guess the chick isn't used to being turned down. She isn't bad looking. She's attractive. I wouldn't have screwed her if she weren't.

"You're a fucking asshole," she huffs dramatically before she turns and walks away. Seconds later, I hear the door slam.

"Can you believe that bitch?" I look from Mason to Matt and then back to Mason. Matt looks pissed. Mason has his eyebrows scrunched together. "What the fuck are you both staring at? I handled her the only way I could. So what if I was an ass? She's the psycho bitch that showed up here uninvited."

"Dude." Mason chimes in and continues to eye me without another word.

"What?" I demand.

Matt pushes his chair back and walks off.

Just like a pussy. Has something to say, but not the balls to say it.

How am I fucking friends with him?

"Well, what the fuck, man?" I ask Mason.

"It's not how you acted with that chick. It's what you said." He sounds like I should know what he is talking about. I don't. Obviously I don't, or I wouldn't be asking him.

"You're going to need to explain better than that."

"Tara." I look around, but she isn't here. I recall the door slamming, but I don't get why she would leave. She knows I get laid regularly. It's not a secret. "Your comment about never meeting a girl you'd ever want to fuck twice."

His words hit like a freight train.

Shit.

"Fuck," I yell and throw my fist down on the hard surface of the table.

"Yeah." He pushes his own chair back.

I stand and reach into my pocket for my cell. "I didn't mean it about her."

Mason leaves the room without another word. It's not needed. I know he suspects how I feel about her, but he doesn't understand why I won't go down that road. I'll never go down that road with her. Not because I don't want to, but because I won't hurt her. She isn't, nor will she ever be, just another quick fuck.

I locate Tara's name from my contacts and press the call button. Her number rings, then goes to voice mail. That tells me she doesn't have it turned off. She just isn't answering it.

I call her two more times. Still no answer by the third attempt, and my anger flares. I leave her a message.

"Bring your fucking ass home, now." My tone is laced with heat. I know it, and I don't care.

I walk toward the living room. Dinner is trash now, but I couldn't care less about food at the moment.

"You just can't help it, can you?"

"What?" I bark at Mason. He's sitting on the couch flipping through the TV channels. He's not looking at me.

"You continue to push her into his bed, you know."

By him, I assume Mason means Jared.

Prick.

I call her again as I make my way up the stairs. Voice mail is bullshit.

She doesn't return home. I don't see her again until Friday when she shows up at the studio.

CHAPTER FIVE
TARALYNN

"Taralynn."

The first thing that registers in my brain is my name being called. The second thing is that it's Shawn's voice. In all the seventeen years I've known him, he has never once called me by my full first name. I think he started calling me "Tara" because when he was a little kid, he had a hard time pronouncing "L" sounds. When he outgrew his minor speech impediment, he kept calling me Tara.

Finally, there's the tone of his voice, laced with irritation, which brings me to the here and now.

My eyes fly open just as the smell of latex fills my nostrils. Once everything comes into focus, I see what looks to be a pair of black latex gloves bunched into a ball in his fist only inches away from my face. I can also feel him leaning over my back. My cheek is lying flush with Adam's wooden desk, my arm is stretched out, and my hand is still cupping the computer mouse.

Apparently, I fell asleep at some point while going over the business financials.

I don't have classes on Fridays, but what I do have is a part-time job at Southern Ink. I say part-time job because it's only one day a week, but the reality is, I don't get paid for the work I put in here. Adam Manning, the owner of the tattoo studio and Shawn's boss, sweet-talked me into handling payroll for his business about two years ago. The guy has a thick and deep Mississippian accent that's impossible to say no to.

It all started with me coming in every Friday around noon, tallying up all the artists' commissions based on their appointments from the previous week and any hourly wages for non-commissioned staff, then writing checks that were already signed by Adam. What it has turned into is me still doing all that, plus paying the business's bills and ordering all the supplies. So, in essence, I'm doing Adam's job so Adam can continue servicing his clients, not to mention prolonging every appointment because the man was gifted with the art of gab.

"Yeah," I yawn, lifting my head up. Shawn backs away from me, walking around to stand on the other side of the desk.

"What are you doing looking at Adam's banking info?"

"What?" I cover my mouth as another yawn forces its way out. Damn, I've got to stop wasting nights spending time with Jared. Seeing him is only prolonging the inevitable.

"Never mind," Shawn snaps. "Look, I'm finishing up on Cosmo's arm piece. I'll be done within thirty, and I'd like to hit the road then, okay?" Cosmo is a longtime client of Shawn's. He's in a biker club out of our hometown of Tupelo. But when I say "biker club," I'm not referring to the Harley MC types. I'm talking about the BMW MC types.

"Road. Got-cha." I stretch my arms over my head.

"Do you think you can have everyone paid by then?"

"Yeah. Yeah, I have them right here. I don't know what happened. I guess not getting enough sleep the past two nights is catching up with me." Shit. Why did I say that? By the look of his locked jaw, he knows I didn't sleep at home.

"Just . . . be fucking ready to leave." With those words, he pivots and stalks out the door.

I don't know what his deal is. Shawn Braden screws a different skank every other day. Why he cares who I do makes zero sense.

I log off the bank website and close all programs before turning off the computer. I cringe at the mess on Adam's desk, so I straighten it up, making it much more organized than when I arrived. I can't help myself. Things look prettier when they are clean and properly placed. It may also serve to calm my nerves at times too.

If people took better care of their things, our world would be more relaxed and peaceful. I'm sure of it.

I grab the checks I stuffed in envelopes earlier and walk out of the office.

I make it around to everyone, handing paychecks to each person. Leaving Shawn for last, I lay his check down on the side table behind him. His concentration is on Cosmo. Every tattoo I've seen Shawn create is nothing short of beautiful. This one is no less. It's placed on the inside of Cosmo's right forearm. It's the form of a woman, similar to the tattoo Shawn has on the inside of his left forearm. Both are of pretty women.

"Who's the pretty lady?" My question is directed at Cosmo. He opens his eyes and looks down at Shawn's work. Cosmo takes a deep breath and follows with a sigh as he exhales.

"My wife, sugar." That's sweet, but sad too. I know he lost his wife of twenty-five years last year. This piece is obviously honoring her.

"It's beautiful, Cosmo."

"Well, sweet cheeks, I can't take credit for that. That is all on your boy here."

No, not my boy, but I don't say that thought.

I catch Shawn's grin, but that's all I see. His head is lowered, and he's focused on the design. Unlike Shawn's similar tattoo, this one is a portrait of a woman. Her chin is resting in the palm of her right hand, and she's smiling a big, gorgeous smile. One might think Shawn recreated this from a photograph, but I'd be willing to bet Cosmo showed him a few snapshots of his late wife, and then Shawn created this image himself. He's that good.

"I know; he's an amazing artist, isn't he?"

Shawn glances up as if surprised I would think that. I'm not looking at him, but I catch his expression from the corner of my eye. I'm still looking at his client, who is relaxed in the black padded chair that reminds me of the type you'd find in a dentist's office.

"The only person I've ever let permanently mark me up," Cosmo laughs out.

"Don't fucking move, old man." Shawn's voice doesn't have any heat behind it. He's always had a soft spot for the guy in front of me. He's sweet, but I don't know him all that well. Mason and Shawn never have anything but praise for the man.

"What about you, Taralynn? Have you let him mark you yet?"

Cosmo knows my name? That's strange.

Sure, I've seen him a handful of times. At cookouts back home mainly, but I didn't think I had made enough of an impression upon him to actually learn my name.

"I keep telling her she needs a little ink. Her vanilla skin is bad for my business." Adam walks over, throwing his ink-covered left arm around my shoulders and pulling me into his side.

"No, sir," I answer Cosmo's question as I push away from Adam. The word marked has my face heating from thoughts of how I'd rather be marked by Shawn Braden.

"You want any?" Cosmo doesn't wait for my reply. He continues, "You know, he told me," Cosmo lifts his arm, the one that isn't being worked on, and points a finger in Shawn's direction, "these things were addicting. I have to say he was right."

"I don't know." I do want a tattoo, and I want one bad, but I haven't the slightest idea what I'd want placed on my body forever.

"Maybe." I'm not sure I wouldn't wake up one day and no longer like it. That's what's stopping me, I guess.

"What?" Shawn lifts his head and cocks it to the side. "You want a tattoo?"

I shrug my shoulders. I mean, what else am I to do? I don't know what I'd want and I'd probably pick something stupid anyway.

"That's a no," he says flatly.

"It's not a no, Shawn. I want one; I've wanted one for a long time. All of yours are amazing, but I don't know what I'd want permanently branded on me for . . . forever." I'm a book nerd that loves to read and write the stories that play out in my head. I don't have a favorite flower or bird. "There isn't anything I can think of that would look pretty on me."

"If that's the case, and you like all his shit," Adam gestures in Shawn's direction, "then you need to let me tattoo you, seeing how I put damn near all the tattoos he's toting around on him." Shawn glances up briefly before continuing his final touches of Cosmo's tattoo.

"I don't think so."

"And why not?" Adam is clearly offended. That wasn't my intention, and I'm not sure how to smooth this over.

"Adam, you're an excellent artist, obviously. But what I find amazing about Shawn's tattoos is the design. Everything inked on his skin was something he thought up in his head and drew out. It's his work, just placed on him by someone else. If I ever decide to get a tattoo, there's no one I'd let do it other than Shawn."

I glance over in Shawn's direction again. He's staring at me but not saying anything. His expression is strange, as if that was the last thing he expected to come out of my mouth. But every word I said was true.

"Really?" It's a whisper out of Shawn's mouth.

"Yes, really. If I ever come across something I want, I'd only have you do it." I laugh at a thought. "I'll probably be like Cosmo, waiting until I'm middle-aged. But then my skin will be too, and mine won't look as good."

"I'm done, old man," Shawn says to Cosmo as he backs away from the reclining chair and begins cleaning his station. "You're my last appointment for the day. We're about to head to Jackson, so I'll see you out." He turns to me, taking his keys out of his pocket and holding them out for me to take. "I'll meet you in the truck in a few minutes."

I take them and make my way outside.

I'm ready to get on the road. The sooner we get out of Oxford, the sooner we will make it to Jackson, to my brother's. It's been over a month since I've seen Trent.

I'm sitting in the backseat of Shawn's pickup truck with my shoes off and my legs crisscrossed in the seat. We've been on the road for nearly an hour and a half and are almost there.

The closer we get to Jackson, the more excited I become.

I've been working on my novel during the drive and managed to get one chapter written, but that's all. I have my earbuds tucked into my ears, but I'm not listening to music. I'm one of those people that need complete silence to write. I need alone time inside my own head, so to speak, without any white noise. The earbuds are solely to cut down on Shawn and Mason's conversation, as well as the music coming through the speakers in the truck.

It's worked okay, but to be honest, Shawn's voice is distracting. It is pure southern sexiness with a deep drawl and a rasp. What I wouldn't give to hear that sound whispering dirty thoughts into my ear. A girl could get wet just imagining that. And trust me, I have.

Too bad that little fantasy will never be my reality.

"What's with you and brunettes here lately?" Mason chimes in. I don't look up; I know that question is directed at Shawn. I can feel Shawn's eyes on me, so I'm sure he's glanced up in the mirror to see if I'm listening. I don't want them to think I give a damn about his response, and really, I don't. I don't want to hear about Shawn and other women. I am slightly jealous when it comes to him. And yes, I'm perfectly aware I shouldn't feel that way, but it's not like I can control my feelings. I'm not robotic.

One thing I'll give Shawn credit for, and I'm grateful for, is that as much as I know he sleeps around, he rarely bring it around me. I don't know if that's for my benefit or not, but I'm still glad he doesn't. I don't think I could remain living in the house with him if he had women constantly going in and out. It's going to suck when he finds "the one."

"I didn't realize I had to fuck a certain breed." Did he just call women breeds? What the flyin' eff? Mason snickers, and I continue looking down at my laptop as though I'm lost in my own fictional world. I wish I were.

"Dude, you've always been picky as hell." Umm, no he's not. Picky doesn't have sex with tramps like Holly Torres.

Shut it off, Taralynn. Don't go there. You'll only ruin your day by thinking about her. She isn't worth it. Never was and never will be.

So why the hell did he sleep with her but won't so much as consider me?

"What planet are you on, motherfucker?" Shawn snaps back. "Every bitch's legs spread the same way. The only thing I'm after is the end result. As long as the package is decently wrapped, why should I care what color her hair is?" I can hear it in Shawn's voice —Mason is grinding on his nerves. Mase has a knack for doing that.

"Yeah, okay, tell that to someone that hasn't watched and even taken part in that same action. Because you try to fuck every little blonde, but you can only see one."

What does that mean? Okay, I need to stop listening. It's only causing my chest discomfort. Discomfort I do not need or want.

"I don't know what your fucking angle is, but drop it." Shawn bites out the last two words as if trying to get a point across to Mason.

Mason loves dishing out advice, mainly to his roommates, but he is the last person to ever take it from others.

"She can't hear us, and I'm simply carrying on a conversation here."

"Did you put liquor into the Styrofoam cup you're drinking Coke out of? Shut the fuck up, Mason." Shawn's voice is rising, as it does when he gets pissed off.

"Probably not going to happen. Know what I mean?" Mason doesn't wait for Shawn's response, and I don't think it was meant as a rhetorical question. "You could have her instead of letting him hit it anytime he wants."

Her?

I'm lost. I thought they were talking about me not being able to hear, but I don't even know why that would matter except for the fact that Shawn unfortunately knows exactly how much I'm attracted to him and has mercy on me by not subjecting me to all his whorish ways.

"Last time I'm going to say this, so let me be perfectly clear . . ." Shawn breathes in deeply. I can see his shoulders rise and fall dramatically. My head is still lowered, but I can't help glancing up every now and again. "I don't give a rat's ass who Tara bangs or who she doesn't. Jared can have her because I don't fucking want her."

My head snaps up, looking at Shawn's face in the mirror. It's unreadable with the black sunglasses he's wearing, and I can't tell if he sees me, but when his palm connects with his steering wheel, that tells me he knows I was listening and heard him loud and clear.

"Good, then you won't care if I hit it either."

What?

Oh, I'm pretty sure Mason's going to be the one to get hit— right in his penis.

My eyes lower to see Mason reaching for his cup in the cup holder between him and Shawn. Shawn grasps his wrist before he can retrieve the cup. My eyes go back up to the mirror. Shawn's jaw is locked tight.

"Touch her, and I'll break your dick, rendering it inoperable." Shawn releases Mason's wrist, but Mason doesn't respond to his threat. When I look in Mason's direction, he's cupping his lips to hide the curve of a smirk on his face.

Men are complicated, so much more than women.

Mason isn't interested in me; at least I don't think he is. I mean, I haven't thought of him that way, really, and I don't want to.

I'm not even sleeping with Jared anymore. Not that I've told Jared that, and frankly, I'm avoiding that conversation. I wish I liked him the way I like Shawn, but I don't. Jared knows what to say to make me feel wanted, and even beautiful. He's nice to look at, and he's good in bed, but that's where it ends. I don't feel anything more when I'm with him, and I want more. I just wish I didn't want more with the person who doesn't want anything from me. That was said loud and clear a few moments ago. Not that I didn't already know it, because I did, but it still hurts to hear it from his mouth.

Maybe I should forgo men altogether and jump on the chick bandwagon. They have to be easier.

In one sentence, Shawn declares I'm nothing to him. In the next, he has an issue with Mason wanting me. Now that's something entirely different; what's up with Mason?

The truck comes to a stop. I look up to see that Shawn has parked in my brother's driveway.

Thank heavens! After this drive, I need a drink. Then again, maybe that's not why I need a shot of tequila. You should shoot to feel, to experience, and to remember not to forget. I needed this dose of reality. Shawn and I will never be. When will I get that through my head?

I pack my laptop away, storing it in my over-sized Coach purse.

There is one plus side to my mother; she buys me designer things. I know it's really for her benefit, but her desire to see me with nice things works in my favor, so why should I complain? And the best part is the bag is purple. Nothing makes me happier than the color purple.

Shawn and Mason both open their doors at the same time. I pull my purse onto my shoulder and slide into my boots. I open my door and slide out, landing on the pavement and into my Tony Lamas more snuggly.

I shut the door and look up to see Shawn standing in front of me with his tattooed arm above his head and the palm of his hand clamped onto his neck. He's looking down at me as if remorseful. His shades are on top of his head, so his golden-brown eyes are peering into mine. I look away and move to step around him, but Shawn reaches out with his other hand, placing it on my side to stop me from leaving.

I want to close my eyes so I can fully take in the feeling of his touch. I don't. I have to stop this one way or another. I can't continue having these feelings for him.

"Tara." The sound of his voice makes this situation worse. I pray Kylie bought enough tequila for the weekend.

"I want to go see my brother now." I push his hand away from my body and walk off. Shawn doesn't stop me again. He is so confusing. Why does he care? If what he said was how he feels, it shouldn't matter.

I walk in the front door, not bothering to knock. To some, that may seem rude, but this is our family. The door is always open. Too bad that doesn't apply to the home I grew up in.

Walking through the living room area and into the kitchen, I set my purse down on the counter that's covered with full grocery bags. Kylie must have just returned from the store. I look through the kitchen window directly above the sink and see my brother and his friends outside by the pool. I smile at the sight, taking a breath in through my nose to allow the last few minutes of the drive to dissolve.

I'm done wanting something I can't have. I'm going to stick to that plan and get myself over Shawn this weekend, one way or another.

I walk out into the backyard. Trent and Kylie are standing off to the side of the pool. Kylie has her hands planted on her hips, looking up at Trent. Compared to me, Kylie is little. She's tiny in every way. Shane is nowhere in sight, but a couple of my brother's friends are milling about. I notice Shawn and Mase enter through the side gate at the same time I step off the concrete steps leading into the backyard. Well, it's not exactly a backyard since there's no grass or real yard, only a pool.

Trent's back is to me, so I step lightly, trying to make the least amount of sound possible so I can surprise him before anyone notices the three of us. Kylie sees me coming, but I don't think she has said anything to Trent. I increase my speed to a jog, afraid he'll turn around. As I near my brother, I leap, jumping onto his back.

"Surprise!" I yell as I wrap my arms around his front. Trent steps forward, which forces Kylie to take a few steps backward. Trent turns his head to look back at me from over his shoulder.

"It's not a surprise when I knew you were coming, brat." Trent's called me 'brat' for as long as I can remember. He means it as a joke and always says it in an affectionate way.

"Shut your face and tell me you missed me." I cross my arms around the front of his neck and squeeze.

"Oh, I missed you, all right." My brother lets out a quick chuckle before his lips spread into a grin. When his eyes widen, I know I'm in trouble. His hands latch onto the skin behind my knees, digging in so I can't get away.

Oh, crap!

"Trent!" I warn, knowing what's coming and there isn't a chance in hell I'll be able to stop him. Doesn't mean I won't try. "My boots can't go in water!" He doesn't listen and probably doesn't care either because our mother still buys him everything he's ever wanted. The cost of clothes and shoes doesn't faze him one bit.

"Too late for that." Trent laughs.

I don't have a chance to protest further because he takes a few steps toward the water and then launches us into the deep end of the pool. The warm water envelops my body within seconds. Normally, this is a wonderful feeling, but not when I know my favorite cowboy boots are being ruined.

You don't ruin a girl's shoes.

No way is this funny.

Trent releases me, and I push away from him as my head returns to the surface. "Trent!" I scream, pushing my hair out of my face to glare in his direction. He's laughing. Of course he is. "You're a butthole."

I turn away from him and swim to the ladder. Everyone is laughing—just freakin' great. Thank goodness I did not put on makeup today.

"You love me."

"You ruined my boots." Yes, I'm sulking, wouldn't you?

"Oh, what's the big deal, sis? Just get Mom to buy you another pair." As if it's that easy. For him, it is, but mother and I don't have that kind of relationship. But I'm not jealous of my brother. I'm glad he doesn't have to deal with the bitch side of the queen.

"She didn't buy them. I did. They aren't Katherine Evans approved." I pull myself out of the pool and onto the pavement. Water runs down my legs and into my boots. Walking over to a chair in the shade, I plop down and start to remove them.

"What's the big deal? They're just shoes."

Just shoes? Oh, he didn't say that.

Effin' men.

"A fine-ass bitch in short shorts and cowboy boots," Shawn coos. "There is nothing sexier." His voice goes flat. "They were a waste on your sister." Shawn grabs a beer from one of the larger coolers as Kylie walks in his direction.

I guess he wasn't sorry after all.

What an asshole.

"Hey, jerk," Kylie calls, "turn your dick-o-meter off. I'm not having your shit this weekend." Kylie looks like a midget compared to Shawn. He doesn't say anything back to her, just continues looking down at her as he takes a sip from the bottle. Kylie turns to look at me. "Come on, let's get you into a bathing suit and us a drink." I second that, at least on the drink end. I needed one when I walked in, and I need it even more now.

I follow, leaving my boots outside.

Spotting my weekend bag by the backdoor, I scoop it up. Mason or Shawn must have brought our bags from the truck since I left mine.

"I'm going to go change. Can I use your bedroom?" I ask Kylie as we enter the kitchen.

"Of course you can. I'll make us margaritas. Sound good?"

"Yes, please, and with a double shot of tequila on the side." My brother's girlfriend laughs. There is nothing better than a frozen strawberry margarita and a pool. They go together like brownies and ice cream. You can have one without the other, but it's not near as good.

"Coming right up, sweets." Kylie's voice fades away as I reach the hallway that leads to their bedroom, Shane's bedroom, the computer room, and the bathroom. It's a small house, but it is perfect for the three of them.

I quickly change into my black halter-top one-piece swimsuit and then pull on a dry pair of shorts to cover my chunky legs. Without alcohol, I'm overly self-conscious of my appearance around others. Especially when perfection clad in ink, jeans, and a loose T-shirt is around.

Why do I like him? It's an endless question I ask myself too often. I don't get it. Why can't I turn it off?

My thoughts are on finding Kylie and my tequila-laced margarita as I exit my brother's bedroom, so I don't see Shane until I run straight into him.

"Easy, killer." His voice sounds tired.

"Sorry, Shane." As I pull back, I see he's only wearing a pair of boxer briefs, a sure sign that he just woke up. Seeing him almost naked does not faze me in the slightest, unlike the way my pulse races when I see his brother in similar clothing. We've all grown up together, so why would it be any different? Obviously, my body and brain aren't on the same page when it comes to seeing the Braden brothers scantily clad.

"It's fine, precious." He shakes his head as if telling me it isn't a big deal. "I'm heading back to bed. See you in a few hours."

"Back to bed?" It's late afternoon. Who sleeps this late? His brother doesn't even sleep this late.

"The only reason I'm up is that I heard you scream. I couldn't go back to sleep until I took a piss. I pulled a double, so I was at the hospital for over twenty-four hours. I just got home late this morning."

"Aw, Shane, I'm sorry. I didn't mean to wake you." Damn, I feel bad now. Like my brother and Kylie, Shane is also in his second year of residency.

"Don't sweat it, kiddo. It's not a problem."

"Okay, you go back to bed. Kylie was bringing out the tequila a few minutes ago, so I'm going to head back." I nod in the direction down the hall leading toward the kitchen.

"Oh, Lord." He shakes his head again.

"What?"

"You and tequila, precious." That's all he says before walking into his room and shutting himself in darkness. I think I understand why they all have their windows blacked out: when the lights are off, it's pitch black inside their bedrooms. I guess working long hours happens a lot when you're in medical school.

Sure enough, when I walk back through the kitchen, there is a tall glass of deliciousness with a double shot of tequila sitting next to it. I pick up the shot glass, toss the contents toward the back of my throat and swallow. Kylie had limes laid out, but I didn't bother.

"Thank you," I tell her as I start on my drink. "I needed that."

CHAPTER SIX
SHAWN

N ow who is this pretty little thing?

Leaning into the frame connecting the sliding glass door to the wall, I fold my arms across my chest and eye the sexy, strawberry blonde pixie that just walked through my brother's front door a few seconds ago. I've never seen her before, but she followed Jamie in, so I assume they're friends. Good, I can get her to introduce me.

I take a sip of my beer.

Mason is wrong. I don't go after women with a certain color hair.

I take another swig, savoring the hoppy brew as I continue looking them both over.

Jamie is one of Kylie's friends. I think they work together or work out together, or something. I don't know, nor do I care. I banged her this past summer. Decent fuck, nothing to dabble in more than once, but then again, who is?

As I push off the doorframe, someone steps into my path, blocking my easy mark for the night. "You planning on doing anything about that?" Trent points his index finger behind me.

"You're blocking my view," I deadpan, casting my eyes downward to meet his. Trent's now several inches shorter than my six-foot two-inch frame. If he thinks he can still get in my face and order me around like he did when I was a kid, he has another think coming. For the most part, I've always liked Trent. He's not a bad guy, but he's Shane's best friend and always came first. You'd think blood would be thicker than water, but not with Shane. Trent glances behind him, taking in the scantily clad redhead who's now smiling back at me.

So I've caught her attention. This'll be easy-peasy.

"Hmph," he blows out as he shakes his head. I peer around him and give the little hottie a once-over so she knows I'm interested. "Worry about who to stick your dick in later, and go do something about that shit out there before I have to."

"You're a big boy. I'm sure whatever it is, you're capable of handling it. And if you can't, call Shane, 'cause last I checked, I'm not your bitch." I go to walk past him, but I halt when he lays a firm hand on my shoulder. I don't know what his problem is, but the last thing I need is this shit. "Careful, Evans."

"It is your job to watch her and make sure she doesn't do anything stupid." By 'her,' I know he's talking about Tara. Trent is always quick to remind me why she lives in my house, why I'm forced to see her on a damn near daily basis, and why it's my fault she makes dumb decisions without thinking them through. "So I suggest you handle Mason. You can get his hands off my sister, or I will. I really don't want to hit my girlfriend's little brother, but I will if he doesn't stop touching Taralynn like he is right now."

I pivot, doing a one-eighty before he even has time to take his hand from my shoulder. If I thought his words alone caused me to see red, I was dead wrong. The scene in front of me has my body on fire. Mason is lying down, practically flat on his back, on a lounge chair in front of the pool. Tara is straddling his hips, holding what I think is a bottle of tequila. My best friend, who I'm about to lose it on, is smirking up at her while running his palm up her bare thigh. Tara is wearing a black bathing suit that molds to her perfect body like a second skin. It's a one-piece that barely covers her plump ass. It dips too low in the back and ties around her neck, causing her already voluptuous tits to push together, sitting high on her chest. My eyes zero in on his right hand that continues to skirt up her outer thigh.

I remove my cell phone from the pocket of my shorts and quickly press his name under my contacts and watch, waiting for him to answer. It doesn't take but a few seconds before he grabs his own phone lying on the table next to him. He answers without taking his eyes off Tara. I'm going to murder him tonight.

"I'm busy." His voice is laced with irritation and heat.

He's turned on. She has him turned on. Tara brings the bottle to her lips, tosses her head back and takes a swig. The fuck? Since when does she drink like that? Yeah, I know she loves beer and has a few shots of tequila occasionally, but still. She takes another swig before bringing the bottle back down to her side and lowering her face to Mason's. He parts his lips and she releases the liquid into his mouth.

"Get. Your. God. Damn. Hands. Off her, you stupid motherfucker." Murder red, the color of blood, is all I can see surrounding their bodies.

"Like I said, I'm busy, so piss off."

And with that, the line goes dead. He drops his cell phone on the table. As his left hand goes around her ass, I walk out of the house. His right hand goes further up, along her belly, and over her chest until he reaches her neck, where he pulls her down, only inches from his face. Right before their lips meet, I reach the pool area, squat down on the side of his lounge chair and wrap my hand around his throat, squeezing only tight enough to get his attention. Tara looks up, giving me a strange drunken look before blushing like she's been caught doing something she shouldn't be doing.

I look down at my best friend. "Sure you want to do that?"

Mason lifts his hands off Tara as if saying he surrenders. Good decision on his part.

"Remove your hand from my neck, now," he throws out. It's a threat; I hear it in his tone. Mason is the fun, don't give a shit type, but he isn't a pussy in any way. He doesn't take shit from anyone, not even me. He'll go toe to toe with men bigger and stronger than him without thinking twice.

I release him and stand. Tara sinks down on top of Mason, laying slightly off to his left side, and looks up at me. "Don't rain on my fun, Shawn. Now, if you want to join in . . ." She trails off as she gives me a sexy, albeit drunken smile before glancing down, eyeing my shorts before returning her eyes to mine.

Did she? Did she just suggest what I think she suggested? Mason starts to laugh, and Tara follows suit while I stand looking down at both of them, dumbfounded. She's obviously wasted.

"Is that what you want, Taralynn? You want Shawn and me to fuck you together?" Mason runs his palm up her arm.

Tara goes silent. She looks from me to Mason as if contemplating it.

I don't think so.

No fucking way.

Not waiting a second, I grab her by the wrist, pulling her up and in front of me before bending at the knees and tossing her over my shoulder. I don't want to hear her answer. I'm afraid of what it might be. If it were 'no,' I think that would solidify things. I know she's a good girl. Tara isn't meant to do the things I'd do to her given the chance. But if it was a 'yes,' I'm not sure I'd have the strength to turn her down. I know I couldn't allow Mason to touch her, not in that way.

"Shawn," she slurs.

"You're drunk. You're going to bed."

I make my way across the yard and into the house. Trent nods in my direction, but I don't address him. It should have been him to stop that shit. It should be him to put her in bed, not me.

"Put me down, Shawn." I walk through the kitchen and down the hall, rounding the corner to my brother's room. I should be placing her in Trent and Kylie's bed, but I don't. "Shawn, stop, please. I'm going to throw up."

I halt, turning around and taking the two steps toward the bathroom. I set Tara right side up and back on her feet, and she grabs onto my shirt for support. I pull her closer, telling myself I'm only doing it to steady her.

It's a lie.

I want her heat, her smell, the feel of her body pressed against mine.

I open the bathroom door and guide Tara inside. She goes down on her knees in front of the toilet, making a gagging sound as I grip her hair in my hands.

She pukes her guts up for nearly a full minute. When I'm certain she's done, I release her hair and grab the hand towel by the sink. I wet it and pass it to her. She cleans her mouth off and then goes down on her ass.

I squat, opening the cabinet under the sink. I spot what I'm looking for and grab the mouthwash. I pour a large amount into the cap, placing it on the countertop. Reaching for Tara, I pull her up into a standing position.

"No, I want to lie down."

"This is the bathroom. You're not going to lie on the floor." I shove the cap filled with mouthwash in front of her face. Her head pulls back as she tries to focus her eyes. When she realizes the contents, Tara lifts her hands and takes it from me. She shoots it back into her mouth, but just to be on the safe side, I admonish, "Swish that, don't swallow."

Tara tosses the cap onto the counter and grabs onto my waist before leaning to the side to spit into the sink. Then she pulls herself closer to me and lays her cheek on my chest.

"Mmmm . . . you feel good," she purrs.

"Let's get you to bed."

"And you?"

"Tara," I warn.

"Haven't you ever heard the phrase, don't knock it until you try it?" She's serious, drunk serious, but serious nonetheless. This is why I don't like dealing with her when she's like this. Her brother should be the one here right now; she wouldn't be spewing this crap.

Tara thinks she wants me.

She doesn't, or at least she shouldn't. She doesn't need me like that.

She needs a man that can give her everything. I'll never fit in with her family. I'd never get their blessing. Hell would have to freeze over first. *Their* opinions matter a little too much in Tara's world. Given all that, I know it'll never work. Why torture myself with it?

"Wrap your arms around my neck."

"With pleasure." I scoop her up without addressing her previous question. Of course I've heard the saying, but if I never get a taste of something, then I'll never know what I'm missing.

Once I have her on the bed, I turn away to search for her clothes. Her bathing suit is a little damp. I don't want her to sleep in a wet suit. She could get sick.

"Where are you going?" Her voice is hopeful, and it causes a heavy ache in my chest. I'm not leaving her; I don't want her to throw up again and choke on her puke.

"To find your clothes." That seems to satisfy her. Her head falls onto Shane's pillow, and she closes her eyes.

I exit the bedroom and come face to face with a very pissed off Mason. I don't care.

"If I were you, I'd stay away from me right now." He's lucky I don't punch him for that shit after I warned him early today.

"Well, I'm not you, Shawn. I'm not turning down the best thing offered, especially when it's being offered so freely."

"What the fuck is that supposed to mean?"

"It means you have until graduation to make her yours. After that, I'm doing all I can to make her mine, and I won't quit until I do, brother."

I advance forward, shoving him back into the wall. "Touch her and I'll break you, motherfucker."

Could I take Mason on? Sure. Could I win the fight? Maybe. Mason and I are almost the same height and weight. He's an inch or two shorter, but we have the same build.

"Both of you cut this shit out." Kylie's voice rings out. She pushes me off, away from her brother. Kylie's little, but don't let that fool you. What she lacks in size, she makes up for in brains and mouth. She also knows how to handle Mason and me, and I can assure you, she isn't the least bit intimidated by our size. Kylie has no reason to be. Both of us would do anything for this woman who has her palms on the center of our chests at this very moment.

"I'm done here," I say, taking a step back, eyeing Mason before turning and going into Trent and Kylie's room to retrieve Tara's bag. Once I have it I come back out. Kylie and Mason have cleared out, but Trent is waiting for me.

Fucking A.

I blow out a breath as I shut his door.

"What do you want? I have a drunk girl to attend to, seeing how you won't handle your sister."

"Are you saying you're not the man for the job?" What is he talking about?

Trent loves riddles. It's stupid as hell.

"Look, dude, if you have something to say, say it. I don't need you going around the world to get your point across." Why can't people just say what they mean? What is the point in all the other shit?

"For whatever reason, Taralynn likes you, so maybe it's time you grow a pair and do something about it before someone else does."

"Did it ever cross your mind that I don't want her?"

"It did, but then again, you've always been a lying little shit."
With those last words, he turns and walks off. Probably the best
thing he could have done. I don't want Tara to wake up and
discover that I beat up her brother.

I enter Shane's bedroom. Tara is still lying on the bed, but she's
rolled onto her side. She would offer me such a fine view of her ass.

Crossing over to the bed, I place her bag on top of the
mattress, then I look her over. Man, she has one fine-ass body. I've
got to get it covered before my dick no longer has breathing room
inside my pants.

Looking away from her and down into her bag, I move things
around until I find a T-shirt and pajama pants. No way am I
putting a tank top on her tonight. Holding up the T-shirt, I can
already tell it isn't going to be long enough, so I toss it back into the
bag. Not needing it any longer, I move the bag onto the floor.

I then crawl into the bed with Tara. When I gently roll her
onto her back, she doesn't make a sound. She's out cold. That's a
good thing for me because turning her down, even drunk, is getting
old.

I place her pants to the side and pull my own T-shirt over my
head. Assessing Tara, I try to decide the best way to undress her
and re-dress her without causing myself any more discomfort. I
don't see a win-win here. Even if I don't see a thing, I have a very
vivid imagination when it comes to the woman lying in front of me.

This is going to be one long-ass night.

I pull my T-shirt over Tara's head and proceed to pull her arms
through each hole. Her bathing suit is a halter top, so that's easy. I
untie it and then reach under the shirt, with my eyes closed tight, to
pull the material down her body. I stop before I reveal her center.
That's when I open my eyes. I need to make sure she's still covered.

I may be a dick, an asshole for sure, but I'd never take
advantage of her in any way. My T-shirt comes down almost to her
mid-thigh, but it's not covering her because I had my arms under it
to pull her suit down. I adjust and then finish taking off her damp

bathing suit. I toss it behind me so it lands on the floor. I quickly pull on her pants, lifting her slightly to pull them over her butt.

Once done, I pull the cover out from beneath her body so I can cover her.

I fall onto my back on top of the covers and lie next to her. I don't know how I'm going to get any sleep being this close to perfection. The smell of Tara is all around me, smothering all other scents. It's not helping the hardness inside my shorts.

I force my eyes to close.

It's hours later before I'm able to doze off.

CHAPTER SEVEN

TARALYNN

T wo uneventful weeks flew by after we returned from our weekend at my brother's. Shawn has been acting like a douchebag ever since. Mostly he's been avoiding me, but when he is home, he's a brooding dickhead.

He may have saved me from making a major mistake with Mason the night of Kylie's party, but I'm not about to go telling him that. Frankly, I'd like to forget that ever happened. It's not that Mason isn't attractive. He's more than attractive, in both the looks and personality department. The man is gorgeous, but even more important is he's funny as all get out. However, Mason and I as a couple? I just don't see him that way unless, of course, I've had a bottle of tequila.

Gosh darn Patron.

If I didn't need something from Shawn, I wouldn't be waiting around the studio late on a Friday evening. I was supposed to work tonight at Mac's Pub, but I called in, feigning a headache.

Shawn is cleaning up his station when I walk over. The only other person still here is Kenny, and his station is toward the front of the large room, near the receptionist's area.

"Can I talk to you?"

He stands up from wiping his chair down and tosses the used paper towel into the trash bin a few feet away from us.

"Sure, what's up, Tara?" He looks down at me.

I place my hands in my back pockets and rock on my heels. I haven't the slightest idea how to start out this conversation.

"If it's that damn serious, maybe you need to take a seat." He gestures to the chair he finished cleaning moments ago. He has a good point. Maybe sitting will calm my nerves. I don't even know why I'm so itchy. Nothing is probably going on, anyway. It's all probably in my head. I've never run a business. I'm probably way off here.

I go ahead, taking the seat he's offered.

"You're never here this late, so what's going on, Tara?" he prompts, looking concerned. Shawn's arms fall to his side as he awaits my reply.

"Um," I pause. Where do I begin? "I don't know. It's probably nothing; it's just things aren't adding up." I stop talking. One, I'm rambling and not making sense. Two, my voice was increasing with every word. That happens when I get nervous and jumpy. I look around to see if Kenny heard me. He looks up but doesn't look curious.

"You don't want Kenny to hear us?" Shawn looks from Kenny, back to me. I nod my head. "Lie back in the chair and unbutton your pants." He turns away from me.

"Excuse me?"

Seconds later, he's standing next to me, holding what I know is transfer paper with a design. I can't see what's on it.

I look up at Shawn, confused. Did he tell me to take off my clothes?

"You don't want anyone to hear us talking, so I'm going to act as though I'm positioning a design on your hip bone."

"Why my hip?" This isn't making any sense.

"Do you want me to listen or not?" His eyebrows furrow.

"Fine." I lay back and pop the button on my jeans. The self-conscious feeling I get when I'm around him starts to set in the moment my jeans and panties lower to reveal the skin surrounding my hipbone. It's not like he can see anything substantial. All my girly parts are still covered, and Shawn's seen more of my flesh when I'm in a bathing suit than in this moment. Still, there has never been a more intimate moment between us than right now. I don't know what to do. How am I supposed to talk while lying in this position?

All I can think about is him looking at the pudginess of my stomach. I'm pretty sure I have a stretch mark or two from my weight fluctuation.

Shit. How did I even get in this predicament?

"Now would be the time to start talking, Tara."

Shawn lays the paper against my skin, rubbing his hand thoroughly over me to make sure the marks take to my skin. His hands feel amazing, even if it's not full contact and there is a thin sheet of paper between us.

Shoot, my breathing starts to accelerate.

Calming breaths are what I need.

"Today, Tara, I'm not getting any younger." He isn't looking at me, so I doubt he can see the way my cheeks have started to heat. I take a slow deep breath and exhale even slower.

"It's about Adam. Well, the studio, actually." That causes him to pause his hand on me to look up. His palm remains flat against my body as his brown eyes penetrate mine.

"What do you mean?" He's curious and looking at me intently.

I'm starting to calm. As I do, I'm able to relax further back into the cushioned seat.

"Over the last few weeks, I've noticed things."

"What things?" If he would give me a chance, I'd tell him without him having to ask. Shawn's impatient when you pique his interest. Actually, the only time Shawn isn't impatient is when he's working. It's an appealing thing to watch. Shawn is totally and completely calm and in his own world when he's hunched over someone with a tattoo machine firmly clutched in his hand.

I don't know if you can compare the two, but his mom is the same way when she's in her element. Pamela Braden is a pediatrician. She was my doctor until I graduated high school and technically became an adult at eighteen. Both of Shawn's parents are doctors. Mr. Bill is a cardiologist and works at the largest medical facility in north Mississippi.

"Adam's finances with the business," I tell him. I chew on the side of my lip as I look for the right words. I'm no expert here. I'm a double major at Ole Miss—English and Accounting. My dad's doing, of course, because one major wasn't enough to please him. "I've always handled just the payroll side of things." I don't know why I'm starting out this way, but I feel the need to explain in detail.

"I know this already, Tara. You've been doing it for two years now."

"Yeah, but when Adam got me to start paying the bills and ordering stuff, he gave me—" I'm not able to finish because Shawn cut me off.

"He what?" He's looking at me a little dumbfounded when his eyebrows close together, forming a tight crease in the center. "So he has you doing his job now? What else does he have you doing?"

"Besides payroll, I pay all the incoming invoices and order everyone's supplies." I bite the inside of my mouth behind my lips. If this is pissing him off, what I tell him next may flip his lid. "He also asked me to interview a piercer he has coming in next Friday."

"Are you shitting me?" He's seriously shocked. I didn't think it was possible to shock Shawn.

"Yeah. He only asked me today if I'd do it. He said he was going out to Vegas and didn't want to reschedule the guy's interview." Maybe Shawn was the wrong person to bring this to. Heck, I haven't even gotten to the point of what I wanted to talk to him about.

Shawn removes his right hand from my hip and places it on the smooth surface next to my left side. He shakes his head.

"He's having you do his fucking job, so what, he can take a vacation? Unbelievable." His expression turns hard. "He'd better be paying you more to do all the shit he's supposed to be doing."

Paying me? As if.

"Umm . . ." Yeah, I don't really know how to say this next part.

"He's not, is he? Cheap motherfucker." Again, he shakes his head as if he can't believe the ways of his boss. It's true. Adam is cheap. I mean, I have to bargain shop for the basic things the studio needs, like toilet paper and hand soap.

"He's never paid me. At all," I add.

"Come the fuck again?" His jaw locks and his eyes turn dark. He's mad.

"He doesn't pay me, Shawn, and frankly, I don't think he can." Not after seeing his bank statements. Adam is barely keeping the lights on in here.

"The hell he can't. Business is great and has been for a while now. None of us are sitting on our ass without clients to service."

"Look, this isn't what I wanted to talk to you about."

"Then what is it? Spit it out already because I have a boss's ass to kick. You can't let him or anyone else take advantage of you like that, Tara. What the hell were you thinking?"

"Well, it started off as a favor, and it was working to my advantage too. I was learning things I could use for my accounting classes. And it's not as if I hate coming here. The opposite, actually; it's a job without being a job, I guess."

I've never seen myself doing anything other than writing. My dream is to get published, and it's something I intend on making happen. My father wanted me to go into law like him since it was obvious my brother wasn't going to follow in his footsteps. I'm not either, but for me, that meant also majoring in something I could fall back on if the whole "writing hobby," as my parents put it, doesn't work out.

But it'll work out. I'll make sure of it because I'll be damned if I'm ever going to be financially dependent on a man like my mother is. I don't understand it to save me. I'm not judging; it's just the way I see things. I'll never feel as though I can't make my own way in this world. For me, that means getting out and earning my own living. Bringing my own food to the table, so to speak.

It's the reason I have a part-time waitressing job at Mac's Pub. It certainly isn't because I like the job. I don't. Most of the patrons are nice, but there are always the creepy, cheesy men that make little comments or place their hands on me. Not to mention I have to wear a top that shows off my boobs.

"Look, I'm sorry. Maybe I shouldn't have brought anything up. It's not like I know if anything is going on, but I didn't want to go to Adam without talking about it with someone. And I don't want him to think I screwed something up."

That is my real issue. I'm afraid he's going to blame me for something I know I didn't do, or at least didn't do intentionally.

"What are you talking about? Please explain it to me because I'm not following."

Shawn looks back down at my waist. A few seconds later, I feel the paper being lifted from my skin. I'm dying to see it, but I don't look down yet. I need to get everything out so someone else can confirm that I'm not crazy.

"I've been noticing the online bank statements are way off from the written ledger Adam keeps in his desk. I only use it when I write down anything I pay out. That's it, I swear." I say this like I'm guilty of something when I'm not. "Two weeks ago, I decided to figure out where the discrepancies were coming from. It's taken a while, but I think I figured it out with the help of one of my teachers."

Shawn balls up the paper and tosses it into the trashcan. He's still looking down at me. His eyes are big. Shawn has big brown eyes to start with, but right now, they're wider than normal as if he's in awe. Surely he's not.

"I'm listening." He finally looks up.

"The amounts deposited each week don't add up to what I've been paying each artist based on their commission and what the studio profits off each artist's clients."

"What exactly are you getting at?"

"It looks like I'm overpaying the artists, but Shawn, I check myself multiple times. There's just no . . . I don't know how I could make mistakes like that."

"Tara, stop!" Shawn glances back down to where he laid the design. It's only a second or two, but it's as though he can't stop looking at it. I really want to see it now. "I check my shit every week. I can't speak for most of the jacklegs in this place, but I know Adam and Kenny check their shit too. If you were overpaying one of us, we would have caught it. Kenny is a stand-up guy. He's honest. I'm damn sure he wouldn't let that go on without correcting it, and neither would I."

"Then . . ." I stop, not wanting to continue. Continuing means I'm accusing other people of stealing without any proof. "Fuck," I sigh out in a long breath. Shawn raises his eyebrows in surprise. "Oh, like you've never heard that word come out of my mouth before."

"Sure I have. Maybe once or twice, but only when I provoke you." He smiles his half smile that normally melts me on the spot. "Then what? Finish what you wanted to say."

"Only three people touch the money that comes into this place: Adam, Sabrina, and me." Sabrina is the receptionist for the tattoo studio. She runs the front. Answers the phones, schedules most of the appointments for the artists, and makes daily deposits to the bank. "I would never steal from Adam or anyone. I—"

"Tara, stop defending yourself to me. I know you wouldn't, and not for a second did that thought ever cross my mind." He's serious. I breathe in relief, knowing Shawn believes me. I don't know how much weight that will hold, though; it's Adam that has to believe me. "I'm going to tell you something, but it stays between us until I'm ready for others to know, okay?"

I nod my head once, telling him I understand and agree.

"I'm buying the studio from Adam. I sign the paperwork and hand over the check on Monday. If someone is stealing money from the business, I need to know ASAP. Whether it's my friend and soon-to-be former boss or some little cunt that needs to get a boot in her ass and shoved out the goddamn door, I need to know who, and I need to know now."

I'm startled, but not at his use of the "c" word. I thought Shawn had stopped shocking me years ago, but the confession that he is not only staying in Oxford indefinitely but is also going to be the proud owner of a business in three days took my breath away.

I was worried what would happen after graduation. None of us have really talked about it. I know Shawn loves his grandparents' house, but I also know Chance—Adam's cousin who is coincidentally another of our brother's good friends—offered him a spot at his tattoo studio in Las Vegas. I overheard a discussion about it this past summer. Shawn is a talented tattoo artist. His work should be seen everywhere, and there's no better place to get his name out there than in Sin City.

"What do you want me to do?"

"We need to figure out who's taking the money. I gotta say, I don't see this being on Adam's shoulders. I mean, it's his business. I know he's disconnected from it and simply put, he sucks at managing—which is another reason I decided to give it a go—but I don't see him as a thief."

"So you're thinking Sabrina, then?"

"I don't want to think anyone I work with day in and day out would stoop that low, but sometimes you don't really know people. People are out for themselves, and a lot don't care if they harm someone else in getting what they want."

I stop and think about everything from the past few weeks that I've been mulling over. I didn't really consider someone taking the money. I think I was too worried that Adam would think I screwed up. And even though I know I'm thorough, I considered the fact that maybe I did mess up. A light bulb comes on, and I peer up at Shawn.

"You keep an appointment book of everything, right?" I know he does, which is why I don't wait for his reply. "Sabrina keeps an appointment log for all artists too. If I can add up the costs and what should be deposited daily, that will tell us if someone is taking money out before it hits the bank."

"True, but it won't tell us who."

"Then I don't know what to tell you."

"I'll figure something out. Lie back. Let me wash this shit off you."

"No way, I want to see it." I smile and rise, but Shawn places his palm on my shoulder and stops my movement.

"I don't think so."

"I do think so. Now move." I push his hand off and sit up. I'm dying to see what a tattoo designed by Shawn might look like on me. I've wanted one for so long.

"Tara, just let me clean it off." He looks really nervous. I don't know why. "It's not anything worth seeing. It was something I drew up for a chick that decided not to get it done."

Again, I'm getting the feeling that isn't true. Shawn isn't usually one to lie, as in ever.

I push him back and get out of the chair before he can stop me. A long mirror runs the length of the back wall. It starts from the ceiling and ends where the countertop begins. The counter is thigh-high, so that artists can reach for anything they have on it when they are sitting down.

What I see when I look in the mirror has liquid pooling in my eyes.

Freakin' hell, it's beautiful and perfect.

Oh, my God.

This is it.

The one.

I have to have this inked on me.

"Shit, Tara, I didn't mean to make you cry. I told you to let me wash it off. Fuck." I look in his direction as a tear slides down. God, I'm such a girl sometimes. Shawn looks almost hurt and maybe disappointed.

"I want it," I declare, because I really do love design. "Oh, my God, this is the prettiest thing I've ever seen."

"Huh?" He shakes his head. "No, you don't. Let me clean you off now."

"No way, I'm absolutely serious. I want this tattooed on my body, and I want it now."

The design is a thick storybook, opened and placed on my hip. The spine of the book is on my hipbone. There are swirling words and birds set as if they are flying from the pages. Little black birds are flying in every direction, trailing words behind them. Words like love, hate, joy, tears, drama, pain, and so on. There is even a slightly larger one trailing the letters "HEA" behind it.

There are almost no words to describe what I'm looking at.

Perfection is the closest.

"Now?" He's questioning me. I don't think he understands the way I feel, and I have to make myself clear if I'm going to talk Shawn into letting me have this and doing it himself.

"Yes, now. Come on, do this for me, please. Besides banging the first tramp you see in a bar, what do you have to do tonight? There will still be plenty of time to screw a random whore after you do me."

That last part came out wrong.

"Tara, a tattoo is permanent." Well, freakin' duh. Does he think I'm stupid?

"Really? I had no idea. Thanks for the heads up, Mr. Genius." He huffs at my sarcasm. He deserved that.

"No, I'm not doing it. I'm not going to put something on you that you might regret. No, Tara, not happening."

102 N. E. HENDERSON

"What the hell makes you think I'm going to regret it? I wouldn't. Shawn, you're an amazing artist. You're the only person I'd want tattooing me, but if you aren't going to, then I'm going to get someone else to do it." Apparently, I'm not above blackmail here. "I want this design, and I want it tonight."

The chime of the door sounds. Shawn and I turn our heads just as Adam walks through the door.

"Forgot my GD phone." He looks in our direction and is taken aback when he sees me. "You're never here this late. What are you doing here, girlie?"

"Adam," I sing at the same time I turn to face him. "What do you think of this?" I widen my smile into a toothy grin. If I have to pretend I want Adam to tattoo me to get Shawn to do it, then so be it.

"Nerdy, but hot on you." He strides over, not taking his eyes off my body.

"Shawn won't do it. Will you?" I raise my T-shirt up a little to give him a better look.

"Besides the nerdy side of it, it's a pretty rockin' tat, and it looks killer on her. What gives, brother?" He aims his question in Shawn's direction. I glance over, taking in the hard eyes staring at Adam. I don't know if it has to do with the tattoo I want or what I revealed to Shawn about the business he's buying.

"Because I said she's not getting a tattoo. Period. End of fucking story."

I'm getting this done whether he likes it or not.

You see, the thing about Adam is, he likes a girl with an extra-large chest. I don't flaunt what I have around here. Heck, I don't flaunt it anywhere, really. But if I need to use it to get what I want, why the hell not, right?

Taking the hem of my shirt into my hands, I pull it up and over my head in one swift move.

A girl's gotta do what a girl's gotta do.

"You haven't seen it all. It goes all the way up my ribs." The birds stop an inch below my bra line.

"Fuck." Adam's eyes aren't on the side of my body. He's staring at the center of my chest. "I'll do it."

"Like hell, you will." Shawn grabs my elbow, pulling me away from Adam. "Put your fucking shirt back on." His face is on fire. I'd laugh, but I'm not trying to piss him off, at least not in that way.

"The lady wants a tattoo. The lady shall get what she wants." I twist, or attempt to, in order to face Adam. He's saying everything I want him to say.

"What part of *no* do you not understand?"

"Shawn, stop." My voice is stern. He needs to know how serious I am. "I really want this, and if you aren't going to—"

"Fine." Shawn throws his hands up. "If you're determined, then it'll be me that does it."

"Thank you. That's all I wanted." I smile up at him as I wrap my arms around his neck. Shawn closes his eyes for the briefest of seconds, as if savoring the moment. I know he's not. That's only wishful thinking on my part.

He sighs and pulls away from me.

"You know this is going to hurt, right?"

"Probably." I've seen every expression imaginable in this place. Tattoos bring some to tears. Others seem to experience pure bliss. There are even those whose whole being seemed locked in terror. "I'm guessing needles poking into my skin hundreds of times, over and over again, won't feel peachy."

"Peachy?" Shawn shakes his head, but he smiles. "Get in the chair. You want this, let's do it."

I step backward and sit down, swinging my legs onto the seat, and lean back.

"Put your shirt back on, please."

"Wouldn't it be easier if I—"

"Tara, please." It's a plea.

"Fine, whatever." I sit back up and pull my shirt over my head.

"Tuck the right side into your bra." I do as he says, but I still think it would have been easier to leave it off. "Are you really sure about this?"

What's a girl gotta do to get a damn tattoo tonight?

"Yes, Shawn," I force out as I fall back into the chair. Why is he making such a big deal about this? His work is flawless and beautiful. The moment my eyes landed on this design, I knew it was the one I wanted.

"Then relax. We're going to be here about an hour."

That hour turned into two. Apparently my threshold for physical pain isn't as high as my capacity for mental pain. The needle jabbing into my hipbone and rib cage was enough to bring on the waterworks. Shawn eventually had to get Adam to talk me through it, because he couldn't do that and concentrate on the tattoo process. Adam not only talked to me but also let me hold onto his arms, never complaining once.

He's a great guy like that. I don't think he could have stolen from his own company. I don't see that in him at all.

CHAPTER EIGHT

SHAWN

It's been a week since I inked the book tattoo on Tara. The morning after, she freaked. I initially thought she was acting nuts because she regretted getting the tattoo, but then I realized she thought something was wrong. When I discovered it was just a little plasma leaking from the fresh wound, I laughed. She didn't find the same humor in the ordeal that I did. She was okay once I explained that what was happening was perfectly normal.

I have to admit, her hysteria was cute.

It's a Friday night, and like any other Friday night after work, I'm at Mac's Pub. Eventually I'll make it out to a club if I don't find a prospect here.

The two jackasses standing at the bar catch my attention. They were having a pissing contest when I walked in the door half an hour ago. Doesn't look like their conversation will be mellowing any time soon. Mac needs to get his ass out here and end this shit.

This may be a local hole-in-the-wall bar, but it's a good spot to chill after a long day. Drama doesn't have a place here. These two old fuckers either need to take their shit outside or go sit at the opposite ends of the bar, as far away from each other as possible.

"Hey man, that was a pretty cool piece you did on Calvin's leg."

My attention on the two drunk middle-agers at the bar arguing is interrupted by my now ex-boss. I'm now the proud owner of the tattoo studio I work at. We haven't made the announcement yet, and I don't plan on announcing it until I find out who is stealing money from the company. Adam and I had it out on Monday morning. He swears up and down he'd never do something like that. I believe him, and we both found it laughable that Tara believed either of us would think she was capable of something like that.

"Yeah, I thought it turned out pretty good too." I glance in his direction momentarily before turning my sights back onto the bar. Calvin's been a client of mine since my first week at the studio here in Oxford—that was over three years ago. I've been fortunate enough to do every bit of ink he has on his body. It's a cool feeling to know someone trusts you—and only you—enough to permanently mark their skin.

The old fucks' conversation is starting to escalate, and Mac is still nowhere to be seen. He doesn't stand for BS in his bar. People come to drink and chill out after a stressful day at their jobs.

Honeysuckle blonde waves catch my eye. I glance a few feet from the confrontation, seeing Tara and Holly talking. Tara looks frustrated. She can't stand Holly, and the feeling is mutual.

At a distance, you might think their looks are similar. Holly has blonde hair too, but it's straight and bleached. She's of average height. Tara has an inch or two on her. They are both well endowed, but where Tara's tits are real, Holly's double D's are enhanced with silicone. Tara is all curves with a plump ass, whereas Holly has no ass to admire—or waist, or even legs, for that matter. Up close, Holly is a big ol' mess.

Something about Holly's stance is off, though. Tara clearly wants away from her, but Holly grasps her elbow. Yet, she's looking past Tara. I glance in that direction, turning my eyes to the men I was previously watching.

Their argument has escalated, and now they're pushing and shoving each other. I glance down, noting the glass item in one guy's hand. He's holding it too tight. I don't register my quick movement in their direction until a body crashes into my chest. At the same time, a beer bottle smashes against my shoulder blade, making me clench my fist around blonde strands. A quick intake of air is pulled into Tara's mouth, followed by a soft moan.

"Son of a bitch!" I shout, releasing Tara's hair. She steps a fraction backward, looking up at me in confusion.

"Oh fuck." I hear a tone of fear from behind me. Tara looks past me, and I pivot around with what I'm sure is the threat of death coming from my eyes. The guy I've only seen here on a rare occasion releases the remaining broken bottleneck of the beer from his hand. "I-I . . . I'm sorry, man," he stutters.

"You're sorry?" I snap. "You're fucking sorry doesn't cut it."

I walk forward, grabbing a handful of dirty T-shirt and shoving him backward.

"Had I not seen what was happening and stepped in, you would have hit her in the face with a beer bottle instead of me." I jut my finger out, pointing in Tara's direction. Everyone eyes at her. The asshole looks ashamed, but I don't care. His carelessness almost hurt Tara.

"I'm sorry," he says again, but it's directed at Tara. She stands there, not knowing what to do.

"Get out of my bar." Mac's voice comes out loud and fierce from somewhere behind the bar. "I don't want to see either one of you back in here again." Both men leave without another word. The guy that swung the bottle has his head lowered as he walks out. He may regret what he did, but that doesn't change what almost happened.

I take a deep breath. The pain in my back is starting to make its presence known. I turn around, and when I do, I see Holly's mouth is agape. That little scene didn't play out like she wanted. I know she doesn't like Tara. I even know why she doesn't like Tara. Me. But I never thought she would outright try to cause Tara harm. That pisses me off further. "Get out of my sight." She knows it's directed at her. She huffs but does as I say, stomping off.

"Your back, Shawn." Tara's voice is a whisper. She looks more distraught than I do, and I'm the one with blood running down my body. "Come on, I'll fix it." Tara grabs my hand and tugs me along. When we reach the back of the bar, she pushes through into Mac's office, and I pull the door shut the door behind me.

"Um, sit down and remove your shirt." She releases my hand, then walks over to a metal cabinet behind a wooden desk. I take a seat on the coffee table in the middle of the small office. Pulling my T-shirt over my head, I take in the torn material on the back. The shirt is ruined, so I toss it into the trash can off to my left.

Tara approaches, holding up another T-shirt. This one is white, whereas the one I tossed was black. It's folded neatly, displaying the red emblem of Mac's Pub on the front.

"You can put this on after I clean and bandage you up." She places the shirt on Mac's desk. His desk is in the corner of the room next to the office door.

Tara walks over to stand in front of me. She bends, placing the bandages, alcohol swabs, and paper towels next to me. She pulls my shoulder forward, making me lean into her. My palms wrap around the edge of the table, and I turn my head to the side, trying not to breathe in her scent.

You'd think with her working in a bar that she'd smell awful. She doesn't, and I really don't need her this close. Hopefully she'll hurry this up so I can get out of here. Looks like I'm going to make it to Level sooner than I thought.

"It's deep. You might want to get it stitched up so there isn't a big scar." She pulls back and looks down at me at the same time I glance up.

I shouldn't have tipped my eyes to hers. Fuck, she's beautiful. I snap my eyes back down, but when I do, her tattoo catches my attention. It's poking out between the gap where her jeans and tight shirt meet.

"Just handle it."

Tara doesn't dress as skimpy as most of the wait staff here, but it's almost worse. Tara leaves a lot to the imagination. Her blue jeans are ripped up one leg, showing a little of the tan skin on her thigh. They are also torn on the backside at the knee and a small tear under the cheek on the left side of her ass. The golden skin of her stomach is slightly exposed, her pants riding low on her waist. She doesn't normally wear them this way, but with her tattoo still healing, she has to keep tight clothes away from the wound. The white T-shirt emblazoned with Mac's Pub logo is fitted, stretching across her ample chest. Tara has a nice-sized rack, and this work top shows it off. The sexiest thing about this outfit, though, are the rips at the top of the shirt that reveal a hint of her cleavage if you look close enough.

To me, this is worse than if she wore short shorts with a low-cut top because I'm led to wonder what she'd look like without a stitch of material covering her body. I'd be willing to bet every man in here has thought the same at some point.

The stinging sensation of the alcohol catches me off guard. My hands come off the table and wrap around her thighs, squeezing the burn away. Tara takes in a quick breath of air and tenses right before releasing a breathy moan.

Fuck me if that sound didn't turn me on and cause a small discomfort in my pants. I release the pressure, but I don't remove my hands from her jean-clad legs.

To set the bottle down, she has to lower herself and lean over me. Tara's movements quicken, as does her breathing. All thoughts of what's happening above her waist cease to exist in my brain because my eyes close as I pull in a long inhale of her powerful scent.

The way I grabbed her when she poured rubbing alcohol on my back has her turned on.

I can smell it.

I bite down on my tongue. I'm trying to stay still so I don't do something stupid, but there is no use reasoning with myself when my dick takes charge.

I feel the bandage seal over my wound, and in the next second I'm standing. I don't know if I'm trying to run or what.

Tara looks up at me, and that's my undoing. The decision is made without my consent, even if I'm the one in motion. I pick her up by the thighs, moving one hand under her ass. I use the other hand to wrap her leg around me. She moves the other around me next. In one long step forward, I have her back against the door and my lips slamming against her mouth.

My movements are fast. There is nothing slow about the way I'm handling her. I run my free hand up under her T-shirt. Tara has one palm resting on my bare shoulder, and her other is in my hair, running her fingers through the strands.

She moans again for the third time tonight, causing her mouth to open and my tongue to enter. She tastes divinely sweet. If I could get my tongue down her throat, I think I would in an attempt to draw more of her luscious taste into my own mouth. Tara's tongue melds with mine. She returns my passionate kiss. My hand glides up her stomach and over her bra. Her nipple is hard, and it's something else I want to savor.

Her fingers tighten through the strands of my hair. I move from her mouth down to her jaw. Tara lifts her head toward the ceiling, allowing me access to her neck. I kiss downward, one hand squeezing her ass, the other constricting around her breast.

"Oh, hell."

At the sound of her voice, I stop all movement. It's as if reality smacks me in the face. What am I doing?

Tara isn't the girl you fuck in a bar, no matter if it is behind a closed door in an office I doubt anyone's going to walk into. Tara is the kind of girl you make love to in a bed, and the simple fact is, I don't do love. I certainly don't fuck in a bed. I haven't since high school. I'm after the quickest release from the easiest woman I can find.

That isn't Tara.

Tara needs and deserves a man that can cherish every inch of her mind, body, and heart.

I'm not worthy of the last two.

"Shawn?"

I release her legs, and they fall to the floor. I can't look her in the eyes, so I grab the T-shirt she got for me, pull her away from the door and walk out without looking back at her.

What the fuck did you just do, you stupid motherfucker? I berate myself as I walk back into the bar, getting the hell out of there as quickly as I can. The bartender has my credit card on file. There is no need to settle up. He'll charge my tab before he closes out at the end of the night.

Stupid.

Stupid.

Stupid.

CHAPTER NINE
TARALYNN

Holy cow—that kiss! My lips are still tingling from his mouth ravishing mine. Half an hour has passed, yet I'm still dazed.

His erection against my stomach was solid as a freakin' rock.

I always knew one simple kiss from Shawn would knock me sideways. Yet, it wasn't a simple kiss at all. It was a kiss that defies all kisses that have ever come before him. Not that I've been kissed a great deal, but still, his kiss was like silky smooth chocolate, spiced with habanero peppers—sweet and luscious, but so burning hot it left me tingling.

Thank God Mac let me leave an hour before my shift was supposed to be over. After Shawn abruptly pulled himself away from me and walked out without saying a word, I had to get out of there. There was no way I could think clearly enough to finish my shift. Not that any clear thinking has really happened since I left the bar. It's like my brain blanked out after that kiss, and I'm left wondering what happened and if I imagined the whole thing.

When I walk in the front door of my house, it dawns on me that

I drove home from work, but I don't even remember starting the ignition, much less the drive home. God was surely watching out for me tonight. As usual, I'm hit with loud music as I enter, so I force a smile, telling my body to relax and not overthink things. After all, Shawn had been drinking, probably had a long stressful day at work, and I was just in the right place at the right time for once in my life.

Luck was on my side. That's all it was.

I want to go straight up to my room so I can soak in a hot bath, but before I can make that happen, I'm grabbed by the arm and dragged through the hall and into the kitchen by Amanda. "Hey, look who I found coming through the door."

She turns and smiles at me. It's a fake smile. I've known Amanda Clayton long enough to know she has an agenda. I look past her to my best friend, who happens to be her boyfriend. I love Matt. God knows I do, and not in the "I want him for my boyfriend" way.

I'm not jealous of her in the least. My love for Matt is because he's my best friend and has been since the first day we met, but I'll never understand what he sees in her. Sure, her body and face are attractive, but that's all. The only thing underneath that prettiness is bitch topped with more bitch.

"Get over here, Taralynn." Matt chimes in. "I would like to introduce you to my new buddy."

Great, he and bitch Barbie are playing matchmaker. Why my BFF thinks he needs me to date, I do not understand. He thinks I'm hopelessly in love with Shawn. He's not wrong, but he wants me to get over it already. I slug my way toward him, but obviously Amanda doesn't think I'm walking quickly enough. She loops her arm through mine and practically tosses me onto the guy next to Matt.

Awkward.

For a short prissy little thing, she packs power. I guess cheerleading did make her somewhat of an athlete.

"Hi," I say as I force myself to halt a few feet away before Amanda shoves me completely into this guy.

"Hello," he greets me back. And please forgive me for this, because I know it's wrong to judge a person before you get to know them, but I immediately don't like him. It's his voice. It makes me think of a slithering snake. I hate snakes. They are the devil, and I want nothing to do with them. So that pretty much makes me want nothing to do with him, either.

It's not just his voice, though. It's the whole package. His hair is dark and slicked back on his head. The easy look isn't doing him any good unless he's going for the unclean and dirty thing. I like clean. He isn't. He's wearing a black T-shirt and black jeans. The T-shirt is too large for him. He's not a small guy; he's about Matt's size in height and build, putting him about two inches taller than me.

I think I need to find the quickest way to my room. That bath is definitely more appealing. I'm starting to feel dirty just standing near this creep.

"Matt tells me you're an English major like him." Why on earth is Matt talking about me with this guy? I've never seen him before, and Matt doesn't make friends that easily. He's a lot like me in that regard, so I don't understand how I'd even come up in a conversation.

"You need a drink," Amanda announces. "Here."

I take the black Solo cup she thrusts at me. Seriously, she is freaking me out here. She's never nice to me. What is going on today? I turn back to the snake-like guy whose name I don't even know. Nor care to know.

"I am," I sputter. He smiles, which is a huge turnoff. I take a sip of the beer that is clearly draft and definitely not Corona.

"Derrick here," Matt says, tipping up his own cup before finishing, "is a sophomore this year." I stop hearing Matt at that point because frankly, I'm not interested. I want my bath, and I want to remember the feel of warm lips on my skin. I take a large gulp of beer and relish in thoughts of Shawn's kiss.

I don't know what I could have done differently for him to continue. He seemed really into it, and heck, he's the one that grabbed me and slammed me into the door. I don't think I've ever been more turned on than in Mac's office. I love being manhandled. Jared knows how to handle my body to get me off, but Shawn wasn't even attempting to grant me a release, and I was on the edge. A minute more of his erection pressed into me as his lips melded with mine, and I would have come.

I snap out of my thoughts as my empty cup is taken from my hand and replaced with a full one by dirty Derrick. I force a smile to thank him, even though I didn't want another drink. At least not whatever's in my cup. I have plenty of my own beer in the fridge and even tequila sitting on the counter. Those options would taste better, but I don't complain. Instead, I bring the cup to my lips and sip. Maybe the more I drink, the more I'll stop questioning what happened back at Mac's.

Did I do something wrong or turn him off?

Should I have done something differently or felt him up the way he was doing me?

I don't know. It all happened so fast, and in the blink of an eye, it all stopped.

I look around the kitchen when I take another pull of liquid into my mouth. Unease settles into my gut. Matt and Amanda aren't in the room. No one is; it's just Derrick and me. The back door is open, and I hear voices from the deck area.

I look down at my cup, which is still half full. Shoot. Screw it. I lift it to my lips and tilt the cup all the way back, letting the beer flow into my mouth and down my throat, drinking it like it's a shot of tequila.

Definitely not the same.

I breathe out and then wipe my mouth with the back of my hand.

I shake my head to clear the dizziness that I'm sure is caused by gulping down half a cup of beer. I blink and offer him a smile.

"Well—" I begin, but he doesn't let me finish. Derrick shoves another cup into my hand and latches onto my elbow. My skin crawls so much from his touch that I want to rip it from his grasp and scratch the area.

What is wrong with me? Why am I being so . . . judgmental?

Hell, I don't know. I just want to go lie down. I really need to lie down.

"You can't call it a night yet. We haven't gotten to know each other, and I want to get to know you, Taralynn."

I take a quick sip, maybe more than a sip, and sit the plastic cup on the granite countertop of the island in the center of the kitchen. I offer another smile.

"I'm exhausted," I explain. His fingers press into my skin. "I'm sure I'll see you again. My roommates are always having people over on the weekends."

He's digging into my skin now, and my eyes start to get hazy. That feeling in my gut is increasing. My fight-or-flight instincts kick in, and I can tell you now I don't have a whole lot of fight.

Which is why I yank away from his grip and take off toward the living room, hoping to find Matt or even Mason.

I'm scared even though I don't know what's wrong, but I do know something isn't right.

I don't know why, but I have a very bad feeling.

CHAPTER TEN

SHAWN

Walking in the front door, I exhale the breath I've been holding. The scream of Five Finger Death Punch hits me as I kick out of my boots. Not even good music can settle my nerves at this point. I didn't make it past the parking lot at Level before I turned the ignition back on and headed back to Mac's, only to learn Tara went home before the end of her shift. Evidently the moment we had in Mac's office threw her for a loop too.

Her car is here, but that doesn't mean anything. She could be at Jared's for all I know. I certainly don't want her to be at that jackass's house. I don't know what I'm going to say to her or how to excuse my behavior, but I have to see her right now. Running my palm through my hair, I take a deep breath and force my legs to move.

When I enter the living room, an array of people sit around. Mason and a few guys are standing in front of the flat screen, drinking beer, watching a basketball game and shooting the shit. Amanda and two other chicks that she probably brought with her from Starkville are on the couch chatting. Matt's walking away from her, but pauses when he sees me heading his way. He's got a scowl on his face and looks highly irritated. Amanda can do that to people. Why he's still with her, I haven't a clue. He's been dating that bitch since sophomore year of school. Pretty sure that's the only piece of ass he's ever had, which might be the reason he's still with her.

"Hey, man," Matt greets me. "You're home earlier than usual."

"Yeah, I suppose I am." Before I can ask him if he's seen Tara, she comes running into the room from the kitchen.

"Matt." Her voice is breathless, and her eyes shine with panic. I don't like this. "Something's not ri . . ." She grasps his biceps, but seems to need to catch her breath, not finishing her sentence. Looking to my left, I see a guy waltzing out of the kitchen, where Tara came running from. The irritation on Matt's face intensifies before shaking out of Tara's grasp. His eyes pin the guy that comes up behind Tara with a hard look. I already don't like this guy even though I've never seen him before tonight.

"What the fuck, Derrick?" Matt almost yells it in his direction. "Do I need to take her upstairs and fuck her for you too?"

My eyes widen, and I feel rage bubbling from inside me. I'm close to ripping him a new one but Tara stumbles backward, pulling my gaze back to her, where her expression looks like he's slapped her across the face with his words.

"No worries, man, I got this." Derrick, as I now know his name to be, oozes sleazeball. I can see why Tara wants nothing to do with him. He grabs her elbow and then pulls her into his chest with a hard yank. "Just point me in the direction." He laughs.

I don't think so, motherfucker.

What the hell is Matt's problem, anyhow? He's supposed to be Tara's best friend. Instead, he just threw her to the wolves.

Tara snatches her arm out of his hold, and the movement causes her to stumble forward. Something is way off here. She looks drunk, but I know that's not possible. She was sober when I left her at Mac's less than an hour ago. When he reaches for her again, I step toward her, wrapping my hand around her waist and pulling her front flush with my torso. She grabs onto my T-shirt with both hands like she'll never release me again. Part of me doesn't want her to, but I need to put that out of my head so I can figure this situation out.

"Taralynn." Matt's voice booms throughout the room as all eyes turn our way. If I didn't have her standing in front of me right now, I would have dropped him on his ass already. I place my hand around Tara's lower back, pulling her as close to me as possible.

"Dude, what's your deal?" Derrick whines. "Are you trying to cock block me?" This guy is a joke. I don't have to cock block anyone, let alone this dipshit loser. "Not cool, man."

Before I can address this doucheprick and kick him out of my house, Tara lightly calls out my name. I almost don't hear her, but when I realize her hands are loosening from around me, I glance down. When I do, time freezes for a split second. I witness Tara's eyes start to roll to the back of her head as her body falls backward.

After shaking myself back to the present, I tighten my arms around her just as she goes completely limp on me. I'm shocked for a small amount of time. I look up to see the same shocked expression on Matt's face. My head snaps over to Derrick, who's got that flight look in his eyes. The moment it registers, he flees, running for the door.

"Mason," I scream my best friend's name. "Stop his ass, now. He did something to Tara." I feel it in my fucking bones. Mason immediately high tails it after the motherfucker. Two of the guys he was standing around follow him out. I look at Matt. "What did you let him do to her?"

"I . . . what the . . . Taralynn." He can't make full sentences. He's floored and isn't grasping what's going on.

"Get your ass out that door and find out what he did to her." Matt's eyes snap to mine. It's sinking in, causing he stumbles with realization before walking away from me. "Lawson," I call out Matt's last name. He turns. "Once you have an answer, beat that motherfucker within an inch of his life." He nods, swings back around and leaves.

"Tara, baby," I call out to her as I gather her, hooking an arm under her knees and hoisting her up. I take her over to the couch. "Move," I demand from Amanda and her friends.

They comply immediately, not for Tara's sake but out of fear. My anger is palpable. I gently lay her down and brush her hair off her face.

"Tara." I call again, but she doesn't respond. I know I need to call an ambulance. My parents' voices ring in my ears. They are both physicians and taught my brother and me well.

I'm scared shitless at this moment. I know I have to check for a pulse. I'm not medically trained, but I know the basics. Fumbling for her wrist, I secure my fingers around her. Concentrating on her pulse, I conclude it's strong and steady.

I glance up, scanning the room for Mandy. When my eyes land on her and I know she's looking at me, I instruct her on what I need. "Go get me a cool, wet washcloth." She crosses her arm and scrunches up her face. "Amanda," I bite out. "You can get me a goddamn wet washcloth, or you can take your ass back to Starkville tonight. What's it going to be?"

She huffs, but spins on her six-inch heels and goes off to do as I requested. I turn my attention back to Tara. "Tara, please wake up," I plead unsuccessfully. "Fuck."

A few minutes later, Amanda strolls back into the room and tosses me the rag. "You took your sweet ass time," I snap at her.

"You know, Shawn, she's probably just drunk. I doubt anything is wrong with her except blowing it with some guy that finally showed her the time of day." This bitch needs to thank the stars my mom drilled into me that a man never lays a hand on any woman in a bad way. I've never in my life wanted to strangle a girl until now.

"Tara," I call out again, knowing futile. I'm not going to reach her, she can't hear me.

Pulling my cell phone from my pocket, I unlock it, knowing I have no choice. I have to call an ambulance. The noise of people shuffling behind me catches my attention. Before I can input 911 into the phone, I see Mason walk in, his body drawn tight and fists clenched together at his sides. Matt follows in behind him, sporting a busted lip. A few more guys come in as well. More than the two people that went out with my friends. They are guys from the neighborhood.

"Rohypnol." Mason says the word like it's a nasty taste in his mouth.

The fuck? That's the date rape drug.

"He fed her a roofie." It's not a question. I clearly heard what Mason said. I'm stunned. I had no idea people could still get that shit. I've been around the college scene as long as my friends have. Longer, really, since all of us used to come up here on weekends when my brother lived here. I've never seen nor heard about anyone giving or receiving the date rape pill. This is blowing my mind, but I've got to get her to the hospital. I don't know much about this. For all I know, people could overdose and die from it. I look back down at my cell. The screen is back to black, so I input my code again.

"What are you doing?" It's Matt that asks the question. I want to beat his ass so bad. He let this happen. I witnessed him push her onto that fucker.

"I'm calling 911. What do you think I'm doing?"

"You can't." Panic has set into his voice. I stop before entering the last number.

"Excuse me? You let that piece of shit drug her, and now you don't want to take her to the hospital? She could die!"

What the fuck is going through his head?

"Oh, please!" Amanda's voice is nails on a chalkboard. "Let her sleep it off. She'll be fine."

"Get that bitch away from me." I point my index finger in her direction. She gasps, and I want to throttle the fuck out of her.

"Upstairs," Matt orders his girlfriend. Amanda cuts her eyes to Matt, giving him her best "I hope you die" look.

"Lindsey, Trena, let's go. We're leaving."

Good. I hope the door hits her on the way out.

"That goes for everyone in the house that doesn't live here. Get out." I eye everyone standing around to make sure they heed my words. They do, so I look back at Tara before putting the last digit into my phone.

"Shawn, I'm serious. You can't. Think about it," Matt argues.

"Think about what? Making sure she lives through the night?" What in the flying fuck is wrong with him? Maybe Tara needs to rethink who she's friends with, and maybe I need to rethink who I let live in my grandparents' house.

"She's Jacob Evans's daughter. This isn't just some local college girl being drugged. The media will pick that shit up, and it'll be, 'Well respected Tupelo lawyer Jacob Evans's college daughter OD'd at a party last night.' That's what will be on the news tomorrow morning. Tara will flip out."

"That's ridiculous." It's not really. In all honesty, it's something I can see happening. People around here love gossip and don't care if it's factual or not.

"Her parents would disown her for sure. Her mother is waiting for her to screw up."

I have to get her checked out. I can't sit here and play the waiting game. I don't think it's a serious enough drug to cause lasting damage, but then I don't know medical shit outside of how to take care of a fresh tattoo.

There is only one option I can think of, and I'm the one who's gonna feel the blowback. They're going to kill me for letting this happen.

I clear the number on my phone and search for the contact in my favorites. When my eyes land on the number I need, I press the button to initiate the call even though I'm dreading the conversation.

"Did you not hear a word I said?" Matt growls.

"Yeah, I heard you," I bark. "I'm calling my mom."

Matt relaxes, and Mason walks over, placing his palm on my shoulder.

"I'll watch over her. You go call Pam."

I stand, leaving Tara's side to walk into the kitchen.

The call is answered within a few rings. I'm sure I'm waking them. It's after 11 p.m. as it is.

"Shawn, baby, what's wrong?" My mother has never grown out of calling me baby. I hated it as a kid, but now I kind of love it.

What am I going to say?

God, give me the strength I need to get this out.

"Mom, I need you to come to the house." I take a breath and finish. "Bring any medical supplies you have with you, please."

"Shawn, you're scaring me."

"How fast can you be here?"

"I'll be there in forty, baby." It's an hour from my hometown to the place I've come to think of as my real home. Good to know my mom is taking this seriously.

───────

"TARA?" I call out for the hundredth time. I can't help myself. I know it's no use, but I won't stop calling her name in hopes she will eventually answer me. This isn't how I envisioned tonight ending. Her anger, I can handle. Tara upset and crying, I can deal with— even though I wouldn't like it. Tara lying on the couch unconscious, not so much. I'm holding myself together by a thin thread.

When is my mom going to get here?

"Why do you continue talking to her? You know nothing is going to change." I'm about ready to handle Matt the best way I know how—my fist connecting with his face.

I push off the floor and get in his face. He backs up, and I advance.

"This happened because you let it." I point behind me in Tara's direction.

"Back off, Shawn." Oh, he's angry, is he? Well, let me give him something to really be pissed about. I grab the material of his polo, fisting it in my hands.

"Make me, motherfucker."

"Shawn Douglas." My mother's voice calling me by not only my first name but also my middle name hits my eardrum, causing me to release his shirt, but I don't back off.

"What the hell is going on here?" my dad bellows.

Shit. Of course she brought him. I knew she would, and I also knew he wouldn't let her come alone. I don't blame him. I'm sure if I had a wife I loved, I wouldn't let her crawl out of bed in the middle of the night to run to her adult kid's beck-and-call alone, either.

"What's wrong with Taralynn?" My mother's voice turns to concern. She practically runs toward the couch. My mom has a bond with Tara that I don't exactly understand, but I don't dislike it either. They are close. "Honey?" My mom has called Tara "honey" for as long as I can remember. I'm certain she loves her as though she was her own daughter.

"Shawn, start speaking. Now," my father demands. It's a voice that makes me feel like a child again. I step away from Matt to look at my parents. Shit, my ass is about to get it. I inhale through my nose and force the air out through my mouth.

"She was drugged." My mother gasps. My father's eyes widen in shock. "The date rape drug." Now my mother's eyes do the same, and I press on. "He didn't touch her. I got to her before anything bad happened."

"You don't call this bad?" my dad yells. "Why isn't she at the hospital?"

I don't have a response to that. I look down. I knew I should have made a different call.

"A word, Shawn," my dad says through clenched teeth. "Now."

I follow him into the foyer. Disappointing my parents isn't something I'm used to doing. I've screwed up in the past. I screwed up a lot back home before I moved to Oxford, before I got out into the real world and found my place. Before I grew up, I guess. Never once, until this moment, have I ever felt like I've let my mom and dad down.

This feels like pure shit.

"Where did I go wrong? Please explain to me where I messed up on the parenting road because I was pretty damn sure until tonight I taught you better than this." His eyes are boring into mine hard.

"You did, sir."

"Then why is she laying in that room unconscious when she should be in a hospital?"

"I don't have an excuse, Dad. I mess—" Before I can finish, the front door flies open, and in walks Trent.

Great. Who the fuck called him?

"What the hell did you let happen to my sister?" He grabs me the same way I had Matt, pushing me backward. I have to grip the railing on the stair banister so I don't fall back onto the steps.

"Trent," my dad calls out. "Let him go."

Tara's brother doesn't, and I don't shove him off me either. I deserve this. If I hadn't kissed Tara earlier tonight, none of this would have happened. She wouldn't have taken off work early. She wouldn't have been here for it to happen in the first place. I'm just as much to blame as Matt, maybe even more so.

"I asked you a question. Answer me, damn it." Trent is screaming in my face.

"Let him go, Trent." My father pulls Tara's brother off me. "If you want to go see about your sister, I suggest going in there." My dad points to where she is. Trent eyes me hard, but does as my father says.

I push myself off the railing and stand back to full height. My dad is looking at me, waiting on me to speak.

"I'm sorry. I know I messed up, Dad. It's just . . ." I shake my head because, ultimately, there isn't an excuse for not taking her to the hospital to be checked out. My mom is a pediatrician, and my dad's a heart doctor, but neither one of them works in emergency medicine.

My dad steps closer, wrapping his hand around the back of my head, and then he pulls me into him. I rest my forehead on his shoulder.

"At least you called us, son." My dad and I both sigh at the same time. "Just promise me, in the future, you will call for immediate help. That means an ambulance."

"There won't be a next time," I assure him.

"Son, you can't predict the future. None of us are promised tomorrow. You have to make decisions today to the best of your ability and hope that there is a tomorrow. You're my son, so I know the best of your ability is better than the call you made here tonight. Learn from it. That's all I'm asking."

"I hear you." I pull back, nodding before walking back into the living room to check on Tara and ask my mom if she'll be okay.

When I enter the room, I freeze. What I see is unexpected. Sure, my mom is a doctor, but I didn't expect her to whip out an IV bag in my living room. She turns, taking in my surprise.

"It's just normal saline to prevent dehydration, and I'm hoping it will bring her around sooner rather than later. Depending on the dosage she was given, she could be out for a full twenty-four hours."

A mother-loving day? Shit.

"So she'll be—" Tara's brother interrupts my question to my mom.

"Can someone explain how my sister was drugged?" Trent bites out his words at a slow pace. He's seated in the recliner next to the couch with his elbows pressed into his knees.

I can't answer his question because I don't know much of the details.

"He put a pill into her cup at some point tonight," Mason tells the room. I guess Matt got that information out of the son of bitch when he made the fucker tell him what he did to Tara.

I walk the short distance to where Tara is. I need to be closer to her. I need my mom to reassure me she's going to be okay. I know she is because if she was in any danger, my mother would have called the medics by now. Something I should have done even though Matt deemed Tara wouldn't want that.

"Shawn called his parents because we knew your parents would flip out," Mason continues. Why he feels the need to defend me to Trent, I don't know. I fucked up; I knew that before my father confirmed it.

The banging sound of someone beating on the front door causes me to turn in that direction.

Who the hell is here now?

"I'll get it," my dad says and turns away from us.

"They would," Trent comments. I look back at him before lowering myself down in front of Tara. He nods a look of understanding in my direction. I don't want it. I should have made a different call, regardless of their parents. "As much as I know she should have been taken to a hospital, they wouldn't have let her live this down. It wouldn't have mattered to my mom that she didn't do anything wrong."

She has to stop letting them treat her this way. Parents are supposed to love their children, faults and all, and Tara doesn't have one damn fault.

"Jared." My dad's voice is a warning, and I pivot, standing straight up.

"Get the fuck out." I'm not dealing with his ass right now. Jared and I have an understanding. Meaning neither one of us enters the other's home, and when we are in the same place, we stay on the opposite sides of the room. He's crossed a line.

I make a leap forward, but Mason halts my progress.

"I'm not leaving until I know she's okay." He peers past me, looking in her direction, and I'm seconds from losing it. "Taralynn," he calls out.

"She's unconscious, you idiot." And he isn't about to touch her —not in my house. It'll be over my dead body.

"Who did this to her? All I know is she was drugged. What happened, Braden?"

"That about sums it up. I think you can leave now." He's pissing me off. He doesn't have a right to her.

"Not until you tell me who did this to her." His face is red, and his body is strung tight. He wants to hit something. Probably me.

"Boys," my mother soothes.

"It's been handled." At least I assume it has. Matt only had a bleeding lip, but if he knows what's good for him, he better have kicked the fuck out of that shit-prick before letting him go.

"A name, Shawn."

"Derrick Landers," Matt answers him.

Good to know. Now I know who to go find.

Jared turns to leave but stops and looks back at Tara. I don't like the fact that his worried expression is for her. He's sincere, and I can see he cares.

I care about her. He shouldn't.

A heartbeat later, the door slams.

"Is she okay?" I look down at my mom.

"She will be. I'll need to check her out in the morning or when she wakes, but I believe she will be fine. She'll most likely have a killer headache and hurt all over her body when she wakes up, though."

"I'm taking her to her room. You and Dad can have my bed."

I don't wait for anyone to tell me different. My mom had already removed the IV before Jared showed up, so I scoop her into my arms and leave the room.

CHAPTER ELEVEN
TARALYNN

"Ughhhhh," I groan before blinking my eyelids open. They snap shut immediately. Jeez, that was the wrong thing to do.

The bright light.

My head!

God, it hurts so bad.

Why?

I squirm, trying to move from my spot, only to realize something is constricting my movement. When realization dawns on me, my body goes solid. That something is actually someone, and they're practically wrapped around me from behind. A heavy arm is draped over my side with a large hand splayed across my bare lower belly.

This is what has me freaked out, not to mention the massive weight leaning against my back.

"Relax," he says. "It's only me." At the sound of Shawn's deep, raspy vocals, my body is instant jelly, melting into him.

Then another realization dawns on me. Shawn is in my bed. Shawn is wrapped around me. And in the position I'm lying, partially on my side, but mostly leaning over onto my stomach, Shawn's hand is cupping a whole lot of belly bulge; as in my fat.

I'm not saying I'm fat or anything, but at five-foot-eight and weighing one hundred and fifty pounds, I could certainly stand to lose ten or fifteen pounds.

Suck it in, Taralynn, I tell myself. Suck as much in as possible.

"Relax is not a cue for going stiff and sucking in your gut."

Life hates me. That has to be it, because it certainly isn't working in my favor.

Freakin' hell.

I release the air I've been holding and then relax into the mattress and his hold on me. I have to say it feels nice. Even with the thumping inside my brain, I could get used to this easily.

Why the heck is Shawn in my bed?

Why does my body hurt all over? Possibly even more than my head does.

"Why do I feel like I've been run over by a truck and then beat up on top of that?" Did I get into a fight last night? Surely not. Me . . . fighting? That is laughable. I mean, I think I could hold my own. I don't think I'm physically weak, but I've never been in a fight in my life.

Shawn scoots away from me, but pulls me with him. He falls onto his back with his head resting on one of my pillows. I roll to my other side so I'm facing him. When I do, what I see is a shock.

Dear mother of God, Shawn looks like he was hit by a Mack truck.

"Hell, Shawn, you look like I feel. What happened?"

"What do you remember from last night?" He's scanning my face.

My eyes instantly go to his lips when I remember the feel of them on me. My mouth goes dry at the thought, and I have to jut out my tongue to moisturize them.

"After leaving the bar. When you got home." Well, that tells me he knows exactly where my mind went. I don't know why, but when it comes to him, I can't shut off my facial expressions. I'm good at it with everyone else, but never him.

I think, trying to access my memory when the image of a face from last night enters my brain. My eyes go back to Shawn's, silently asking him to say something, anything, because right now I know the button to my blue jeans is undone and the zip pulled down. My pants are much lower than I'd wear. Even with my tattoo healing, I didn't have them this low.

Oh, my God.

What happened?

What did I do?

That guy.

No.

No way!

I'm on the verge of tears when Shawn's hand cups the side of my face. "Nothing happened. I promise you that, Tara. I didn't let him touch you beyond your arm." His words should bring relief, but why are my pants not fastened?

"Then why are my jeans down, and why does my body feel wrecked?" I like a little rough sex, but never once have I woken up feeling this bad. This is beyond bad, and I don't know how to describe it. I'm not one for sleeping with strangers either. Casual sex is one thing, but it was always with Jared, and I've known him forever.

"Calm down."

"Easy for you to say. You aren't about to have a heart attack."

"Didn't you hear me? I didn't let that motherfucker do what he had planned. I pulled your pants down so the tattoo could breathe." Shawn's palm runs behind my head. His eyes close, and his forehead lowers onto my throbbing one. "He drugged you."

Holy crap balls.

This is bad, so bad; my parents are going to murder me.

"I don't remember anything. I mean, I do, but everything is hazy. I remember Matt being a douchebag, some guy I couldn't lose, and then your face, but after that nothing. Everything else is blank. How did this happen, Shawn? I'm not that stupid, am I?" Apparently I am. I don't need him to confirm that.

"No, Tara, you're not. You didn't do anything wrong. He put something into your drink somehow. You were at home. You should have been safe, and I let this happen to you. I'm sorry." Why is he sorry? This makes no sense. He can't control what happens. He wasn't even home when I got home last night, so there was nothing he let happen.

Shawn releases me as he falls onto his back.

I rise up, placing my left hand on his stomach when I do. I'm about to tell him he isn't at fault when I see the cotton with clear medical tape covering the crease in my arm where my elbow bends. That's a sure sign that there was recently a needle in my arm.

Panic sets in.

Oh, please tell me I wasn't taken to a hospital. I really am dead.

I guess Shawn interpreted my facial expression for what it was. "My mom gave you something to prevent dehydration." My eyes go to his.

"Pam? Not a hospital?" I question, and he nods. I relax at the thought. This is messed up. My first reaction to being drugged shouldn't be how my parents are going to react.

"My parents are here. I'm sure my mom is working on dinner now."

"Dinner?" I ask. Sure, Pam loves to cook, but rarely does she start on a big meal before early afternoon.

"You were out for over twelve hours. Are you hungry? Do you need anything?"

Holy cow. That's a long darn time.

What do I need? For a start, new parents. That's what I need.

My stomach rumbles as if answering his inquiry. Usually I snack on stuff at the bar during my shift, but we were so busy last night I never got a chance to eat anything. Of course, losing a meal probably doesn't hurt me any, and with Pam's delicious calorie-infused dishes, it's best to skip a few.

"I'm starving, but I feel dirty. Can I shower first?" Why am I asking permission? Of course I can.

"Yeah. Does your head hurt?"

"Like a mother." Shawn laughs at my nonuse of "fucker" to finish that sentence. I don't see the need for excessive cuss words when so many other words available. Shawn does it enough for everyone in this house as it is.

"I'll go start your water. The heat should help ease the pain, and I'll grab you some aspirin." Shawn rolls in the opposite direction of me before climbing out of my bed.

"Cherry powdered aspirin, please, and make it two packs." I turn to my left side to get out of bed as well.

"What is it with you and Mason taking excessive amounts of aspirin? Jesus, Tara."

"Some of us want relief fast." Plus, when you take over-the-counter medications for so long for pain, your system seems to get used to the medicine, and they aren't as effective anymore.

When I was in high school, I started getting back pain because the size of my boobs increased at a rapid pace. It seems like these babies showed up overnight. Sometimes it's a plus having double D's, but it usually isn't worth the hassle. At least I didn't have to buy my chest. Nope, these are God-given.

I stand up too quickly and have to grab the bedside table for support so I don't fall. My eyes close to ward off the dizzy spell.

"Whoa. Easy, Tara." A large frame is before me, and warm hands encase me. It's nice; I'm not going to lie. Before I open my eyes, my legs are being removed from the floor. I open them to look at Shawn. "I got you."

This is all too weird, Shawn being in here and him taking care of me. I get it, I guess. It happened in his house, so he feels somewhat responsible even though he shouldn't.

"I understand why I feel like dog crap, and I'm sure I look

worse than I feel, but why do you look so rough?" His brown eyes are red, he has dark circles under his eyes and his hair is a mess. He's still beautiful, but a beautiful mess at the moment.

"You look fine, Tara." I doubt that. Shawn starts to move, walking toward the bathroom, I'm sure. "I haven't gotten much sleep. I've been awake since I got up yesterday morning."

Damn, I feel bad.

"Because you've been taking care of me?"

"My mom took care of you. I simply watched you to make sure nothing happened." Shawn places me down on the lid of the toilet and then turns away from me. Seconds later, the water is running, and he's rummaging through the medicine cabinet above the bathroom sink.

"I'm sorry." I need to pee really badly. He has to leave.

"There isn't anything for you to be sorry about. Here, take your excessive amount of pain killers." He hands me two open packs. I toss them onto the back of my tongue like they're a shot of tequila. I wash the powder down with a cool glass of water Shawn hands me.

"I need to use the bathroom now." That's the politest way possible to tell him to get out so I can use the toilet.

"Are you good, or do you need help with anything?"

"Nope, pants are already undone. I think I can handle the rest." Shawn turns his face away from me. I'm not certain, but I think that might have been a blush. Today is bizarre. "Thank you for everything. I don't know what all happened last night, but thank you."

He nods and exits the bathroom, closing the door behind him.

I make sure to lock the door and then shed my clothes.

He's right; the heat of the water does help ease the tension inside my brain. I don't want to get out, but my stomach is in need of food. Especially since I know Pam is here. My mouth is practically watering.

I towel off slowly so I don't have another dizzy spell and wrap the white fluffy material around my body.

Quickly as possible, I brush my teeth and rinse my mouth with minty mouthwash. After about twenty minutes of being awake, I'm feeling slightly better than when I opened my eyes.

The last step is to throw on some comfy clothes. I open the door to my room and jump backward when I see Shawn on my bed. His legs are at the end of the bed with his feet on the ground, but he's reclined onto his back with his arms behind his head. As if he hears me, Shawn leans up, resting on his forearms. His eyes scan my body from head to toe. I grasp the towel covering my nakedness even tighter, though I want nothing more than to release it. If my pain wasn't so prominent, I'd be tempted to drop the towel just to see what Shawn would do.

"I didn't think you'd still be in here."

Shawn's eyes close, and he drops back down onto the bed.

"You had a dizzy spell when you got up. I didn't want you to fall coming down the stairs." His eyes open again, but he's staring at the ceiling, or so I'm guessing.

"I'll be fine. You can go. You don't have to babysit me, Shawn. I know this isn't your style." I walk over to stand in front of my dresser.

"Yeah, and what is my style then?" Shawn pushes off the bed. I see him in the mirror as I pull out my sweat pants and a T-shirt. He walks up behind me, getting close without touching my back. He places his palm down flat on the smooth surface of the dresser. He looks at me through the mirror, and I look at him. I don't answer his question. I don't know how. "Are we going to address what happened in Mac's office, or are we going to pretend it didn't happen?"

It happened. There is no way I'll ever forget a moment of his lips on mine or his hands on my skin, and I don't want to either.

"Do you want to forget it happened?" I ask meekly.

"I asked you that question."

"And I countered."

"Tara," he warns. Shawn's eyes close as his forehead falls forward, down toward the damp skin between my neck and shoulder. He pulls in air as if pulling my scent into his nose. The heat from his exhale causes my body to shiver as goose bumps break out across my skin. "You can't handle me. I don't know if there is a woman that exists that can."

"And you'll never know because you won't take the chance to find out." He looks back at me, staring into the eyes of my reflection. I do the same to him.

"You're probably right." Shawn pushes off the dresser, turns, and walks out of my bedroom.

I don't understand him. He has the perfect parents and a great childhood. Why is he so against relationships? It's something I shouldn't concern myself with. Even if Shawn was interested in a woman more than once, it wouldn't be me.

He's wrong, though. I could handle him if given a shot.

I huff out a breath of air and finish grabbing my necessities to put on clean clothes so I can go see Pam.

CHAPTER TWELVE
SHAWN

I've been riding four-wheelers since I was a small kid. I love it. Having a machine between my thighs and riding until my thumb is numb from holding the throttle button is my idea of relaxation. I don't need a beach. I just need dirt and a Yamaha.

My parents discovered an ATV park in another state when I was in junior high. We traveled there so often that my parents bought a smaller second home near the park. Since then, it's had a few upgrades. The kitchen was redesigned the way my mother wanted, and an in-ground pool was installed five years ago. So, for the past ten years, Thanksgiving in Georgia riding four-wheelers, eating good food, and enjoying our family time together has become a family tradition.

You only live once, might as well enjoy it to the fullest and do the things you love. That's my parents' motto. I like it and try to follow suit.

Tara and I arrived at the Georgia house this morning. My parents came yesterday so Mom could prepare everything for the meal we enjoyed earlier tonight. Shane arrived a few hours ago. Everyone else—my other roommates, Tara's brother Trent, Kylie, and Mason's other sister Layla—should arrive within the hour. Tomorrow we all plan to spend the whole day riding.

It's been nearly two weeks since the drugging incident, but it's never far from my mind. I want to beat the shit out of the guy who tried to rape Tara, and if I ever see him again, it'll happen. I'm certain of that. The son of a bitch should be in a cell right now. No, that would be too kind. He deserves far worse.

Mom and Dad tried to talk her into going to the cops about the incident, but Tara refused. It pisses me off that a grown woman—a fucking adult—still gives a damn that her shitty parents would blame her for what happened.

Oh, I'm certain her bitch of a mother would lay blame on Tara, but she shouldn't care what her mom—or anyone else —thinks.

The parties at my house have mellowed since then. We've all been hanging out at Mac's more and more, which suits me just fine. When Tara works, I get impeccable service. But I'm hoping to get her to quit working at the bar once I get everything squared away with the studio. She still has another full semester of school when this year ends, plus her writing and the two jobs. I don't see how she manages everything. Something will have to give. Now that she's getting paid for working at the studio, I think it'll be a no-brainer.

"Here, son." I glance up to see my dad holding a bottle of Corona out, offering it to me. I gladly take it.

"Thanks, old man." The cap is already removed, so I bring the cold glass bottle to my lips and take a sip of beer. We finished eating half an hour ago. I'm stuffed, and I'm sure my dad and brother are too. Shane headed off to bed a few minutes ago. Mom's cleaning up the mess we all made, and Tara is seated down from me at the other end of the couch with her nose buried in her e-reader.

"So what's this I hear about you buying the studio from your boss?" I roll my head in his direction to my right, laying a thick glare toward Tara's head. She isn't paying me a lick of attention, but I'll have a word with her later. It's not that I'm keeping secrets from my parents. I don't need to hide this from them, but the fewer people that know my plans, the smaller the chance of it becoming public knowledge before I'm ready. Meaning before I find out who's stealing money from the shop.

My lower leg is being nudged, so I turn my attention back to my dad. He's shaking his head.

"Your grandmother," he says as if clarifying that it wasn't Tara that spilled the beans. "You're lucky she's in Florida and doesn't live back home any longer. That old lady can't keep anything to herself. The whole congregation of her church probably knows too. You know how she brags." He shakes his head while laughing about his mother-in-law.

That I do. Old people are something else. If all old men do is sit around with their buddies drinking coffee and talking about the weather while old ladies talk about everyone and their mother, then please kill me before I get old. There's got to be more in life than sitting around, waiting to die.

"What else did she tell you?"

"She told your mom—who told me, of course—about buying the studio and the house." Of course she did. They tell each other everything.

"That about sums it up." I polish off the last of my beer.

"Sums what up?" My mother walks into the room carrying a glass of white wine. When she gets next to my dad's chair, he pulls her down into his lap with ease so she doesn't spill. I'm used to this. These two are all about public displays of affection and always have been. It's been normal all my life, so it doesn't gross me out like Mason. I've witnessed him turn and leave a room when his parents kiss.

"Me buying Southern Ink and Grand-maw and Grand-paw's house." Tara shuffles a few feet from me. I look up to see her standing up. She grabs her empty bottle of beer and walks past me with a slight stumble. I raise my own empty. She takes it without me having to request another one.

"Bill?" she questions before leaving. Her voice is smooth. Most wouldn't realize she's past the buzzed stage and is well into a drunken state.

"I'm good, darling." He holds up his bottle to show her he isn't close to being done. I guess I drink too fast, but then my dad isn't a big drinker. He has an occasional beer, but that's usually on the weekends or a holiday like tonight. Tara and I started drinking hours ago. I'm certain she's polished off one of the two twelve-packs of Corona we brought today.

"That is major, Shawn." My mom smiles beautifully at me. Her smiles always touch her eyes. "If all I can complain about is that my baby lives an hour away from me, then I'm doing pretty darn good." She relaxes onto my dad's chest.

"Major how?" I already live there and have for several years. I think of it as my home already. As far as the studio is concerned, it was either buy it or move to Las Vegas. It's not that I'm opposed to the latter option; I'd just rather stay where I am. Chance offers me a spot every time a vacancy at his tattoo parlor opens. He's been on me to come join his team for two years now. I can't bring myself to accept his offer.

I look up as Tara extends a cold bottle of beer to me. As I reach for it, my finger brushes across her wrist when I pull it toward me. Any possibilities of other reasons I can't leave are washed down my throat when I swallow the cool liquid.

Tara sits, picking up the electronic device to begin reading again. I look back at my parents when my mom speaks.

"It means you're putting your own roots down somewhere. You're choosing Oxford as a home." She sips her wine. "I'm proud of you is all I'm saying, son."

"Okay, Mom." I leave it at that. Sure, I love hearing compliments from my parents, but they make me feel strange—not at ease. I never know how to respond.

"I'm going to head to bed soon since we have a long drive tomorrow," my mom says to my dad.

"I know, love, but stay and watch the football game with me for a few minutes." My dad doesn't take his eyes off the TV when he speaks to her, nor does she respond to his request. Instead, my mom leans further into him, nestling into his front.

They're perfect—my parents, that is. I've never met two individuals that pour off unconditional love the way they do. They are each other's missing half. If I believed in soulmates, I guess that's what they would be. But I don't.

Maybe I just don't believe in it for me. I don't know. I've never given it much thought, and I don't plan on starting now.

I glance in Tara's direction. Her eyelids are closing and opening slowly. I'm surprised she's still awake. We've both been drinking heavily for hours.

"Night, son." My mom brushes her lips across my forehead. I nod my own goodnight to her before she walks past, doing the same to Tara. My dad mumbles something similar, following suit less than five minutes later. Tara and I are left alone with the light from the TV shining through the room.

I look in her direction. She's leaning toward the right side of the couch, her legs tucked under her body, her head propped in her palm. Her eyes are fully closed now. Her purple night shorts are riding high, causing my mind to wander places it shouldn't go.

The vibration in my pocket brings my thoughts to a halt. Retrieving my phone, I see it's a text message.

Mason: Almost there.

Might as well call it a night. They'll be here any minute, and with the long drive, they will surely all be ready to crash out.

"Tara," I call out as I stand, shoving my cell back into my pocket without sending him a reply. "Get up. Let's head to bed."

"Uh huh." She moans but doesn't budge from her spot. Taking a few steps in her direction, I grab her device before it falls to the floor and place it on the end table.

"Tara," I call out once again. She doesn't reply this time nor does she move to get up. I know I'm going to have to carry her, and as much as that thought sends a surge of energy through my body, I don't want to touch her. Touching her does things to me I don't like. Things I refuse to acknowledge wanting.

She tempts me with the impossible.

Herself.

I polish off the last of my beer and set the empty bottle on the table. Bending down, I gather Tara from under her knees and arms, lifting her off the couch and into my arms. A soft purr falls from her lips as her head rests on my shoulder, stirring thoughts of what she'd sound like lying beneath me with my cock buried deep inside her.

Get a fucking grip, Braden. It'll never happen. You don't want it to happen. It cannot happen, ever.

Tara is perfect too, like my parents. She's beautiful, sweet—way too sweet—and good. Everything I'm not. You know what happens when you mix oil and water? It doesn't blend, not even a little bit.

I head toward what's still referred to as the kid's rooms with Tara in tow. Each room has four bunk-style beds and conjoining full bathroom that connects the rooms. Before I make it there, Tara grasps my bicep, pulling herself closer into my body.

Not this shit. Not tonight.

Tara turns her face into my neck, inhaling as if she's pulling my scent into her lungs. Who am I kidding? That's exactly what she's doing, and it sends chills running down my spine and increases the constriction I'm feeling in my pants.

"Mmmm," purrs from deep in her throat. That sound only helps to spur my dick upward.

Drunken Tara equals bold Tara. She's never like this when she's sober. Sober Tara would never have the guts to come onto me. Drunken Tara is a whole other person, and this isn't the first time I've been in this situation. I wasn't expecting it tonight, though. Usually tequila is involved when this occurs.

I shake my head, trying to give her a hint to stop and be still. It doesn't work. She pulls herself closer by running her palm from my bicep to my neck and pulling harder.

"You smell good." Her voice is a low, sexy rasp, and her breath is warm against my skin. "You smell like you." I ignore her words the best I can. Talking to her only encourages Tara.

Tightening my grip around her legs, I use my other hand to open the door. Walking in, I bypass turning the light on. The room isn't very large. There are two bunks on both sides of the wall to my left, a dresser, a closet and the entrance to the bathroom to my right. Turning left, I hunch down, depositing Tara on one of the bottom bunks.

She doesn't release me when I pull backward.

"Goodnight, Tara," I bite out. The sooner I stop touching her and get into my bed, the sooner I can shut off my brain and stop having unrealistic thoughts.

"It can be a good night." I can see the smile play out on her lips thanks to the moonlight shining through the windows. The kids' rooms don't have blinds or curtains, which is my mother's way of ensuring everyone gets up at the butt crack of dawn. I complained a lot as a teenager wanting to sleep in, but now I see it differently. Not that I don't like sleeping in; I love it, hence my non-eight to five job. The missing window accents ensure we get all the ATV riding time possible.

"It will be a good night as soon as I'm asleep. You should do the same. Tomorrow will . . ." My words die on my lips as one of Tara's hands slips underneath my T-shirt. "Tara," I call out as her warm palm moves north.

At least it wasn't south . . . oh fuck, I thought that too soon. The same palm glides downward, stopping above my jeans. "Stop this and go to sleep."

"No."

My eyes snap to hers. "You don't want to play this game with me, little girl."

Laughter erupts from her deep inside her throat. "Little girl, really? I'm three months older than you, Shawn." She lets out a soft sigh. "I most certainly do want to play."

She wants to play? All right then, I'll call her bluff. Tara can't handle me, no matter what she thinks.

I bend down so my hard chest lightly brushes her soft, plump tits. Everything about Tara is soft and something I need to stop thinking about at this very moment. Her breathing labors, making her chest rise and fall faster. Skimming my lips across her cheek, down to her ear, I whisper, "Are you sure?"

"Y-y-yes." Her stutter is breathy.

I run the palm of my hand down her side, over her ass, and across her thigh. Her shorts are riding high on her hips, and the skin on her legs is heated. Moving back up her outer thigh, I slip my hand under her shorts and continue my path until I'm cupping her full round ass. My hand is seated between the thin material of her cotton shorts and what feels like silk panties.

"Please." That one word falling from that beautiful mouth almost makes me forget what I'm doing. She can't want this—want me—not really. If she would take a minute and think about it, she'd realize what a mistake I'd be. I won't be her mistake.

Faint noises from outside catch my attention, and then I hear the sound of the front door closing.

Our friends are here.

Without thinking further, I rip myself from under Tara's bunk, moving lightning fast. I turn away from her, hearing a soft whimper of protest.

Kicking my shoes off, shucking my jeans, and pulling my T-shirt over my head takes mere moments before I jump underneath the bunk across from Tara. By the time my head hits the pillow, the door is opening and in walks Mason and Matt. They are as quiet as possible before climbing on top of the bunks above Tara and me.

It's hours before I'm able to sleep. The feel of Tara's flesh burns on my hand for a long time.

It'll never happen.

"Damn girl, that was delicious." Kylie looks up from her empty plate to compliment Tara on the breakfast we all just ate. A compliment that isn't needed, not really, since even Tara knows she's a great cook.

"Thanks, Ky," she replies as she gets up from the table, taking her own empty plate to the sink. I mirror her actions, moving from my spot at the high-top counter.

"I'll second that," Trent chimes in.

My parents left an hour ago, heading back to Mississippi. The eight of us remain and won't be leaving until Sunday morning. I've been looking forward to riding my four-wheeler since the last time I was here nearly three months ago.

"Now I'm not so sure if it's a good idea for you to move in with us. You'll make me fat if you're living there too." Kylie laughs, but the room goes quiet. My thoughts of riding vanish.

I am standing directly behind Tara, waiting to place my dishes in the sink.

"What's she talking about?" Tara's body stills at the heat laced in my voice. My tone is harder than it should be for a casual conversation, but at the moment, I don't care.

Tara can't move to Jackson. I don't give a fuck if it's only a two-hour drive away. Less the way I drive. Why would she even want to live in that cramped three-bedroom house anyway? It is half the size of my house. It's tiny for the three adults that live there now.

She doesn't move or turn around to face me. Trent pipes up though.

"I asked my sister to move in with us when she graduates in June." His voice is cool, but I didn't miss the unsaid words coming from Tara's brother. I jerk my head toward where he's still seated at the table. Trent's smirk has me wanting to wipe it off with my fist.

Turning to look at the back of Tara's head as she tries to scoot out of my way, I grab her hip with my free hand. Leaning forward, I place my dirty dishes on top of hers in the sink, whispering into her ear as I do it, "Are you?"

"I haven't thought about it much." Her voice is also a whisper with a hint of sadness. "I don't know yet." She presses into my palm, so I release her, and she moves away from me.

"God, grad is only half a year away," Mason groans. "I don't want to think about becoming an adult in that short amount of time, so let's go get dirty."

"You're already an adult, loser." That's Layla. She's the middle sibling between Kylie and Mase. She lives in New York and is only down for the holiday. Layla's an actress that performs on Broadway, though I've never seen one of her plays. I don't intend to. I'm sure she's good, but it's not my thing.

"Yeah, maybe in years, but he is most certainly not an adult. Are you, little brother?" Kylie asks. Mason and Layla fight like cats and dogs way too often, so it's a good thing they live far away from each other. On the other hand, Kylie adores Mason and will do anything for him. Maybe it's being the youngest, I don't know, but he has her wrapped tight around his finger.

"You know it, sis."

"Are we going to chat all day or ride, people?" Matt asks the room, his question addressed to no one in particular and everyone at the same time.

"Ride. I need a break from you motherfuckers." Shane stands. "Taralynn, breakfast was great as always, sweetness. I'm going to gear up. See y'all outside in a few." With that, my brother leaves the room, and everyone follows suit.

Even though we'll all be riding together, but on separate machines, we each have a device inside our helmet that allows us to talk to each other when we want. We don't talk much, though. Being free, out in the open on dirt and lost inside our own heads is what this is all about.

"I'll never understand my sister's infatuation with you." Here we go again. Wonk, wonk, wonk. This speech was old when I heard it back in high school.

Only Trent and I remain in the kitchen. The others followed Shane's lead and are prepping to ride.

"That makes two of us," I reply flatly. I don't get it either. Tara should want someone good, deserving. Someone like her, and someone that fits.

"I get why you want her."

"I don't want her," I snap back.

"Lie to someone that hasn't known you since you were still pissing the bed." He spent the night with my brother numerous times when I was a little kid. Only once did he witness that accident.

"I was five, fucker." *Asshole.*

"Like I was saying, I get why you like Taralynn. Everything about her is good, kind, loving—unlike the trash you wet your dick with."

"Just because I'm not still fucking the same chick I lost my virginity to doesn't mean everyone I screw is trash. I'm sure a lot of them are plenty nice. I just don't care to find out." What would be the point? Pussy is a dime a dozen. There are always women willing and ready to be screwed.

"She won't always be waiting for you to wake up, you know."

"I'm done with this topic. See ya outside." And with that I leave the kitchen to change into my riding gear. The sooner I get onto my four-wheeler, the sooner I'll have a clear head. Last night's close encounter with Tara needs to cease existing in my mind.

CHAPTER THIRTEEN
TARALYNN

It's the week before Christmas, and all my finals for the semester are complete. Thank God. One more semester to go, and then I'll officially be an adult. At least that's the way I see it. No more school, and the real world will begin.

I don't know if I'm excited or dreading it. Maybe a little bit of both. None of us have spoken about what happens after graduation. I know Shawn is staying here. Mason, I'm not sure of. Matt and I can do our jobs from anywhere.

Matt wants to be an editor. Freelance work is everywhere. He's done it for years, editing papers for high school classmates, which continued in college. He's gotten more and more work every year. I don't see him having any problems. He's my editor, actually. I like having an editor that hates all things romance fiction related. I think they catch more errors.

Mason is a computer engineer. I don't really know what that entails because when he talks about his work, it's like listening to someone speak a different language. I know he's brilliant at designing websites, but that doesn't covers even half of his knowledge when it comes to computers.

I'm sitting in a posh breakfast restaurant at the moment,

waiting on my mother to arrive. To be honest, I didn't know these places existed in Mississippi outside of Jackson. Apparently at least one does. Who knew?

It's not like her to request my presence like this. She said she wants to talk, which translates to she wants to talk while I sit receptively and listen like the good little southern girl I'm expected to be. I need a throw-up bag. I'm over her crap.

Well, that's a lie.

I don't understand why my parents' approval is so important to me. Logically, I get that it shouldn't matter what they think of me. But I can't seem to be content with my own inner value. I need to learn how to be happy with myself.

"Taralynn," her voice sings. It's not a loving melody. It's a snooty, you're a waste of my time, hateful sound. "So glad you could drop by to chat with me."

Drop by? I drove an hour out of my way to come see her. I wouldn't call this dropping by.

"Certainly, Mother." I don't call her Mom like my brother does. I don't even refer to her as Momma, like Shawn and his brother call Pam. No, she's always been Mother. This is at her request. Demand, really. It's so formal, like her, and I hate it. I never want my kids to call me that word.

"What can I get you today, ladies?" I look up to see a tall, lanky waiter in black attire standing before us.

"A sparkling water for both of us." I don't like sparkling water. I hate the fizziness. It's like drinking flat, tasteless champagne, but I bite my tongue. I've learned to choose my battles with her wisely.

My mother doesn't look at the waiter when she relays her order. She generally doesn't look at many people—except those she tries to resemble. "I'll have an egg white omelet, no salt, all vegetables." She didn't even open her menu. I guess she comes here often.

"And for you, Madam?" He smiles down at me.

"Pancakes, please, and real maple syrup." I close the menu.

"The egg white omelet is a must, Taralynn. You should try it."

"I like pancakes, Mother." And I don't have them very often. Surely an uppity place like this should make delicious sweet goodness.

"They like your thighs too." Ouch. She's starting early. The server's eyes widen. I smile up at him as if her words don't faze me. They do, but I won't let anyone see that everything she says to me hurts, especially her.

Our waters are delivered almost instantly. After witnessing how she spoke to me, I'm betting the waiter has correctly assumed he needs to pay special attention to our table. That's probably a good plan. Katherine Evans isn't afraid to request a manager when service takes longer than she feels it should or that the restaurant staff doesn't act in a manner she prefers.

"Your brother only has two more years after this one to finish up his residency." She takes a sip of her water, pinky raised, and continues. "He'll be choosing his fellowship program soon."

"Yes, he will." I know this already. "I'm sure he and Kylie will end up at the same hospital in or around Orlando." Trent wants to be a trauma surgeon and work in an ER. Kylie wants to be a plastic surgeon. She loves Orlando and has always wanted to live in Florida.

"Right," my mother bites out. "Jackson needs someone with your brother's skills. North Mississippi could use someone like him as well. My son has a lot of options in front of him." She always refers to Trent as her son, but I've never heard her call me her daughter. I used to think it was odd, but then I realized my mother doesn't like me very much. I've never known why. I don't know what I could have done to lose her love. If I knew, maybe I could have fixed it a long time ago. Problem is, I've always gotten the feeling it has to do with the fact that I was born. So, maybe I never had her love to begin with.

"True." I'm not going to argue with her. Trent doesn't want to stay in Mississippi, and neither does Kylie.

"You graduate college in six months, Taralynn. What are your options?" So *this* is why I'm here. Freakin' awesome.

"The same options they have been since before I started college, Mother. You know I want to be a writer. I am a writer. That hasn't changed. It's not going to change." I emphasize the last sentence. This isn't a conversation I want to hash out with her again. It's been done over and over, and she doesn't understand. Although, maybe she does and doesn't care.

If something doesn't fit into her little box, it's wrong.

"That's just not going to work, and you know it." Our food arrives at the same moment those words spill from her lips.

"What is that supposed to mean?" I can't help myself. Writing is the one thing in my life that centers me. I can get lost inside my head, letting everything bottled up inside me flow out into words, exiting forever. I can't do that any other way. And she can't take that from me. I won't let her take that from me.

"Your father and I have built our name from the ground up. You and Trent have a duty to uphold and honor it. Trent is doing that well. You, on the other hand, are not. Writing fairy tale trash is not only laughable, it is disgraceful. You might as well label the word garbage across your chest." She neatly cuts her food and takes a bite as her words sink in. She's never been this harsh before.

I've lost my appetite. Eating will only make the food come back up.

She really is a bitch.

That's loud and clear to see.

"Mother." I don't get further than that word. My voice cracks, and I won't allow her to see my tears. Never will I allow that. I breathe in through my mouth and exhale the same way.

"Young lady, you have six months until graduation to make the right decision for your future. I've done all I can do. The rest is up to you." She takes another bite of food. She obviously isn't having the same issues in the eating department that I am.

"You're going to have to explain better than that, Mother."

"Preston will make a fine husband and son-in-law to your father and me. He will make our family proud. You would be smart to grab him up before someone else is smart enough to do so. Do you understand what I'm saying now?"

"My plans don't include getting married any time soon. I don't even like Preston. I thought that was obvious months ago." There was zero chemistry. It's not going to happen. She can bet her most expensive Louboutin heels on that.

"Yes, well, he is still interested in you. God only knows why. He has long-term plans for the future. Don't be dumb, wasting your time on a boy who doesn't want you, not to mention doesn't fit into our family."

She's talking about Shawn. She knows I like him and have liked him since I was a little kid. I told her so when I was a small child and still believed in the possibility of having the mother-daughter relationship that I so desperately craved.

Just because Shawn doesn't fit into her idea of what our family is, doesn't mean he doesn't fit into mine. Hell, I don't fit into my family. I never have and evidently never will.

"Stop judging him. You know nothing about Shawn." She should since he's been around since I was five years old.

"I know more than you think. About him, and about you, young lady. I know you work in a low-life bar and hang around that tattoo place Shawn Braden calls a job. I mean, really, that boy will never grow up. He will never be husband material, Taralynn. Stop dreaming and start making an effort in this family." She polishes off her omelet. I haven't even touched my breakfast. I don't plan to either, and I don't plan on staying here any longer. I'm sick of her crap. I'm sick of being her daughter, and I'm sick of taking her verbal abuse.

I'm done!

"Shawn is a tattoo artist. He has more talent than you'll ever know."

"You call that talent? Oh, please. Wake up, Taralynn. I'm

trying to help you. What he does is not talent, and neither is what you call writing." She takes a sip of her water as I push back my chair. "Where are you going? We aren't done, and you haven't even touched your meal. If I'm paying for it, the least you can do is eat. After all, you're the one that ordered it."

"I'm done, Mother. I'm not hungry any longer, and that tattoo place I hang around," I form air quotes to drive my point home, "is a job." After Shawn found out Adam wasn't paying me, he made sure the following week I was writing myself a paycheck too. I have to admit, I'm making more there working a few hours a day than I do in crappy tips at Mac's three nights a week.

I stand, but she isn't finished.

"Think about what I've said. I'm serious, Taralynn. You have until graduation. If you make the wrong decision, then your father and I have no choice but to make a decision of our own. If you want to continue being a member of this family, you will grow up." She looks down at her empty plate as if dismissing me.

I don't respond. Instead, I walk away knowing that if my parents want to give me an ultimatum regarding my life, then so be it. I'm a big girl, and I'm determined. I will make it.

What she says will not affect me.

As much as I want that to be the truth, I'm not sure I believe it.

CHAPTER FOURTEEN
SHAWN

Tara arrived two hours ago. She told me the day before that she'd probably be late because she was having brunch or breakfast or some shit like that with her mother. She wasn't, though. In fact, she arrived a few minutes after I did. I was setting up my station for my first client of the day when she walked in.

I don't think her encounter with the evil queen went so well. Tara wears her feelings across her face, so it's easy to tell when she's upset. She normally masks it when it comes to her parents, though. That shit has got to bother her. The way they treat her, it would bother anyone, except maybe me. I don't let petty stuff get to me so easy.

I spray my chair with cleaner and wipe it down with a paper towel. I do the same to my rolling table workstation, discard my latex gloves, and toss them into the trashcan.

Samantha, the girl I just finished tattooing, is a classmate of Tara's. Apparently, she and Tara were talking last week about Samantha getting her first tattoo. She had planned to let a local artist in her north Mississippi hometown pop her ink cherry.

I've heard of the place. Kenny apprenticed there years back, so when Tara mentioned Samantha's plans in front of me, there was no way I could let the girl go through with it.

I don't know the girl well. In fact, her coming in today was our first meeting in person. We talked on the phone a few days ago about what she wanted tattooed. I played around with some designs, two of which I shared digitally with her.

She responded immediately that she loved both drawings but picked the shield with a bright blue shining light behind it. Her dad was a cop. He lost his life in the line of duty a year ago. She wanted to honor him with a brand on her shoulder for all to see. You could tell she was proud of her dad the way she spoke of the man.

I'm proud of my own parents in the same way. It's the reason I had a stethoscope inked on the back side of my left bicep with my mother's name written in script and my father's name written in block letters.

I normally can't schedule a first-timer appointment for at least seven weeks out, but I ended up having a cancelation today. Sometimes things work out perfectly. Tara seems to really like Samantha. I would have stayed late one night this week to do it had someone not canceled. The girl was too impatient. She would have gone through with letting the other, less experienced artist permanently mark her body.

I hope I did her father justice. Memorial tattoos are always difficult. You never really know if you hit the nail on the head. She teared up when she saw it complete, so I sent her to the back office to find Tara. After today I guess it'll be my office—or Tara's, however you want to look at it. If she accepts my offer, and I hope she does.

Samantha has been back there for about ten minutes now. I need to talk to Tara before I meet with everyone else. The big announcement about me taking over ownership of the shop is taking place in thirty minutes, so if I'm going to ask her to stay on permanently as my accountant, I better get moving.

When I open the office door, Tara is sitting on the edge of the wooden desk, and Samantha is relaxed in one of the two chairs in front of Tara, being careful not to lean on her right shoulder that I've just tattooed.

"She sounds like a total bitch." Samantha shakes her head. "How do you deal—" They both turn to look at me as I walk in. Tara jumps off the desk.

"Sorry."

"Sorry for what?" I question Tara as I push the door closed. I notice the loose hinge on the upper portion of the door. It's funny the things you start seeing when you own them.

Adam opened this place close to ten years ago, and it's past time for some improvements and upgrades. A new name is my starting point, but I plan on cleaning and polishing a lot around here as soon as the change is official.

Tara doesn't answer my question. Attempting to divert my attention from the conversation I just interrupted, she fusses over Samantha's new ink.

"My God, Shawn, it's beautiful," Tara coos, gesturing toward Samantha. She walks closer to where her friend is seated, looking down to admire the fresh tattoo. Until a few weeks ago, I didn't know Tara even liked tattoos. Now that I do, I can't stop getting ideas for intricate designs I want to tattoo on her. I don't think I'd place one on the outer part of her arm, but I know what I want to ink on her next. I just have to figure out a way not to give myself away when I approach her with it.

"She's right, you know," Samantha agrees. "You did an amazing job. I'm glad I let her talk me into getting it done by you, Shawn. Thank you." Samantha smiles up at me. "I don't know if you know how much it means to me, but thank you. I love it."

I nod in her direction. I like praise; what person doesn't? But I'm not one to gloat. Once you tell me you're happy, then it's over and done. Time to move on.

"Good deal." I rotate my face to look at Tara. "You got a minute?"

"Yeah, sure." Tara looks away from me, but before she can say anything to Samantha, the girl speaks up.

"I need to get going. I have an hour and a half drive home. See you in a few weeks?" Tara laughs and leans forward to hug her friend. Samantha is a few inches shorter than Tara.

"Yeah, see you in the new year." Both women release each other. "Have a safe drive, and text me later."

"Will do." She turns to walk past me, and as she does, she says, "I can't wait to show it off. You nailed it, Shawn." She closes the door behind her. I move to take the seat she vacated.

Tara leans back on the edge of the desk.

"So how was mommy dearest this morning?"

"A fucking bitch as always." My mouth drops. Tara rolls her eyes. "Oh, close it. I can say the f-word, you know." True, but she doesn't drop it very often.

"The f-word and the b-word in the same sentence, though. How crude," I tease. "Damn, she must have come on strong."

"You have no idea."

"So tell me." I didn't intend to ask about her mother, but since seeing her so obviously distraught when she arrived a few hours ago, it's been bothering me. I'm curious, so I probe.

Tara looks to the ceiling briefly before sighing dramatically.

"She gave me an ultimatum."

The fuck for?

Her head falls forward, and she looks me in the eye. "Stop writing. Marry a douche bag. Pop out a kid or two and be the perfect doting little wife she is, or lose my family privileges." She smiles sarcastically as my jaw locks. Tara married to some lame shit-fuck doesn't sit well with me. In fact, it pisses me off.

"Someone needs to cunt punch that bitch." I'm dead serious. Tara snickers, waving my comment off.

"I don't want to talk about her anymore. Tell me about today.

How do you think the team is going to take the news?" We don't have so much as a team currently, but I hope to make that a welcomed change. No business or organization can thrive without a solid team. I will demand loyalty, and those that won't give it to me can leave.

"Kenny knows," I tell her, and she looks surprised. I'm sure she is. I hadn't intended on anyone here knowing except Adam and Tara. I wanted to know where his head was and where others stood. Kenny's a people person, and I know everyone talks to him. He's a lot like Adam, really. "He and I talked about it last week. He thinks a couple of the guys will be supportive, and others will buck it. I think the same. We'll know here in a few minutes."

"What do you mean? I thought you were telling everyone late this afternoon?"

"Adam wanted it over and done with, so he managed to sync everyone's schedule up for a meeting. It worked out this way, but I have something I want to discuss with you beforehand."

"You want to hire an official payroll clerk, don't you?" She looks a little disappointed; at least I think she does. It could be me reading into this.

"I do."

"I figured. I didn't think this would be a long-term thing anyway." She laughs. Her mother now appears to be the last thing on her mind. "It's lasted a heck of a lot longer than I ever thought."

"Women," I state. "Y'all assume too damn much."

"What? But you just said—"

"I want you." I mean that in more ways than one, but I can't tell her that. I've thought about this since I bought the place. Graduation is only six months away. If she takes my offer, I can ensure she stays in Oxford and possibly in my house, or my soon-to-be house when I buy it from my grandparents. I'm going all in here. I'm not ready for Tara to exit my life. She won't ever fully leave, and I know that. She's too ingrained into my family, but I'm not ready for her to move back home, or anywhere else, for that matter.

"Shawn, I'm not even qualified for that position."

"You've been doing a fine job of it so far." I know she wants to be a writer. Hell, she's a writer, and I don't want to take that from her. I'm nothing like her parents. I'd never crush her dreams. Well, except for one—me, and she just needs to trust that I know what's best for her because it isn't me.

"I don't know. I think you would be better to find someone that can do it long-term. I don't know what's going to happen after graduation, and—" I cut her off.

"Then what's stopping you? You just said you don't know what's going to happen six months from now. It's not going to stop you from writing. You can do this job, which pays, finish school and write too." Shit, I have to convince her, and I will one way or another. I need Tara. Fuck, I don't know what I'm doing here. Sure, I want to own my own business and turn this studio into a success, but I don't have a clue what I'm doing. I'm bullshitting my way through. "I'm buying the house from my grandparents. You can stay; there's plenty of room."

"Come on, Shawn. I'm only there now because you felt obligated." She throws her hands up.

"What the fuck is that supposed to mean?"

"You know exactly what it means."

"I'm not obligated to anyone, and if I didn't want you there, you wouldn't be." Maybe that's a stretch—I do owe her big time. Even without her brother on my ass, I knew that four years ago. "I need you, Tara. I don't know what the fuck I'm doing."

"You don't need anyone. Isn't that what you've always said?" She looks away from me, but not before I catch a glimpse of the pain reflecting in her dark eyes.

I recline into the back of the chair, hitting the back of my head against the wall in frustration.

"That's a low blow, don't ya think?" I pull my head forward to look back at her. She shrugs. "Look, I'm telling you now that I need you. Please, Tara. Help me make this place the success I know it can be." I've never begged or pleaded with anyone in my life, but that's exactly the way I feel in this moment.

She's silent for close to a minute.

Tara continues to stare at me. I know she's thinking, but I'm not sure what. I'm hoping it's in my favor.

"How about for now we say I'll continue on until graduation. By then, I'm sure I'll have a plan for my future."

"Are you not sure you want to stay in Oxford?"

"Shawn." She pins me with a hard stare. "It's not about what I want. I've never gotten what I want a day in my life, and it doesn't . . ." She doesn't finish her statement, but it doesn't take a genius to know where it was headed. We both look away from each other as the sound of the office door opens.

"You ready to do this thing or not?" Adam pokes his head in. Tara hops off the desk and leaves, squeezing around him and out the door.

"Might as well."

I stand as he turns to walk away. I follow until I'm out in the open, where everyone is scattered around. It's not an overly large space. There are four stations on each side of the room, with one being walled off in the back corner for piercing. Two of the stations toward the front have been vacant all three years I've worked here. Yet another reason this place needs new blood running it.

Adam starts the meeting off, as he should.

"I appreciate some of you coming in earlier than your usual schedule. I don't think this will take long, but I needed you all here." He takes a seat on a rolling stool, and looks around the room. I'm propped against the wall with Tara seated next to me in my chair. "I was approached a while back. Someone wanted to purchase the business." He gestures around, indicating the studio even though it isn't necessary. They're all smart enough to know what he means.

"So what's that mean to us?" Hunter's stupid ass pipes up.

"I'm getting to that man." Adam's annoyed with him as usual, yet has never done anything about Hunter's attitude or work ethic. I already know he and Tyler won't make my cut. Tyler is the shop's piercer. He only became one after he couldn't hack it as a tattoo artist. The boy does shit work no matter what he tries. Hunter is just a shitty person, and I can't stand him. He has a piss-poor attitude, and I won't have that type of person working for me. "It means I've sold, and as of today, we all have a new boss."

"So, not even a heads up before now." Hunter, again. "That's shitty, man."

"I had my reasons. All of which did not concern you, or anyone else in here, for that matter. Piss off if you don't like it." The day he stops being the boss is the day he decides to grow a pair of balls.

"Are you leaving?" Sabrina pipes up, looking at Adam as if she's mad. She's probably beginning to realize this is the end of her run. She's going to soon find out it's not only the end of her stealing from me, but that ass is about to be canned.

It took long enough, but I finally have the proof I need to know she has been stealing from the company for nearly a year. Chance, my brother's tattoo artist buddy in Vegas, gave me some good advice. He is successfully running the tattoo shop he owns, so I'm confident he knows a thing or two about business.

"No, I'm not going anywhere. Jesus." I find it funny that he's annoyed.

"So who's the new owner?"

"I'm getting to that if you motherfuckers would shut the fuck up for a minute." He runs his palm through his hair. "Fuck, you bitches talk too much."

"I'm the new owner," I pipe up, letting Adam breathe. All eyes

162 N. E. HENDERSON

turn to look at me. Most looked stunned. Only Tara, Adam, and Kenny knew before this moment that I bought the place.

"Oh." Sabrina voices her thought. It's the way she screws up her face and rolls her eyes that piss me off. "Couldn't that have been relayed via text or something? Even an email? Did we all need to come in early for that news? I mean, really, it's Shawn. He's one of us. Nothing will change except the name signed on my paycheck."

Adam shakes his head with the slightest of movements before he turns his head in my direction.

"I'm going to leave that one with you, brother," Adam says.

"What?" Sabrina looks at us both as if missing a key piece of information. She is.

"That's where you're wrong," I begin. "All of you need to listen up. Things are about to change. That is one thing I promise you right here and now. I'm not saying anything Adam did or didn't do was wrong. What I'm saying is that everything before this moment is irrelevant."

"Irrelevant? Like how?" Sabrina chimes.

"Before today, I wasn't your boss. I didn't give two shits what you did, didn't do, or how good any of the work was that you put out. Today, that changed." I look each person in the eye, giving them time for my words to sink in. "A lot is about to change. Probably fairly quickly too. Some of you won't make it, that I'm sure of. Others, I hope you'll see this as an opportunity to improve —not only your skill but yourself as well. We're here to work, not shoot the shit." I look at Adam when I deliver the last sentence. Tara has opened my eyes to things I hadn't noticed.

"All right, boss," Jon says, so I turn my attention in his direction. He's sitting on top of his storage cabinet, legs crossed, looking me in the eye. His expression is masked. I can't tell if he's on board with me or not. Jon isn't a bad guy, and from everything I've seen, his work is damn good. "Enlighten us on these changes."

"First change is the name. It's changing to Wicked Ink. I have a new sign on order that'll replace the one in the parking lot. Shirts with our new logo should arrive by Monday. Commissions will stay the same; 60 percent goes to the artist, with the shop retaining 40 percent."

"So far, everything I'm hearing from you is sitting okay with me," Jon continues. "What else?"

"I'm going to meet with each of you individually at some point today, going over my expectations, answering any questions you may not want to voice in this room, and getting an idea of who's staying and who's going." I huff, breathing out air and taking more inside. "However, what I will say to all of you, here and now, is that if you want to continue working here, I expect your loyalty—to the business as well as to me. When I said some of you will not make it, I meant it. This studio will not put out low-quality work. Every person employed here will give one hundred percent from the moment you walk through the doors until the moment you walk back out."

The end of today can't come soon enough. All in all, I'm glad Adam decided to get this over and done with.

"Are you saying we don't give a hundred percent now?" Tyler asks. He's standing near Hunter. They are good friends and goof off together. Tara thinks she isn't qualified, but she is—a lot more than I am. I need her, and I see that now more than ever. She brought a lot of things to light for me—especially Tyler and Hunter.

"I'm not saying everyone isn't," I laugh because, frankly, that's all I can do. "Several of you don't even put in 50 percent around here. That will change. Know that and believe it. There are those of you that never have a full schedule. If you aren't going to make the studio money, then I don't have a place for you. Is that clear enough for you, Tyler?"

"Crystal, boss," he bites back.

Yeah, he will not be here much longer.

"One last thing I want to announce before you all get back to

work is that I've made Tara the official studio manager, so she'll—"
I'm interrupted before I can finish.

"Wait a minute, that's my job." Sabrina jumps off the table she
was sitting on.

I glance in Tara's direction. I never actually got around to
telling her that minor detail. Her eyebrows are raised.

"No, that was never your job." Adam barks at her. "Your job is
to greet customers, make, change, and cancel appointments.
Answering the fucking phone is your job. Running the cash register
is your job. Never in your job description did it mention
management."

"Adam," she calls out.

"Enough. I think I was clear, but to finish what I was saying,
Tara is the studio manager. She'll continue doing payroll, ordering
supplies, and everything else she's been doing. Nothing with Tara is
changing; I'm just making it official. You all feel me?"

"Yeah, brother, we hear ya." Kenny answers for himself and
everyone else.

"Good deal. Y'all are free to get to work." I lean off my table
and walk toward the back office. I need a breather, away from these
people.

When I reach the door, I open, walk through and shove the
door with minimal force but enough so it'll close behind. As I make
my way to my desk, I realize the door never shut. Before I sit down,
I see Tara propped up against the frame.

"Yes?" I question as I plop down. She just stares at me. "It's just
a title, you know. You were already doing the duties."

"I know." Tara turns and leaves without another word.

BY THE TIME the sun goes down, I'm ready to get the hell out of
here, but I can't. I have roughly three hours left. My last client
should be here in about an hour, and since I finished the last one

earlier than I thought, I have an important detail to wrap up before then.

Sabrina Gold.

"Hey, you texted me to come back?"

I look up from where I was cleaning my station to see Tara. I had sent her a text message thirty minutes ago, asking her if she could return to the studio tonight. Tara told me earlier today that since she's been making more money working here, she doesn't want to continue working at the bar. She spoke to Mac and gave her formal notice, effective immediately.

"Yeah, I need a favor," I tell her in a low voice so no one else will hear our conversation. I wave her closer, and Tara obliges. The sweet and spicy scent of her perfume envelops me, but I keep my expression neutral, not allowing her to see the effect she has on me. Thankfully she doesn't know how strongly I'm affected by her.

"Sure, what do you need?" Her eyes dart all over the room. Trying to determine why I'm keeping my voice low, I'm sure.

"I'm about to fire Sabrina. Adam has agreed to be in the room with me, but I need you there too."

"Me? I don't know anything about firing someone, Shawn." Confusion is written all over her face.

"I don't need you to actually do anything except be in the room." I don't know a whole lot about owning a business, but Chance made one thing clear. Do not fire her without witnesses. He was adamant about at least one witness being a female so if she tries to claim sexual harassment or anything else, I'd have people to cover my back.

"Oh." Realization dawns on her. "You just want me to witness in case she tries to start something later?"

"Exactly. You okay with that?"

"Sure, it's no problem, but what are we going to do about the rest of the week? Who's going to work the front?"

I turn my warmest smile on her, hoping she'll throw me a bone.

"Me?" she questions, but before Tara can tell me no, I clarify. I know she'll be returning for her last semester of school in January, and I'm not asking her to manage the studio plus be the receptionist.

"Just tomorrow and Monday. When we get back from Christmas after next weekend, I'll get someone hired, I swear." *I'll beg, Tara, but please don't make me.* I'm silently projecting those words from my brain. If she only knew that she's the only person on earth I'd beg something from, then she'd know just how much I hide my feelings for her.

"I guess." She doesn't sound enthused.

"I'd do it myself, but I have a full schedule." I wrap both my hands around her shoulders. "I appreciate it. I really do. And I'll make it up to you, okay?" Her eyes fall to my lips. The moment lasts only seconds before her face heats. Quickly, she turns, making my hands fall from her.

"Yeah, sure. Um . . . where should I go?" I don't acknowledge her embarrassment or the reminder of the hot kiss we shared weeks ago.

I look in Adam's direction, giving him a quick jerk with my head toward the office. He nods as he makes his way toward the back.

"Go wait in the office with Adam. I'll bring Sabrina back there in a few minutes." Tara doesn't say anything else, but she does as I ask, walking fast, following in Adam's direction.

No sense in delaying this any further.

I turn and walk toward the front. As I near, I notice Sabrina placing the deposit bag into her purse. This isn't unusual, as Sabrina has always been the person who handles taking the deposits to the bank. That was a huge error on Adam's end.

"You got a minute?"

She glances up before retrieving her purse and lifting it onto her shoulder.

"Sure, what's up?"

"You know I wanted to meet with everyone today. Let's do that in the office before you leave, okay?" I keep my voice neutral and my face blank. No need to scare her or let her think there is a problem.

"Okay, but I was just headed out."

"Your shift doesn't end for another thirty minutes." Wow, she really doesn't give a rat's ass about her job, does she?

"I know, Shawn." She laughs, but there isn't a lick of humor behind it. "I always leave a few minutes early so I can stop by the bank on the way home."

"And here I thought the banks close at five."

"Well, ours doesn't." Her reply is condescending. Did I know our bank or any bank for that matter, stayed open past five o'clock? No, I did not, but the bitch doesn't have to have an attitude.

"Fine, okay. Let's go talk." I don't wait for her to argue further. Instead, I turn around and head toward my office. Stupid bitch is going to wish she were a little nicer. This shit has been weighing on my mind all day. Maybe she needs the money. Hell, maybe she has major medical issues going on that we are all clueless about. But you know what? Fuck that. Stealing is stealing, and it's wrong no matter how you look at it.

I walk in, and as I do, I open the door wide so she can follow. Adam is leaning against one wall, and Tara is seated behind the desk, leaving the two chairs in the room vacant. I don't opt for one of the seats. Instead, I round the desk and lean against the wall closest to Tara. She begins to stand, but I shake my head, indicating I don't want her to move.

"Um, what's going on?" Sabrina has a worried expression masking her face, but I doubt she has a clue just how worried she should be.

"Have a seat, please." I motion to the chairs. She closes the door before making herself comfortable. "I thought you and I were going to have a one-on-one conversation. Isn't that what you said this morning, Shawn?"

"It is, but that isn't what we're here to do. I told you this wouldn't take long, and I meant it, so I'll get right to the point, Sabrina. I know you're stealing money from the company." Her eyes widen in shock, but her lips remain sealed. "Have known for a while now, but I didn't have the proof until two days ago."

"Look, I don't know who has been talking to you, but they are lying."

"Save your breath, Sabrina. I said I have proof, and I do. Wednesday, when I had you run that errand, I calculated all transactions myself against the schedule." Two days ago, I sent her out on a quick run for the studio. She was gone just long enough for me to add up the money. "What was deposited into the bank account was six hundred bucks shorter than what you left with."

"That . . . that can't be right, Shawn. I didn't do it. Someone else must have taken the money out before I left." I can see the sweat form on her brow.

"You're just digging yourself a deeper hole, so shut it."

"I said I didn't fucking do it!" she booms. I'm certain she could be heard outside this room.

"Stop lying, Sabrina." Adam chimes in. About fuckin' time too. He's the one she's started screwing over in the first place. He should be pissed.

"I'm not. Why don't y'all believe me?" She throws up her hands in a dramatic gesture before slamming her back against the chair she's seated in.

"Maybe because Shawn has proof like he said." Tara's voice is raised from the soft sounds that usually come from her mouth.

"Butt. Out." Sabrina grinds her teeth with each word. Her demeanor changes, then her eyes roam back to me. "There's no way you have proof. It's your word against mine, in fact. For all I know, you took that money out just to have a reason to get rid of me. I'll sue." The bitch smiles like she has just one-upped me.

"Like hell you will." Tara is on her feet, about to pass me, when her words and actions sink in. I reach out, grabbing her by the waist and pull her into my front without thinking it through. My palm slides easily beneath her T-shirt to rest on the skin above the waistband of her blue jeans. I do this to calm her down, to bring her emotions into check, but in doing so, skin-to-skin contact with her has the opposite effect on me. She instantly relaxes against me, whereas the muscles in my body are coiling.

"Is that a threat, Taralynn?" Sabrina lifts her torso, straightening her back.

"You're lucky he isn't calling the cops and having you arrested for stealing." She attempts to pull away from me, but I place my free hand on her other hip, keeping it on top of her clothes. No way I could get away with calling the first time a 'slip of the hand' if I do it again.

"Again, it's his word against mine." This time she crosses her arms across her chest.

"Give it up already." Adam shakes his head.

"This ends now," I assert. "You're fired; end of story. Tara is right. I could easily press charges against you, but I'm willing to let this go. Just walk the fuck away, because my patience with you is shortening by the second. My suggestion, and I really hope you take it, is to pack whatever shit you have that actually belongs to you and get out. You won't get a last paycheck from me; I think you've taken enough money already."

Her mouth falls open.

"I installed security cameras above the register earlier this week. You don't have a leg to stand on." Before she utters another word, I decide to provide a bit of caution. "If you speak, if you do anything other than stand and leave, I won't let this go. I'll do whatever it takes to make sure you're prosecuted for stealing from this company."

She hesitates, only for a few seconds, and then does exactly what I suggested she should do. She stands and walks out of the door without another word. But before she can make it all the way out, I stop her. I shake my head. Did this bitch really think she was that fuckin' slick?

"Don't you think you have something that belongs to me, Sabrina?" She stumbles, and then her body freezes. She looks back at me with hatred in her eyes. They bore into mine, but that's okay. She obviously isn't too smart. "I watched you put the deposit bag in your purse before we came back here. Did you honestly think I forgot already? Hand over the money, then get the fuck out," I bark, my tone loud and harsh.

She has fear in her eyes now as she hands over the bag to Adam and then scurries out the door like the pest she is. Finally, the only smart thing this bitch has ever done. She's lucky that little move didn't warrant a call to the cops. She's gone, and I'm fucking over the whole situation. This is done. It's over, and the company can move on. I can move on and concentrate on everything I need to improve around here.

"I'm outta here, man. See ya both tomorrow." Adam drops the bag on the desk and then follows Sabrina out, leaving Tara and me alone in the office. Her back is still pressed against my chest. My hand is still on her skin, and I have no idea how to alleviate a situation that is now awkward.

It would be so easy to slide my hand up to cup her breast. I still remember what they felt like when I did it in Mac's office. Her skin is soft, like velvet, and her tits are firm, and fuck—I have to get her away from me right now, or she's going to feel something pressed against her ass that she shouldn't.

I rip my hand out from under her clothes and gently push her away with my other hand.

"I need to . . . I have a client waiting . . . probably. See ya later." I'm sure I do . . . maybe . . . hell, I don't know. I can't think, and I need to get away from her and the way she smells like things I want to taste.

I walk away, leaving her in the office.

Shit, I need to get laid.

CHAPTER FIFTEEN
TARALYNN

After the fallout at the studio last week, I didn't think today would ever get here. As I lay in bed, my thoughts keep returning to all the shop drama. Not only did Sabrina get fired for stealing, but Tyler and Hunter got canned a few days ago too. Apparently, all three of them were in on it and were splitting the money.

What a flippin' shame.

Hunter had an attitude problem, sure, and he lacked a decent work ethic, but the guy could tattoo beautifully. I don't get it. If it was about the money, all he had to do was work harder. He never had a full schedule. He might do two or three tattoos in a day. Hunter always dragged them out. A simple one-hour design would take him three times as long to finish as anyone else.

As much as I don't want to see anyone lose their job, Adam should have let Tyler go a long time ago. He didn't work out as a tattoo artist. Then he was given a position as a piercer. Not that I want any other piercings than in my ears, but if I did, I'd never let Tyler touch my flesh.

I interviewed a potential piercer for Adam a while back, but he didn't show up with a portfolio that would have given me a glimpse of what he would bring to the studio. I'm still learning the ins and outs of the tattoo and piercing world, but one thing I know for sure is that an artist—a real artist that's serious about his or her profession—would never show up without a display of their previous work. If you take pride in something, you show it. At least that's what I've heard from both Shawn and my brother's buddy Chance Manning in Vegas.

"Taralynn." My dad's whisper of my name brings me out of my thoughts as he enters my bedroom. I'm not asleep, obviously, but he doesn't know that. It's early Christmas morning—real early —and I'm lying in my bed at my parents' house. "Wake up, sweetheart."

I've been waiting on his arrival for about half an hour. We have a tradition that I look forward to every year. Ever since I was a little kid, he's always woken me up before anyone else gets up to give me a Christmas present that's just from him and him alone. It's our secret. I've never breathed a word of this, even to my brother. I don't know why my dad does this, and I've never asked. Once a year, every Christmas morning between three and four, I get my daddy the way I've always wanted him. Needed him. In these moments, I feel like a kid loved.

"I'm awake, Daddy." This is another rare moment when I call him that particular word. It's usually Dad. At least it is in front of my mother. Her rule.

He sits down on the edge of my bed. I rise, pulling myself into a sitting position. He's holding a box, resting it on his leg. I can see the outlines of the sharpness in the dark. Excitement spurs within me, making me feel like a small child.

He reaches over to the bedside table and turns on the lamp. Thankfully, the lamp is dimly lit, so the brightness doesn't sting my eyes.

"Merry Christmas, baby girl." He places the wrapped present on my lap.

"Merry Christmas to you too." I smile, looking at him

expectantly. He knows what's coming. I can't help myself. "What is it?" I'm way too giddy for a twenty-one-year-old, but I don't give a crap.

"Child, every year since you learned to speak, you've asked that same question." He laughs lightly. "I've never told you before, and I'm not telling you now. Open it, Taralynn, if you want to find out."

It's heavy and several inches thick. When I pick it up, it feels solid, so I give it a shake. Nothing rattles. My dad laughs again. The wrapping paper is the same every year—Santa Claus. I don't know how he manages to pull that one off, but he does. I lay it back on my lap and proceed to tear into it, quickly learning that it isn't a present inside a box. The present itself is wrapped. It's a book, and a thick book at that. Flipping it over to the front, I read the title. It's a thesaurus for writers.

I'm floored—maybe even shocked. I was not expecting him to give me something like this. I look up, confused. Not because I don't like it, and not because I'm ungrateful. I'm both. In fact, I think I love this. It's the best gift he's ever given me, but coming from him, it doesn't make sense.

"You don't like it?" His question is full of disappointment. That's the last thing I want my dad to feel, so I quickly dispel that assumption.

"Yes, sir, I like it a lot. A lot a lot even. It's just . . . I don't get why you would give me something like this. I'm confused, but I love it."

"Confused how? You love to write, so I thought it would be something useful for you."

"It is. It will be very useful, but you hate that I want to be a writer."

"Sweetheart, I don't hate it. You enjoy it, and I get that, but I'm your dad. I want what's best for you. I know you don't like to have been forced to graduate with two majors, but it's my job to ensure that if one option doesn't pan out, you'll have a second option to pursue."

"That doesn't make any sense to me. And it's contradicting the ultimatum you gave me just a week ago." Why would he have her tell me I have to give up writing and settle down if he doesn't disagree with my passion for writing?

"What are you talking about? I haven't given you any sort of ultimatum. Ever."

"That's not true." My voice falters, allowing the hurt inside to filter out. "Mother said that if I don't give up writing after graduation and marry someone worthy of this family, I wouldn't be a welcome member of it any longer." Who does that to their children? Aren't you supposed to love them unconditionally? Accept them for who they are, the good and the bad?

He stares at me. It's as though I've rendered Jacob Evans speechless.

I haven't given any thought to what my mother said after I told Shawn. I wouldn't allow myself to dwell on it; I knew the moment I did, the emotions would overcome me. I was right. The tears come and fall from my eyes before I'm able to keep them at bay. I didn't want this. I didn't want to cry in front of him. I didn't want to ruin the one moment I get to enjoy my dad the way I've always dreamed.

I turn my face to look away, but he grabs my jaw firmly between his thumb and index finger, pulling my head back around to face him. He's angry.

"Let's get one thing straight right now." His normally light blue eyes are dark. Almost scary looking as they bore into mine. "Nod so I know you're not only going to hear, but you're going to really listen to what I say." I do as he says, nodding my head. "The moment you were conceived, you were my daughter. You became a part of me for forever in that moment, and you'll always be not just my daughter but as much a part of this family as anyone else in it. Am I clear on that, Taralynn?"

"Yes, sir, but she said—" He cuts me off before I restate my mother's words to me last week.

"Katherine does not speak for me. She should not have said what she said to you, and I'll address that with her." He releases my jaw and places his palm gently around the back of my head. Leaning forward, my dad plants a soft kiss on my forehead. It's tender and sweet and something he hasn't done in years. "I'm sorry, baby girl. I'm sorry I'm not the father you need nor the father you've always deserved."

"Don't say that." I feel awful hearing those words come from his mouth. Not because it isn't true. As much as I don't want to face that reality, it is true, but I didn't think for a minute that he thought he was a bad dad.

"Don't state a fact?" He raises an eyebrow. "Taralynn, I know I've been less than a father to you your whole life. I don't have an excuse. Do I have my reasons, sure, but that doesn't make them right. And I'm sorry for that. More than you know. One day." He pauses, then looks up toward the ceiling as if to gain control. Of what, I'm not sure. "One day I'll tell you. I owe you an explanation for so much. It just won't be today, but don't ever think you don't belong here, that you don't belong in this family. You do, more so than others in fact. You're an Evans by blood. For me, blood is everything and all that matters . . . now. Go to sleep, sweet girl. Katherine will want everyone awake in a few hours."

He stands, turns, and then walks to my door to leave.

"Daddy," I call out. He turns to look back at me as he opens the door. I raise the book off my lap. "It is pretty awesome. Thanks."

"You are pretty awesome, daughter. That's just a book, but I'm glad you like it. See you in a little while."

He leaves, and I'm left thinking about his words.

Blood is everything and all that matters . . . now.

My mother isn't blood.

He made it sound as though he loves his children more than his wife, but is that true? I don't know, and I don't want to contemplate it. I'll never come up with an answer.

After I place the book on the nightstand, I scoot my body down the bed and pull the covers up. I am tired, and sleep would be nice.

So that's what I do.

I sleep and sleep well until I hear that harsh voice I've dreaded since I left Pam and Bill's on Christmas Eve.

"IT WASN'T SO BAD," my brother says. I roll my head toward Trent, fixing him with an annoyed stare. We just left our parents' house after Christmas dinner. We're headed to a party at one of Trent's high school buddy's house after a quick stop to pick up our gang. Kylie's parents' house is just a few blocks over, and Shane's parents' house is directly across the street from that.

"Not for you!" I plead. "You're the adored one." Dinner was hell. Any amount of time spent in my mother's presence is torture.

Taralynn, don't slouch. Taralynn, you really shouldn't be eating bread. Taralynn, I'm talking to your father. Do not interrupt. Taralynn, have you returned Preston's calls? Taralynn, stop slouching. For heaven's sake, stop making me repeat myself.

Oh, for the love of God, I wish she knew what it felt like to carry around the weight of my boobs. She'd slouch too. It's not that I don't appreciate what God gave me. I do, and normally I like my large breasts, but sometimes they are a pain in the butt and cause lots of pain in my back and shoulders.

"Adored? Really, sis?" He chuckles, and I know he's hoping I drop the sentiment. He and I both know our mother dotes on him and always has. I also know it's something Trent hates. Not because he doesn't love our mother, he does, but he doesn't like that she treats us differently. Deep down, I think Trent fears it'll eventually cause a rift between the two of us. It won't, of course. I love my brother; I look up to him, in fact. He's the one person in my family I don't think I could live without. I certainly wouldn't want to.

"Yeah, really." It's Christmas. I don't want to put him in a foul mood. "I'm sorry." I draw out. "I shouldn't have said it like that. I just don't get her. What did I ever do to piss her off so bad that she hates me?"

"She doesn't hate you." I roll my eyes, not believing him for a second. I doubt even he believes that statement. "Look, let's forget about Mom and Dad for the night, okay?"

"Yeah, okay."

"So have you thought any more about moving down to Jackson?" Trent takes his eyes off the road for a moment to show me his award-winning, 'you're going to agree to what I want, and you know it,' smile.

"Not really," I deadpan. This is not a topic I want to discuss. I have thought about it. I should want to move and get away from home, from Oxford, my parents, but I don't, not really. My parents, yes, absolutely, but . . .

Even I don't want to admit it inside my own head.

"And why not? You graduate in six months." He sounds exasperated.

"Don't start with that crap, Trent. I heard it from Mother last week." Now I'm the one that's annoyed.

"I'm not Mom, and I'm not giving you an ultimatum. I'm not asking you to give up your dreams. You can write anywhere." Trent was more than pissed when I told him about my brunch with our mother. He wanted to call her, but I begged him not to. I knew, and so did he, that confronting her would only make things worse. Thankfully, he agreed to let it go. "You can't live there forever, Taralynn."

Great. He's going to bring up Shawn.

"I realize that. Can't we just forget about this conversation and enjoy tonight?" Jeez, what's with him? He's not usually all up in my business.

"Look, I know how you feel about him, but," Trent pauses as if searching for the right words so he won't tick me off. Probably smart on his part. "Maybe leaving for a while would be good for the two of you. Show him what he's missing."

"Ha!" I laugh out loud. I can't help myself. "The only thing Shawn Braden will miss when I leave is my cooking. You and I both know that. I'm not stupid, Trent. I know he doesn't like me the way I like him." God, I'm so over this conversation.

He's driving at a snail's pace. We should have arrived already. Kylie's parents' house is less than a mile from our parents' house.

"I don't know if I believe that," he chimes. "I don't think I've ever believed that. When he thinks no one is watching, he stares at you. Shawn always has. I think you confuse him. I also think that he thinks he's supposed to want a certain type of girl and won't allow himself to be with anyone different. Shawn doesn't take chances, if you haven't noticed."

"You're wrong, Trent. He just bought a business, one that will be challenging for him to manage and still enjoy tattooing. That place needs a lot of work. If that isn't taking a huge chance, a risk, then I don't know what is."

"I'm not talking about taking a chance with his brain. I'm talking about his heart, Taralynn." I start to refute his statement, but he doesn't give me the opportunity. "I just want my little sister to be happy. If he can one day make you happy, then that's what I want for you. I want you to experience what I have with Kylie. I can't describe it. There are no words. She completes me, and I know deep down that the moment she becomes my wife, I'll never want for anything again. You deserve that too, sis."

Wow. I can't lie. I do want that. I want that and more, but I also know Shawn isn't going to be the man to give it to me. I would love nothing more than for him to, but I can't realistically believe it'll ever happen.

"Brother, I love you, and I love that you love me so much that you want that for me too. I do want it. You know me, and you know I do, but it won't be with Shawn Braden. As much as it sucks, as much as I pretend it doesn't hurt, he's made it perfectly clear on more than one occasion that he doesn't want me. Not now, and not ever. Just forget about it, okay? I'm tired of dreaming unrealistic dreams."

"I think you're wrong, little sis."

I need to change the subject.

"So when is this wedding going to take place? Because you've been engaged for three years!"

"It'll happen. Once we finish our residency and get settled somewhere. Florida, I hope. It'll happen."

"And then?" I can't contain the excitement in my voice.

"Then what?" He takes his eyes off the road briefly to glance in my direction. "You coming to live with us is about as far as my future plans go right now."

"Kylie wants a baby. I know she does. She loves kids." She still reminisces that Mason made the most perfect baby doll ever when she was a little kid. I can see that having a real-life baby to play with versus a plastic one would have been way cooler.

"Then she'll get a kid. She can have as many ankle biters as she wants when we get married."

"But do you want a baby?"

"Sure, why not?"

"You don't sound very convincing there, Daddy-O."

"I'm not opposed to having a kid. I don't have a desire to have one. For Kylie, she's looking at motherhood as another step in completing herself, to fulfill something inside her. I guess . . . I guess I already feel as though I got that fulfillment with you."

"I'm sorry." Dang, was I that much of a burden for him?

"No, Taralynn, don't say that. I'm not sorry. You're taking that wrong." He removes one of his hands from the steering wheel to grasp onto mine and squeeze. "When they brought you home, you were the coolest thing I had ever seen. Any opportunity I got, I'd feed you, and it was fun because you never threw up on me like you did with everyone else. And I could talk to you for hours. Did you know my name was the first real word out of your mouth? You have no idea how neat that was." He releases my hand to grab the wheel as he pulls into the Morgans' driveway. "I don't know . . . I don't have a desire for a kid like she does, but if it's what she wants, then it'll be what she gets."

Kylie is one lucky woman.

If I find someone that treats me half as good as my brother treats her, then I'd consider that a score. Trent is a rare find.

THE FOUR OF us arrive at Weston's house half an hour later. When we get inside, Trent quickly introduces me to his old buddy from high school. I vaguely remember the guy. Pretty sure he was on the soccer team with Trent, but he isn't looking so fit and trim now. Tonight he's sporting a beer belly underneath his polo shirt.

Trent hands me a bottle of Corona that I gladly take from him. The cap has already been removed, and a lime wedge has been shoved inside. Perfect! I take a sip.

"I'm going to head out back with Ky. Come with and hang out with us."

"Mason is over there." I point toward the television where Mason and a few other guys are standing around talking and probably watching some sporting event. The TV is blocked from my view, so I don't know what's on. "I'm going to walk over there and talk for a few, but I'll come out in a bit, okay?"

"You sure about that, sis?"

"Yeah, Trent, of course. I'll be out there soon. You know I want to soak up as much time with you before you head home." He raises an eyebrow. What? I'm not lying. I do want to spend time with him. I don't see my brother nearly enough.

"Not what I meant. Your mouth might have said Mason, but your eyes were on Shawn." I turn away. He's right, but I didn't think I was being obvious about it. "Look, until he's ready to man up, there is no sense in torturing yourself by watching him hit on some random slut."

"How do you know she's a slut? Aren't you being judgmental?"

"Is the Pope Catholic?" I say nothing in response. "Okay, then. Look, go hang with Mase, then come join me out back. I just want you to have fun when you're hanging with me." He makes me smile. I roll my eyes, but I'm not annoyed, and he knows it.

"I'll be out there in a little while. Go to your friends."

He walks off as I down more of my beer. I must be a glutton for punishment, standing here and watching Shawn Braden lay the moves on another woman. He's leaning against a wall in the living room. The teeny tiny female standing in front of him, well she looks like a little girl in his presence. Is she even over five feet tall? Surely he would crush her. Not that she seems to be weighing that as a con. She clearly wants him. Her front is pressed against his, and her arms are wrapped around his waist. The strain in her neck has to be killing her by the way her head is leaned as far back on her shoulders as it will possibly go just so she can see his face.

I am not jealous.

I drain the liquid from my bottle in one long swallow without breaking my eyes from the other side of the room.

As if feeling someone's eyes on him, Shawn looks up from little miss hoochie. His eyes lock with mine, and I know I've been caught. I don't look away, though. I'm done pretending, acting as though I don't have strong feelings for him when he and everyone else know I do. I'm done lying to myself that this doesn't hurt.

I think my brother is right. Not about Shawn having feelings for me that he won't admit, but about me needing to move after graduation. I wonder if distance and time are what will make me forget about him. Can I forget how I feel? If it's a possibility, shouldn't I do whatever it takes to try?

Shawn's eyes turn hard moments before I feel a hand snake around my waist and another beer comes into view in front of me.

"I think that one's finished. I brought you a fresh one." I smile, wrapping my hand around the bottle and taking it out of Jared's hand. He takes the empty one from me. Turning, I wrap my free hand and the one holding the beer around his neck for a hug.

"How have I gone over a month without seeing you?" I exclaim. I've missed Jared. He can be a good friend when he isn't trying to bring the subject of "us" up. Don't get me wrong. Jared is great in bed, and I wish I wanted a relationship with him. It would make life easier and cause less pain in my heart, but I can't force myself to feel something that isn't there, just as I can't force myself to stop feeling something that is there with Shawn.

Love sucks.

Why is it marketed in all hearts and roses and pretty colors? Lies. All lies. B freakin' S is what love is.

"Life, baby." He turns his seductive smile on me and I know he wants something.

"What? Just spill it, Jared Dawson."

"Can we talk?"

"Sure. What do you want to talk about?"

"Not right here. Let's go upstairs where it's quiet." I raise my eyebrow. I'd say he can't be serious, but this is Jared. "Not for the reasons you're assuming, but I'm not opposed. You know that." He brings my body flush with his own. "I'll never be opposed to that, Taralynn."

I push him backward, but I already know I'm going with him if he wants to talk away from everyone else. Jared knows that too because he grabs my wrist gently, wrapping his palm around it and pulling me toward the stairs.

I ascend the stairs, following behind him giving me a nice view of his jean-clad rear. It's a very nice view, especially naked. His butt is taut, tan, and sculpted to perfection. There have been numerous times I've wanted to smack his the same way he enjoys hitting mine. I've never tried, though. Jared brings a wild side out of me, but I've never had the guts to really let go.

I long to be with someone that provides me with total comfort so I can just be me. Do the things I think about, write about, the stuff I watch on my phone when I'm alone in my bed at night.

I have this fear, genuine fear that I'll never experience that kind of relationship, that I'll never find that person.

The sound of a door gently closing brings me out of my thoughts. I'm standing in an empty bedroom. It's a small kid's bedroom. It must belong to a boy because there are superhero things everywhere in here. The Batman emblem adorns the black comforter on the bed. Must be a pretty cool kid. I'm a sucker for boy toys. Maybe it's because Trent would give me his stuff when he deemed himself "too old" to be playing with something. Of course, it never stopped him from playing with them with me after he gave them to me.

He places both hands on my shoulders and slowly runs his palms down my arms. He's standing directly behind me. With his chin, he moves my hair away from my neck. Closing his hands around my wrists, he runs his lips from behind my ear, down my neck, and stops before coming in contact with my sweater. Ever so lightly, he plants a kiss on my skin.

For a second, I let my eyes flutter shut and forget where I am.

"Taralynn." Jared calls out, so I turn, facing him. He's so darn sexy-cute, and I can tell by the twinkle of hope in his eyes that talking isn't all he hoped for. Well, buddy, I don't think so, especially not in some little kid's bedroom. Eww.

"Jared, you said you wanted to talk."

"I do, but I can't fight the temptation to touch you. I've missed you. I've missed the feel of you." His eyes glance down to where he kissed my skin. "What do I have to do to convince you to give this a try? Us a try, baby."

I don't know how to convince him there will never be an "us." This is why I stopped sleeping with him a couple of months ago. I hate feeling like I continue hurting him because I can't give him what he wants. "Baby, we're good together. We fit together like a glove."

"Jared, don't. Don't do this now. We've—" I don't finish because he cuts me off. He doesn't want to hear the same speech over again. I don't want to give it, but here we are. Again.

"All I'm asking is that you give us a real chance. You never have. You always blow off any possibilities of a relationship."

"I'm not blowing anything off." God. What does he want from me? I've spelled it out, haven't I?

"Then what is it? We have fun; sex between us is fucking phenomenal. Why can't you give a relationship a shot?" He blows out a breath in frustration.

"I don't want a relationship."

"You don't want a relationship, or you don't want one with me?" What am I supposed to say to that? I don't know, so I remain silent. I don't want to do this. I don't want to hurt him. He deserves more than what I can give. "I'm willing to give you anything. Braden won't give you shit. He doesn't look twice at you, but it's still him you want. I don't fucking get it."

"I'm not asking you to." I take a step closer toward him, but Jared backs up. I can't blame him. "I like you, Jared. I even love you, but I love you like a friend. You deserve someone better than me. Someone who you can go all in with and can equally go all in with you. It's not me, but she's out there. If you open your eyes, I know you'll find her."

I don't wait for his response. Instead, I step around him, walking the few steps toward the door, but before I walk out I hear him.

"I want it to be you."

I don't know what else to say, so I leave, shutting the door behind me. I can't convince him, that's obvious now, but maybe time will. He'll see. Jared is such a great guy. He was a douche in high school, but who wasn't? Now he's fun and caring, and he has so much to offer someone.

He might want it to be me, and on some level, I wish it were.

Reaching into the front of my dress, I take my cell phone out from where I have it tucked in the center of my bra to check the time as I descend the stairs. Without a purse and no pockets, it's the only place I can store it because I don't want to hold it all night long.

Once I see it's just after ten, I swipe the screen and type in my code to unlock it since I have a text message I didn't realize I had. But before I'm can open it, someone latches onto my wrist and yanks me forward. I stumble off the last step, and my body is jerked around the stairwell. I'm pulled into a bathroom so fast I don't know who has a hold of me.

Panic sinks in as the door slams shut. I'm disoriented from the quick and unexpected capture. It's a man; I know that much because I'm pressed against his hard chest.

The slight case of vertigo I just experienced dissipates as my senses return. It's the scent of him that makes my body relax automatically into his. My eyes snap up to Shawn's, and then a soft, inaudible moan escapes my lips at the sight of the intensity behind his brown eyes. The flakes of gold are glowing. I know he's pissed. Why, I'm not sure, but it's such a turn-on. I couldn't tell you why that is, either. Another unexplained effect he has on me.

"Did you fuck him?" His question catches me off guard, and I don't respond as quickly as I guess he thinks I should. Releasing my wrist, he grabs me by the waist with both hands and then yanks my body closer to his front. "Did you?"

"What?" He takes my cell phone out of my hand and places it on the counter next to the sink.

"Don't do that. Don't play stupid, because we both know you aren't." It takes a second for what he's asking and telling me to sink in, longer than it should anyway. Being pressed against his crotch isn't helping my intelligence shine.

"Jared?" Okay, dumb question. It's obvious that's who he's asking about because he saw me with him earlier, but it's like my mind is on delay at the moment. "No?" The dumbness just continues. Why did I say it like a question? Like I'm asking him if that's the right answer. And why the flipping eff does he even give a rat's behind?

"Did he touch you?" I nod. Speaking isn't working out for me in my current position. Shawn's hands tighten around my waist. "Where?"

Is he . . . is he getting hard? I can't think pressed against him like this. My brain can't keep up. My body wants to mold against his, but somewhere within, I know I need to turn this off. I'm getting whiplash. It's been so long—too long—since my vagina has seen a man's attention. I could've had it earlier tonight, but Jared just isn't who I want.

Sure, attention from Shawn is hot. I'd be lying if I said I didn't want to take this as far as he's willing to let it go, but he seems to only want something from me because he thinks Jared got it.

I shove forward, then push myself away from him, taking a step back only to be met with the flat surface of the bathroom door. Breathing in, I pull in a large quantity of air. It allows my mind to catch up. Not being in contact with his body grants my own a break, bringing me down from the heated high I didn't realize I was experiencing.

My break is shorted-lived. Shawn takes a step forward to stand only inches away from me.

"Where?" Oh, are we still on this? Again, why does he care?

"What's the matter, Shawn? Tinkerbell isn't cutting it." He and the little blonde tramp are laughable. She's like two feet shorter than he is. Who finds that attractive anyway?

Stupid men.

No response from him; his lips are pressed into a firm line.

"Is it past her bedtime? Did she need to get home?" That was low. I don't know how old the girl is.

My jealousy is really shining, but then what do you call what he's in here doing?

His eyes flash right before I realize he's made a move to grab me by the arm and flip me around. Within a split second, my back goes from being pressed against the door to being pressed against Shawn's front. My chest is now pressed firmly against the door.

He just took this to a whole new level, and not a bad one. No, a flaming hot one this is. I'm not a whore, but sometimes I think I feel like one from the dirty things that filter through my mind.

"I'm not in here to talk about her." He leans down to my ear. "I asked you where he touched you. Now I expect you to reply with an answer." If he's going to play this game, he's playing it to the end. I'll be damned if I allow him to leave me hanging like he did a few months ago.

Reaching behind me, I hook my fingers into the front pockets of his blue jeans and yank forward, pulling his crotch snug against my butt. He's still hard. Harder, in fact, and I like it a lot.

"He kissed me." I lean my head back to get closer to him. I want more contact. I want as much contact as possible. I already have on too many clothes, and so does he. Shawn is liable to gain his senses and stop whatever this is that is starting.

I don't want that to happen.

"Hands on the door." I comply almost immediately. "Where? Where did he kiss you?"

"My neck." My voice is getting breathless, yet he's barely done anything except take control over me. My weakness. "The exact spot where your chin is resting." I flex my hips, making my butt push into his front. Shawn pulls his face away from me. I moan in protest, but he's only gone long enough to move my hair out of the way.

I might like a man to take control, but I'm an active participant too.

Shawn places his tongue on the spot, swiping warm heat across my skin. Goose bumps erupt as the cool air trails behind. At the same time, he raises the hem of my sweater dress up my body.

"Ahhh, don't you dare stop this." He has to know I'll kill him if he even attempts that.

His hand dives into my hair, where he fists the strands into a tight bunch. Pulling me an inch or two backward, his mouth goes back to my ear. "Not a word. Not a fucking word, Tara."

Does he think he's punishing me for allowing Jared to kiss me? If this is punishment, then please give me more—lots more.

His lips move away from my ear, going down to the spot he licked. He swipes the area again with his tongue. More goose bumps follow seconds before he bites down on me. I clamp down on my teeth, locking my jaw so sound doesn't escape my lips. No way am I going to mess this up.

Shawn's hand, the one clutching my dress at my waist, slips to my hip. For a moment, it rests there, covering the strip of material holding my bikini panties in place. In another swift move, he swings us both to the side so we face the mirror that spans the wall over the sink. I grab the edge of the counter to brace myself as I find his eyes in the reflection.

He latches onto the string of my underwear but doesn't take it further. I want him to pull them down or rip them off. Anything, but not nothing. Seconds pass as we stare at each other.

I realize he's waiting on my consent. Shawn may be in charge of this show, but he isn't a man that would ever take something not freely given to him.

I nod, letting him know I want more. I'm not anywhere close to leaving this bathroom. I feel the material stretch before loosening and falling down my legs, telling me he went for the quickest route and ripped them.

I might complain later. I sort of liked that pair. They match the black bra I'm wearing. Sexy underwear is easy to find. But sexy and equally comfortable underwear is not so easy to find.

His hand slides down my leg, causing my skin to tingle. His fingers aren't rough, but they aren't soft either. They're just right, large and firm the way a man's touch should be. He encompasses my thigh in his palm, bringing my leg up and outward until I feel the bottom of my riding boot stop, bracing on the lid of the toilet. Shawn still has his other hand wrapped in my hair, holding my face in place to look directly into the mirror so I can't look down.

His hold on my hair tightens, eliciting slight pain. It's a good kind of hurt, and the start of a promising painful pleasure. He begins to suck on the area of my neck that he's licked several times. The palm of his hand runs from my inner thigh to the top and then behind my leg, where he continues until he cups my rear. His hand leaves, but quickly returns with a loud smack, causing heat to shoot through me.

"Mmmm . . ."

I can't help the sound that escapes. I wasn't expecting to be spanked, but he can do that again.

His mouth relaxes on my skin, replaced with teeth against me. "Shhhh."

"Continue that . . . and . . . I'll be screaming." Oh, but please continue. He locks back onto my skin, sucking again. I'll have a bruise on that spot before this is over.

Shawn steps to my side, keeping his front pressed against me so I can feel the hardness inside his jeans. I want to feel all that solidness inside me, but apparently he has other plans at the moment. His hand goes underneath me where his fingers breach my folds. Continuing, he runs his finger through my wet center until he reaches my clit. Without stopping to pay it a lick of attention, he runs the same finger in the opposite direction only to slip it inside me. I have to suck in my bottom lip to bite to suppress a moan.

God, that feels good.

He withdraws all too soon and is running back up my length. When his finger stops at my clit this time, I feel his thumb being submerged into me.

Have freakin' mercy.

His thumb pumps in and out a few times before he withdraws

again. This time he inserts his middle finger along with another digit inside, but that's not what has my body on alert and my eyes snapping up to look into the mirror. Shawn's wet thumb stops, pressing against the tight hole in my backside.

He's still sucking on the skin of my neck while pumping into me. His thumb starts to slowly run back and forth against the tight area. His head doesn't move, but his eyes lift and connect with mine. In this moment, looking into his eyes while he's doing these things to me, I feel overwhelmed, scared it'll all be taken away, but most of all, the beginning of what I think is freedom. Free to be me. Free to feel human and not my parent's puppet.

I push back, pressing into his thumb. Shawn doesn't stop, but the speed of his finger going in and out of me slows.

No. No. No.

"Please. Oh, please." I don't feel the least bit ashamed for begging him to enter me both ways. This is my dirtiest fantasy come true.

He's so easy to read right now. There has never been a clear moment like this between us when I could look at Shawn and tell what he was thinking or wanted. He wants this. He wants to do this to me. And that makes me burn hotter within. He's the one in charge, but I feel empowered. It's a heady cocktail that makes me feel tipsy yet alive.

His thumb slips lower where he dips it in, coating his flesh with my juices. Once his thumb is lubed up, he positions it back against the hole, where he starts to press inside. His other fingers resume a better speed, going in and out at a constant rhythm. He's met with a pressure of resistance but isn't deterred. Shawn continues easing in, slowly, gently.

His other hand releases my hair, moving down my back, over my waist until he gets past the material of my bunched-up dress and connects with the flesh on my belly. His palm is warm as it moves downward. When he stops, no time is wasted; Shawn presses two fingers against my clit. He doesn't move them, just presses firmly into me as his other fingers continue their path in and out while his thumb starts to retract.

"Oh, my God." Small shudders develop within me, making me tighten my grip on the edge of the counter. Shawn enters me both ways simultaneously, going in and out, over and over again. It feels amazing. It's too much yet not enough. My head falls backward. Tingles cascade from my sex outward, going down my body and up through my chest.

It's not until I'm coming down from my high that I feel his teeth biting into my skin. I'm panting hard, harder than I ever have before this night. It's like I've exerted all my energy. Maybe I have, but I didn't do a thing.

He withdraws, and I whimper.

When I force my head to lean forward, looking at him through the mirror, Shawn looks at the mark between my neck and shoulder. It's red and angry.

"Shit." His eyes close. Remorse? Is that what I saw? "What the fuck?"

Hell no.

I twist, turning around to face him. He steps back, but I grab the front of his jeans. Without allowing him time to process what I'm doing, I quickly pull his belt buckle open. His brain must catch up, because he stops my hands from unbuttoning his pants.

"Tara, no. I . . . shit, I'm sorry. I shouldn't . . . I gotta go." He pushes my hands away, but I just bring them up to his chest, pressing against him to stop.

"Let me." I want to give back all the pleasure he gave me. I want to show him this is good. We could be good if he would just give it a chance. "I want to."

"No, you don't. I shouldn't have taken that as far as I did. Shit." He breathes hard. His eyes skate down to the mark he made. "I'm sorry about that."

"I'm not, and you're not either. Don't lie to me. I know you liked doing that to me just as much as I liked you doing it. I saw it,

Shawn. I know you did, so do not lie to me and say it should not have happened."

"Liking something has nothing to do with if it should or shouldn't have happened. It won't happen again. I really am sorry. Move." His body is tense. He won't look at me anymore.

"Why are you so against this?" I gesture between us, but he's not looking, so I clarify. "Something more between us."

"I'm not right for you. You know this."

"No, actually, I don't know this." I mock his words. They're ticking me off. "Let's stop skirting around this. You know I want you. Why won't you give in?"

"I just did, and I shouldn't have. This isn't happening again. Drop it, Tara."

"No." Okay, that came out a little childish. I might as well have stomped my feet.

"Don't you get I'm protecting you from me?" He sounds exasperated.

"What?" That's absurd. "Why?"

"Tara, protecting you from me is my goddamn mission in life." With those last words, he pushes me to the side and walks out. I'm left alone in a bathroom where he gave me the best orgasm of my life only a few minutes ago. Damn . . . if that wasn't the hottest thing I've ever experienced in my life.

In a bathroom.

Eff my freakin' life.

CHAPTER SIXTEEN
SHAWN

"**D**arlin', a fuck is just a fuck. Doesn't matter if it's in a warm bed or up against a cold concrete wall inside a bathroom."

"But we haven't—" I press two fingers against her lips to silence her. The same plump lips that I only remembered thirty minutes ago were wrapped around my dick last month. I'm pretty certain I fucked her too. What a wasted night.

"Honey, I'm not in the mood tonight. You asked to share a cab ride, which I graciously allowed. That's all this was, and I have no desire for a bedmate. Ya feel me, babe?"

"Yeah, Shawn," she bites those words out with a stunned look marring her overly made-up face as she grabs the twenty-dollar bill still slid between my index and middle finger before sinking back down into the back seat of the taxi.

I'm sure she thinks I'm a complete dick, but hey, I paid her cab fare home. I can't be that much of a dick.

I push the door closed, turn on my heel and make my drunk-ass way up the driveway to my house. I can hear the music playing from outside. It's not loud enough that the neighbors will call the cops. Hell, I bet half of those motherfuckers are inside right at this moment. Probably a few passed out and scattered throughout my place too. Parties are getting back into full swing around here since that night Tara was drugged a few months ago.

I haven't laid eyes on that shit-fuck, but when I do, he'll wish he'd never crossed me. That's a day I'm looking forward to.

As my feet land on the last step leading to the porch, a figure catches my eye, demanding I look that way. The first thing I see is a tangled mess of blonde waves. It's shielding her heart-shaped face from my view because her head is bowed, but I know it's Tara.

It's been six days since our heated bathroom moment on Christmas night. I've done a good job of avoiding her like the plague. Not only at work, but at home too. It's easy when I stay out so late that she's already in bed by the time I get home. When I finally get up in the morning, she's usually already left for her classes. I even missed family dinner night earlier this week. I regretted that. I should have manned up and faced her, but I didn't.

Mason and Matt prefer to get hammered in walking distance of their beds. With parties gathering at my house on the weekends again, I can understand why she's still awake. A moment of concern flashes in me, remembering what happened those months ago with the guy that drugged her.

"What the hell are you doing out here?" I stop to ask, but she doesn't move or look up. It's then that I take in the rest of her. She's wearing a tight pale purple tank top and matching shorts. The light color of the material against her tanned, flawless skin is striking, not to mention too sexy for my liking. Tara wouldn't dress like that around others. That's the type of clothes she sleeps in.

The sight of her in next to nothing has my heart racing.

Fuck me. No, please do. Really!

Yeah, like that will ever happen. Don't hold your breath, Braden. You'll never let it happen. You told her as much last weekend.

It has to be below thirty degrees out here. I can see my breath as I blow the air out of my mouth, so what the fuck is she doing out here in those skimpy pajamas? It's New Year's Eve. Well, since it's after midnight, it's actually New Year's Day. She shouldn't be outside. Not dressed like that.

"Earth to Tara," I bark. Still nothing. "Hello?" I walk over, hunch down in front of her and place my palms along the bare portion of her outer thighs. "Shit, Tara. You feel like ice." I flinch at the point of contact. It's then she looks up at me. That one look is like a knife stabbing straight through my heart. A heart that only beats when I'm in proximity to the beauty sitting in front of me now.

Two tears fall simultaneously out of both of her eyes. My jaw clenches, and my hands tighten around her upper legs. I'll kill a motherfucker, that's for damn sure. Her shoulders start to rise and fall as her tears stream down. Her face is red and blotchy. She's been crying for more than a few minutes, and just by the feel of her skin, I know she's been out here for a while.

Then, catching me by surprise, she leans forward and wraps her arms around my neck. It's not that I've never had her in my arms. Sure, there have been more than a few drunken moments when I've toted her to bed, but she's never willingly reached out for me. Not like this. This is different.

This girl is going to be the death of me. She has the ability to bring me to my knees, and she doesn't even realize it.

"What's happened, Tara? Did someone hurt you?" I ask the last part through clenched teeth as I run my palms up to her waist. She shakes her head from side to side, but her silent shudders don't stay silent as she starts to cry harder and louder. When she fists her hands around my T-shirt, I slide my hands down and under her ass to scoop her up as I stand. Her legs wrap around my hips, connecting behind my back.

"I'm taking you inside. You're freezing." I turn and walk the short distance to the front door. Once I'm inside, I use my boot to kick the door closed. I head to the stairs directly in front of me, not paying attention to the others yelling my name from the living room off to my right side. Taking the steps quickly, I land on the second floor in seconds. I turn to the right and head down the short hall toward her room.

"No. Please don't take me in there." I halt my legs immediately. Well, fuck, where the hell am I supposed to take her? After a moment of contemplating I pivot, turning around and heading to my room at the opposite end of the hall.

Once we're inside and the door is closed, again using the heel of my boot, I stride over to my bed and place her down gently on the mattress. She releases me and immediately pulls her legs up to meet her chest and then wraps her arms around herself. Tara is staring directly at my chest, but not actually looking at me. I can tell she's spaced out, but she's also shivering. I can't fathom why she was outside in this weather. Granted, Mississippi weather is bipolar. One day it's seventy degrees, and the following day it's twenty. We are a screwed-up state, but that's just the South for you.

Tara hates cold weather too, so the fact that she was sitting out there like it was no big deal is throwing me off. Not to mention the tears. I know something major is wrong. Tara doesn't let people see her cry. I'm pretty sure her mother ingrained that into her at a young age. With a house full of people downstairs, I don't know if someone hurt her feelings or worse, but I plan on finding out. And if I need to shove someone's face into my fist, well then, I can do just that.

I pull my long sleeve T-shirt over my head; once I have it off, I start to pull it down over her head. Getting her warm is my first priority. Once I have it perfectly over her torso, I tell her, "Give me your hands." She complies without looking up at me. It's almost as if she isn't herself, lost in another world, but hearing everything I say. Tara writes a lot, so it isn't unusual for her to get lost inside her own head. I've often heard her say it's her favorite place to be.

I place her palms flat against my abdomen. My muscles clench at her freezing touch. How long was she outside? Her hands are like ice. I cover her hands with my own, running my palms in an up and down motion, trying to heat her from the outside.

"Tell me what happened." I keep my voice gentle. Taking a step closer, I keep one hand covering hers but move my other palm to cup the side of her face. Placing my thumb under her chin, I lift her head to get her to look at me. Her eyes meet my own and what I see is crushing. Tara has always worn her emotions plastered onto her face. And tonight, she looks heartbroken. Something inside me tightens. I don't like this. To my knowledge, she isn't dating anyone. She hasn't really dated since high school, and everyone knew back then that anyone she dated was her mother's doing.

Katherine Evans, or the evil queen as Tara dubbed her when we were kids, is all about image and money. If you don't have a certain amount in your bank account then you might as well be the dirt under her shoe. Funny thing is that Katherine's money is all Jacob's money, her husband and Tara's father. Katherine doesn't have a job and has never pulled her own weight from what I've seen.

When Tara shakes her head and drops her eyes, I try again. "Tara, baby, tell me what's wrong, please."

Shit, that was a slip-up. It happens every now and again when I'm on edge, or when she's drunk and I know she won't remember. Not knowing what's wrong or what's causing her sadness has my body and head ticking like a bomb ready to explode.

"I can't fix it if you won't tell me." I take the buzzing cell phone out of my pocket. I don't recall anyone ever calling me this much in one night. Every time I've attempted to answer it, something or someone distracts me. This moment is no different; she snaps her sapphire eyes back up to my own before dropping a bomb the size of Mt. Everest on me.

"My brother is dead." My phone slides from my hand, dropping somewhere on the floor, as liquid pours from her eye. Oh fuck. I bring her head forward, and release her hands so I can pull her to me. Tara has been connected to Trent's hip since the day I met her. If it wasn't for the age difference and looks, you'd think they were twins.

I move away from her, falling onto the mattress, letting my back land against the headboard on my bed. Once I've adjusted myself, I pull Tara into my arms. She latches onto me, pushing her face into my neck, one hand digging into my bicep and the other squeezing the side of my neck opposite her face.

"I'm so sorry, baby." There I go again, but fuck me, I don't know what else to say or do. I'm in new territory here. I've never dealt with death, or at least not someone so close to me. Granted, Trent and I weren't friends in any form, but like Tara, he was a fixture within my own family for so long. He's my brother's best friend—or was my brother's best friend. Shit. Shane. Kylie. I can't think about them at the moment. Tara needs me, and I'll give her anything she wants right now.

Her crying starts again. Tears, I hate. Tara wailing, I can't take. I don't know what I have to do, but I know I have to do something to help her.

Moving my hand up, I place it onto her lower back and wrap my other around the back of her head, pulling her as close to me as I can possibly get her. "I don't know what to do, but whatever you need, I'll do it. Just tell me." I bring my forehead forward, touching it to the top of hers as I close my eyes. I exhale a breath of air, feeling as though I'm at a loss.

"Make it go away. Take it away and make me forget," she begs, making my lids snap wide open. I only know one way to make her forget, and that is the last thing I'm prepared for. She doesn't need meaningless sex, not tonight, and not ever. Tara is better than that.

Is she even asking me to fuck her? I have no clue right now.

"Tara?" Her name comes out as a question, but no other words follow. I don't know how to ask her to clarify or how to tread around her with what's happened tonight. I certainly don't have any intentions of hurting her. And adding sex into this will hurt Tara. I know her feelings for me are serious. I've known it for a long time. It's always written on her face, but I also know I can't give her what she deserves or wants. I don't do relationships. I never wanted a relationship. I don't fit into her family the same way she fits into mine. It would never work, so it's pointless to even go there.

"Please, Shawn. I've never asked you for anything. I need a break." Her voice cracks. "Even if it's a small one. I can't take feeling like this. It hurts so bad, and I want it to stop." She lifts her head, causing me to pull my own back. "Please."

I let my head fall all the way back against the leather padding on my headboard. This can't happen. I've worked too hard to keep her untouched by me. There have been so many times I've wanted to kiss her lips. So many times I've gotten off just picturing her body in my mind. Truth be told, I can't masturbate without thinking of her. I've wanted her just as much as she's wanted me, maybe more. But she's never once come right out and told me, and I keep my desires buried down, not even admitting it to myself before tonight. Shit.

"Tara, I'll take you home. I'll even take you to my parents if that's what you need, but this—" She cuts me off, which is probably good because I don't know what I'm saying. I'm rambling, and I never ramble.

"No. I need *you*. You said anything. Please, Shawn." She plants her right palm on my chest and pushes up. "You'll screw anything with tits but me. What's wrong with me?"

"Nothing." My reply is immediate. And there isn't. What Tara doesn't grasp is that she's perfect. She fits too perfectly in my arms. She isn't too short or too thin. Her body molds to mine a little too well. "You just—"

"Don't." Her voice is final. "Don't tell me what I do or don't want. I have parents for that." She removes her hand from my chest, and I know she's about to pull herself off my bed so I reach forward, gripping her waist. I quickly pull her back to me, before flipping her onto her back in the middle of the bed. My body hovers over hers.

"Damn it, Tara, I'm not. But come on. You want more than a

five-minute fuck, and you know it. Same as I know you're better than that."

"What I know is I want you, but you don't want me, so move and let me up."

I drop my head, knowing I'm going to regret this. Maybe not tonight or even tomorrow, but in the long run, I will regret this night one way or another.

I crash my lips to hers. My left forearm is planted on the mattress next to her side, so that I remain above her without crushing my full weight on top of her, but I let the lower half of my body land down on her thigh. She doesn't think I want her or have ever wanted her? Well, then I'm going to prove that theory wrong. "I don't want you? That's what you think? Baby, I'm pretty sure I have a hard dick pressed against you that would say differently."

I'm pissed now, and I don't know if it's because she can't see how much she turns me on or because I can't deny myself the one thing I've wanted since I realized what my dick was meant for.

"I'm giving you one last chance to back out. Think about this, Tara." I might be telling her she can walk out my door, but my eyes are begging her not to, and my right hand has found her ass. I squeeze before slowly moving lower, onto the back of her thigh, before yanking it up, encouraging her to wrap her leg around my waist. "Don't fucking regret me tomorrow." My words are whispered in a plea as I reach back up, fisting the band of her shorts and panties.

"Never." She lifts her head, meeting my lips as I glide the material down her legs. Her mouth opens, allowing my tongue access to the sweetest thing I've ever tasted. The night I kissed her in Mac's office at the bar has nothing on this moment. I wanted to kiss her last weekend, but I knew if I did, I'd be in the exact spot I'm in now, about to fuck her.

Tossing her bottoms behind me, I bring my hand back up, bunching the material of my T-shirt. I need all barriers removed so I can feel every inch of her. If this is going to be my one and only time with Tara, I plan on taking my time. By the time I wake up tomorrow, I want to have every inch of her memorized. Burned into my brain so I'll never forget.

"Get this shirt off now." I lift myself, twisting to reach the bedside table to access a condom. Before I slam the drawer closed, I feel her. Tara is in a seated position in front of me. She removes my belt from the loops of my blue jeans, and as I turn back around, her tongue lands on my abdomen. The warmth from the heat inside her mouth radiates through me. She kisses and nips along my skin. To my shock, it causes a fire to radiate inside me, running down all the way to my cock. Before I realize it, the button on my pants is popped open, and the zipper is down. Tara immediately pushes my jeans and boxers down my legs all at once.

When her lips brush against the head of my dick, I suck in a strong pull of air. Holy . . .

Grabbing the back of her hair, I yank her mouth away from my junk and push her down onto her back. I was seconds away from losing my shit. There is no way I'm allowing this to end prematurely. I just need a minute to gain my control back. I take both of her hands, bringing them above her head and clasping my left hand around her wrists, holding her securely.

Shit, the sight before me halts my movements to discard the rest of my clothes. Tara naked is something to cherish. She's beautiful lying beneath me, her tan skin on display just for me. Her full, round tits are positioned high on her chest because I have her arms raised. God, they are gorgeous. I want to taste them, suck and bite them. I want to fuck that beautiful rack until I paint her chest with my white, creamy cum. I'm growing harder just thinking about the dirty fantasy that's played over and over in my mind for years.

My head lowers until my lips meet her left nipple. Tara's body jolts when contact is made. My tongue juts out, licking from below her nipple to the top of her breast. The upper half of her body lifts, pushing her breast into my mouth. I accept it, sucking as much as I can in. As I slowly pull back, I swirl my tongue around her tight peak a few times before my mouth pops off.

"Don't stop," she demands.

"I don't plan on it, baby."

My lips and tongue go to her other breast, paying equal attention. I've never been this attentive to a woman in my life, but Tara deserves it. More importantly, I want to do it.

My palm skims down her ribs, gliding over her lower abdomen until I reach the bare surface of her pussy. I smile around her nipple before lightly biting down. Tara's hips lift an inch or so off the bed as my middle finger slides through her slick folds, slipping inside smoldering liquids. Her insides grab onto my finger before I can draw back, trying to hold me inside her.

My mouth works its way back up to her neck, where I lick, kiss, and lightly suck until I reach her lips again. I take them, rougher this time around. At the same time I reenter her pussy, adding another finger. This time, I slam my way to the hilt because after last weekend, I know she likes it hard.

"Ahhh," Tara moans into my mouth. "Again, please again."

My digits slam in and out of her, over and over. Tara arches her back as her eyes flutter closed. My mouth moves slowly away from her lips, across her cheek, until I'm pressed against her ear. My thumb presses hard against her clit.

"Are you close, Tara?" I know she is. I can feel her all around my fingers. If I could fit my whole damn fist inside her, I would, just to feel her insides contracting around me as she is now, but that won't happen. Tara is snug inside her wet pussy. When she doesn't say anything, my other hand tightens around her wrists. "Tara, answer me."

"Yesss," her voice is soft, low and breathy.

"Come for me, and I'll suck every drop of cum from your pussy." I didn't get a taste last weekend, and I'm dying for that chance now.

"Oh, go . . . ahhhhhh. Oh." Her walls rapidly contract around me as she orgasms. My fingers slip out as her body slows. Her chest heaves up and down. And I do something I don't ever recall doing before this moment. I bring my fingers to my lips and suck her cum into my mouth to taste her. She's sweet yet tangy. It's light and wonderful and definitely something I want to do again.

It's not that I've never gone down on a girl before. I have, but it's not an act I do regularly. What the hell am I supposed to get out of it? Nada.

Keeping my promise, I release her wrists and move down her body until my eyes land on the wet, dark pink flesh that calls out for me to devour. My flat tongue swipes up from the bottom to her clit.

"Shawn," Tara moans as she pulls her off the mattress. My eyes snap up to hers as I dip my tongue inside her. Her eyes widen as she pulls air in through her mouth. Tara tries to scoot backward, but my hands wrap around her ass, tightening so she can't move further away from me.

"I don't think so, baby. You're not going anywhere until I'm done." I pull her a few inches closer to my face. "Stay just the way you are. Watch." With that, I look back down and take another sweep upward. With my fingers, I pull Tara's skin back so I can latch onto her clit.

"Too . . . ahh . . . sen—oh, my God." My eyes roam back up. Tara's head has fallen back to her shoulders.

"Uh-uh. Watch me, Tara." Her head rolls forward until she's looking down the bed at me.

"I'm too sensitive." Tara takes a breath, closing her eyes and reopening them to look at me. "Please, put on the condom and . . ." Her voice trails, not finishing, but I press her for the rest. I want to hear her say it.

"And what, Tara?" I ask, then swirl my tongue around her clitoris. When she doesn't answer, "Tara." I suck her clit between my teeth and bite down. Not hard, but with enough pressure to get her attention.

"Fuck me, Shawn. Just fucking fuck me already." God, fucking hell, if that didn't solidify my dick, hardening me to the point I need to plunge inside her and come like I've never needed to before.

I come up onto my knees, grabbing the foil package. Within seconds, I rip it open and sheath my dick in record time. After tossing the wrapper, I bend forward, falling over Tara and capturing her lips with mine.

"Say you're sure." I need reassurance. I've always been confident, except when it comes to her.

"I'm sure." I press a gentle kiss to her lips as I press inside. Bliss doesn't come close to a word to describe what's going through me at this very moment. She's snug around me. Her muscles contract every few seconds, making my thoughts blank. My dick is encased inside an inferno that I never want to exit.

After pulling back, I ease back in slowly, making love to Tara. Making love for the first time in my whole goddamn life.

With each thrust, I pull out slower than the last. I want this to last as long as humanly possible. The problem is, I can't slow down the rapid rhythm of my heart or gain any control over my cock. When I come, I come hard.

The only thing I manage to do is swallow her scream down my throat when she follows me over.

How I'll ever go back to having meaningless sex again, I do not know. I don't want to think of anything else but these feelings taking over. This is good. So damn good, but I'm not an idiot. She's too good for me.

CHAPTER SEVENTEEN
TARALYNN

I feel his chest expand from underneath me before he blows out a heavy force of air. "You're thinking too hard."

What does that mean? It's impossible for Shawn to know what I've been lying here thinking for the past ten minutes since I woke up. Maybe I should have eased out of his bed and left before he awoke. At least that way we wouldn't be left with the awkwardness of what this could turn into. But I couldn't do it. I spent the first five minutes trying to talk myself into it, but this feels too good to ruin.

Lifting my head, I look up to meet his gaze. His normally self-assured expression is nowhere in sight. It has been replaced with uncertainty and what I think looks like a touch of fear.

"Do you want me to leave?" I don't want to, but you can only live in a fictional world for so long. Eventually reality comes back to life.

"You really think I'm that much of a dick that I'd kick you out of my bed the moment you woke up?" Shawn sits up and turns to look at me, the hurt evident in his gaze.

"I don't know? I can see you're in uncharted territory here. This isn't exactly your normal." His eyebrows furrow, so I clarify what I mean. "Me in your bed—any woman, for that matter, in your bed." Realization hits and he nods.

"You're right," he states with a sigh. "I don't know what to do, but I'd like to think you don't believe I'm so much of a jerk that I'd boot you out." He wraps his arm around me, pulling me close, comforting me like only he can.

He is a jerk most days. Maybe he just doesn't see it. I mean, he has his sweet moments. Shawn isn't an uncaring person like he would like everyone to believe. The truth is, he loves hard if you're a part of his circle. He takes care of those he cares about. In his own way, sure, but the point is that he does.

At the thought of my brother, everything before Shawn coming home crashes down on top of me like a building set up with dynamite to implode, and I again feel the pit inside me growing.

That phone call was my undoing. The moment Shane said my name, I felt the arrow pierce the skin on my chest in front of my heart. His voice was weak, and I could tell he had been crying. It was so apparent I could feel it within my own body. He struggled with his words but eventually got out that there had been an accident.

Tears sprung to my eyes because there would only be one reason he was calling me, and that meant it involved Trent. I couldn't speak. I didn't want to ask the question screaming inside my head. When Shane told me my brother was gone, I stopped breathing, and my cell phone fell out of my hands. I bolted from my bedroom and out of the house. I needed the air that had been ripped from my lungs. It didn't matter, though; the cold January night did nothing to assuage the emptiness in my chest. I didn't start breathing again until I realized Shawn was hunched down in front of me last night.

"How did it happen?" Shawn's voice brings me out of my reverie. There is no need for him to explain his question since I'm sure it's written all over my face that I'm thinking about my brother. I've often been told I wear my feelings loud and clear for everyone to see. That's both true and false. Although that's the case when it comes to most people, with my family, my mother mainly, I hide my feelings well. It's hard work, but I usually do a decent job. It's just easier than dealing with her judgments.

Taking a deep breath, I slide myself off Shawn, pulling the creamy blue sheet with me as I do. Wrapping it around me to cover my naked chest, I flop down, landing flat on my back next to Shawn. My movement knocks him back into a laying position. He twists, rising onto his elbow to face me.

"A wreck is all I know." I feel the tears pooling in my eyes. "Shane called me late last night around eleven. Trent was on his motorcycle, got hit by a car, and died at the scene of the crash." I can't hold them back. The liquid spills over, down the sides of my face and into my ears before pooling on the pillowcase under my head. This is the first time I've let the facts fall from my lips. Saying it out loud makes it so much more real. I'm never going to see him again, talk to him, even if it's through a stupid text message.

His right hand cups my face, and his forehead comes down to rest on top of mine. It's comforting. "Fuck." He breathes the words out. "I'm sorry, Tara. I should have been here. Fuck, I'm sorry." I don't know why he's telling me he's sorry. It's not his fault. Maybe it's just what people say, I don't know. I've never dealt with death before. This is new.

Before I can tell him he has nothing to be sorry for, his lips land on mine. My mouth parts in automatic response to his touch. I could lose myself in his mouth alone. Last night I did just that and more. Had Shawn denied me, I don't think I would have made it through the night. I don't know if someone can die from a broken heart, but that's exactly what I imagine a slow death feeling like.

It's not a passionate kiss, nothing like the kisses from hours earlier. This kiss is an apology, and I still have no idea why.

"Shawn?" I breathe his name into his mouth. His slow movements come to a halt, but his lips remain on top of my own. I can't pull back. I'm already pressed into the mattress as it is with him leaning over me. "This isn't your doing." He lifts, pulling back an inch or two to look at me.

"I know, but my phone kept blowing up last night. I never checked it, but if I had . . . Had I answered, I would have been home sooner." I can see pain and regret in his eyes. It shouldn't be there. He had no way of knowing.

He clenches his eyes together.

"Shawn, you didn't do anything wrong. You did everything right. Thank you." Did I really just thank him for sex? Yeah, I guess I did, but I don't care. I needed everything he gave me. He told me not to regret him when I woke up. He needs to know I don't. I could never.

His eyes open, but he isn't looking into my eyes. From the looks of his, he's staring at my lips. I'm not stupid. I might write romantic happily ever after's, but I know they aren't real. When I leave Shawn's bed, I'll never grace it again. Knowing that doesn't do anything to wash away my hope. I'll never stop wanting him.

"I have no regrets, Shawn." His eyes snap to mine. "None."

Shawn wants me to stay on at Wicked Ink after graduation, but I already know I can't. I can't continue living in a fairy tale world that will never come true. I've lived here with him for nearly four years. It's been the hardest four years of my life. Being so close to him yet never having the chance to be together is painful. It's too hard. It's just too much, and I can't keep it up.

His mouth crashes down onto mine, urgently this time, and again my lips part automatically, accepting him. The moment his tongue touches mine, I feel him start to expand from underneath the sheet. His hardening cock is pressed against the back of my hand and hipbone, on the same spot he inked the most beautiful work of art onto my body just a few months ago.

I've never felt this kind of frenzied need prior to him. I've always enjoyed sex; well, except the night I lost my virginity. That was an inexperienced mess, not to mention a waste of my time. But right now, I need him inside me again. Especially if this will be the last time. I want to savor him, relish every part of his body. My mind may have accepted my reality, but my heart and body aren't ready just yet.

I reach out and grab his shaft. Shawn lifts his body slightly, allowing me to move my hand up and down his length in its entirety. I do so with slow strokes.

"Fuck, Tara. Shit, that feels . . . fuck." His right arm disappears underneath the covers, his palm running down my bare torso until it meets the top of my legs. He slows, wrapping his hand around my thigh and pulling it back to part my legs. My body is open for him to explore once again.

Jared and I have had plenty of sex, but never four times with five orgasms in a matter of hours. Who the hell even knew that was possible? Not this girl. Shawn's mouth is just as skillful as the cock I'm stroking right now.

"Tara, baby." I could get used to him calling me that. I know not to. Shawn's palm moves back to my center. He doesn't waste any time and runs his middle finger up and down the length of my folds, disappearing inside me.

"Ahh," I moan at his swift entry. "More."

"Tar—oh shit, don't fucking stop, baby." I increase my pace, tightening my grip a little. "We used all the condoms last night."

Shawn adds another finger, then starts a pumping motion, exiting and entering me over and over again. It feels divine. His lips find mine, and I open my eyes to peer into his. I've never shared eye contact with someone during an intimate moment before Shawn. This is like nothing I've ever experienced; it's erotic, passionate, uninhibited, and yet vulnerable. This kind of intimacy is so different that it scares me. And it feels so good.

Before I can make another plea for more, his thumb brushes against my clit. I want to scream, but instead, I clamp my teeth together. His thumb circles as his middle and ring fingers pump into me, faster and harder. I feel the beginnings of my free fall starting. I increase my speed on Shawn's cock. I want him ready to come when I do.

Between the kissing, our tongues molding together, my legs spread and accepting his assault, and the intense strain on my hand that's pumping him to his own orgasm, I don't realize the door to Shawn's bedroom is opening until Mason's voice halts us both, ruining what I was seconds away from receiving.

"Hey man, have you—" Mason stops. "Holy fuck." Shawn's head and mine turn to see Mason and Shane standing in the doorway. Mason is shocked. Shane looks distraught, perhaps even angry. He's the first to leave, turning and disappearing. Mason just stares like he doesn't know what to do.

"Get the fuck out, dude!" Shawn yells as he rips his fingers out of me.

"Yeah, sorry." Mason turns, closing the door.

"Ah, fuck," he whispers and then rolls off me, away from me. I look up at the ceiling. I don't like it, but there's zilch I can do or say. Realization has probably dawned on him. He told me last night not to regret our night, and I don't, but I don't think he can say the same.

I sit up, holding the sheet against my chest to look for my clothes, but all I see are my panties and Shawn's T-shirt. I stand, getting dressed in my underwear and his tee.

"Tara," he pleads. I don't look at him. I'm scanning the floor for my clothes, but I still can't locate them.

"I need a shower. I'm—"

"Tara," he says, louder this time, but I'm not doing this. I know what this was, and I know what it wasn't. There is no need to hash anything else out.

"Don't, Shawn. Let's leave it here." And in my head, where I'll replay every intimate moment of our time together in his bed. Later. Right now, I need out of this room. Shawn doesn't say another word, and I give up looking for my clothes. I leave, heading to my room so I can shower and prepare for today. I don't want to face it, but I've got to stop living in a fantasy.

My brother is gone, and I'll never get another second with him again.

———————————

ONCE I'M DRESSED and my wet hair is pulled back into a ponytail, I head downstairs. The steaming shower did nothing to ease the pressure bearing down inside my chest, unfortunately. It's back at full force, as strong and severe as it was last night before Shawn got home and temporarily took away the pain.

I hear the racket in the kitchen before my feet land at the bottom of the stairs.

"Would someone tell me what the fuck is going on?" Mason demands. His voice has none of his normal playful tone. I enter the kitchen, and all three—Shawn, Mason, and Shane—turn to face me. I look directly at Mason.

"Trent . . . he's gone. He's dead." The last word comes out choked. It's the second time I've verbalized that word, and it's as gut-wrenchingly painful as the first. I don't want it to be my reality, but it is. My brother is gone. Why?

"What?" Mason's question tears me away from my thoughts. His eyes bug. Turning toward Shane, he says one word, asking about his sister. "Kylie?"

"At your parents'." Shane's response is a mere whisper.

"Oh, fuck." He turns back to face me. "Taralynn . . . I . . ." He can't make a full sentence. He's in shock and worried about his sister, I'm sure. Mason may be the youngest of the three Morgan siblings, but he's as protective of his sisters as Trent was of me.

"Go to Kylie, Mase. She needs you." My voice comes out calm, but I feel anything but that on the inside. He steps forward, grabs the back of my head gently and pulls my forehead to his lips.

Seconds later, he's out the door. I'm left standing in the kitchen with Shawn and his brother.

I don't look in Shawn's direction. I can't. Thoughts of last night and this morning need to be forgotten as quickly as possible.

I realize there's not a chance in hell of that happening, but I can't think about it. Instead, I force my legs to move forward and walk up to Shane. Without words, he wraps me in his arms, fusing me to his chest. I feel the gush of air as it leaves his lungs. It's as if he's been holding everything in until this point. Maybe he has. I had Shawn last night. Who did Shane have?

"I'm so sorry, sweetheart." I know he has nothing to feel sorry about the same way I'm sure he knows it too, but this is what people do in situations like this. I don't understand it and probably never will.

"Here," Shawn says. I pull away from Shane to turn toward Shawn. He's holding two coffee mugs in front of us. I nod a thank you and take the one intended for me. Immediately I take a long gulp into my mouth, letting it swirl before swallowing. It's made perfectly, just the way I love it, but I don't sweet flavor.

I don't feel numb. I almost wish I did because the pressure inside is almost too much to bear. It's taking everything in me not to collapse and cry out, but what use would that do? It won't bring him back. I'd do anything to get Trent back, but that won't happen. That isn't reality. Screw reality.

My mind reels as I quickly swallow each drop of caffeine. I set the now empty coffee mug on the island countertop.

"So, what—" Shawn's cut off when Shane interrupts him.

"Why didn't you answer your phone last night?" His tone is accusing and possibly laced with hurt, but Shane has always turned pain into anger. Trent once told me that a girl in high school cut him to the core. He loved this girl, and when they ended, Shane was never the same. I don't remember a lot from then. I was in sixth or seventh grade and likely wrapped up in Shawn the same way I still am today.

God, I'm pathetic. Here I am, just a few hours after learning my brother was killed, and Shawn is still first and foremost in my mind.

"Dude, I'm—" I cut Shawn off from the certain apology he was about to offer.

"He was with me, Shane." That's true for the most part. He wasn't here when I first found out about my brother's death, but when he got home . . . he made me forget, just like I asked him to do. It might have been a short reprieve, but it was the temporary relief I needed.

Shane trains his blue-green eyes on his brother. They're usually bright with a glow to them, but not today. He wasn't happy with what he discovered when he walked into Shawn's room earlier. That much was clear then, but I don't care, nor do I need his approval.

"Not exactly the type of consoling I needed you to do, brother," he bites out the last word.

"And it is none of your damn business, brother," Shawn's words are an equal bite back. "So back off."

"Shawn." It's a warning from Shane through clenched teeth, but I've had enough. I won't have Shane ruin what happened between Shawn and me.

"Stop it, both of you." I can't stop the tears that pool into my eyes. Before I can swipe them away, Shawn grips my bicep and pulls me into his arms. He wraps one arm around my back while the hand from his other clasps the nape of my neck. My face plants in the center of his hard chest, and without getting the chance to wipe my tears away, they soak into his T-shirt. He doesn't seem to care.

The sound of the door closing, followed by Pam's voice a few moments later, has me pulling away from Shawn. Before I turn, I brush the back of my hands over my wet cheeks. For a moment, I'm met with resistance from Shawn. My eyes go up to his, but I can't read him. His expression is neutral, and then he releases me.

"Can someone tell us what happened? We woke up to the sound of an ambulance in the neighborhood and saw it outside the Morgans' house." I twist around to see Bill walking up behind his wife. They both look distraught. If I had to guess, I'd imagine I look similar. "All I could get out of Brock was that Kylie had a panic attack over Tr . . ." She pauses, unable to say my brother's name as tears of her own fall. Bill puts his hands on her shoulders. "And none of you were answering your cell phones."

"Tell us Brock was wrong and he isn't . . . gone." Even Bill can't say the word either.

I just shake my head because saying that ugly word again will be my breaking point, I'm sure of it.

Pam's sad eyes flick back and forth between Shane and me as if she's unsure of whom to go toward first. Bill squeezes her shoulders before walking to Shane and pulling his son into a hug. Pam's eyes remain on me.

"Honey." It's the only thing that comes out of her mouth as she raises her arms to offer an embrace. Pam has a pet name for not only her own two kids but also for Trent and me. She's always called me honey for as long as I can remember. It's rare that I hear her call me Taralynn.

She always refers to Shawn as Baby, Shane as Bud or sometimes Buddy, and Trent . . . Trent was Kiddo, which never really fit in my opinion. Then again, I've never seen my brother as a kid.

I walk to her and allow the warmth of her motherly arms to envelop me. I don't break, though. It's hard, but the tears stay at bay. Normally, I don't hide my emotions from Pam. She's one of the few people I'm comfortable around and feel safe just being me. I think I'm holding back to protect myself from more pain. I can't handle anything more right now.

"So what happened last night, Shane?" It's Shawn that voices his parents' question again. Even if my heart isn't prepared for it yet, I want to know the full story too.

"We were heading home on Interstate 55 after leaving a friend's house," Shane began. "Kylie wanted to beat the New Year's crowd and be able to see the ball drop on TV. Trent was on his motorcycle. Kylie and I were in her car, following. It was late, but it wasn't that late. I guess the time of day doesn't really matter when someone drinks too much and decides to drive."

"What?" I ask, because I don't want to assume my brother would do something so stupid. Trent's smarter than that; he wouldn't. "My brother wouldn't drive after drinking—especially not on his motorcycle." I'm the one that's gotten on the back of Jared's motorcycle numerous times after drinking, sometimes too much. Trent would never be so careless.

"Not Trent. But the guy that hit him? I'm certain he was drunk."

"What makes you think that?" Bill inquires.

"Seconds before he slammed into Trent's bike, I noticed his car swerving in the lane beside Trent. After Trent took the impact, the car veered into an embankment, and the man was ejected from the vehicle. He was also pronounced on the scene." He breathes. "I'm sure they'll have to do an autopsy on him to confirm any traces of alcohol."

"Honey, grab your purse, okay? We'll take you home." Pam squeezes me before releasing me.

My parents.

I haven't thought of them. God, I'm awful. What they must be going through at this very moment. I should be home.

"I . . . I need to pack a few things. I don't have clothes at my parents' house." Unlike Pam and Bill's house; I have a dresser full of clothes there.

"Okay. No problem. We'll leave when you're ready."

I look back at Shawn before exiting the kitchen. His eyes are sympathetic, but otherwise, I can't read what he's thinking. I can't dwell on it either.

CHAPTER EIGHTEEN

SHAWN

It's the day of Trent's funeral.

Man, it's surreal. I just saw him a week ago on Christmas night at a party. It's not like we were tight, but I sure as hell didn't think I'd be standing in my old room at my parents' house, in front of this mirror, putting on a black suit for this reason.

I don't think I've been to a funeral since I was a little kid. I don't remember much about it other than the awkwardness of not knowing what to do or say when random people hugged me and started crying.

Will that be me today? No, it won't, but I do know one person who will be in tears. I'm a master at masking my emotions; Tara isn't—except for when it comes to her parents.

I haven't laid eyes on her in three days. She's been at her parents' house since my parents dropped her off there Sunday morning.

As I tighten the knot on my gray tie, a sound draws my attention to the here and now. It's a soft melody. I've heard it before, and I'd know the sound anywhere. It's been nearly ten years since Shane has played his guitar.

So why today? I wonder.

He didn't stop playing because of Trent. He stopped because he lost Whitney. I was a kid in middle school back then, but even I know Shane loved her. Even though he won't admit it, it's also why he hasn't moved on. I don't think he can.

I drop my hands from the shit job I'm doing. Yep, I'm a man that doesn't know how to tie a tie.

Walking out of my room, I step into the hall and then make my way down the short distance to Shane's bedroom. I don't knock; I doubt he'd hear the sound over the guitar. He's also been distant. He won't talk to our parents about how he's coping. Except for yesterday, I've been here since Sunday afternoon. I had to go into the shop and reschedule my clients for today and tomorrow.

I open the door to see Shane sitting on his bed with his back leaned against the headboard, legs crossed, his guitar resting in his lap. He's dressed the same as I am, but without shoes, just black socks with a black suit.

I lean into the doorframe. He stops playing the moment he notices my presence.

"Wanna talk about it?" He looks up at my question.

"Nothing to talk about."

"Bullshit!" I holler out. Pointing my finger in his direction, I tell him, "The guitar, the song, they both say differently, man. They tell me you have something you need to get off your chest."

"Go away, Shawn. Not today." He breathes hard.

"Don't play that card with me." I shake my head to emphasize my point. "You're not in here moping over your best friend's death. You're in here thinking about *her*." He glares at me before cracking.

"So what if I fucking am?" Shane shoves the guitar off his lap and onto the mattress. "No one understands what I go through every day. What I've gone through and lived with for the last ten years."

"You're right, I don't, but if you've been keeping that shit bottled up that long, it can't be good, man." I remember Whitney a little bit. When she wasn't with my brother, she and Kylie were always together, so I saw her from time to time when I would be over at Mason's.

"What would you know?" He snorts. I'm sure most people would take offense to that, but not me. He's right.

"Not a damn thing. Doesn't mean you can't talk to me, though. I am your brother." His eyes soften slightly, but they also take on a deep sadness.

"I feel fucking awful. Today is my best friend's funeral. I'm not pissed that I'll never see him again. I'm not reminiscing about all the things we've done. I'm too angry that I lost the only girl I've ever loved, and I can't get over her. It's been ten years. A fucking decade, and a day doesn't go by that I don't think about her. She's the last thing I think about before sleep takes over and the first thing that crosses my mind when my eyes open in the morning."

"Shit, bro." What do you say to all that? What do I say to all that?

"You know," he laughs, but there isn't a lick of humor behind it. "I was jealous. Jealous of Trent and Kylie and what they had. And seeing them together every day, I envied them. I wanted *that* back. I had what they had, but it was taken from me, and it wasn't fair." Another sardonic laugh drips from his lips. "That's fucked up, isn't it?"

"No." I don't think it's messed up at all. "I think if I was in your shoes, I'd be angry with God too."

"I'm not angry with God. God wasn't the one that took her from me. Her asshole parents did." That last sentence is full of resentment. Hatred, even.

"How did they cause her death?" Something isn't adding up. Was she on life support after the crash, and they decided to pull the plug?

"Whitney isn't dead," he tells me, then gives me a look like he thinks I'm stupid or something. If that's true, then why aren't they together if he's so much in love with her? That is, if she's the one he's talking about.

"What? No, dude, I remember Mom and Dad telling you she didn't make it after she was taken to the hospital." I was young, but not young enough to have gotten that screwed up. I was in the living room when they told him. I witnessed him break apart. That night was the only time I've ever seen Shane cry.

"That was a lie. Her parents told Mom that. The next day, Dad saw her during his rounds in the ICU. She was still unconscious at the time. Even though it violated HIPPA regulations and could have cost him his career, he told me. I'd never been more relieved and happy in my life. That was short-lived. Her parents wouldn't allow me to see her. I tried, man. I tried to get to her every way I could. Nothing I did worked. They kept her from me. As soon as she regained consciousness, they immediately transferred her to another hospital and moved away."

That's fucked up. That's beyond jacked up. What kind of people do that to kids?

"I don't know what to say, Shane. I can't imagine something like that."

"Dad spoke to her attending physician. When she woke up, she didn't remember anything. Her whole life before opening her eyes in that hospital was gone."

"Do you think she ever gained her memory back?"

"I don't." The way he says it makes me think he knows more than he's sharing.

"What makes you think that?"

"If Whit remembered us, if the girl I knew remembered herself, then she would have found me." I never knew how heartbroken my brother was. Damn. "A few months back, I stumbled across her Facebook page. She's married and has a kid."

Shit. This story keeps getting worse by the second.

"Damn, brother, I'm sorry."

"The kid looked to be about a year or two. There weren't any photos of her husband, which is probably a good thing. I don't think I could have handled seeing that much of her new life.

Whitney looked amazing, but not like my Whitney. My Whitney hated dresses. Refused to ever wear them to church on Sundays. But in every photo on her page, she was wearing a dress. Reminded me of the way Taralynn dresses when she's in her mother's presence." He pauses, taking in air through his mouth. "So, yeah, I don't think she remembers me or anything else from before the accident."

"That is rough, brother. I hate that I never knew." Why didn't I know? He's my brother. I should know that shit. This makes me realize just how far apart we are. I don't like it. We're family. Hell, my family is close, but where the hell have I been?

"I'm done with this today. My mind should be on Trent." Shane swings his legs off the bed and stands up. He looks at me and shakes his head. "You still can't tie a tie for shit, can you?"

"I'm not meant to wear these things." I reach up and fist the material in my hands.

"Come here, little brother. It's time you man-up and learn."

I walk toward him. That will never happen. Suits and ties aren't for me. No woman will ever get me down an aisle in a monkey suit, so why bother learning? While Shane jerks on the material, pulling me closer toward him, my mind flashes to Tara and impossible things that will never happen. I shove those thoughts away. No need to let a mind want things it won't ever get.

CHAPTER NINETEEN
TARALYNN

"Taralynn." Her commanding tone from directly behind me freezes my feet to the ground. I slowly twist around to face her, not wanting to deal with whatever crap she's going to throw my way now. She's been impossible to deal with for the last three days.

The problem is, I don't have my car. I've been stuck at home with my mother since Sunday when I was brought home after waking up with Shawn to find Shane, Pam, and Bill at my house. I've tried to help with arrangements and things, but according to the bitch that is my mother, everything I do is wrong. Everything I've always done is wrong in her eyes, so why would this time be any different?

"Yes, Mother?"

Her eyes criticize me from head to toe. From that look, I can already tell she's found something wrong with my choice of attire. I haven't the faintest idea why, though. I'm dressed in a solid black, sleeveless A-line dress with a modest neckline that falls just to the top of my knees that are appropriately covered in tan pantyhose. I'm wearing the black, patent leather, closed-toe Jimmy Choo pumps she bought me for Christmas. My hair is neatly curled and swept up in a half up-do. I've completed my chaste, good little southern girl look with black diamond studs in my ears. The only thing I can imagine she can complain about is that I'm not wearing the matching black jacket to cover my arms.

My mother often tells me my arms aren't slim enough to wear anything sleeveless. Considering we are at my brother's funeral, you would think what I look like would be the last thing on her mind. But my mother is always concerned about outward appearances. Knowing this, I'm ready to explain I got hot in the jacket earlier and accidentally left it on my old bed at my parents' house. I'm sure she'll be happy to know I've already regretted my error. I'm cold, and nothing seems to warm the chill in my body.

"Do you need something, Mother?" I ask again, drawing her eyes up to mine. There isn't one crack in her armor. You would never guess this is the mother of the man lying in a casket in the next room. How can she look so put together when I'm a wreck? The person I love the most is gone. I'll never see Trent again. How am I supposed to be okay with that? I'm not ever going to be okay with that.

"Yes, I do." She takes a deep breath, bringing air in through her mouth and exhaling the same way. Maybe I'm wrong. Maybe she does have feelings and is trying hard to remain strong. I stopped trying to understand my mother years ago. "I need you to tell Shane he's needed as a pallbearer."

Has she lost her damn mind?

"No, I won't." Shane is a mess right now. How could she fathom he could do that? She was supposed to arrange everyone needed for that duty. She knows plenty of people, and my dad has a lot of relatives here that can do that.

"You will. I don't have time for an argument with you today. Go." She waves her hand, dismissing me.

Not today.

"I said, no, Mother." I've never come right out and denied one of my mother's requests, and I know my voice was much louder than I really intended. I don't care, though. This is the most absurd thing she's ever asked. Shane was my brother's best friend. She can't expect this of him, and I will not allow it. If that means standing up to the evil queen, then so be it.

"Taralynn, keep your voice down," I glance away from her at the sound of my father's voice to see him walking up next to her. "I do not need any extra stress today. Whatever it is Katherine asked of you, please do it." He always takes her side, no matter what. Rarely does he ask what's going on. He doesn't care and never has.

"No, Dad, I won't. And neither of you can make me." I cross my arms across my chest and stare my mother down. She's livid. I can tell by the way her eyes are trained on me. They're hard, and her jaw is locked as if she's trying to stop herself from saying something.

"Tara?" His voice is questioning. "You okay?" Shawn's hands land on my hips as his front meets my back. My body relaxes into his as if on reflex.

I glance toward my dad to make certain he understands my stance on his wife's request, and if I didn't know better, I'd think my dad's eyes were wrecked with panic. He's no longer looking me in the eye. He's glancing back and forth between Shawn's face and where his palms are resting on my body. My dad knows how I feel about Shawn. If I'm honest with myself, everyone—including Shawn himself—knows I've been attracted to him for as long as I can remember. But I also know, just as my father does, that I'm not Shawn's type. The look my dad is giving us, though, is throwing me off. I push thoughts of Shawn to the back of my mind and focus on the problem in front of me.

"She wants Shane to carry the casket after the service, and I told her no." My father's jaw locks, and Shawn's hands tighten. He doesn't like the idea any more than I do.

"Stop acting like a child, Taralynn," my mother scolds. Why does she have to be such a bitch, all the time? "I'm burying my son today, and I need his friend to step up to the plate today and do this."

"Katherine."

"I won't—" My dad and I both speak at the same time, but I'm not able to finish because Shawn cuts me off.

"I'll do it." He bites out the words. "Tara is right. My brother is in no shape to be a pallbearer. I'll do it in his place." His voice softens, but I can tell he's angry with my mother for even wanting Shane to take on that responsibility. Shane's barely holding it together as it is.

"Thank you, Shawn." It's my dad who speaks. "Katherine, we need to head to the chapel." My father turns, walking away without my mother. She glances at Shawn before peering back at me.

"I expect you to be in the chapel within fifteen minutes for the service. Until then, please take yourself to the lady's room and sort out your face. Show your brother and everyone that came to show him respect some decency and go make yourself presentable." With her harsh words, she turns and stalks after my father. And I bolt, yanking myself from Shawn's grip.

I'm out the door from the main lobby within seconds. The blast of icy wind hits me in the face with a smack, but I don't care. I don't know where I'm headed. I just know I can't do this, not today, not ever. Trent is gone, and I feel utterly lost. He didn't do anything to deserve to die.

"Tara." At the same time Shawn says my name, his arms wrap around my waist, halting my movements away from the funeral home. I twist in his arms, wrapping mine around his shoulders. I'm holding on for dear life. I know it, and I'm sure he feels it too.

"I can't do this." My words are mumbled as my face is buried into his neck. With my four-inch heels on, I'm just an inch below Shawn's six-foot-two stature.

"You have to, and you will." He snakes his hand further around my waist as the palm on his other hand glides up my back, stopping at the nape of my neck. "For Trent, you can." He squeezes the area of my neck reassuringly, and I pull back, sniffling the snot that wants to roll down my nose back up.

I nod my agreement. He's right. I have no choice; this is my last moment to see my brother. Even if he is lying in a box that will seal shut and never open again.

"I got you. I promise." His words are like a healing balm to my shattered soul.

About the time that I'm going to release him, a soft hand graces my shoulder and squeezes. I disconnect myself from Shawn, turning to find Eve and Chance standing next to us.

"Hey, baby girl." I practically leap into her. I'm a few inches taller than Eve Matthews, but she's no ordinary petite woman. Like Kylie, Eve makes up for her size in attitude and spunk, not to mention color. Eve is a lot to take in the first time you meet her. Chance calls her his living, breathing canvas. Colorful ink adorns her entire body. She really is a beautiful, breathtaking sight, as are the photographs she takes.

"You came." They're the only words I can get out. The tears are starting to pour. The harder I try to hold them in, the more intense they seem to want to flow. I pull back from her and nod to Chance. He and Eve are best friends, practically connected at the hip. They both grew up with my brother and were all really great friends, but Chance and Eve dropped out of high school early. Eventually, Eve and Chance left Mississippi and moved to Las Vegas, Nevada, to pursue their art. I know Chance has tried to get Shawn to move out west. I'm not sure why he never took the opportunity. Sure, the studio is doing great, but Shawn would get a lot more exposure in a big city like Vegas.

Eve's voice brings me out of my thoughts.

"There aren't many things that could get me to come back to this state, but I could never forgive myself if I didn't come to say goodbye to him." Eve is strong; I've often said she seems bigger than life. Emotions I've never seen her display are written loud and clear on her face. Her eyes are rimmed with red, and her lip trembles slightly when she breathes out.

Chance latches my wrist and pulls me into his warm arms for a brief hug.

"Hey, sweetheart." Chance cups my face, applying a small amount of reassuring pressure, and then looks deep into my eyes briefly. He's equally as striking as Eve, with all the ink decorating his skin. The majority of his tattoos are covered by the dark suit he's wearing, but a dragon's paw with its claws digging into the skin on his neck is peeking out of his collar. Chance has jet-black hair, tanned skin, and a pair of stunning diamond blue eyes. He belongs on the cover of one of those tattoo magazines, or maybe on a billboard. "He got you?" He gestures in Shawn's direction, and I nod. Chance does the same and releases me. "We're going to head in."

Shawn pulls my back to his front once again, and I soak up every ounce of affection he gives me. "We need to do the same," Shawn whispers. "Please go see him one last time."

Trent.

My head bobs. It's the best I can do. I need to do this.

Lord, please give me strength.

And He does.

Moments later, I find myself standing in front of the shiny black casket, peering down at the body inside. It's not him, not really. I know that, but it doesn't stop me from wishing he would open his eyes, making this all one cruel joke.

This reality blows.

I can't bring myself to touch his body. I don't want to remember him as being cold and stiff; that was the opposite of who my brother was. My earliest memory is of my brother being kind, warm, and loving to me. He used to take me everywhere he went. He never left me behind when I was a small kid.

"You were the greatest brother a girl could ever have. I hope you know that. I'm sorry if I never told you. I love you so much,

Trent, and I miss you. It shouldn't have been you. You shouldn't be gone. It's not fair!" The tears are falling hard now. So hard, making the form in front of me a blur. "You were always there for me when I needed you. It's like you had this sixth sense or something when it came to me. You just knew, and you were there. Now you're not here, and I'm all alone. I don't want to be alone."

Large hands wrap around my hips. Shawn has been standing behind me this whole time. He steps into my space. His chest meets my back, and I have to admit it helps to have him here. It's comforting and eases a fraction of the weight centered on my chest.

"You're not alone, Tara. You'll never be alone." His voice is a whisper for my ears only. He's wrong, but I don't correct him on it. I don't want to let our night in bed together jeopardize the friendship that has grown deeper since he confided in me about buying the tattoo studio, but deep down, I know being friends will never be enough for me now that I've had a taste of how good we could be together if he just gave us a chance. "It's time to go into the chapel."

I give Trent one last look before I let Shawn lead me away. Away from my protection, away from the only love I've ever trusted, away from my big brother.

I miss you, Trent.

Every pew in the funeral home chapel is filled with bodies. Some I recognize. Most I don't. Shawn leads me to the front row where my father and mother are seated.

"You were supposed to be in here ten minutes ago," she whisper-yells as we walk past.

"Katherine," my father whisper-yells back at her. It sounds like a warning, but after what happened outside earlier, I doubt it'll do any good. He's back to taking her side. Everything he said on Christmas morning must not have meant jack.

My father doesn't utter another word, but his eyes scrutinize us as we take our seats. I sit next to my dad, and Shawn sits down next to me. He rests his arm on the back of the pew behind me, and he takes my hand with the other. Within a few seconds, the hand he has resting behind me moves closer. Shawn places his warm palm on the back of my neck, stroking softly. His touch allows me to breathe a little easier.

The preacher conducts the service. I'm sure it would be considered lovely, but I can't view it as such. This is the worst day of my life. This is even more difficult than the night I found out he died. This makes everything too real. And then there are Kylie's cries coming from behind me—it's all I hear the whole time.

CHAPTER TWENTY
SHAWN

The funeral ended with a graveside service. The entire day has slowly crept along. I'm spent, but fuck, I can't leave Tara now. I may be a regular jerk, but I have to set aside my desire to just get the fuck out of here. For Tara.

It's nearing nightfall, and everyone close to Trent is at the Evans's home. I'll be heading to my parents' house around the corner to crash at some point. I want to talk Tara into coming with me. She's spent enough time around that bitch she's forced to call Mother. She needs to be around the ones that love her effortlessly and endlessly: my family.

Matt's voice in my ear rouses me from my thoughts.

"Damn," Matt breathes out with a slight shake of his head and a small remorseful laugh. "You guys remember when Trent got so pissed off and wanted to murder Shawn for getting Taralynn sent to in-school suspension for five days?" My eyes snap up to hers. She's staring at me from the comfort of Matt's lap. They've been off for months now, but you couldn't tell it right now. He's finally acting like a best friend should. Comforting her when she needs it.

My gaze is the first to falter as the memory of that day sinks into my head, playing out like an old movie right in front of my eyes.

"Mr. Braden," Principal MacIntyre blows out as he leans forward in his oversized black leather chair from behind his equally oversized dark wooden desk. "I'm at my wit's end here. I'm at the end of my rope with you. I've tried for nearly four years. I've tried to get through to you. Nothing has worked!"

Wonk, wonk, wonk.

It's the same speech I get every time I'm in his office, sitting in this same ugly brown chair. As often as I'm in here, you'd think I'd become accustomed to the hard, uncomfortable wood underneath my ass. But I haven't, and I swear the man keeps me in here longer each time.

"Mr. Mac, it's not you. It's me." I stifle the laugh that's trying to escape my mouth. He doesn't like my humor. Oh well, I do.

"This," he fumes with a stern tone as he points his finger at me, "Mr. Braden, isn't a laughing matter. There isn't any humor in the situation you've gotten yourself into today." I toss my head back as I grip the sides of the chair and slouch down until my head meets the hard surface behind me. What the hell is his damn problem? I sit up, looking him in the eyes once more.

"It was a stupid joke. Come on, even you've got to find the humor in it." He takes a deep breath, pulling air in through his nose before releasing it from his mouth.

"No, Shawn, I don't. That's just it; no one but yourself finds the things you do funny."

"Now that's just hurtful. Plenty of people were laughing throughout the halls earlier."

"Shawn, you're failing to grasp the severity of this."

"If you're planning on suspending me, then please go ahead and get it ove —" There's a light knock on the door before I can finish my statement. As Mr. MacIntyre looks past me, I turn in my seat to see who's decided to prolong my stay in this chair. Without being given permission to enter, the door opens slowly. Tara appears within seconds with a nervous, scared shitless expression across her face. If I didn't already know she worked in the principal's office during third period, I'd think this was the first time she's ever been in here.

Tara is the good girl. No, let me take that back. Even good girls get into *trouble every now and again. But not her, not little miss perfect. Tara reminds me of a rose, just as it's starting to bloom: exceptionally beautiful, perfection in all things . . . superior. Like I said, perfect.*

"Miss Evans, what can I help you with? And please make it quick. I'm in the middle of something." He looks back at me, only briefly, but I know I've been successful in getting on his nerves today. Ah, the joys of high school.

Tara enters the room, closing the door behind her, then proceeds to walk closer to where I'm sitting. Her hesitant eyes meet mine, only for a moment, before she takes the seat to my right and looks straight ahead at Principal MacIntyre. She doesn't say anything for a few long beats, as if she's trying to collect her thoughts. I'm baffled as to why she's even in here.

"I have . . ." Her whispered words are followed by a short pause. She looks down, then glances back up as she straightens her posture and takes a gulp of air. "I need to tell you something, Mr. Mac."

"Go on, Taralynn, I'm waiting." Mr. Mac's voice is much softer as he speaks to Tara versus when he was addressing me. Go figure. She has him wrapped around her finger too. I sit back in my chair, proceeding to lean my head back and slouch down once more. I'll never find a comfortable position, but I might as well make the best of it while she takes her sweet time.

"It was me." My ears perk up. Why do I get the feeling she's in here about me? Was it the look she gave me, the emotions in her eyes, or her words? I'm not sure. "I did it. I wrote Holly's number across the lockers, not Shawn."

Silence.

The room is silent. I sit up, looking to my right where Tara is sitting, not looking at me but chewing on the left side of her bottom lip as she awaits Principal Mac's reply. Hell, I'm waiting for it too, because I'm not sure I heard her correctly. Did she really come in here and confess to something I did? Not Tara. No way did I hear that right. What the hell is wrong with this girl? Why on earth would she take the blame for me? Tara may not hate me, but she surely doesn't like me.

"Miss Evans." Mr. Mac finally speaks. "You don't expect me to believe that, do you?" His eyebrows are pulled in, and he's staring at Tara as if he's trying to read her. He probably is. He's always doing that. He thinks he can read me like a book, but I'm not that transparent to anyone.

"Mr. Mac, with all due respect, and I really mean that, I'm not sure it actually matters what you believe in this case. I'm telling you I did it. And you don't have any real proof Shawn wrote that message, do you?" Her hands clasp together in her lap, and she's squeezing them tightly as if she doesn't want to chicken out and back down from the lie that just spilled from her lips.

Taralynn Evans just lied.

Holy shit, I never thought I'd see the day. On top of it, she lied for me. I have no idea why, either. It makes no sense. It's not like I'm scared to get in trouble. The worst he can do is suspend me from school for a few days, maybe even a week. Okay, been there, done that, not a big deal. A few days off will be nice.

"Considering he gave his confession in my office and the fact that he and his friends were laughing about it, I'd say I have enough to go on. Now, Miss Evans, I'm going to overlook this. You're going back to class, and I don't want to see you in my office again unless it's during third period and you're working in here. Is that clear?" So he does have a fierce voice when it comes to the perfect one. Hell, his tone might be bordering on scary . . . if I were a girl.

"No, Mr. MacIntyre, I'm sorry, but we aren't. I'm telling you, it was me, not Shawn. And based on what you just said, you don't have any real proof Shawn did it." I'm getting whiplash, I think. Tara's voice has taken on a bold confidence I've never heard before. I might even like it, if her dumb ass weren't in here trying to get me out of trouble.

"Very well, Ms. Evans, I'll humor you." He relaxes into the softness of his plush chair, leaning back as he continues to speak to the crazy chick I'm wondering if I know at all. "Please explain to me why on earth you would write, 'For quick and easy fun, call x number,' and that number being Holly Torres's home phone number? Please tell me, because I'm dying to know that reason." Sarcasm is dripping off his lips.

Tara is silent for a moment, searching for an answer, I'm certain. If I weren't still in shock, I'd probably be rolling on the floor laughing. This is laughable. She's laughable. No one in their right mind would believe the story of Taralynn 'perfect' Evans being malicious to another person and destroying school property in the process.

Maybe I did take that stunt a little too far, but the way I see it, that bitch *deserved it. I told Mason and the others it was because she went around telling people at school that we were dating. We aren't. I don't date. I screwed that whore once, just like any other girl. I don't do seconds, but the real reason, the reason I don't want to even face, was Tara.*

Holly had sex with Tara's douchebag of a boyfriend. Not only did she sleep with him, she recorded it on her phone and sent the video to Tara via text message. I guess the only bright side of the deal was that Tara broke up with the loser.

I'm ripped from my thoughts when the feel of Tara entwining our hands catches my attention. She still isn't looking at me. Her attention is on our principal. I cut my eyes to him as well. He's staring at our tangled limbs too. An eyebrow is raised, but other than that, he isn't giving anything away, and I can't read him.

"I was jealous."

Come again?

"Say what?" *He's as stunned as I am, I think.*

"Jealousy. You know, the green-eyed monster. When someone—" *He stops her.*

"Taralynn, I'm aware of what it means, but I don't understand why you would be jealous of her." *He scrunches up his nose. Holly is pure trash. I don't say that about many people, but the bitch is. My dick didn't seem to care when I fucked her, though.*

"Because," *she glances my way, giving me a look that tells me she wants me to go along with whatever she says.* "She made everyone in school believe Shawn was dating her." *Her hand tightens around mine as her words come out.* "He's not with her." *She says it as if it's obvious. To me it is. To everyone, it should be obvious. I wouldn't date that bitch if she were the last chick on earth. If I were smarter, I never would have had sex with her in the first place.*

"Taralynn." *Principal Mac breathes her name out.* "That's all well and good, but—" *He doesn't get to finish.*

"He's with me." *Say what?* "That's why I did it. She deserved it. Don't you understand that?" *Damn. If I didn't know better, I'd believe Tara and I were dating. She sounds like she believes the words coming out of her mouth.*

"You want me to believe the two of you are dating?" *He holds up his hands* before Tara says a word. "Not only that, but you were the one to degrade a fellow student's self-worth and deface school property? Does that sum it up, Taralynn?"

Dude sounds a little ticked off.

"Yes, sir."

His eyes cut to mine. With that look, I know he's asking me if I'm going to allow her to take my blame. That look also pulls me out of whatever it is that's been going on since she took my hand. I'll never admit to anyone just how great it feels to have her hand in mine. I can't let Tara do this. Her parents will flip the fuck out.

"Tara, come on." I slide my hand out from hers and sit up. Turning in the chair, I face her. "There's no point in this. I can handle what Principal Mac dishes. I always do."

"No, Shawn." Her words are bitten out, then she turns to face me. "Not this time. He's not going to suspend you. He's going to expel you. You won't graduate."

I'm speechless. For the first time in my life, I have no words.

This isn't good.

"How did you know that?" Mr. MacIntyre is as stunned as I am.

"It's true?" What the fuck? "It was a joke."

"Shawn, you've done too much over the last four years. This was my last straw. You need to be taught a tough lesson."

"One in which I assure you he has learned."

"Taralynn, go back to class. This does not involve you."

"I disagree, since I told you I did it, not Shawn." He huffs from frustration before glancing away from us. He looks to the ceiling. "Shawn, tell him it wasn't you."

I really do not know what to do right now.

I don't want to be expelled, that's for damn sure. I really don't have a choice. I have to go along with this, but why is she the one bailing me out?

"Right. Um . . . what Tara said." I feel so lame right now.

"Are you certain you want to stick with that story, Miss Evans?" He's not only pissed, but I'm pretty sure I see disappointment in his eyes. "Be sure.

There is no going back. You realize I will have to punish you for these transgressions?"

"Yes." I hear the uncertainty in her voice. It's clear as day, but I cannot not graduate. That is not an option, so I remain silent.

"Monday morning, you are to report to Coach Parker's room for ISS. You'll have five days of in-school suspension for your actions. You also have to apologize to Holly. Lastly, you are responsible for the bill to re-paint all the lockers in Hall B. We're done, Miss Evans. Please return to your class, now." He dismisses her.

Once she exits and the door is closed, a very pissed off man stares back at me. One which I may be a little scared of at the moment. No longer do I see my principal. He's angry. I'd be willing to bet that angry is not part of his job description while in the presence of a student.

"I hope you're happy."

"I wouldn't call any of this happiness, sir." No point in pushing his buttons any more today. Maybe not even the rest of the year.

"You don't have any idea what just happened, do you?"

"I was here. I heard every word, sir."

Can I please go? I think to myself, feeling like I want to crawl under a rock.

"Taralynn will be graduating with honors. Until two minutes ago, she would have received a full scholarship to college. With a suspension on her record, she won't be getting it now. That's what you did. That's what you took away from her. To save my soul, I have no idea why she did that for you, but I hope one day, you make her sacrifice worth it. Out of my office, Shawn."

Oh, shit.

"What did you say?" Katherine's vile voice tears me away from the memory of four years ago. "You-you did what?"

Tara turns into Matt, mouthing something I can't make out, then turns her head toward her mother. "Yes." I want to laugh, but I hold it in. Tara's tone has a bite to it.

"Why on earth would you do that?"

"I'd like to know the answer to that as well, young lady." Her dad comes to mirror Katherine's stance.

"Well, you see," Tara's voice is rich with sarcasm, "some people care about their friends so much that they're willing to make sacrifices for them. Something I don't think either of you knows anything about."

"You ungrateful little—"

"Katherine," Jacob silences his wife. Probably the best thing he could have done. I won't physically hurt a female, but I have no issues with lashing out at one verbally. "Taralynn, we'll talk about this later, but know that whatever you think you are doing with this boy, it isn't worth it. I just . . . I can't believe you right now."

Tell me how you really feel, Jacob. Not that I didn't already know.

Self-worth to these two is on a whole other plane that I'll never get to.

"Don't you dare, Jacob." There is venom in my mom's voice. "Don't speak about my son like that."

"Oh, come on, Pam. Don't sit there and tell me you can't see it as clear as I can. Do you want history to repeat itself?"

What the hell does that mean?

"Enough!" My father stands. "Jacob, a word." My dad stalks toward Tara's father. They both stare at each other before turning and walking out of the room.

Tara's mother remains. The look in her eyes is unmistakable. Hatred. Her green eyes are trained on Tara as Tara is looking back at her too. Looking at them both, you'd never guess they were related. Tara's skin is tanned like Jacob's. She doesn't share any resemblance to her mother the way Trent did.

Tara pops up off Matt's lap and walks away. She doesn't want Katherine to see her cry. I could tell she was on the verge. She makes her way to the stairs, ascending them until I can't see her anymore. When I turn back around, my mother and Tara's are glaring at one another. If I hadn't seen it for myself, I'd have never believed it. My mom hates Katherine.

My parents left after Dad had a private talk with Jacob. I don't know what they discussed, and I don't care. Tara's parents are fucking assholes. She's perfect, and they don't deserve her.

Tara's been alone long enough, so I head upstairs to find her. When I reach the top of the steps, I stop in front of Tara's bedroom door. It's wide open, but she's not in there. That tells me I'll find her in Trent's old bedroom. I don't knock before entering the room. I can see from the crack under the door that it is dark inside. Night has finally taken over. It's been one long day. One I want to see end sooner rather than later.

She doesn't stir as I gently turn the handle and push the door open. Her body is stretched out diagonally across the bed. I can tell she's sleeping from the rhythmic rise and fall of her torso. She's lying on her stomach with her hands underneath her face, making the hem of her black dress rise to meet the top of her thighs just a few inches below her ass. Memories of my lips kissing that same area of flesh filter in. I remember being so turned on by biting her ass cheek while my fingers were inside her. She came the same moment my teeth bit down, coming all over my finger and running down my wrist.

The shit she does to me. I don't want these feelings, but not because I don't want her. I've wanted her longer than I care to admit. But I'm realistic. I know a relationship with this perfect girl lying in front of me would never last.

"Tara." I won't leave her here. Evidently my mother feels the same way, since as she was leaving with my dad, she barked an order at me, insisting I bring Tara when I come home. "Tara, wake up," I call out, a little louder this time.

I place my knee on the edge of the bed and lean over. Giving her a gentle shake, she stirs. I let go of her shoulders, and she rolls onto her back, propping herself on her elbows. Tara looks around the dark room briefly before her eyes land on me.

"How long was I out?"

"Not long; less than an hour. I'm here to collect you. We're going to Mom and Dad's. You can crawl back into bed when we get there."

"Um . . ." She looks torn. If she thinks she's staying here after the way her parents treated her, she can think again.

"You're coming. Now get whatever you need for the night, and let's go." Luckily she doesn't argue. She grabs a purse and a large white bag. I take the bag from her shoulder and push her toward the door.

Five minutes later, we are parked outside my parents' house. I turn off the engine. Neither of us has spoken since we left the Evans house. What do you say to someone that lost the only person in their family that gave a damn about them? Loved them. I can't relate to that. I'm not bragging when I say this, it's just a fact; I have an amazing family. One I'm grateful for every single day.

She opens the passenger door and slides out. I grab my keys and do the same, following her inside and up the stairs. Remaining silent, we each head for our bedrooms. As soon as I enter mine, I remove my jacket and tie and toss them on my bed. I've been itching to do that all day. I hate suits.

As I unbutton my shirt, I turn to walk over to the dresser, but stop as I see Tara standing before me.

Damn, she's beautiful. Even sad and tired, she's stunning. She doesn't even know how enthralling she is, and I think that's what has always captivated me. Okay, that's a lie. She captured my attention from day one.

My gaze drops to her lips. "Need something?" I ask. Those motherfucking lips. So plump and naturally crimson. They are perfect to suck on, bite, and kiss.

I need to get her out of my bedroom. The last thing she needs is another unbridled sexual ravaging from me after the day she's had. I may know there isn't a future in store for us, but that doesn't mean I don't crave seconds, and thirds, a whole fucking feast, for that matter.

"You." The word is a whisper, but it's like a shout-out to my already aroused dick. I shut my eyes. If I can't see her standing in front of me, in that black dress and bare feet, then I can imagine something else. Something I don't desire.

"You should get in bed, Tara. Get some sleep." Her body steps into mine. Her palms slide over my hips. This isn't helping matters any. I'm trying to do the right thing here.

I don't want to be her crutch. I don't want to just be the mechanism to help her forget her pain any more than I want to be her regret.

Damn it . . . I'm not supposed to want more than I deserve.

Her hands slide up slowly over my shirt. Her knee wedges between my legs, pressing against my hardened cock.

I want her more than I want to wake up tomorrow.

That realization has my hands fisting into tight balls at my sides.

Her movements halt, then I feel her back away from me. My eyes fly open. What I see reflecting at me causes constriction inside my chest. Her dark blue eyes are crushed. Why?

"You—" Her voice cracks. "You don't . . ." She doesn't finish her sentence. Instead, she turns and runs. I scrub my palm over my face, through my hair, and back down. I don't understand. What the fuck did I do?

The sound of the front door closing jolts my body into action. She can't leave; she doesn't have a vehicle here. It's back home in Oxford.

By the time I make it outside, I witness her running behind Mason's house. His bedroom is on the back side, and he has a door leading outdoors. Shoving my hand into my front pocket, I grab my cell phone. My hands fumble to unlock the motherfucker, but once I do, I call his number.

The call rings through to voice mail. I'll do this all night if I have to. I'm doing him a favor by calling instead of walking over. It's already after nine at night. Mrs. Naree will shit a brick if she finds his friends coming and going this late at night.

I press end and repeat the process. After five rings, he picks up.

"Want to explain?" Mason answers, and I hear a door close. I'm guessing he stepped onto the deck outside his bedroom door.

"If I could, I would. What did she say?"

"Nothing . . . yet. She walked in crying just as you called. Didn't take a genius to put two and two together."

"Man, I don't fucking know what I did to upset her. Can you let me talk to her?"

"Yeah . . . no. Look, whatever it is, I'll find out and defuse. Talk to her tomorrow after she's slept." I won't get any sleep until I know what happened back in my room. I need to speak to her. I know she's had a rough day, but . . . fuck.

"Where is she going to sleep?"

"My bed. Layla is in bed with Ky, but I'm not shoving Taralynn in a room alone."

"Mase." I breathe. "Please don't—I mean, if she asks you to—"

"I'm your best friend. Don't fucking insult me like that, bro. The way I see it, you've already claimed her. You just better back that shit up." The line goes dead.

I haven't claimed her. I can't claim her.

CHAPTER TWENTY-ONE

TARALYNN

"**M**ase, your penis is stabbing me in the butt," I tell him with agitation as I attempt to squirm from his hold around my waist. When the hell did this happen? Ughhh.

"It's a cock," he states blankly.

"Not to me, it's not." It almost comes out as a laugh, but seriously . . . ew! Well, Mason is hot in a cute sort of way. He's my friend, but certainly not the friends with benefits type for me. And there's also the fact that I'm not drunk. So, again, ewww.

"No?" I can feel his smile spread across the back of my head. "I don't think that's what you were thinking two years ago when you sucked the motherfucker off."

Well, hell. Why couldn't he have forgotten about that? "Nope, it was a penis then too." And it was. Not that I didn't enjoy blowing him, because, well, I like giving blow jobs. But it was a one-time thing. We were both drunk. Very drunk. So drunk that I didn't remember it happening until later the next day.

"God, you sure know how to kill a bonner," he jests as he releases me and rolls off his bed.

When I got here last night, Mason didn't ask questions. I know he spoke to Shawn on the phone, but I don't know what was said, and I didn't ask. He tossed me a T-shirt and a pair of boxers, and I was out within minutes of washing off my makeup and crawling into his bed.

"Thanks for letting me crash here last night." I feel bad showing up the way I did, unannounced and so late. I know his parents have rules about friends not coming or going after a certain hour, and I'm sure he'll be hearing from his mom this morning about it. I want to be gone when that happens. That lady scares me. She's tiny, just like Ky and Layla, but fierce.

"You doing okay? Because you know if you aren't, you can talk to me about anything." The playful Mason is gone. Concern is etched in his voice. I love him for it. Mason is a great guy and a wonderful friend.

"I'll make it." I turn my face, giving him a small smile. I don't know how I'll make it in life without Trent, but I guess I have to.

"And last night?"

"Just a misunderstanding. No biggie." I was an idiot to try anything with Shawn again. He's made it clear he doesn't want to be with me. I guess being around him most of the day yesterday with all that physical contact gave me hope. Evidently, I wasn't thinking clearly. "I sent Matt a text last night before bed. I'm going to ride back to Oxford with him this morning."

As if on cue, my phone chimes, telling me I have a message. Picking it up, I confirm it's my best friend.

Matt: Waiting outside.

"He's here. I was going to change and get my bag out of Shawn's truck." Mason stares at me but doesn't say a word. I grab my dress off the top of the dresser and make my way into the bathroom, but I'm stopped as I place my hand on the doorknob.

"No need to change into your clothes from yesterday. Just grab a pair of gym shorts from the bottom drawer over there." He points toward the tall chest of drawers across the room. He's not looking at me; instead he looks to be texting on his cell phone.

Thinking about it, I really don't want to put back on a dress that will only be constricting. Loose, comfortable clothes are exactly what I want right now. Mase's will do until I get home to shower and put on my sweats.

"Okay, thanks." I pull out a pair of black basketball shorts. After I have them on, I roll the band a few times because I can't stand them falling past my knees. When I'm done, I grab my purse and head toward the door that leads to the backyard. "Thanks again. You coming home today?"

"Yep." He smirks down at his phone. I wish I were in on whatever is so humorous. I could use a laugh right now.

Exiting, I stop by Matt's car and place my purse inside.

"I need to grab my stuff. Be right back." He doesn't say anything, but nods.

Walking up to Shawn's truck, I open the back door. He always leaves his truck unlocked at home and at his parents'. I'm not sure why. Probably isn't smart, but it's not like the neighborhood is shady.

Before I'm can reach in and grab my heavy tote bag, someone wraps their hand around the bend at my elbow and yanks me backward. In a quick motion, I'm turned, and my back meets the steel of the side of the truck. It doesn't hurt, but I'm caught off guard.

"What the hell, Tara? Why did you take off last night?" I look up to see hurt eyes looking back at me. I wanted to avoid this conversation. That's why I asked Matt to pick me up this morning. I didn't figure Shawn would be up this early.

"I don't want to deal with this. Let's forget it ever happened. I'm going home." I point toward Matt's car to indicate my ride is here and waiting.

"Well, too bad. We are dealing with this. Right now." He crosses his arms over his broad chest and leans back a few inches.

He can go blow smoke up a bear's butt. I don't give a crap. I'm leaving, and I'm leaving right now.

244 N. E. HENDERSON

"No!" Screw it. He has to come home eventually. I'll get my things out of his truck then. I move to get past him, but Shawn quickly stops me by stepping in my path.

"You aren't leaving. We need to talk."

"Move," I bite out. Last night was embarrassing enough as it is. I don't need to hash it out, not with him, anyway.

"Not until you listen." I don't think so. I step in the other direction, only for him to mimic my move. "Just hear me out."

"Why?" I don't give him time to respond. I don't want him to. "There's no point. Bye. See you later."

I don't get a chance to move an inch past him. Instead, I'm picked up and tossed over his shoulder. He starts to walk, but not in the direction of where Matt and Mason are standing next to Matt's car. My guess is he's walking toward his parents' front door.

"Put me down."

He doesn't comply.

"Shawn, put me down."

Nothing!

When I'm jolted up and down a few times, that confirms my thoughts of him taking me into Mr. and Mrs. Braden's house. The door swings open, and he enters with me.

"Grab that for me and close it, would ya, Tara?" He sounds smug.

"Put me down!" I yell.

"That's not gonna happen, darlin'." I watch as he raises his leg to kick the door closed with his boot.

"Shawn Douglas, what do you think you're doing?" Pam's voice rings out. Thank God. She will make him put me on the ground, hopefully soon too, because I'm getting dizzy. "Put her down."

"Stay out of this, please, Mom." Shawn ascends the stairs. I'm once again jolted, which only makes the vertigo worse. I have to close my eyes.

"Shawn!" I call out. He has to stop soon.

"Zip it, Tara." He hits the landing and then turns. I'm pretty sure he's headed toward his bedroom. Although mine is across the hall from his, so he could be heading to either one. I keep my eyes closed. A door opens, and then I'm propelled backward, where I land on a plush surface.

Opening my eyes, I see it's a bed. His bed.

I move to get up, but get nowhere when he straddles my torso. Oh, hell!

"Why did you run from me last night?"

"You know why." I don't want to do this. Why can't he leave it alone? After everything I've been through the last few days, I want to feel nothing. I want to block everything and everyone out—especially him. He makes me feel too damn much. Want too much.

"If I did, I wouldn't be asking you." I stare up before turning my face to look away. I can't look at him and say this. I don't want to see the truth in his eyes.

"God, Shawn, don't—please don't—I know you didn't want me. You don't want me. Hell, you've told me over and over again. You would think I'd learn by now." He grabs my jaw, gently turning my face to look at him. The one thing I don't want to do. He lowers, getting inches away from my face.

"I'm pretty sure my hard dick said otherwise. Fuck, Tara." Now he sounds pissed.

"Just because your body reacts to mine doesn't mean you want me, wanted me. I saw you. You were standing in front of me. You were doing everything possible not to—"

"Get off her, Shawn. What is the matter with you?" I can't see Pam because Shawn's body is blocking his mother's.

"Mom, please stay out of this." He blows frustrated air into my face. I hate how it reminds me of what he tastes like when his tongue is in my mouth.

"Bill!" Pam yells out. Great! Shawn's in for it now. This will not end well for him if Mr. Bill walks in and he's on top of me.

"Shawn, get off, please," I big him.

"Leave, Mom."

"This is my house, son, now get off Taralynn!" she commands.

"Sweetheart, what's . . ." Bill begins. There's a pause, too long of a pause. "What the? Shawn!"

I hear feet stomping toward the bed, and a heartbeat later, Shawn's body is ripped away from me. Mr. Bill shoves him backward toward the window. I know Shawn, and I know that he would never lay a hand on his dad, but I don't want to chance anything happening.

I jump off the bed, and before I process what I'm doing, I find myself standing between Shawn and his dad. My back is to Shawn.

"Mr. Bill, please, it wasn't as bad as it looked." It probably was, but no need to confirm that for his parents. It's not like Shawn intended to hurt me. He would never. Shawn is many things—manwhore, asswipe, jerk—but abuser is not one of them.

"Taralynn, I need to speak to my son." He looks down at me. "Alone." His tone leaves no room for argument, but that doesn'tstop me.

"What are you going to do to him?" I ask as Shawn places his hands on my hips and pulls me back toward his chest. Shawn's parents have always been reasonable. They talk things out. Bill doesn't look like he wants to talk anything out. This concerns me. Apparently, his dad reads that from me because his brows turn inward.

"Have you ever seen me lay a hand on him, or Shane, or you?" He breathes hard. "I just want to talk to him. That's all."

"Tara," Shawn says from behind me. I twist, looking over my shoulder and lifting my eyes to meet his. "Head home with Matt. Take Mason too. I won't be long behind."

Nodding, I do as he says, walking away from him and out the door.

CHAPTER TWENTY-TWO

SHAWN

I didn't come home right after I left my parents' house like I told Tara I would. That was thirteen hours ago. My head was so messed up . . . it still is. I drove. I thought if I could step foot out of this state, if I could just get a few hundred miles of distance, clarity would come. It didn't.

I slam the gearshift into park. I'm home. Tara's somewhere inside the two-story house I'm staring at through the windshield of my truck.

You've never been a pussy, so why are you being one now?

I open the door and hop out of the truck, noticing the car in my driveway that I've never seen before. After trudging up the steps, I open and walk through the front door.

The house is quiet, but I know someone other than my roommates must be here. Soft voices filter down the foyer. They're coming from the kitchen. I hear a female voice. It's familiar, but not Tara's. I head in that direction.

I enter to find Matt leaning against the countertop in front of the sink, Mason sitting on a bar stool with his arm stretched out on the granite island, and the source of the female voice, Samantha,

I'm certain, is sitting on top of the island counter. The three of them are engrossed in conversation.

"Where's Tara?" My question causes them to turn their heads my way. "Samantha, right?" I nod in her direction.

"That's it, but you can call me Sam if you like. Most people do. Taralynn is in her room. I was up there about fifteen minutes ago."

"Is she doing okay?" I know it's a dumb question, but it's the one that's been on my mind all day.

"As good as can be expected right now." She has a point. She would know too. Samantha, or Sam as she wants to be called, lost her dad a year ago.

"How's the tat healing?"

"Great. You made my mom cry, though." She smiles.

"We were talking about what pizza to order since there's no food in the house." Mason slides off the stool and walks to the fridge. When he opens the door, all I see is beer. He grabs two and returns to his bar stool, handing one to Sam and flashing her one of his smooth smiles. She's definitely his type. If blondes are my type, then redheads are his.

"Okay. I need to talk to Tara. Catch you guys a little later." I don't wait for any response, but I notice the smile Sam tries to hide before I turn, walking back down the hall. Rounding the stairs at the front of the house, I jog up until I reach the landing.

I knock on Tara's bedroom door, but there's no response from the other side. I knock again. Still quiet. I turn the knob and walk into an empty room. Everything is immaculate except the ruffled covers on the bed. The sound of running water draws my attention toward the door leading into the bathroom and closet. She must be taking a shower.

I'll wait.

Walking over to the bed, I straighten the covers before sitting on the edge of the side facing the dresser. Looking into the mirror, I determine I look like shit. I didn't get any sleep last night, I

MORE THAN LIES 249

haven't eaten today, and being cooped up in a truck for hours hasn't helped. I'm fucking tired.

I lean back, allowing my body to rest on the mattress while my feet remain on the floor. I throw my arm over my eyes to shut out the overhead light from the ceiling fan above me.

I'm not lying there long—maybe a minute or two—when I hear the clicking sound of the bathroom door opening. I breathe out a long puff of air. I'm clueless about how this will play out. And fuck me if I'm not a little scared, maybe even more than just a little.

"Shawn." She sounds shocked. Perhaps she didn't expect me to come see her when I got home. I should have been home long before now. We need to finish our conversation from this morning. My dad was so pissed at me. Probably still is. Who knows? I didn't stick around for a lecture. I walked out within five minutes after Tara left.

A shadow crosses over my face, telling me Tara is standing at her dresser so I pull my arm away to peer up. Her back is to me, but she can still see me through the mirror. A black towel is wrapped around her body, and her wet hair dangles across her shoulders.

"When did you get back?" I hear her words, but forming a response isn't working. Raising my torso, I sit on the bed to take in the rest of her. My eyes fall to her bare legs. Shit.

"We need to talk."

Ignoring my statement, she asks, "How did things go with your dad?" She squats to the floor, pulling open one of the bottom drawers, where she pulls out a set of pajamas.

"Not about that." She stands and places them on top of the dresser. "We need to discuss what we were trying to talk about before they interrupted us." She closes her eyes and lets out a puff of air before opening them back up to look at me again through the mirror.

"Let it go, please," she pleads.

"That's not going to happen, darlin'."

Tara pulls open another drawer, pulling out a pair of panties. When she pushes the drawer closed, she bends at the waist to step into the navy blue material. With one hand, I grab the opening of the towel, and with the other, I open her palm, causing her to drop the underwear to the floor. My eyes glide up her body until they meet hers. Pulling lightly on the towel, Tara steps closer toward me until she's standing between my legs.

"Can't we forget it happened?"

Tugging on the soft towel untucks it from the top, allowing it to fall down her body. I release it from my hand as it joins her panties on the floor. Tara stands before me naked, beautiful, exotic and tropical with her tanned skin, wet hair, and dark blue eyes. Her breasts are large. I know she wears a DD cup; hell, I've lived with her for years. They are perfect. She's perfection.

"What part would that be?" My voice is a cross between a whisper and a growl, full of desire. My hands glide up both sides of her smooth thighs until I settle at her waist. "The part where I fucked you with my fingers five nights ago? When I tasted every inch of you with my tongue? Or when I made love to you in my bed? Two things, I might add, that I've only done with you."

"No." That word comes out as a moan. "Not those." Sliding my palms behind her, I cup her ass and pull her forward until her middle meets my lips. Her skin is soft, just the way I remember it. The way I've imagined it for the last longest five days of my life. I kiss her just as softly.

"So the part where you think I don't want you, then. Is that the part you want us to forget?" Squeezing her ass cheeks in each hand, I flip her onto her back, where she lands on the bed with me towering above her. "If my dick wants you, then I want you. Do you think the last few weeks—a couple months ago, even—are the only times I've ever wanted you? Been affected by you? It's not true."

Her chest rises and falls at a rapid pace. Her dark eyes are dilated, and her skin is hot to the touch.

"What are you saying?"

"I want to fuck you right now. I want to wake up next to you and make love to you tomorrow. Then I want to repeat that over and over and over until we don't want to do it anymore." Something in the back of my mind tells me that day will never come, but I don't verbalize that thought. It scares the fuck out of me. Instead, I bury my face and mouth into her neck, where I kiss her. Moving to the muscle between her shoulder and neck, I bite down.

"Ahhh." She likes it when I do this. Her hands skim the skin underneath my shirt. "You have too many clothes on."

I push up and straddle her. Lifting from the hem of my T-shirt, I pull it up and over my head.

"Better, baby?" She rakes her eyes down my chest.

"No, you're still too covered up." Her hands slide down my torso and grab my belt buckle, unfastening it and ripping the belt from the loops. "Lose the jeans and boots. I want you as naked as I am." She smiles expectantly. There's confidence in her eyes. I like it a whole fucking lot. She's changed this year.

Hopping off the bed, I give her what she wants: me wearing absolutely nothing.

"Now we're talking." She rises onto her elbows, but she isn't looking at my face; her eyes are zeroed in on my cock. That look is causing my already stiff shaft to harden even more. When she wets her lips, I can't take any more. I pull a condom from my wallet and toss it on the bed.

That was the only stop I made before coming home. After last weekend, I needed more. I knew then, somewhere in the back of my head, that I'd have to have her again. That night wasn't enough, and tonight won't be either. I have no idea where this leads, but I'm not willing to let it go just yet.

Grabbing her by the leg, I yank her toward me until I'm able to latch onto her thigh. I flip her onto her belly and then pull her the rest of the way back until her ass meets my crotch.

"Are you hungry?"

"What kind of question is that?"

"Our friends are ordering pizza. I need to know if you want it quick and hard or slow and savoring." My palm lands down on the meaty flesh of her outer thick with a loud smack.

"Mmmm." She pushes into me. "Rough and hard, but I don't want this over for at least an hour, maybe longer."

A smile crosses my lips.

We don't make it down for dinner. There's no need for food after we fill up on each other.

CHAPTER TWENTY-THREE

TARALYNN

I walk into Wicked Ink at two thirty. It's Saturday, and I'm covering the receptionist for lunch at Shawn's request. They're always this busy on Saturdays, so I don't know what's different about today other than it's my birthday—which falls on Valentine's Day—and I could be sitting in my oversized comfy chair with my e-reader. I only have hundreds of books on there just waiting for me to pause and read. I'd much rather be living in someone else's fictional world for a few hours than in my own reality.

Trent is gone. My brother is never coming back. You'd think I'd be happy today, that I could put that sad fact in the back of my mind just for one day and enjoy turning twenty-two. But I can't.

Trent was a huge part of my life, especially on my birthdays. He always made it a point to do something exceptional to make my special day extraordinary. From the cheesy voice messages of him singing happy birthday to the single purple rose he had sent to me every year, Trent never failed to make me feel treasured. I'd never seen a purple rose before I received my first one on this day of my high school freshman year. Trent has always denied he was the one that sent them to me, but I never believed him for a minute. That was the same year—the same day—he started sending Kylie red roses.

So, instead of being at home, I'm here, about to work. Well, let's back that up; I'm about to do more work. I spent five hours this morning cleaning the wreckage from last night's house party. That's in addition to the ton of laundry I washed, dried, and folded. I hate housework, but more than that, I hate a messy house, so I'm stuck. I have no choice. I have to clean.

"Hey, Nat." I walk behind the front desk, where Natalie is hanging up the phone. She looks like she partied way too hard last night. Her blue eyes are dark around the rims, and she has mascara smudged underneath. She doesn't look like she's slept or showered. I like the girl, but gross.

"What are you doing up here today?" Oh, great. Did Shawn not tell her?

"Shawn asked me to cover you for lunch." When her eyes glance in his direction, mine follow. He's at his station, leaning over a pair of legs. Looks like he's inking the back of a woman's thighs. I frown. I can't help myself. Her shorts are practically nonexistent. *Slut.* The fact that they have to be short for him to tattoo her properly does not take precedence over the fact that he's eye level with her butt hanging out of the material.

"Well, okay. He didn't mention it, but I am about to leave. See ya in an hour." Natalie grabs her purse and walks from behind the counter toward the front door. Laughter catches my attention, and I turn toward the back of the shop where all the artists' stations are located. That laughter came from Shawn's table. I roll my eyes as the phone rings. Looking away, I turn around to answer it.

"Wicked Ink, this is Taralynn. How can I help you?"

"Hey, baby doll." Chance's voice greets me. I smile. "I wasn't expecting your bright voice on the other end of this line. I thought Miriam trained the new girl well? So what are you doing answering the phone? Happy birthday, by the way."

"Mir did an excellent job with Natalie. I'm just covering while she stepped out for lunch. Thanks for letting us borrow Miriam for a week." Miriam works for Chance in Las Vegas. She's his studio manager and runs the front desk as well. Thankfully, when Shawn finally hired a replacement for thieving Sabrina, Chance and Miriam agreed to have Miriam come to Mississippi to train our new receptionist. Two weeks later, Natalie is killing it up front. Not only that, the customers love her.

Other than looking like she came in wearing what she wore the night before, she's great. Her customer service skills are awesome. She has an extroverted personality and can talk to anyone. She doesn't sport any ink work on her arms, but the dragon tattoo covering her back with one paw hanging over her shoulder and its tail wrapped around her legs is pretty neat.

"You're welcome, doll. We're both glad we could help Braden out. Tell him I'll catch him later. I only called to see how well the new chick answered the phone and if Miriam's training was retained. I'll take your word that it was. Later, sweet girl."

"Later, Chance. Tell Eve I said hey."

"Will do." I hang up the phone. When I turn around, my bitch-o-meter dials up a notch thanks to Slutty McSkanks-a-lot squeezing on Shawn's arm. He's finished the tattoo, and they're standing. I guess she likes the job he did.

Shawn pulls his arm slyly away from her grip. He looks uncomfortable, I'll give him that.

As if feeling eyes on him, he looks in my direction. His eyes grow bigger as if he thinks he's been caught. He's not technically mine, so he doesn't really have a reason to feel guilty. I'm probably just reading too much into that look, so I turn away.

Less than a minute later, I feel a presence behind me, and then I see Shawn's client standing on the other side of the counter in front of me. She isn't looking at me. She's ogling his sexy body and shooting him a flirtatious smile. Didn't she have enough time to get all that out when she was lying on his table? Tramp.

"Tara will take care of you." Shawn brushes his hand over my hip, squeezes, and then walks away. She watches him the whole freakin' time. I quickly scan the appointment log to find out how much she owes.

"That will be seven hundred and fifty bucks." She finally looks my way. After pulling out her credit card, I scan it through the card reader. This is a recent addition to the business. The studio is no longer cash only.

"So do you know if he's seeing anyone?" She nods in Shawn's direction.

Be polite, Taralynn. Be polite.

"He's not the dating type, honey." That is true. Shawn and I have been sorta seeing each other for over a month. We have sex. That's all it is. Great, awesome, phenomenal, I can't get enough of him sex, but just sex. Only sex. We aren't dating. He made it clear weeks back when we returned from Tupelo that he didn't want anyone to know we were sleeping together. Talk about a crusher.

"Well, now, I'm not opposed to a little fun. Maybe I'll see him around then." Her eyes brighten, then she turns and walks away after retrieving her credit card from my hand.

Happy birthday to me.

"Happy birthday." Shawn perches his elbow on the glass countertop and leans into it. I look over. There's only about a foot of distance between us.

"You told me that this morning before I got out of bed." Oh, the memory.

"I said it when my mouth was on your pussy. It doesn't count." He smirks. That smile and those eyes . . . I have to look away. Glancing down, I scan the appointment calendar looking for Shawn's next client. Hmmm . . .

"Your schedule is blocked off, but it doesn't say who your next client is."

"She's already here." I look up, but there's no one waiting in any chair. Turning my head, I look Shawn in the eyes.

"Where?" Seriously, who the heck is he going to tattoo? A ghost?

"I'm looking at her, babe."

"Me?" His eyebrow lifts. "I'm not following."

"I want to give you a birthday present. I want to tattoo you, and I want you to allow me to do it and let it be a surprise." He's joking, right? "You trust me, don't you?"

"Yes." I do, but to permanently ink me without me seeing the design is crazy. That's messed up. No one in their right mind would let anyone do that to them. He's lost his damn mind. "No way!"

"Come on."

"I'm not opposed to another tattoo. I'd love one, in fact." Cosmo was spot on. They are addicting. Once you get past the week of non-stop itching, you forget about any misery associated with getting a tattoo, and you want another. "But I want to see it first."

He looks at me like I just burst his bubble.

Sooorry. Too bad, buddy.

He huffs air out through his nose.

"At least let me put the transfer on, then you can look and decide. Will that work?"

"Yeah." I'm excited. "So we're doing this now?"

"After you." He holds his arm out, silently telling me to walk toward his table. I do so with a little pep in my step.

After he cleans my skin and dries it, Shawn applies the transfer. When he finishes, he pulls the paper off and quickly balls it up before I can see. Shawn looks at me. His eyes tell me he's nervous. He shouldn't be. I know the design will be beautiful. All his work is amazing. I have no doubts that I'll love it, but there was no way I could go through with it without seeing it first.

"Can I look?"

"I guess." Is he sweating? Shawn Braden? Okay, today just became bizarre. I hop up and swing my legs to the ground so I can stand. Taking a step toward the mirror, I raise my arm.

Shawn placed the soon-to-be tattoo on the underside of my left bicep.

What I see in the mirror has confusion and tears springing to my eyes. It's the rose. The purple one. The transfer displays one single rose not quite in full bloom, with a stem and a ribbon. The ribbon says, *Beautiful* in a pretty script font. The reason I don't understand is that I've never told anyone what the ribbon attached to my annual birthday rose said. Only the sender and I would know. Right?

"You don't like it?" His voice is soft. Disappointment is etched in it.

"It's beautiful. I love it more than the one on my hip . . . but how? How did you know about it?" Did Trent tell him? Did he see the rose without me knowing?

"It's not obvious?" If it were, would I be asking? I shake my head. "I'm the one that sent you the rose every year on your birthday."

Talk about a revelation.

The tears come harder. Shawn has just revealed he's thought about me with affection as far back as high school. He thinks I'm beautiful. Or he wants me to think I'm beautiful. I'm not sure which. And it was never . . .

"It was never my brother." The words come out. I don't mean for them to, but they do. It's not because I'm sad that the roses weren't from Trent. Okay, I am a little, but that's only because he's gone.

"You thought it was Trent?" His eyebrows pull together. "Shit, I'm sorry, Tara. I didn't know you thought that. I wouldn't have . . ." He stops mid-sentence.

"No, don't. I'm happy to learn who the roses were really from. I just would never have thought you sent them to me." This isn't like Shawn at all. At least I don't think. I've known him a very long time. He doesn't do this type of thing. Why me?

"I know you're having a hard time with Trent's death. You can talk about it. You can talk to me about it." Concern. That, on top of everything . . . it's all too much. I bow my head, letting the tears fall to the ground.

I haven't cried in public in weeks. I was doing so good, holding back the tears until I was alone in the shower where they could fall and not be seen. I don't want to talk about his death. I don't even want to talk about his life. I certainly can't verbalize that to people. I sound awful. Who doesn't want to remember one of the most important, beloved people in their lives that was lost way too soon? I'm that awful person, and I don't want anyone to know it.

"Come on." He takes my hand in his and gently tucks me behind him. I follow until we are behind closed doors in his—our —office. I use the space more than he does, but he is the boss.

Shawn twists around, letting his back hit the smooth surface of the closed door. Then he pulls me into his arms and wraps them around me. I love this. Being in his embrace does something that no other person has ever accomplished. I can relax into him. I can't do that with anyone else.

"Get it out, Tara. Talk about him. Scream, yell, cry, or even hit something if you need to. Hit me. Just get everything out before it swallows you. I know you're struggling. I just don't get why you don't talk to me, or Mason, or even Matt."

Because I can't. It's that simple, but I don't say that. I tried explaining all this to Matt weeks ago, and he didn't get it. I only frustrated him, and now he's pulled away again. I miss my best friend.

I shake my head, hoping he takes that as an answer and drops it.

He doesn't.

"Tell me, Tara. Tell me something," he pushes. I don't want to be pushed.

"I'm okay. I'm better than I was when it happened." I pull in air and blow it back out to calm my emotions. "I love the tattoo, and I want it."

"Why don't you think about it, and if you still want it, we'll do it when you're ready." I want it now. I need it now. The pain will only help purge some of the suffocation I feel inside.

"I'm ready." I force a smile. He sees right through me. Another tactic will be needed. I rub my palm down his crotch.

"Tara." I like the sound of my name as a warning. I wonder if I can get some type of punishment out of this.

I drop to my knees. I'm in blue jeans, and the floor is carpeted, so it's a good thing I'm not wearing a skirt. I wouldn't want burns on my knees when I'm done making him cum.

"I'm going to make you believe me." I rub over the front of his pants again. He grows hard; I can feel it through the material.

"You want the tattoo? I'll give you the tattoo now, and we can do this later." He pushes on my shoulder.

"You don't want my mouth on your dick?" He likes it when I call his cock a dick. He thinks my mouth is too clean, so it turns him on when I use dirty words. "You don't want me to suck it down my throat?" He licks his lips.

"Yes, but this might not be the best time or place, baby."

"But I sit in this office—in your chair—every week and fantasize what it'd be like to get the boss off." I pop the button on his jeans. "In his office." I slide the zipper down ever so slowly. "Just like this."

His chest rises and then falls in hurried pants. After I pull his pants down to his knees, I lean forward into him and smell as I work my mouth up to the black band on his boxer briefs. He smells nice since it's only been a few hours since he took a shower.

I open my mouth, and my tongue slides out, licking the skin just above the band, making a slow swipe across his lower abdomen.

"Shit." His words make this worth it. I love that I can do this, turn him on so quickly. It turns me on too.

With my hands, I gather the material between my fingers and pull down. As I do this, I kiss a path down his happy trail. The trail that leads me to the very thing I want to pull into my mouth. I continue kissing down his shaft. He's hard. Hard and ready for me.

I release his underwear when they meet his pants at his knees.

Shawn bends, grabbing my T-shirt from the hem in the back. When he rises, he takes my shirt with him, leaving me in my bra and jeans.

"That's better, but I want them out." Placing my palms on my breasts, I squeeze the material of the bra, making my cleavage grow. Shawn sucks in another breath. Running my hands inside, I release my breasts, letting them spill over the material. "God, I love your tits."

Reaching up, I cup his balls and gently massage. With the other hand, I fist him at the base of his cock. He's warm. I pull my fist forward as I continue looking up at him. I love watching him when I do this, when I suck him off. It makes me so wet.

Lowering my head, I lick the tip. When I take him into my mouth, I only suck on the head for a few seconds before gliding him all the way into my mouth. Working my mouth and fist together, I find a rhythm.

"Fuck, baby." He grabs my hair, fisting the strands in both hands and tightening his grip. I love my hair being pulled. He can do more of that, and I'll be a happy woman.

When I pull away from his base, going up to the tip, I swirl my tongue around, making sure I dip the tip of my tongue into the slit in his cock. He loves that. Shawn hardens more, and his fingers grip tighter. He's about to come, so I quicken my pace. Sucking up and down, up and down, until I feel hot cum squirt toward the back of my throat. I swallow as it comes into my mouth. He's salty.

When I know he's almost to the point of being too sensitive, I relax my mouth and pull back. His head is resting on the back of the door. His jaw is locked tight so he didn't make a sound alerting anyone to what we are doing back here.

I stand and start to pull my breasts back into my bra. Before I can reach down to the ground for my shirt, Shawn grabs me by the waist and fuses my chest to his. Then he lays a kiss on my lips.

That makes me feel good about what we did. I love knowing he liked it.

"You have the right idea about dirty fantasies in this office. I think I just developed one where I fuck you in my chair." He smiles.

"You should definitely do that soon."

"Now seems as good a time as any." His eyes rake down to my chest, and his palms slide down to squeeze my butt cheeks.

"You have a tattoo to finish." I raise my arm.

CHAPTER TWENTY-FOUR

SHAWN

Walking through the hall toward the kitchen, I smell the first scent of what's to be a good dinner. It is Sunday night. Tara is obviously preparing another wonderful meal.

When I enter the room, I stop dead in my tracks. Damn, if she only knew how hot I think she is. She's leaned over the counter, her nose in a book, I think. She's wearing a tank top and black yoga pants. That ass is screaming for my hands to mark it. I never would have thought I'd be a man who enjoys spanking a woman, but I've found it incredibly sexy. She has the perfect round ass for it. Seeing my handprint on her flesh just does something to me. I can't explain why, but I like seeing it after I plant my palm on her bare skin.

The house is quiet. I didn't notice anyone in the living room when I passed by. Our roommates aren't around, so I'm free to touch Tara the way I want. I make my way toward her and stand directly behind her. Placing one hand on her hip and snaking the other around her front, I pull her into my chest, inhaling as I bury my nose in her hair.

I'll never tire of this smell. She is springtime and honeysuckles.

"Is there a reason I woke up alone this morning?" I ask, moving my hand to reach under her shirt, careful where I touch her. I finished the tattoo on the underside of her arm a little over twenty-four hours ago. It's still fresh, and the wound needs time to heal.

"Yeah, you don't get up until noon, and I had to go grocery shopping." She laughs as if sleeping that late is unheard of in her world. Oh wait, it is. She's up at the butt crack of dawn every day.

"I require my beauty sleep, baby." I kiss her on her cheek before flipping her around to face me. "What are you cooking? It smells great."

"You say that about everything I cook." She tries to turn back around, but I don't let her. I like having her in my arms this way. Every way.

"Nothing special. It's just a roast." She points toward the crock-pot. "It's been cooking all day. I didn't really do anything."

Dinner is in the crock-pot tonight. That means she doesn't have to stand over a stove to make sure nothing burns.

I bend my head and plant a soft kiss on her lips. I know I'm being risky. Our friends could walk in at any moment, and we'd have to come clean about what's going on between us. But I'm not ready yet. I like it just being her and me. The thought of anyone coming between us and ruining what's just started has me tightening my grip on her and increasing the intensity of our kiss.

I'm becoming obsessed with Tara. I want her all the time. I can't get enough of her. When I'm at work and she isn't there—or even when she's working back in my office—I'm thinking about her. When I leave her bed or she leaves mine, it feels wrong. But I know wanting her this much isn't right either. There should be a healthy balance, and I don't have it.

Her parents would shit a brick if they knew she was with me this way. They'll ruin us if they find out. I can't let that happen, so I have to keep us as just us until I figure out how to keep her longer.

I worry that she's growing tired of me. That she's starting to see what her parents see. That thought kills me.

Tara deserves what my parents have. Best friends and lovers, connected forever.

She pulls back, breaking our connection.

"I need to study. I have a test tomorrow." She once again tries to turn away from me.

"Yeah, well, your pussy sitting on my face sounds more appealing than whatever is in that book sitting behind you." She gasps, telling me I have her just where I want her, and within a few minutes, I will have her pussy riding my face. "Come on, baby. Homework can wait." She nods. Turning, I take her hand in mine and pull her behind me.

If no one is in the house, I intend to make her scream. I've yet to hear my name fall from her lips when I make her come. This keeping quiet bullshit is grating on my last nerve.

CHAPTER TWENTY-FIVE
TARALYNN

S hit. Shit. Shit.

Shawn's mouth is rubbing off on me. Well, inside my head anyway. I'm starting to cuss like a sailor inside my own brain. Before too long, that shit will be coming out of my mouth as easy as it does his. It's not that I don't cuss or have anything against it. There simply are too many other words that can be used instead. Usually, funnier words, at that.

This is the third time I've jacked up payroll today. It's Wednesday, and I'm only here because I have to get payroll done now so I'll be ready to leave for our Georgia trip in two days. I need out of this state. I need away from school and just everything. Stuffing my face with crab legs and riding through dirt, dust, and mud is the exact escape I need.

Two months.

He's been gone for two whole months today.

Samantha said the pain would get easier to handle over time. That hasn't occurred yet. When is that going to happen? I want to fast forward to that day. Every day in my life sucks. I feel so alone. I have no one to talk to. Not because they haven't offered. Samantha's tried plenty of times. You'd think with her going

MORE THAN LIES 267

through something similar, it would be easy to open up to her. It's not. It feels wrong for some reason. Logically, that doesn't make sense, but it does to me. My roommates have tried, Shawn the hardest. I want to talk to him. I don't want to talk to him. I'm scared to talk about it.

It takes another hour, but I finally complete my task and get the checks written. Natalie is going to hand them out for me on Friday. She's been great for the studio. If she knew accounting, she'd be able to do my job, and I'd be able to get back to writing. I haven't written a single word since before Trent . . .

I'm such a loser. A pathetic loser who can't even say what happened to my brother or even think it. The pain isn't getting easier. It's getting harder. At times I feel like I'm suffocating from the inside out. How freakin' logical is that?

My cell phone rings.

Picking it up off the desk, I read the caller ID. It's Mac.

"Hey, stranger." It's been a while since I've been to the pub. I miss it, if you can believe that.

"Hey, sweetie." His voice is always soft when he's speaking to one of his girls. That's what he calls his waitresses. He's a sweet old man in a daddy sort of way, and very unlike my own father. "I'm hoping you can bail an old man out of a bind."

"I can try. What can I do for ya, Mac?"

"Holly called out sick. A new girl I hired last week quit. I'm short tonight, and I was hoping you were free and could work tonight."

Shoot, it's family dinner night. Damn it, but I can't leave Mac hanging.

"Sure, I can do it," I agree before I chicken out. The guys will just have to understand. We leave in a couple of days. I can always make it up to them over the weekend.

"Thanks, girly girl. You're the best. Can you be here in an hour?"

Crap.

"Yeah, I can make that happen."

We hang up. I stack the envelopes with the checks inside them on the desk with a sticky note attached that has Natalie's name scribbled on it.

Walking out, I start a group text to my roommates letting them know the bad news about dinner.

Me: Guys, Mac is in a bind, and I told him I'd help out tonight. I'll make dinner up to y'all in GA. Sorry!!

I'm hoping I can get past Shawn and out the door before he sees his phone. As I walk by, he looks up and gives me a half smile and nods a goodbye. I dodged that one. He was busy applying a transfer on some guy's leg.

My phone dings twice simultaneously as I slide into the driver's seat of my car. I need to get home and change quickly so I can get to the bar on time. A shower is out of the question, but I can freshen up and change clothes.

Matt: You're kidding, right?

Mason: WTF. That's bullshit.

I knew they wouldn't be happy. Coming between men and their weekly promised food isn't the smartest thing one could do. I'll have to hear about this one for a while.

Another text message comes through when I put the gearshift into drive. Keeping my foot on the brake, I read it before pulling out of the parking lot. This one isn't part of the group text.

Shawn: You couldn't stop and tell me that before leaving?

Me: You were busy.

Shawn: And you're a chicken shit.

Ass.

I don't respond.

Instead, my mind wanders to the person I try every day to forget. I don't want to forget him, but if I did, I wouldn't have to feel this pain any more. I really am a weak and crappy ass person.

CHAPTER TWENTY-SIX

SHAWN

"Hey Shawn, how's it going?" Removing my eyes from Tara, I glance to my right to see a chick sliding into the booth next to Kenny. Her voice is familiar. When she settles into the seat, she looks up at me, smiling, and places her hand on my shoulder. "It's good to see you again." Her lips are curved into a flirtatious grin.

I reply with only a brief grin to acknowledge her. This shit is getting old, and it's not what I want to deal with tonight. I know who the girl is. I inked two bow ties on the back of her thighs a week ago.

Before I'm can slide away from her touch, I sense another presence to my left. The sound of bottles clunking together and being placed on the table tells me it's Tara with our drinks.

I turn, looking up to see a flash of anger directed toward the chick that just joined our table. Tara removes her phone from her back pocket. When she looks at the screen, she huffs out a frustrated gush of air.

"Um, Taralynn, honey?" Adam calls out in a question. I look at him as he holds up a Coors Light. He doesn't drink that type of beer. That's when I peer down at the rest of the drinks that aren't what she knows we all drink.

"Yeah?" she questions back while dropping the hand holding her cell to her side. Her expression changes when she realizes she brought us the wrong drinks. "Shit. I'm sorry, guys. I'll be right back." She places her cell on the table in more of a toss than sitting it down. Tara grabs the bottles by their necks and walks off.

My earlier assessment of something being off or wrong is confirmed. Then again, her brother was killed eight weeks ago. She's still dealing with a lot of emotions. Emotions she won't talk about, so really, one could say she isn't dealing with things as she probably should be.

Wanting to know what caused her frustration, I snatch up her phone. The screen isn't locked, and even if it was, I know her code. Her text message app is opened to a text conversation between her and Jared. My jaw locks at the sight of his name. Not liking the thought of her speaking to him, I unashamedly read the messages starting about an hour ago.

Tara: I feel like I'm drowning. Like I can't breathe.

Jared: Come over when you get off.

Tara: Don't. That's not why I texted you.

Jared: Then what was your reason?

Tara: I need someone to talk to. I don't know. I don't have anyone, and I need a friend.

Jared: Baby, you know I'm your friend, but I can be so much more too.

Tara: Don't do that. Don't complicate it.

Jared: Just come over, babe. You know I can take the pain in your chest away. I can replace it with the pain you crave. The pain you need.

Tara: Can't you just talk to me instead of it always turning into more?

Jared: I want more, Taralynn. I want you. ALL OF YOU.

Tara: No you don't.

Jared: Yes, I do. I miss you in my bed.

Tara: Jared, stop!

Jared: Damn it, woman, I love you. Let me fucking love you. I will make you mine. Until then, just come over and let me give you whatever it is you need. My dick or my mouth is yours to do with as you please, baby.

Jared: Respond to me, please. Braden doesn't want you. Not like I do. You know that just as well as I do.

The fuck? Over my dead body. She's mine. I'm going to murder that dickhead.

"Shawn." I hear the girl call my name as I place Tara's phone back on the table, but I ignore her. Looking out into the bar, I see Jared sitting with his friends on what we've agreed to as "his side" of Mac's Pub, and where I am is my side. He's staring hard toward the bar. I glance in that direction to see Tara grabbing our beer bottles off the counter.

"Shawn."

For the love of God, would this bitch leave me the hell alone?

I don't address her. Instead, I look back over at Jared. If he continues watching my girl the way he is, separated sides aren't going to keep me from beating the fuck out of him.

He loves her? He can't love her. I don't fucking think so. He's a douche-prick.

I'll be damned if I let Jared put his paws on her again. And what the fuck does he mean by replacing her grief with the pain she craves? I'll kill that motherfucker if he hurts her. I know she likes rough sex, but pain?

His face is slowly turning in my direction, which tells me Tara is walking back over. I hope he sees me looking his way. From the messages I just read, he either knows I'm sleeping with Tara, or he's playing on her feelings for me to get into her pants. That thought alone makes me want to rip the fucker's dick clean off his body.

It's not until a breathy voice speaks into my ear that I feel a hand running up the length of my thigh and another on the back of my neck. "You know, handsome, I really want to get to know you a lot better. Much better, in fact. What do you say?"

I look up to see Tara slamming the glass bottles on the table before grabbing her phone and storming off. Liquid spilled out, but I'm not sure how one of them didn't break from the force she used.

Fuck my life. That did not just happen. Of course it fucking did.

I turn in my chair so the woman stumbles back, but not before grabbing my arm for support. "Don't ever lay your hands on me again. And no, Lacy, is it? I don't want to get to know you better."

I jump up, leaving my beer on the table to go look for Tara. She walked toward the back.

Passing the bathrooms, I enter the storage room at the back of the building. It's dark inside, but I see Tara standing with her palms on top of what looks to be a deep freezer in the back of the large room. Moving quickly, I walk up behind her, running my right hand underneath her T-shirt to rest on her warm belly and fusing my chest to her back. I need the contact. I need her to feel me and me only.

"Baby." For the briefest of seconds, two, maybe three at the most, she relaxes into me, but it doesn't last, which doesn't settle the tension coiling in the back of my neck.

"Don't." She tries to pull away, but I don't allow her to. "Just leave me."

"No," I state firmly. "I didn't realize she was touching me, or I would have stopped it. I'm sorry, Tara." *Make her believe you*, the voice in my head tells me. It's the truth.

"Yeah, right."

"You think I'm lying?" I don't give her a chance to answer before I spit out another question. "You think I want her?" Irritation sinks its claws in me.

"She was practically sitting in your lap, Shawn. Her chest was pressed against your arm, and her mouth was on your ear." Her words are forced. "Are you saying you didn't feel any of that?" She twists around to face me. "What about when she not so quietly begged you to fuck her? she snaps as her anger flares to match mine.

Yeah, she's pissed.

When she puts it that way, I can't really blame her. I was the same way when I read those messages between her and Jared.

"I was distracted, so no, I didn't feel her until I heard her. And then I saw you. If you hadn't left, you would have heard me tell her not to touch me ever again. I don't want her. I have you. I only want you. Jesus." What does she want from me? I'm being honest. Doesn't that count for anything?

"You don't have me, and I don't have you. You're free to go screw her if you would like to. Hey, use the public bathroom. You're accustomed to them anyway, right?"

I step closer, invading her personal space before reaching under her thighs and lifting her ass to sit down on the flat surface of the deep freezer. Tara's blue jean skirt rides up due to me standing between her legs.

"What the fuck is that supposed to mean? If I don't have you, then who does? Jared?" His name comes like a bark. "Are you fucking him too?" My anger is about to explode. I don't want to be an asshole to her, but hey, that's who I am. After reading her text messages with him, I need somewhere to aim it before I come unglued.

"Leave him out of this."

"Fuck that. Answer the goddamn question. Are you fucking both of us?"

"Why should I answer that? God knows I don't want to know who else you're screwing on the side."

"No one," I yell, getting closer to her face.

"Oh," she laughs sardonically. "So, I'm convenient for you. You don't have to work for it any longer since I'm always available. Is that it, Shawn?" She shakes her head. "You know what, don't answer that. Move. I'm done."

"What the hell are you talking about? I've been under the impression we were having a good time. Great sex every night and every morning. Is my dick not enough for you? You need Jared's too?"

Her palm connects with my face, but instead of it pissing me off or shocking me, it lights a fire straight to my cock. As quick as my hand will move, I grab a handful of her hair at the back of her neck, yanking her face forward until our lips connect. Her lips part, allowing me full access.

When I retract my tongue, she sucks my bottom lip between her teeth. She bites down, not soft, but not painfully hard either.

She slides off the edge of the freezer, so I have to step back to allow her feet to fall to the ground. Tara goes for my belt buckle. When she has it undone, she pops the button of my jeans and then lowers the zipper. We are both in a frenzy.

Releasing her hair, I flip her around so her back is to my chest. I reach down, grabbing the hem of her skirt, and pull the denim upward until it's seated at her waist. Next, I jerk my jeans and boxers down my legs at the same time. I need inside her, and I need in her now.

"Bend." She obeys, leaning over the deep freezer, which pushes her ass out, angling it just the right way. I fist my hard cock in one hand and pull her panties to the side with the other. I ram in harder than I ever have before, taking her hard.

"Ahhh," she gasps when I'm all the way inside. Her walls tighten around me when I start to pull out. "More."

"Don't worry, baby, I won't be done with you until you know you're mine." I ram in again. Releasing her panties, I take control of her hips with my hands, then I guide her off my dick only to yank her back until her ass bruises my groin.

When I push her away this time, she clamps down on my cock, causing me to suck in air through my mouth. I love and hate when she does that. It feels amazing, but I can't last for shit when she does it multiple times on purpose. She knows how to milk me, and she'll milk every ounce out of me if she can.

"Faster," she pants. "Harder." My speed increases on her demand, pushing in harder and pulling out faster than the last. She's coming, but I know she's clamped down on her lip to keep herself from screaming. I do the same as I come inside her because if I open my mouth right now, the whole bar will hear me.

I still both of us, pressing myself against her to catch my breath. Fuck me, that was good. Better than it has . . .

"Fuck." Holy shit. I did not . . . "Tara." I'm still inside her and scared shitless. What am I supposed to do now?

"Move off me." The heat in her voice has returned. Does she not realize what we did?

I pull out and look down. My dick is wet with our cum. My head is mixed with being turned on by the glistening image of us and terrified because I've never had sex without a condom.

She twists around as she fixes her panties in place. We both look up at the same time then her expression changes.

"We didn't use protection." She's as shocked as I was moments ago.

"No shit." The asshole comeback probably could have remained unsaid.

She pulls her skirt down, and I pull my boxer briefs and jeans up my hips then button and zip up.

"I get a Depo shot regularly. We're fine. Well, at least you are. Please, Shawn, please tell me you've never had sex without one before now."

Does she think I'm *that* stupid? Definitely shouldn't verbalize that with the look she's giving me.

"No, I haven't. What's a Depo shot?"

"Birth control. Okay, then." Her voice rubs me the wrong way, and I don't know why. Good that she's on birth control, though, because I want to do that again. I grab her in my arms and pull her closer.

"Does that mean we can do that again without anything between us?" I turn a smile on her.

"We won't be doing that ever again, with or without a condom. Move." My smile falls. What the fuck? That shit was good . . . great, and I know she thought so too.

"Come again?" She can't be serious. Jared. Did his words get to her? Does she believe him? Surely I've shown her repeatedly just how much I want her.

"I'm done with this." I'm speechless as she points back and forth between us. "I'm done being just a convenient lay for you. I'm done being the woman you only want for sex, but not to date. The one you don't want anyone to know you're seeing. I'm better than being someone's dirty little secret."

"Tara, you aren't. I don't see you as any dirty secret." Where in God's name did she come up with that bullshit?

"Don't lie to me." She shoves me back. My mind can't wrap around any of this, so when she pushes me, I stumble back several steps. "You said yourself you didn't want anyone to know we were seeing each other. You've told me that several times. The morning we woke up in bed together after we came home from Tupelo after Trent's funeral, you said let's keep 'us' to us."

I did. I said that, but doesn't she understand why?

"Tara, listen to me."

"No, I'm done, Shawn. Done! Until you want a real relationship—if you want one out in the open where our friends and parents know—you can hang this up. I'm not going to be used for a good time. You can find plenty of actual whores for that."

She storms past me.

What just happened?

I'll fix this. We'll be in Georgia this time tomorrow, and she'll be back in my bed. I guaran-fucking-tee it.

Fucking women.

CHAPTER TWENTY-SEVEN

TARALYNN

I went home as soon as I left the bar after leaving Shawn in the storage room. I then packed and left again. This time I went to my parents' house in Tupelo.

It was my last resort, that's why. I couldn't stay at Shawn's. He would have come home and talked his way back into my bed. He's gifted that way. I couldn't go to Pam and Bill's. What would I have said? Hey, I'm in love with your son, and I've been sleeping with him. He doesn't want a real relationship with me, though, only sex, so I ended it and can't face him like a big girl now. Yeah . . . no.

I should have gone to a hotel. A smart person would have thought of that. But not me, because I'm an idiot, apparently.

When I got to my parents' home, my dad wasn't there. My mother's car was in the driveway, but she must have already been asleep because the house was quiet. I showered and crashed, sleeping over twelve hours. That is unheard of coming from me. I'm always awake by seven, no matter how many hours of sleep I get.

I pulled on a pair of yoga pants and put a bra on under the T-shirt I slept in, then came down the stairs only to be greeted by my mother's wrath. She was hosting lunch. In attendance was her best friend, Judy Reed. The nasty woman matches my mother in every way, from believing her shit doesn't stink to their idea that if a wife is employed, then it must mean their family is poor.

After my mother got over the shock of me being there, she reluctantly introduced me to her other two lady friends, one of which was Preston's mother. *Great.* After the introductions, she took me out of earshot and made it clear that loungewear was not appropriate attire for the middle of the day on a Thursday afternoon. She followed that up by asking me if my father knew I "defiled my body with a disgusting tattoo." She noticed the one on my hip. The sleeve of my T-shirt covered the rose, so she didn't see that one.

I should probably not mention the next one I'm thinking about having Shawn ink on me. Something tells me it wouldn't go over well with her.

That all took place yesterday, less than twenty-four hours ago.

Last night was even worse. My parents threw a dinner party, and wouldn't you know it, Preston showed up with his parents. Talk about an awkward dinner. Being the one with zero in common with anyone at the table—minus blood—was uncomfortable. I usually have my brother to distract me and talk to at these things. Not anymore.

I did learn, though, that Preston is now a junior lawyer at my dad's law firm. He also has aspirations of becoming a partner within a few years.

Yippee ki-yay for him.

When I tried to excuse myself with the excuse of needing to pack because I'd be leaving for Georgia this morning, my mother plastered on the biggest fake smile I've ever seen. Then she announced she thought it would be the greatest idea if Preston took the day off work and came with me, so he and I would have a better chance to get to know one another.

I looked to my dad, thinking he might intervene, because what father wants a man to go away with his unmarried daughter for the weekend? He said nothing. I don't even think he heard a word of the conversation during the whole dinner. It was like he was off in la-la-land.

Preston made it known that he'd love to come with me, and by the time they left the party, it was set in stone that he was going. I never breathed a word. I didn't agree to this. I didn't want this, yet here I am. I'm sitting in the passenger seat of his Mercedes-Benz. I guess he got rid of the douchey Corvette.

We are five minutes away from Pam and Bill's second home in Georgia. I'm silently flipping my own shit, fearing Shawn will flip his shit when I walk in with Preston. Shawn hasn't called or sent me a text since I left Mac's the other night. For all I know, he's moved on and doesn't give a rat's behind about what we did or didn't have. It was sex, but why couldn't it have been more? I'm such a girl.

"Take the next right." I close my e-reader and shove it into my purse.

"No worries, the GPS will get us there." He points toward the center dashboard of his car. His voice annoys me, so in lieu of starting a conversation, I lean my back against the back of the seat and close my eyes. I read the whole six hours of the drive, and now I wouldn't mind taking a nap.

The car comes to a stop, so I open my eyes. We are here.

Finally.

Grabbing my purse, I exit the vehicle and grab my large tote bag from his trunk when Preston pops the lock.

There are at least ten vehicles here. Shawn and Mason are friends with a lot of the locals. When we come here, the house is always full of people, much like it is back home on the weekends.

Walking through the front door, I head straight to the bedrooms in the back to drop my stuff off. Since Shawn's parents aren't here, he'll most likely take the master bedroom. He usually does unless Shane beats him to it. Since Preston is here, that will free up a bunk for him to sleep in.

Walking in, the rooms are already junked up. I see Mase and Matt already have their crap everywhere. Shawn's stuff isn't in here, which confirms my guess that he took his parents' bedroom. I toss my bag and purse on my bed, then gesture to the other bottom bunk behind me. "You can take that one."

Turning around, I look at Preston, who's eyeing the twin-size bed. He doesn't look thrilled. Oh, freakin' well. Maybe he shouldn't have invited himself to come. I fake a smile and walk out. Making my way down the hall, I continue through the living room until I reach the kitchen. It is mid-afternoon, and I could use a beer, so I go straight toward the refrigerator and take out a Corona. After searching for and finding some sliced limes, I pop the cap off using a bottle opener and push a slice inside the bottle. Tipping it back, I take a swallow as my eyes close to savor the crisp taste.

"About time you . . ." Mason stops mid-sentence. I reluctantly reopen my eyes to look at Mason. He's peering over my shoulder. When I glance in that direction, I see Preston coming toward us. I look at my beer, then back at him, remembering he's a wine guy.

"We probably should have stopped by a liquor store. Sorry." I hold up my beer. "I didn't really think about that. My roommate's mom might have some wine in a cabinet over there." I point toward the cabinet above the stove that houses most of the liquor Bill keeps. I guess if Pam had wine, it'd be there.

"I'll tell you what. I'm going to live a little this weekend and have what you're having."

"Okay, they're in the fridge." I turn toward Mason. He grabs me by the elbow and pulls me out of earshot.

"What the fuck is he doing here? Shawn is going to flip the fuck out, Taralynn. What the hell were you thinking?" He swipes my beer from my hand and takes a swallow. "Jesus Christ." Mason shakes his head from side to side, then takes another sip.

"Shawn's not going to flip out." He's totally going to flip his lid.

"Why is he here?" Mason's eyes glance in Preston's direction before landing back on mine. "You didn't like the guy when you went out with him last year. Are you trying to make Shawn jealous?"

"I'm not trying to do anything to Shawn. He's here just because." Because I don't have the guts to stand up to my mother or tell her where she can shove it. That's the real reason.

Don't lie to yourself, Taralynn. You know you're hoping Shawn gets jealous.

Well, yeah, of course I am, but the likelihood of that is slim.

"When do we eat?" I'm hungry, and I'm tired of this conversation.

"He was dropping the legs when I walked inside to get a beer."

"Can I have my beer back now?" He gives me a look before turning around and walking off. I huff and get another beer.

"Legs?" Preston questions.

"Crab legs," I clarify. I've been looking forward to them for weeks.

"Food's on the table." Shawn's deep voice follows the sounds of the screen door opening to the backyard.

I look in his direction. He's staring back at me, and then his eyes slide toward Preston. Shawn's expression changes as anger flashes in front of me when his eyes land back on mine.

He's pissed. Walking fully inside, he stalks forward.

"A word," is all he says as he takes my wrist into his hand, tugging me, and I have no choice but to follow. It's either that or land on my face.

Shawn drags me into the bathroom before I can jerk my hand free of his. I doubt I would have managed to get loose from his death grip. The last time I ended up alone with him in a bathroom was the start of how I got into this mess with him in the first place. Now that I've had him, I don't need to be alone with him. I know what he's packing, and I know just how it feels when he uses that beautiful man-junk in his pants.

"Couldn't you have said whatever you need to say outside the bathroom?" I cross my arms, cock my head to the side, and pin him with a stare that says I'm annoyed. Not because I am. No, it's so I don't reach out and touch him. My hands need to stay to myself. Why does he have to be so freakin' good-looking?

He takes a step in my direction, making him only inches away from my body. His hand slides smoothly over the material of my yoga pants where the band is seated at my hip until he reaches skin.

Son of a freakin' biscuit. Apparently he has no qualms about touching me. My eyes widen when in reality, they want to close and savor his warm touch. Instead, I push him away. If I don't, I'll cave.

"Don't." That one word is all I can muster. I'm weak, but I have to pretend I'm not. It's his fault I'm this way. He provokes feelings inside me I wish weren't there. Life would be much easier if only . . .

Why did I have to fall in love with the unattainable? Does God hate me? My own mother does, so maybe he does too.

"I haven't touched you in two days. I want to feel you, Tara."

Well, too effin' bad. We don't always get what we want. I never do, so why should I give him what he wants only when other people aren't around?

"What about this—" I point between us—"not happening again did you not understand? You can go back to banging every whore that crosses your path, and I'll go back to . . ." I stop, not knowing what to say. Pining over him, probably. "Go back to doing whatever it was I did before I started sleeping with you. Are we done?"

"No, we're not done." His words bite into me, making me step back. "What were you doing before you started fucking me? The asshole out there?" He nods his head at the door. He's talking about Preston. As if. "Why is he here? Why did you bring him here?"

Is he mad? Gee, I just don't give a crap.

"Leave him out of this." I don't answer any of his questions. I need out of this small space. Angry Shawn may be a turn-on. I'm so messed up in the head.

"No," he barks. "Why is he here?"

His persistence causes a huff to escape my mouth. I stare at him.

"Answer me this, where have you been since you left Mac's the other night? Sam said you didn't show up for class yesterday."

"Why are you talking to Samantha?" My eyebrows draw inward toward my eyes and I place my hands on my hips. He raises his own eyebrows as if to say he isn't answering my question if I'm not going to answer his. I breathe out, making it loud. "I went to my parents."

"Samantha was at the house when I got home from work." He doesn't get home until after ten, sometimes even eleven. Why was she there? "What's he doing here, Tara?"

"The evil queen. Okay?" God. What does he want from me? I'm not with Preston. If he knows me at all, he knows that much. He continues to stare. Then he crosses his own arms across his chest. "My mother invited him along with me. I didn't ask him to come."

"So why did he end up here? Why didn't you tell him to fuck off?"

"Because it was easier than dealing with the crap she would have thrown at me had I not let him come with me." Hell, she was already threatening to kick me out of my own family. That's probably going to happen in a few short months anyhow, so why should I push for it to happen sooner?

"I'm not buying that shit." His facial expression is hard.

"Oh, so now I'm a liar." Well, wasn't that a foot in the mouth. Apparently he thinks the same thing because an eyebrow rises again. "I don't care what you believe." Keep the lies coming, Taralynn.

"I think you brought him to piss me off." That may have been half the reason, but I'll never admit it.

"Again, I don't care what you believe. It doesn't matter now, does it? You'll have another woman to get you off before nightfall. That is if you don't already."

I turn, open the door and walk out. No way do I want to see or hear him confirm my fears.

CHAPTER TWENTY-EIGHT

SHAWN

"Hey, Shawn." Kammy's voice filters into my ears. I look up as she walks my way.

It's nightfall. The sun buried down toward the west a few hours ago, but I still have my sunglasses sitting on the brim of my nose. Obviously not because it's bright out. With them on, I can watch a certain blonde without her knowing I'm looking.

Right now, Tara is lying across from me, stretched out on a lounger, nose buried in her e-reader. She's been at it since before the sun went down. Pretty much since we finished eating and got a fire started, actually. It's March, so the night air outside is still too chilly for just hanging out.

Tara glances up when she hears Kammy call my name. Earlier today, Tara's plan to make me jealous succeeded when she showed up with that douche-prick lawyer. She wants to claim her mother forced bringing the guy she went on one date with months ago on vacation with her, but I don't believe for a second that's the only reason. After what happened with us a few days ago, I'm betting Tara has something to prove to me.

Two can play this game, baby.

"Kams!" I exclaim. "Hey, doll, how's it going?" She stops next to the lawn chair I'm lounging on. I haven't taken my eyes off Tara, even though it appears I'm looking up at Kammy. It just so happens I might have fooled around with her last summer. And by fooled around, I mean fucked. If I happen to make Tara as jealous as she's had me all day, then so fucking be it.

That's the least she deserves.

"Better now that I've made it and you're here." Kammy's folks and mine are friends and a lot alike. Her family also loves trail riding on four-wheelers and side-by-sides. Where we stick to coming to Georgia to have fun, her family vacations all over the United States searching for new trails to ride.

Setting my beer down on the table frees my hand to run up her leg, starting from her calf and going up behind her thigh. From behind my shades, I can see Tara's eyes follow the movements of my hand. That's it, baby, let that green-eyed monster take over.

Kammy bends, sitting on the edge of my chair. Tara swallows hard and her mouth opens in a gasp of air. Pain is evident on her face, making my guts tighten. Shit. I didn't think this through. I didn't mean to hurt her. I just wanted to piss her off. Make her as mad as I am.

She snaps the cover on her e-reader closed and turns away as she jump up, leaving the yard where we're all sitting around the fire. Well, most of us. *Princeton* is nowhere in sight and I'm A-okay with that.

Kammy leans down, slides her hand up my chest, and whispers for only me to hear. "Can we have some fun together tonight? I've missed your cock." My eyes snap up to hers, where she's smiling down at me.

God*dammit.*

I grab her around the shoulders and push gently, making her move backward as I sit up.

"Sorry, Kam." I shake my head. "Not going to happen." Her smile falls. "I'm seeing someone." Her lips turn into a frown. If this is what it's going to take to get Tara back in my arms, then it's what

I'll have to do. Fuck the consequences, because I want her far too much to let her go now.

"You don't have to lie to me, Shawn. If you don't want to fuck me, just say so." She stands, turns, and stalks off before I can explain.

I do the same, heading in the opposite direction. Tara is walking up the steps, bypassing the back door and making her way across the wraparound porch toward the front.

I jog to catch up with her in time to see her stop just before rounding the corner as if something caught her attention.

"Tara, wait," I call out to her, but she throws up her hand as if she wants me to be quiet. I don't say anything else, and she doesn't move or turn toward me as I near her. When I'm standing behind her, I place my palm over her hip. It's not skin-to-skin contact, but it'll do until I convince her to give us another chance.

With my other hand, I pull her hair away from her cheek, pushing the strands to the other side so I can see her face. She looks a bit shocked or surprised, but also sad. It's then I hear a solitary voice close by. Follow the sound with my eyes, I focus in the same direction as Tara's incredulous gaze stares.

Preston is sitting on the steps on the front side of the house, talking on his cell phone. I pull Tara an inch closer into my body as we eavesdrop on Preston together.

"Man, what about she's Jacob Evans's daughter did you not understand? She doesn't have to be my type for me to fuck her or even marry her. She's exactly what I need to fast-track my way to partner. I don't want to wait years. I want it now. Do you think he's going to allow his son-in-law to remain a junior partner in his law firm if I'm married to his daughter? Hell no." He pauses, listening on the other end. "She has a pretty face. All she needs is a personal trainer to tackle that ass, and she'd make the perfect little housewife. I mean, have you seen the rack on her?" After a second, he laughs. My hand tightens around Tara. That motherfucker is about to get the shit beat out of him.

When he ends his call, he stands. I release Tara to go kick his ass, but she knows what I'm about to do and throws her arm out in front of my path. I could easily push through her, but respect for her outweighs my rage, so I don't. Preston walks into the house without realizing anyone overheard him.

Tara turns to face me. When she looks up, a tear rolls down her face. I want to murder him for hurting her this way. Tara's always been a little too self-conscious about her body. Probably has something to do with the evil bitch she's forced to call mother.

"Is that all you see too? A chunky girl with a pretty face and big boobs?" Her voice cracks.

"You want to know what I see, baby?" She lowers her face toward the ground, but I lift her chin, forcing her eyes to look into mine as I say, "I'll show you. Then, tomorrow, I'll make that pathetic little bitch of a man wish he never laid eyes on you." *On what's mine*, but I don't say that last thought out loud.

I don't give Tara a fleeting moment to deny me. I grasp her wrist and pull her behind me as I round the corner, heading toward the front door. If Tara didn't need me more right now, I'd find that pretentious motherfucker and bury his ass.

Walking through the door, I make quick strides through the house until I reach the master bedroom. She may not realize it yet, but she's staying with me tonight. And every night hereafter.

Pulling her inside, I close and lock the door. My brother and Kylie are supposed to arrive in the morning, and I don't want him to walk in on us again like he did a few months ago. It's not because I'm hiding anything this time. I just don't want anyone seeing her in the same intimate way that I do. That is for me and me alone.

There is a full-length mirror on the back side of the door that leads into the bathroom. I take Tara and stand her in front of the mirror.

"What are you doing?" I step behind her, placing both hands on her hips. She looks at me from over her shoulder.

"I'm going to show you what I see." I glide my hands up and grasp the hem of her shirt. "Now get naked."

"What?" She tries to pull away, but I don't let her.

"Either you can strip, or I'll strip you myself." I smile, hoping for the latter.

When she takes too long, I decide for her and pull her shirt over her head, tossing it behind me. She'll cringe if she realizes I did that. I'll just have to keep her distracted. I hook my thumbs into the waistband of her pants and pull down. She watches me through the mirror, fascinated by what I'm doing. I bend, taking them all the way to the floor.

As I stand back up, I glide my hands up the outsides of her legs, over her hips, and come to a stop at her waist, all the while watching her in the mirror. Standing in front of me in navy panties and a matching bra, she's beautiful. The color matches her gorgeous eyes. The lingerie is sexy as hell on her. I almost hate to remove them. Almost.

I run my knuckle up her back, brushing against her skin ever so lightly as I make my way to her bra. I unhook the clasp with both hands. Then I skim my fingers along her shoulders, pushing the straps off. The bra falls to the floor. I run my finger downward until I reach her panties, where I treat them the same as her pants, pulling them down her legs.

When I look back into the mirror to view the sexy naked woman in front of me, she turns her face away. If I'm going to succeed in demonstrating the beauty I see in her, she must watch me. I place one hand over her hip, spanning my fingers and digging into her flesh lightly to get her attention. That doesn't work. She refuses to turn her face. With my other hand, I reach around to her front, placing my thumb and index finger on her jaw. I turn her face to where I want her to look.

"I want you to see what I see. I told you I'd show you, and that's what I plan on doing, Tara." Her eyes close, but only for a moment. "Keep looking in the mirror. I want you to watch us. I want you to watch me and believe everything I say. More importantly, I want you to believe it about yourself, here." I remove my hand from her face to place my finger to her temple, and then I move to place my palm flat against her chest, over her heart. "And here."

"Shawn."

"Shhh, baby. Let me talk. You listen and watch." I bend my head to lay a kiss on her shoulder. I lift my eyes, and when I do, I locate and lock them with hers in the mirror. I move my hand away from her chest to run it through her hair. "This hair." I comb my fingers through the locks. "I like the way it feels when it brushes against my skin when you're leaning over and kissing me at the same time you're riding my cock." Allowing her hair to fall from my grasp, I move to run a finger over her cheek. "This beautiful face, those gorgeous eyes, and those lips. I want to kiss those lips, then I want to fuck them, and then devour them." I move my thumb across her bottom lip and continue down until my palm wraps gently around her throat. Her eyes flutter closed. "Open them. I'm not done."

She complies.

I kiss her neck, making my way up to her ear where I suck in her lobe for a second and then lightly nip it as I pull off. I leave my lips against her ear but move my hand down her cheek until I'm cupping one of her breasts. Tara sucks in air through her mouth. "I love your breasts. They feel nice in my hands. They feel as though they belong in my hands." That causes a gasp to expel from her mouth. "They're perfect, just like you, baby." Pinching her nipple causes her to arch her back. She really does have perfect tits. Those alone would make a man stupid.

Moving down her belly, I skate across her hips until my hand runs over her smooth, round ass. I smirk at her in the mirror a second before my palm leaves her skin, only to return as heat bites into the flesh when my palm smacks her ass with force.

"Ah." Her breaths come out in pants. It's a sound I enjoy. It makes my dick grow.

"This ass, Tara." I squeeze, making her squirm. "This beautiful ass makes my head spin. I love watching the way it moves when I slam into you from behind. The sounds we make when I do are incredible." And the way that motherfucker jiggles is so fucking hot. Her chest heaves. "I want to fuck this ass so bad you have no idea. I know it'll fit my dick like a glove the same way your sweet pussy does, baby." I move, rounding her hip until my hand is flat against her lower abdomen.

How does she not realize how beautiful she is?

"Tell me, Tara, tell me what you see in the mirror." I can tell her these things all night long, but she has to believe them for herself.

The desire reflecting in her eyes vanishes as she looks critically at her body. That's not a good sign that anything I told her took effect. And when she rolls her eyes, it pisses me off.

"A stretch mark."

Is she delusional? Something tells me I shouldn't verbalize that thought.

"I don't see any stretch marks, baby. But even if I did, who the fuck gives a shit? I don't. You're still gorgeous, Tara. You can't stand there looking into the same mirror I am, at the same woman I'm looking at, and tell me she isn't beautiful. She is. Remarkably so. However, on to plan B."

I release her and step backward while pulling my long sleeve T-shirt over my head. It gets tossed aside as I bend to pull off my boots and socks.

"Plan B?" She twists, turning her body to face mine.

"You'll find out soon enough."

It's strange. She's self-conscious about herself, yet she's always been perfectly relaxed with me when she's naked. I wonder if she realizes that. I didn't until this moment. She's casually standing in front of me, hands hanging loose at her sides, watching me undress myself. I love the way her eyes scan my body. If I notice the way she looks at me, surely she can see that I look at her the same way.

My hands go to the belt buckle locked around my waist. Tara's eyes settle on me there, causing a smirk to form on my face. I pull the strap out of the buckle, then release it and go for the button and zipper on my jeans. Once I have them open, I shuck them down my legs until I can kick both them and my boxer briefs off.

"So this is where you show me what plan B is?" She hasn't taken her eyes off my crotch, and as much as my dick is enjoying the way she's licking her lips, I have other plans.

Instead of answering her, I take a step forward, place my hands on her waist and pull her toward me. Lifting her, she wraps her arms around my neck and her legs around my waist. I turn and walk a few steps until I reach the bed. Without releasing her, I yank the covers back and then crawl onto the mattress with her in my lap.

"Do you trust me?" I look her in the eyes when I ask. I need her full trust for what I'm about to do.

"I think so." Her eyes reflect a touch of weariness.

"You either do, or you don't. I want you to trust me, Tara. At least for tonight, we can work toward trust beyond right now." She nods. I lean back, resting my head on the pillow as Tara sits on top of me. The only view better than this one is watching my cock slide in and out of her body. And then there is only one thing that trumps that, and that's seeing her face when I make her come.

I plan on getting an up close and personal show of just that, momentarily.

Tara lifts, but I grab the back of her thigh before she positions herself over my dick. We'll get to that, but not just yet.

"I have something else in mind first." Flipping my index finger up in a hook, I flick it a few times, telling her without words that I want her to come toward me. She bends down, and I accept her lips even though that wasn't what I wanted.

"Baby, I want to kiss a different set of lips. Now bring that pussy to me." Her eyes flash with desire, with want, and with need.

Lifting, she continues to look at me as she maneuvers the bottom half of her body up mine. She positions her ass on my chest and her knees over my shoulder. All I have to do is grab onto her from behind and pull forward to have her where I want her. Before I do that, I need one last thing.

"In order for you to see yourself the way I see you, you actually have to see it." I reach over, grabbing my cell phone off the bedside table where I left it this morning to charge the battery when I arrived. Removing the cord, I unlock the phone and pull up the camera application.

"What are you doing?" Her voice is full of concern.

"I told you, Tara. I'm going to make you believe you're as beautiful on the outside as you are on the inside." Her eyes grow wide. "The look you're giving me is a yes. I'm going to record you riding my face. I'm going to videotape you watching me eat your pussy, you getting yourself off with my tongue, you coming on my face. Then you're going to watch it and see what I see." Her mouth falls open.

"I am not."

I glance back at the phone to set it up for the video app. All that's left is to hit record.

"Trust me. Isn't that what I asked, and you agreed to?"

"Yeah, but it wasn't to record me naked and having sex with you." Her hands go to her hips. "I'm not a whore."

"I never said you were, baby, nor do I think it, so exit that train of thought." I hold up the phone in front of her. "The point isn't to record us fucking because I want to record us fucking. I have a point to make, and I promise when I prove that point, you can delete the video yourself, Tara."

I want to put her at ease before we start this. Sure, I'm a dick, but I'd never allow someone else to see a video or photo of her naked or in any intimate way. I wouldn't want someone else to view her the way I am right now.

"You promise you'll delete it?"

"I said I'd let you delete it yourself, didn't I?" After a beat, she swallows, then nods her agreement for me to go ahead with it. "Don't look so shy."

"Says the guy whose face won't be seen in the footage." I press the red button, flip the phone around to hold it over my face for a few seconds, and then turn the device back to find the best angle.

"Happy now?" After that's done, I position the phone on my forehead to get the best shot.

"Not really. It just got awkward." She peers down at me as she grabs her tits, covering them with her palms. They may be shielded from view, but the way she's squeezing them is turning me on more.

"Then I guess I need to remedy that." Taking my hands, I plant them on her ass cheeks and spring her forward. Her pussy lands directly over my mouth.

"When you get done making yourself come on my face, I'm going to fuck you so hard you won't remember that it's been two nights since I've been inside you. And I damn sure will be inside you every night and every morning afterwards." Wetness drips onto my lips. My tongue juts out, licking her taste off my bottom lip, and then I run my tongue through her slit.

"Oh, Jesus." Her hands release her breasts so she can catch herself from slamming into the headboard.

I don't have to urge her to move. Her body starts that almost immediately after her knees hit the mattress and she adjusts the tops of her feet on my chest. Her rhythm is smooth, like a dance. Tara flexes her hips back and forth over me. She's wet—really wet —and the taste explodes on my tongue. I dip inside her because I'm greedy and want more. Then, applying pressure, I run my tongue up until I meet her clit where I circle it with the tip.

Removing one hand from her ass, I reach under her, and with

my middle finger, I push gently inside as I take her clit and hood of her clitoris into my mouth and suck.

"Oh, God, yes." Her eyes flutter closed for a moment, but then they reopen to find mine again. When our gazes lock, I step up the pace of my finger, fucking her faster and with more depth. When I release her clit, I bring my finger out. Tara whimpers, but when I run the wetness to her tight hole, she lets out a long moan. "Fuck me there." She isn't begging. It was a command. A dirty, sexy command that I'm all too happy to obey.

As my finger pushes inside her tightness, my tongue runs down until I reach her entrance. I slip inside her pussy. Tara's palms go to her breasts again, where she starts to kneed and pinch her nipples. Finding my own rhythm, my finger and tongue fuck her slowly. Her juices escape my mouth, dripping down my cheeks and sliding down my neck the more I enter her.

"Harder." She applies pressure, pressing down on me to tell me she needs more. I give her just that.

Removing my tongue, I lick up until I reach her clit. I take it into my mouth, alternating between sucking, licking, and lightly skimming my teeth over her. With the finger inside her, I increase my speed and go deeper, fucking her ass harder. I add my thumb inside her pussy and apply pressure to her back walls. I can feel my finger move inside her ass from the other side.

"Oh, yes. Mmm." The pitch of her voice increases along with the movement of her body as she rides me hard. Her insides tighten around me, almost to the point of trying to push me out. I don't give in to her force. I continue my assault on her hot, sweet, tight ass and pussy. I clamp down on her clit, sucking, nipping, and stabbing her with my tongue. Tara's eyes close, her head falls backward, and her hands fist her tits. Her thighs close around my head, locking me in where I can't move. "Ah. Ah. Aaaaaah. Aah." Her orgasm explodes and then continues until her movements still and her head bows. She eases back off my face and settles onto my lap.

Unfortunately, I can't allow her recovery. I'm hard as a fucking rock. If I'm not inside her within seconds, I'll explode all over myself.

Removing the phone from my head, I flick it off and onto the bed.

"On your knees. Now." It's my turn for demands.

Her eyes snap open, but before she can make a move, I pull her off my lap. I'm behind her and pulling her into the position I want. Taking my cock into one hand and her hip into my other, I pull and push until Tara and I meet in the middle. Once I'm in her, I let out a breath.

"God, I needed that." She turns her head, looking at me over her shoulder, then pushes into me, telling me she's okay with the fact that I entered her again without protection. She's on birth control, so we should be good.

"You and me both," I agree, but it comes out strangled.

I move, jackhammering into her until my cum paints her walls. My release is fast. This was expected after going two days without sex and then being teased all day by the hot little body my dick has grown used to being inside.

I fall exhausted onto the mattress, but my ass needs to get up so I can grab a washcloth from the bathroom to wipe up the mess I know I just made. I can't fucking move, though.

After a minute, I turn my face away from the ceiling when I hear a sound. I look over at Tara. She's holding my cell phone and staring at the screen. I hear our voices. I get to my knees and crawl toward her until I'm sitting behind her, against the headboard. Wrapping my hands around her waist, I pull her between my legs. She leans back against me. Our bodies are sweaty and covered with the wetness from our sex, but I don't care.

When I have her situated, I look over her shoulder and watch the video with her. Tara is silent, so I remain so as well. The moment I feel my dick thicken, though, I have to close my eyes.

There's no way I can go again, not in the next five minutes, anyway. I don't have the stamina for that shit. She'll fuckin' kill me.

When she comes, and the screen goes haywire from my tossing the phone, she starts to set it aside, then stops. That's when I realize the phone fell in the perfect position to record us having sex: it's directly under her. I can see her facial expressions, the way her breasts bounce, how her abdomen tightens, and just how amazing it looks to see her take my cock. This view has nothing on anything I've ever watched live. This is sexy. This is hot. This is beautiful. She's beautiful, even more so than I thought just moments ago.

It ends, and I want to watch it again so damn bad. I almost hate the fact that I promised her she could delete it. Something that amazing shouldn't be trashed.

"So." I breathe hard. "I guess you want to delete it now."

Her face grows red. "Can I watch it again?" A smile forms on mine.

"Absolutely, baby. Just as soon as you tell me what you saw."

She turns in my arms to face me. She's sprawled across my chest with her neck craned back to look at me. I scoot us down into the bed and turn us to the side so she doesn't have to strain her neck.

"That's how you see me?" Her eyes are turned into my chest. I can't tell if this is good or bad.

"I'm not sure. You'll have to tell me how you saw yourself first." I'm hoping she saw what I saw.

"I." She pauses, chewing on her lip as if searching for the right words. There isn't a right or wrong answer. She just needs to say how she felt watching it. She doesn't keep me in suspense too long. "I might have liked it."

"I already know that because you want to watch it again. Tell me how you saw the woman in the video, Tara. How did you see yourself?"

"Sexy." And so much more, baby, you just have no idea.

"What else?" Her eyes sparkle. This is good.

"I think I'd do her." A laugh bursts out of my lips. Tara smiles, and I bring her toward my lips to kiss her.

"I guarantee you I'd do her." I kiss her again. "Want a shower?"

"No, but it beats taking one in the morning, so yeah."

CHAPTER TWENTY-NINE

TARALYNN

M y eyes peek open. Light filters in through the shimmering white curtains. From the bright sun, I can tell I've slept later than usual. When I glance up, looking at the small digital clock on the bedside table, I see it's a quarter till eight in the morning. Not too bad, considering all we did last night.

My mind recounts, remembering it all, especially the recording Shawn took on his phone. Oh my God, I can't believe I let him do that. Why do I not feel ashamed? Shouldn't I? Maybe even just a little bit? I don't, though, not after watching it. It was hot, and the way it made me feel about myself . . . I can't even explain. I don't know what to say. Do I thank him? Shouldn't I have always seen myself that way?

The way I easily let how other people saw me affect how I viewed myself is a little jacked up, now that I think about it. On the bright side, those feelings are gone. Vanished. I no longer care what my mother or Preston thinks, or anyone else, for that matter. I only care about what I think. Shawn did that. He opened my eyes. So now, instead of focusing on the imperfections—and I do have them, we all have them—I see the positive first.

Throwing the covers off my naked body, I sit up and swing my legs off the mattress. Walking around the foot of the bed, I scan the floor for my panties. My eyes widen at the mess. Would it have been so hard to toss clothes in one direction? Our clothes are everywhere and screaming at me to pick them up.

Seeing my panties near the end of the bed on Shawn's side, I bend and scoop them up fast, pulling them up my legs as I stand again. I would rather have put on a clean pair, but my bags are in another room.

"I think I might rather have that sexy body between my thighs today than my four-wheeler."

I look up at a set of brown eyes glued to my chest.

"My thighs are a bit lower." His eyes lock on mine as his smile widens at my remark. "You're cheery this morning for someone that is not a morning person."

"You rode my dick so hard last night I slept like a baby, and now I'm well rested."

"Me?" I question. "I'm pretty sure I'm the one that was getting pounded. Between our amateur porno hour and when you decided to do me in the shower . . . I was the one that was getting ridden hard."

"Get back in bed, baby, and I'll do it again." His lips turn up even more.

"This shop"—I grab my panty-covered crotch—"is closed for the day. I'm sore."

Unbelievable. The mother effer's eyes sparkle.

"So you'll be feeling me all day, then."

I will not reply to that remark. Instead, I turn my back to him and continue searching for my clothes.

"The trails open in ten minutes. Let's get dressed, wake the others, and get going."

I'm so ready to get in my machine and drive for a few hours. I'm hoping I can clear my head enough so I can make some headway with my current work in progress. I haven't written in a while. My mind is such a jumbled mess right now that I need silence and freedom inside my brain.

"All right." I hear the tussling of covers. Seconds later, hands wrap around my waist, and my bare back connects with the hard planes of Shawn's chest and abdomen. My eyes close for a moment, savoring the feeling.

I can feel his jaw open and close a few times like he wants to speak, but he doesn't. After a beat, he kisses me on the cheek and lets me go. I turn around, but he's done the same and is reaching for his duffle bag. I finish dressing and exit the room to change into clean undies and get my riding gear on.

The house is quiet when I make my way through. Everyone must have gone home last night.

As I pass through the living room, a mop of dark hair attached to a man's body catches my attention. It's Shane, and he's lying face down on the couch. I can't see his handsome face, but I know it's him from the ink work all over his back and side.

Most people don't know Shane has this many tattoos. You rarely see him shirtless. His back and shoulders are covered in ink with varied designs. An angel—the biggest and most beautiful of all his tattoos—hovers below his neckline between his shoulder blades, with lyrics surrounding her in script writing. They're hard to read, mainly because the angel is positioned as if she's covering some of the words.

The one that always catches my attention first is the tattoo of the girl's name written in a slanted design across his ribs and wrapping around his side. It spells Whitney in big letters. I never remember her until I see his tattoos, then my heart breaks all over again for Shane.

I continue on through the room, not wanting to wake him up yet. He sent us a group text late yesterday telling us he and Kylie wouldn't arrive until early this morning. A pediatric case he was involved in ran into complications, so he wasn't able to leave the hospital when he originally thought he would. Shane is following in his dad Bill's footsteps and plans to do a fellowship in Cardiology when he finishes up his residency. The only difference is Shane wants to work with children and become a pediatrician.

When I reach the bedroom I dropped my stuff in last night, I open the door softly and walk in. Mason is sprawled out on his stomach on one of the top bunks. Matt is buried under the covers, so the only thing you can see from the top bunk above my bed is a lump forming a body.

I look at the other bed. It's been slept in, but no one is in it now. I assume it was Preston since his stuff is on the floor beside the bunk.

Remembering why I came in here, I walk to my bed and duck underneath, pulling my stuff to the edge. From my bag I gather a clean pair of panties, a sports bra, and socks, then turn and head toward the closet to grab my riding pants and one of my riding jerseys.

"Mase. Matt. Come on, guys, get up. We leave in five minutes." We won't be leaving that soon, but if I tell the guys to be ready in thirty minutes, they won't get out of bed. And then it'll be an hour before we get out of the house.

I hear them grumble as I leave the room.

The light in the hall bathroom is on. Figuring that's probably where Preston is, I go into the laundry room to change.

After I strip down, I toss my dirty clothes in the baskets, then pull on a clean pair of panties and my dark riding pants. Once I have the straps fastened, I put on my sports bra. As I'm pulling the zipper up, closing up my girls, I hear a voice behind me.

"Where have you been?" Preston demands and I sense accusation in his tone.

Twisting at the waist, I turn with my brows arched, wondering how long he's been standing there while I've been dressing. The way he's looking me up and down would have made me uncomfortable in my own skin yesterday. But not after last night.

This is an awkward situation, but not because I care how he's looking at me. I'd just rather him not view me at all. Quickly, I grab my jersey and pull it over my head, covering the top half of my body.

"I just woke up." It's none of his business where I was. "We'll be leaving soon. Do you want to come riding with us or stick around here?" Please stay here.

"I'll come, I guess." He doesn't sound excited. "What's the plan? Putt around on an ATV for a few hours?" Not even close, dude. I clamp down on my bottom lip to suppress a laugh. He's in for a treat if he thinks all we do is "putt around," as he calls it.

"The only time we're going less than twenty miles an hour is when we're going through a high traffic zone that has speed limits . . . or when stopping." I grab my socks from the top of the dryer and start to walk past him. I won't put on my boots and other gear until everyone is ready to leave. "It's a blast being out on the trails."

"Guess I'll find out soon enough." Yes, he will.

"You should probably change, though. The Georgia clay here will ruin those jeans and that shirt." I know the look of designer jeans, and those came straight out of the Buckle. I turn, facing him, but still walking backward. "Did you by chance bring anything that you don't mind getting messed up and extremely dirty?"

"No. Why would a little dirt ruin my clothes?" He can either take my word for it or find out for himself. Either way, I really don't give a rat's behind.

"It's not just a little dirt. Look, I'm not telling you what to do. Wear what you want. It was just a suggestion." After what I heard him say about me last night, I should let him ruin his stuff.

I turn back around, running smack into a hard chest, a bare chest. I look up to find a set of blue-green eyes looking down at me.

"Sorry, precious." Shane laughs. That tells me he was going to let me run into him on purpose.

"No, you're not." I smile. "Shane, this is Preston." I throw my thumb over my shoulder in the direction behind me. With that, I walk around Shane and head toward the kitchen.

304   N. E. HENDERSON

When I walk in, Shawn's back is to me. He's packing drinks into a cooler. He's dressed in black riding pants but lacks the jersey. His beautiful inked back is on display for me to admire. So I do. I prop up against the door frame and watch him.

Man, he is freakin' fine. Too fine.

"I can feel your eyes on me." Busted. He peeks over his shoulder. A smile forms on his lips, then falls away seconds later as his eyes move past me. I look over as Preston walks up next to me.

Remembering Shawn's promise from last night, I'm on alert. It's not that I care if Shawn beats the crap out of him, but I don't want to deal with my parents over it. Pushing myself away from the door, I walk toward him and slowly shake my head. When he doesn't look like he's going to mellow any time soon, I mouth, "Play nice." That only causes him to breathe hard.

"Why don't you finish getting dressed and kick Mase and Matt out of bed while you're at it? I'll take care of this." I place my hand on the cooler. He looks at me for a moment and then nods. Seconds later, he exits the kitchen.

"What's that guy's problem? He doesn't seem to like me." Preston nears me but doesn't bother to help pack the water or Gatorades into the cooler.

Lazy bastard!

"Nothing. He's like that with everyone." Oh, please let today end without any fights.

I don't say anything else. Instead, I finish packing the drinks and load snacks and pre-made sandwiches into another cooler. We'll eat lunch somewhere on the trail and come in at dusk for dinner.

IT'S BEEN THREE HOURS. Three mother-effin' hours of being bombarded by everyone with non-stop complaining from Preston. *Taralynn, slow down. You almost hit that tree. You're going to get us killed.* I know what I'm doing. No one is going to die. Why did he have to come and ruin my fun? Then there are the guys. Shawn especially has been yelling constantly and demanding that I pull over and stop.

My helmet and my friends' helmets are equipped with radio devices that allow us to communicate with each other. Preston is using one of the old spare helmets that doesn't have that feature. I can hear Preston, and I can hear my friends, but he cannot. He doesn't know they can hear him, and they're all pretty pissed off that he's constantly yelling at me.

"Pull the fuck over, Tara." That was Shawn. I've lost count of how many times he's said that exact phrase.

I'm in front of everyone, leading the way, so I've chosen not to stop. Stopping will get Preston in a whole world of hurt. I can't let that happen on my watch.

"Can you please send that asshole packing? He's ruining my fun." Mason's voice comes out labored. While I'm in a side-by-side and Shawn is on a four-wheeler, Mase and Matt are on dirt bikes. Shane and Kylie didn't come out riding with us when we left earlier this morning. They had only arrived a few hours before we woke up, so he went to his room and crashed back out.

When I look in my mirror, I see Shawn pull out of line and increase his speed, gaining on me. Seconds later, he passes me and slams on his brake. That causes me to do the same, but I have to cut my wheels first so I don't run into the back of him.

This isn't going to be good.

I put the gearshift into park and kill the engine. Shawn's already off his four-wheeler and is removing his helmet, walking this way.

"Out. Both of you get the fuck out of the machine." I roll my eyes but do as he says. There isn't any sense in making this situation any worse.

"What's your problem, man?" Apparently, Preston doesn't feel the same way.

"Just unbuckle and get out." I bite each word out as they exit my mouth.

"You're my fucking problem," Shawn snaps. "You will not continue to talk to her the way you've been doing for hours. I'm not putting up with that shit, and I'm not letting her deal with it either."

Preston turns his head, looking at me as if surprised.

"My helmet has a communication device inside it," I explain.

"You see that trail?" Shawn points off to the side of the trail. There is a narrow entrance to a trail that isn't used often. "Get on my four-wheeler. Take that trail until it forks, then take the right fork. It'll take you straight to the house. You're done here." Shawn walks toward the driver's side of my side by side.

"I think Taralynn and I need to head back," Preston declares. I don't think so.

"That's not going to happen. And one last thing"—Shawn looks at Preston with cold eyes—"break anything on my machine, and I'll break something on you. Get in, Tara."

Preston actually does not say another word. He gets on Shawn's four-wheeler and leaves. I'm happy for once since leaving the house this morning.

When Shawn gets into my side-by-side, he puts his helmet back on. I buckle up at the same time he does. Neither of us speaks; instead, we ride for the next seven hours. Not straight, non-stop riding, because we do stop, rest and replenish with snacks and hydration. We take bathroom breaks. The guys pee in the woods. I go up to the lodge area and use their facilities to do my business. We hang out with other riders.

The rest of the day is nothing but fun. By the time we are heading back at dusk, I'm caked in mud, drenched in sweat, and have dirt everywhere, including inside my mouth.

Shawn speeds through the front yard, passing Mason on his dirt bike, and comes to a stop along the tree line where we park our dirty machines. We'll need to hose them down before showering so they'll be ready to ride come tomorrow morning. We're only riding for two days. Sunday night, we'll head back home.

When he parks, I unbuckle and get out of the machine, removing my gloves, goggles, and helmet. I lay them on top of my side-by-side and run my hands through my matted hair. It's a tangled mess, but it's to be expected.

Rounding the machine, I walk toward Shawn as he's stripping off his gear.

"Thanks."

"For what?" His dirty face looks confused.

"For today. For making him leave and then taking me riding." I love it when Shawn drives my Maverick. He hammers on it, and it's like enjoying a roller coaster ride. I had fun. For the first time in a while, I was actually happy today. Really happy, and I finally got to free my mind for a little while.

"You're welcome, but you don't have to thank me." He smiles. I want to get closer. I want to wrap my arms around him, and the way he's looking back at me assures me he wants the same thing. That warms me on the inside.

"Taralynn." My name is said with animosity. It's Preston's voice. I turn around to see him stalking toward me. Does he hate me now? Oh, I'm so broken . . . not. "We're leaving tonight." He looks at me from head to toe. I'm almost certain there is disgust staring back at me. "Can you go clean up so we can get out of here?"

I'm not able to utter a word. I'm taken aback. Who the hell does he think he is? He can't tell me what to do. I don't think so, buddy. Shawn steps in front of me, blocking my path to Preston.

"She isn't going anywhere with you. She isn't leaving here until tomorrow night. But you? You can pack your shit and get the fuck lost."

I step to Shawn's side, but his arm shoots out, catching me before his hand wraps around my side, keeping me in place.

Preston glances at Shawn's hand, then up to my eyes. He ignores Shawn.

Shawn drops his hand, but I stay, standing at his side.

"I had a conversation with your father. I explained what was going on here, and he asked me to bring you home immediately. That's what I intend to do. We are leaving."

"I told you she isn't going anywhere." Shawn crosses his arms against his chest. He's pissed.

"This is between Taralynn and me. Please stay out of it." Then Preston does something incredibly stupid: he grabs my wrist and pulls me toward him.

Shawn springs forward, pushing against Preston's chest, which knocks him backward and frees my wrist from his grip.

"No, motherfucker, this is about to be between you and me if you touch my girl again."

"Excuse me?"

"Did I fucking stutter? What wasn't clear?" He grabs me by the hip with his hand, pulling me into his front as his other hand wraps protectively around the top of my chest. "She's mine. She was never yours. You never had a chance, and you never will while I exist." My adrenaline is kicking up with every word that falls from his mouth. "Understand this—and you can take it back to Jacob for all I care: she's my girlfriend, and if you ever lay a hand on her, I'll rip you apart."

Preston glares at me. "You're dating this nobody? Seriously?"

Oh, no, he did not.

"You're the nobody, asshole, now leave," I scowl, angry that he would say such a thing. But I'm not surprised, either.

Preston glances between Shawn and me a few times before turning and going straight to his car without any other incidents, thank God.

Once he's gone, I look around. Everyone is either standing on the porch or in the yard with all eyes on us. It's then that I realize what Shawn told Preston. He said I was his. Not only that but he called me his girlfriend—and he said it in front of everyone. My stomach is nothing but butterflies right now. I cannot believe what I heard with my own ears.

"Now that I've made a scene out here in front of everybody, you are my girlfriend, right?" He chuckles nervously.

"Maybe if you ask me." I so totally am.

"Tara, will you be my girlfriend?"

"Sure. Why not." I shrug my shoulders.

"Oh, I'm going to make your ass so red for that nonchalant answer later tonight, baby."

"Promise?" He leans down. I turn my face toward him, and when I do, he kisses my dirty, disgusting mouth. His is equally as dirty, but I don't care. That dirty mouth tastes pretty darn good right now.

CHAPTER THIRTY

SHAWN

My phone buzzes from inside my pocket for about the tenth time. I'm exaggerating, but she's called me a lot today. Taking it out to look at the screen, I confirm I was right. I might as well get this over with; if I ignore her calls any longer, she'll suspect something is wrong. It's gotta beat talking to and staring at myself in this mirror any longer.

"Hey, Mom." I turn around, propping my ass against the bathroom sink to lean my weight against it.

"Hey, baby, happy birthday." Her voice has a calming effect on me. It always has, but then again, she's my mom, so that's probably why. I'm sure other kids' moms have the same effect on them. "Why haven't you answered your phone today? I've been calling since before noon."

It's now a little after eight at night on a Friday.

"Sorry. Been busy with back-to-back clients." It's not a lie, but I feel like it is. I've had time to call her a few times in between.

"Shawn Douglas." That's all she has to say to tell me she doesn't believe my bullshit. "Tell me what's really bothering you. And do not say nothing. I can hear it in your voice."

Ah, hell.

"I'm fine, Mom, just tired. It's been a long day, and Tara wants to go out to celebrate my damn birthday tonight." I run my free hand through my hair. I'm not only going to break one girl's heart tonight; I'm going to break two.

When my mother learned Tara and I started seeing each other a little over two months ago, she was thrilled, beyond thrilled, even. She loves Tara, and I know she's going to murder me after tonight. And I won't blame her. I'll deserve her wrath and everyone else's too.

"That's what you're going with? Okay, fine, Shawn. I'll let this go since it's my baby's birthday. Just remember, Sunday at our house is mandatory. I'm baking you a cake, so I know I can expect you, right?"

"Yes, Mom, I'll be there." *If I'm still breathing, and if I'm still welcome home, that is*, but I keep that thought locked behind my lips.

"Love you. See you then." Damn her sweet, motherly voice. It makes me want to crack and tell her everything. A smart man would have asked his mother for advice. I'm not that intelligent, but I also can't say anything to my mom yet.

There's no way she'd understand or even be supportive of what I'm about to do; what I'm about to end no matter how much I don't want to do it.

"Love you too, Mom. Bye."

I end the call and slip the phone back into my pocket. Turning around, I look at myself again.

You're a stupid motherfucker. I hope you know that.

I do know that, but it's either end my relationship now or do something really stupid down the road and she gets hurt worse. As much as I dislike the asshole, Jared was right; I won't last through the long haul. I'm not relationship material. I'll fuck up and possibly lose Tara forever. I'll figure out a way to deal with not waking up next to her every morning as long as she's still in my life, still living in my house, still working at the studio.

My mind flips to last week when I overheard him and Tara speaking in the back at Mac's Pub.

"What do I have to do to get through to you?" His voice is raised. He sounds somewhat angry. *"This is Shawn Braden we're talking about."* When I hear my name, my jaw locks. What the fuck is he doing talking to her at all, let alone about me?

"Stay out of it, Jared."

"No, baby, I won't." He really should not call my girlfriend baby. He's already pissed me off just by standing that close to her. Now he goes and does that. I haven't fought in years, but tonight I might end that streak. *"Shawn doesn't love you. I love you. He'll never love you like I do, Taralynn. You deserve more than he'll ever give you."*

I'm certain getting stabbed with a knife would have been less painful than hearing another man tell my girl he loves her. Sure, I saw it written a while back in a text message, but it hits differently when hearing it out loud. It makes it real, too real.

"You don't know that." Her voice cracks. *"Stop doing this."*

"No. You belong with me. I need you to see that." Tara looks down, but Jared pulls her chin up so she faces him again. *"He's going to tire of the relationship, Taralynn. I'm surprised he's lasted this long without different pussy. Who knows, maybe he's fucking on the side. Ever think of that?"*

That son of a bitch.

"He's not. He's with me every night, asshole."

"I'm not the asshole here. He is for stringing you along. He. Does. Not. Love. You."

"I LOVE HIM!"

Closing my eyes and shaking my head, I try to get the memory to leave. It's no use. The more I try to forget what I heard, the more I dwell on it, the more my head feels fucked up.

She just thinks she loves me. She doesn't, not really. We've only been dating a couple of months. Love should be nowhere in the equation with us at this point. That emotion takes years to develop.

I can't hide in the bathroom any longer. My last client should be here by now.

I open the door, exit and head back toward the front. When I round the corner into the open space that is the tattooing area, I see Tara standing against the front desk. She's talking to Natalie and her friend Samantha. The three of them are leaning in, deep in conversation together.

Sam has been hanging around a little more lately. She's been a good friend to Tara, and I'm pretty certain my best friend is banging her.

I stop at my station. Once I have everything gathered that I'll need for the next client, I place it on the tray next to my chair. When I turn back around, Tara's standing in front of me.

"Hey, babe." Why does that voice have to be so damn enticing?

"You about to head out?"

"Yeah, I'm going to run home to shower and change. Do you want me to come back here and pick you up? I'll be your designated driver tonight." She smiles, but I can tell it's forced. She knows something's up. Either she can see it written on my face, or she can feel it.

"No, it's fine. I'll meet you at Level when I'm done here. We can cab it home if need be."

"Okay, well . . . see you in a bit." She's reluctant for a second, but when I don't say anything, she turns and leaves.

CHAPTER THIRTY-ONE
TARALYNN

Something's up with Shawn; I just don't know what it is. He's been acting different for over a week now. It's like he's pulling away from me, and I don't like it. With the exception of last night, we've slept in the same bed every night for the past few months, but we haven't had sex in five days. Maybe that doesn't seem like a lot, but for us, it is. Last night, he never crawled into my bed with me. The night before that, I fell asleep in his bed trying to wait up for him.

He's been drinking more lately. Before we started dating, I wouldn't have thought anything of it, but after he made us official, going out clubbing was something we've done maybe twice in the last two months. We'll still hang out at Mac's a few nights a week after he gets off work, but even that's increased this week. He's been there every night and hasn't gotten home until early in the morning.

Samantha and I arrived at Level close to an hour ago. I spent extra time getting dressed tonight, perfecting my makeup and making sure my hair was styled perfectly. It's Shawn's birthday, and I want him to remember tonight. I want him to remember me, so I made more effort than I usually do, just for him.

A few days ago, I came across the hottest dress I've ever placed on my body. It's not a dress I'd normally wear, but I'm not wearing it for me; I'm wearing it for Shawn. It's all white and clings to my body like a second skin. The scooped neckline comes so far down that there is way too much of my cleavage on display for my liking. And it is short—really short. So short that I have to keep pulling down on the hem to make sure it's not riding up my butt.

I can do a little uncomfortable for a few hours. I've got this. I hope.

This dress is so not me, but even I have to admit I look hot in it. It didn't help that Samantha took one look at me in it and screamed. She said if I didn't buy it, she would buy it for me and dress me herself if she had to.

So here I am, in a dress I hate and love at the same time, while my boyfriend is literally walking away from me. Something is definitely wrong with him, and I don't understand why he is shutting me out. Why doesn't he just talk to me?

When he saw me walk into Level, his eyes practically bugged out of their sockets. I instantly knew the dress had the effect I was looking for. Then when I sat in his lap, I could feel the proof pressing into my butt. What I don't get is why he got up and left. Not just left, but walked off and left me sitting in the seat he vacated.

There's this uneasy feeling in the back of my mind. I don't like it, but what can I do about it if he refuses to let me in?

"Taralynn, what's with the look?"

I glance in Matt's direction. He's sitting to my left inside a booth drinking a beer. The guys were already here when Samantha and I arrived. She and Mason are inside the booth too, on the opposite side of him with heads bowed in each other's direction and talking quietly to each other.

"It's not me." I turn my attention back to my bestie. We've been getting closer again. He's been distancing himself from Mandy. I've noticed it, but he hasn't said why. I think that may have something to do with our friendship improving. "Something's going on with Shawn, has been for about a week now, but I don't know what. Have you noticed anything?"

"Not really." He looks at me, confused. I know it's not all inside my head. I know I'm not reading too much into this. Something is way off. I'm not imagining this. "Maybe the guy is just having a bad week."

"No, Taralynn's right. I've noticed his moods this week," Mason chimes in, turning to face us both.

"See," I tell Matt, then turn toward Mase. "What do you think is up with him?"

"No clue. Have you asked?"

"No, not outright." Okay, not at all, but I was hoping he'd want to tell me. I'm his girlfriend. He's supposed to tell me if something is bothering him so I can help him work through it. Isn't that what people in a committed relationship do?

"So, maybe you should."

He makes it sound so simple. Is it that simple? Maybe it is, but I'm being a wuss, afraid it's something to do with me.

I grab one of the tequila shots from the table and shoot it into the back of my throat before swallowing. I'm going to go talk to him. I'm going to act like the woman I know I am deep down, and I'm going to find out what's wrong with my boyfriend. Then I'm going to fix it.

———

"THERE YOU ARE." Locating him doesn't bring the relief I was praying for. Shawn is standing against the wall next to the men's bathroom with his head bowed.

I have to get him to talk to me. I know we can fix whatever is wrong together if he'll simply open up to me and tell me what's bothering him. Keeping me in the dark is freaking me out. Can he not see that?

His head snaps up, and his eyes bug for a split second before he masks his expression. There was also a not guilty in his eyes before he blinked. *Okay, Taralynn, stop this. Now you are overreacting.*

His eyes grow cold. I don't like it, but I don't know what to do. Before I realize what's happening, Shawn grabs me and pushes me through the door leading into the women's bathroom directly behind me. When I enter, he swings me around until my back meets the icy tile wall.

"What are you doing?" For the first time ever, I'm worried while I'm in Shawn's arms. His leg goes between mine, where he pushes my thighs apart. His hands go to my waist, and he moves in closer. "Shawn."

"I'm doing exactly what I'm known for doing. I'm going to fuck you in this bathroom." The way his eyes scan my body is disgusting. This isn't my Shawn. This isn't the way Shawn looks at me, and it certainly isn't the way he treats me. I don't know who this man is, but I want him gone. I want my boyfriend back. Why is he doing this? Treating me like . . .

"No, you're not." I squirm, but he has a firm grip on my waist, keeping me in place. "What's really going on? Why have you been acting off lately? Talk to me."

"I don't want to talk, Taralynn." I hate the way my full name sounds rolling off his tongue. I'm not Taralynn to him. I'm Tara, dammit. "I want to fuck."

"Not in here, we're not. I'm not a whore, and I'm not having sex in a bathroom at a nightclub." I push harder this time, and he releases me, but he doesn't back up. Instead, he places his arm above me, bracing it on the wall, his body crowding mine.

"You're right, Tara. You're not a whore, and I want a whore." My chest heaves as I try to suck in oxygen. He doesn't mean that. "This was never going to work." He points between both of us. "All I'll ever offer a woman is a quick fuck."

"You don't mean that." He can't. We're great together. He's

said it over and over to me. I've seen the way he looks at me in and out of bed. It couldn't have been a lie, could it?

Has everything he's told me these last few months been lies?

"Oh, he means it." That voice. I hate that voice. I look over, seeing Holly sauntering out of one of the stalls.

She walks toward us, and that's when Shawn takes one step away from me, making something in my chest crack. When she's close, she wraps not only her arms around Shawn's free arm, but practically her whole body. I want to come unglued. There's something inside me that wants to be freed and wants to hurt her.

"You didn't really think you'd be able to keep this one, did you?" She squeezes his arm while he does nothing to stop her. I look up, silently telling him to push her away. He doesn't seem to like her being here, but again, he isn't doing shit to make her leave, to make her stop.

I want her to stop touching him. I want her to vanish so I can figure out what's really going on. My head is clouded with pressure behind my eyes, on top of my shoulders, pressing against my chest plate.

"Leave us alone." I bark the words at her ugly face.

She laughs. "Oh, darling, he wasn't asking me to leave him alone a little while ago when he was fucking me against the very same space you're standing now."

Another crack forms, racing to meet the first one, then, as if I can feel it, my heart shatters. That's what her words do to me when they fully penetrate.

I look at Shawn, begging him with my eyes, with everything inside me for him to tell me she is lying. That she's a pathetic liar, but he doesn't say anything. He's silent. A statue. His eyes are void of any emotions. They're blank. Dead.

Is that why I thought he looked guilty? Because he cheated on me? He didn't even have the decency to break up with me before screwing her?

This isn't happening. I trusted him. I loved him. I do love him.

I'm about to break. I can feel it crawling up my throat. I won't give either of them the satisfaction of seeing me fall. I duck under Shawn's arm and leave the bathroom as quickly as my heels will move.

When I'm out of the door, I run. I don't know where I'm running to, but I run through the club. I need to get out of here now. I can't be here.

How could he do this?

Somehow, I end up back at our booth. My friends are sitting around laughing and drinking. I just need my purse. When I see it, I snatch it up. That catches everyone's attention, causing them to look up at me.

"Taralynn, what's wrong? You look . . ." Mason doesn't finish his sentence before he's out of the booth and standing up. He scans my face. I shake my head. I can't speak. If I talk, I'll cry. I can't cry until I'm alone.

"Did you find Shawn?" Mason questions me as he scans my eyes. I nod.

"He's in the bathroom, probably screwing Holly as we speak." I turn to leave and run into a body. When I look up, I see Jared standing there. It's evident by the look on his face that he heard me. "Please get me out of here."

"Come on." He reaches for my hand and I take it without hesitation, needing to escape this nightmare that's my reality.

"Taralynn, what the fuck? He wouldn't." Mason defends his best friend and I can't blame him for that.

"He already did, Mason," I tell him as Jared pulls me forward. In less than a minute, we're outside and walking toward his motorcycle at a faster pace than my shoes were meant for while stepping over gravel.

This wasn't how I saw tonight ending.

This wasn't supposed to happen.

Tonight was supposed to be a good night. It was supposed to be a fun and happy night celebrating my boyfriend's birthday.

Jared was right all along and I didn't listen. I'm in love with someone who isn't capable of being in love with someone else. *With me.* Realization hits, and that's when it happens, the seams come loose and I stumble. If it wasn't for Jared holding onto me, I would have landed on my knees in the gravel.

"You were right," I cry out. He pulls me into his warm chest, and I let my tears fall. "What did I do to deserve this? Why did he do that, and with her, of all people?"

"Nothing, Taralynn. He's an asshole. You did nothing wrong except fall for the wrong guy."

I never thought until this moment—even before Shawn and I started seeing each other—that I fell for the wrong man. But clearly, I did. Clearly, I'm a stupid woman in love with a stupid man.

He carries me the rest of the way. When he sits me down, the tears are still falling. They aren't stopping; if anything, they pour harder as each minute passes.

"Shit, I need to go back inside and get Cole's helmet."

"No. I want to leave now. Let's just go; I'll be fine." He hesitates. I don't know why; he's never cared before. I've ridden with him several times without wearing protective gear. He's always been safe with me, and at the moment, I don't even care if he's not. I want the wind to hit my skin. I want to feel something besides the pain that's taken over every inch of my body. A pain I'm terrified will never go away. A pain that feels like it's consuming me.

CHAPTER THIRTY-TWO
SHAWN

What have I done?

My forehead falls forward, landing with a thud on the wall in front of me. The tile is still warm from where Tara's back was pressed against it. Her intoxicating scent still surrounds me.

I swallow the taste of regret as I replay the look in her eyes when her heart broke right in front me. I did that. I smashed her big beautiful heart. I was cruel. I lied to her in the worst way. I knew I was going to fuck up, and I did because I let her think . . .

This wasn't how I imagined this happening. It wasn't supposed to hurt like this. I did this *for* her because, in the long run, she'll be better off without me.

But the look in her dark blue eyes won't leave my brain. That image will be seared inside me forever. How could I do that to her? To me? To us?

"Now that she's gone, and you've come to your senses . . ." Holly's annoying voice trails off as her palm slides up my arm. My skin crawls at her touch. It's wrong, and I don't want it on me. I don't want her anywhere near me. If she were smart, she'd realize being near me might not be the safest place for her.

"Back the fuck off, bitch." I turn on her so quick that she almost loses her balance. And for the first time, I don't give a shit. I might even take pleasure from watching her land on her ass if I wasn't so fucking wrapped up in what I did to Tara moments ago. "Don't you dare think for one second that I want *you*. I just gave up everything I've ever fucking wanted. You aren't Tara. You'll never be Tara. You were the biggest mistake I ever made. I don't plan on repeating it. Fuck off, Holly. Get out of my fucking sight."

I turn my body away from her, not caring what she does or where she goes.

"You'll regret that." There's venom in her threat.

"Piss. The. Fuck. Off." My back hits the tile, and I slide my body to the floor as the bathroom door closes.

What did I do?

Why did I do it?

Because I know her parents will never accept me with her. Because I know Tara cares too much about what they think. Because she wants to make them proud even though nothing she's ever done has accomplished that.

Fuck, I don't know anymore.

Because I let Jared's words seep into my veins for a minute?

It's all excuses.

She told Jared she loves me. That four-letter word, said out loud, scared the shit out of me. Why would she love me? I have nothing to offer her. I've done nothing to deserve her love.

She deserves the world and someone that can give her everything she's ever wanted. I'm a fuck up. I barely finished high school. I quit college after a whole six months. I'm bullshitting my way through owning a tattoo business. I could fail tomorrow, next month, or even next year. Who the fuck knows. Sure, I can get another job, but I'd still be a failure.

Failures do not get a smart, talented, beautiful woman like Taralynn Evans.

It doesn't happen. And if it did, I'd never be able to keep her.

Eventually she'd open her eyes and see me for me. She'd regret me. I don't ever want to be someone she regrets.

I want her to have the love my parents have for each other. Their love is beautiful, endless, selfless, and pure. It's real.

But don't I want that too?

My eyes close, but her face breaks through the darkness, a realization I've known longer than Tara and I had been dating but too afraid to say it to myself seeps into my skin, into my bones, into my head.

I love her.

I'm in love with Tara.

It's more of an acceptance. Deep down, I knew it all along. I've never wanted anything or anyone the way I want her. The way I need her. I can't get enough of her. It's not just sex, though our sex life is awesome. It's being around her, holding her, hanging out, or doing fun shit like riding four-wheelers. I crave her friendship the most.

Shoving them away and ignoring my true feelings for her never stopped them from growing, though. They were there the whole time. And look what I've done.

Self-doubt penetrating my whole being made me believe I don't deserve her and can't make her happy. But I'll never really know if I don't try. And if I want it bad enough—and I do—couldn't I succeed?

I bang my head against the tile until the pain hurts so badly I can't force myself to do it any longer.

That look in her eyes after Holly told her I cheated on her . . . I'll never get it out of my head. Those dark blue eyes split my heart apart. I filled her pretty eyes with so much pain that I don't know if I can fix this.

How do you mend a heart?

You don't break it in the first place, asshole.

I jump up. I have to find her. I at least have to tell her I didn't fuck Holly or anyone else since I've been with her. I have to convince her of that first. She didn't deserve what I put her through.

I pull my cell from my pocket and call Tara. The phone goes straight to voice mail.

Shit.

I should have known it wouldn't be that easy. I stuff the phone back into my pocket.

Pulling the door open, it smacks the back of the wall as I exit. I round the corner, coming back into the larger room of the club that houses the stage for live bands. I look in all directions, not seeing Tara, so I head toward the table we were sitting at before I ran off from Tara and my friends. Mason and Matt are both still there, along with Samantha.

"Where's Tara?" They all look up at me, pissed. Matt more so than Mason, but my best friend is looking at me with disappointment in his eyes. I know I fucked up. I don't need him to confirm it. I don't need any of their shit. I need Tara.

"Leave her alone," Matt spits out.

"Where is she? Her phone is going straight to voice mail." I will not give up until I find her.

"We all knew you were going to fuck it up with her, but that skank Holly? You couldn't keep it in your pants?" Matt's eyes turn to disgust.

I don't have time for this. Explaining it to them will only delay me getting to Tara.

"Not now, Lawson. I need to find Tara." There is a loud commotion behind me. When I look in that direction, I see a guy pulling Cole to the side. I turn back to my friend.

"She left." Samantha's eyes burn into mine. She hates me right at this moment.

"Where did she go?" Before Sam speaks, the sound of something crashing against a wall draws everyone's attention in that direction. The back wall is covered in liquid. I'm assuming Cole threw a beer bottle. His body is bowed against the table, and the guy looks like he can't breathe. His head pops up, and he looks our way. He looks at me, but that's when I turn back around. "Will someone tell me where my fucking girlfriend is, please?"

None of them are paying attention to my question. They're all still looking at Cole's outburst.

"Goddammit, would one of you . . ." I stop when I feel a hand grab onto my arm. Turning my face sideways, I see it's Cole. "What?" I bark, wanting to punch him for interrupting me.

He doesn't speak at first. The guy looks torn up, not that I even care. Not when all I want is to find Tara and beg her to forgive me.

"Jared laid his bike down on the highway about five miles from here." There's a sharp intake of breaths coming from the table my friends are sitting at. Maybe they care, but Jared and I have no love lost. Our friendship ended years ago. Cole telling me he crashed his motorcycle doesn't affect me. Unless . . .

"Where is Tara?" My voice booms louder. I look to my friends for an answer. They don't answer me.

"How bad?" Mason throws a question at Cole. He swallows hard, his brows furrowing.

"She wasn't wearing a helmet," Cole answers.

No. God, no. Tara isn't hurt. It's someone else. He's not talking about her. My Tara wasn't with Jared.

"Where is Tara?" I yell this time as the music goes dead, as everyone quiets down.

"She's okay, right?" Samantha asks.

"He was . . ." Cole's voice cracks. "He was going pretty fast, they said." He looks at me with sorrow. "They pronounced her at the scene, man."

"This is all your fault!" Matt roars, and his body starts to shake. I look toward Mason. He's frozen. He's looking right at me, but he's frozen solid.

Everything inside me stops, then shatters.

No. No, not Tara. She isn't dead. I don't believe him. He's wrong.

"I'm sorry, man. I'm really fucking sorry. She was my friend too." I rip my arm away from Cole, and I bolt.

I can't listen to him any longer.

My world did not just stop fucking turning.

She isn't . . .

She can't be . . .

I DON'T KNOW how I got home in one piece. I was shit-faced when I broke my girlfriend's heart an hour ago. Getting smashed was the only way I knew I'd be able to go through with it. Liquoring it up for the past week has been the only way I've been able to restrain myself from touching her.

And now she's gone.

She's dead.

I'll never be able to touch her again.

Matt was right when he said it was my fault. I might not have put her on Jared's motorcycle without proper riding gear, but I sure as fuck shoved her to him. Because of me, she wanted out of the club. I'm sure he was waiting for the opportunity to take her from me.

I bring the vodka bottle to my lips, tipping it up so the liquid spills into my mouth. I wanted to numb this feeling, but half a bottle later, it's still there. Pain. So much pain that it feels as though my chest is being crushed.

I was too drunk to drive to my parents when I left the club. I shouldn't have driven at all, but I wasn't thinking that clearly. My head was fogged. It still is. This can't be real. This can't be happening.

A shadow crosses me, but I don't look toward the source.

"I'm sorry. I shouldn't have said what I said." His voice is broken.

"Get out." I don't want anyone around me right now. No one

needs to be around me right now. The way I'm feeling, I'm not confident I won't do something I'll later regret.

Regrets . . .

"Look—"

"I said get out. Leave me alone."

Matt obviously gets the point. Soon the shadow fades, and I'm left alone again. I'm sitting in Tara's bedroom, on her floor against the foot of her bed. I don't know how long I've been here. Not long . . . not long enough to drink the pain away.

What did I do?

They were words. Lies. Lies that ended up being the catalyst that got the only woman I've ever loved killed. Words that spilled out of my mouth like vomit as I watched her break in front of my eyes. Words I'll never be able to take back and words that will still be here tomorrow when she won't be.

The tears come again. I only know because my vision blurs from the liquid pooling in my eyes. My face is actually numb. It's the rest of my body that isn't. I feel sick to my stomach. My knuckles hurt, but that probably has something to do with punching my fist through the mirror on top of her dresser. My skin is prickling all over and hasn't stopped since Cole opened his goddamned mouth.

I'll never get to tell her how sorry I am or beg her to forgive me.

I won't see her laugh or smile again. I'll never be able to watch her eyes when she's in deep thought and having a conversation with herself inside her head.

I already miss everything about her. The way her skin makes my skin tingle when we touch. The way her smell wakes me up in the middle of the night because I can't breathe enough of her into me. Or the way she puts my soul at ease when she's lying in my arms at night when we're in bed together.

I'll never get to tell her I love her, have loved her for longer than I even realized. I'll never get to ask her to marry me or witness my children growing inside her. I'll never get any of that.

Because she's gone from my life forever.

My lies, my doubts about myself and insecurities I didn't even know existed have cost me everything. It cost me our future and her life.

Her beautiful life was taken far too soon. It's not fair.

Why did you take her from me?

But he didn't. My actions caused her to leave with someone else. She was mine. I was supposed to make sure she was safe, and I failed her.

I take another drink, tipping the bottle up longer and gulping as much as I can down until I start to choke. It serves me right.

Slamming the bottle down to the ground, another shadow crosses the door. Why can't they fuck off?

"I said leave me alone! Get out!" I yell, not looking up. They can all go to hell.

"Go to hell. The last time I checked, this was still my bedroom. So, no, Shawn, I won't get out. You can get out."

CHAPTER THIRTY-THREE

TARALYNN

There's a long pause of silence before his face slowly lifts. Shawn's eyes scan up the length of my body until he reaches my face. I flip the switch on the wall, turning the bedroom light on. Shawn doesn't even blink as if he's seeing a ghost.

"Tara?" He says my name in more of a question that makes me look at him a little harder. When I take in his face, what I see looking back at me is a wreck that mirror's my own emotions.

Shawn's been crying, but I don't ask why. I don't care. I won't allow myself to care any longer. He broke me, and not just my heart. Shawn shattered all of me in a way that I don't think I'll ever be the same again.

Glancing around the room, it looks like a tornado tore through every square foot of my bedroom. My bed is disheveled. The contents that were once on top of my dresser are now on the floor. The mirror is broken, and if I'm seeing straight, which isn't one hundred percent with the amount of alcohol I've downed tonight, Shawn's knuckles are coated in dried blood.

"What the hell have you done in here?" Disbelief and shock is what I'm feeling right now, but why would he do this? What did I do to deserve any of this? Hasn't he done enough tonight? "Why?"

He doesn't answer me.

One minute he's sitting on the floor, fisting a bottle of booze, the next moment, he in front of me and looks like he's the one in shock and disbelief. And now I'm pressed against the wall with his lips fused to mine. Everything happened so fast that I never saw him coming toward me.

"I thought . . . God, baby. Fuck, tell me you're real." What does that mean? I don't have time to give it much thought. I'm pressed harder into the wall as he presses more forcefully into my body. His lips smash down on mine in a bruising manner.

"Get off," I manage to get out, but that only grants Shawn access inside my mouth. His tongue dives into mine. It's unwanted. I never thought I'd say that. I never thought, not for a second, not until tonight, that I wouldn't want him. Not anymore. Not ever again. I can't. I just can't. "Stop."

"Baby, I'm sorry." His voice is a plea. I don't care. He doesn't get to play games with my heart.

"Get off me! Now!" I didn't think it was possible to hurt more, but this, him pressed against me as though he wants me, is too much. My body is shattering all over again. I can't take this. I can't take him near me.

"I can't, Tara. I can't let you go. You have no idea, baby. I need you, all of you. Please, Tara." His begging comes out in raspy gasps.

I shove. I shove as hard as I can, and I keep pushing. Raising my knee, I slam it into his crotch. Shawn goes down to the ground, cupping himself between the legs.

"Son of a . . . Fuck!" His fist pounds the carpeted floor. "I deserved that," he chokes out.

This was a bad idea. I should never have come home. I knew better, but I wanted my bed.

After Jared dropped me off at Mac's, I drank more, trying to stop the pain, but nothing worked. This isn't a pain that alcohol can ease or numb. This is a pain that isn't going away any time soon. The longer I'm here, the longer it'll take me to get over him. I have to leave. I have to get out of here. I can't breathe in here.

I rode to the club with Samantha tonight, so I had to have a cab pick me up from Mac's and bring me home.

"Tara." Shawn's breathing is labored. "Listen, baby. I'm sorry."

He's still on the ground recovering from my knee to his balls. I know if I'm going to get out, I have to leave now. I break for the door and run until I'm down the stairs and out the door. Within seconds I'm behind the wheel of my car. I don't hesitate; I start the ignition and back the car out of the driveway.

There's a little voice inside my head telling me I shouldn't be driving, but I don't pay it a lick of attention. I can't be here. I can't be around him.

Not when I still love him.

Even after everything, I love him.

That doesn't make any sense. How can I love someone that cheated on me? Used me, I guess. If he always knew he'd never make a relationship work, then what has he's been doing the whole time we've been together?

He used me.

For sex? He could have gotten that from anyone. I don't understand.

I press the gas pedal harder with the only destination in mind that I can think of in my state.

CHAPTER THIRTY-FOUR

SHAWN

She's alive; that's all that matters.

How is it even possible? He told all of us she was gone. But she isn't. She was here. I saw her with my own eyes, I felt her, and then I let her go.

My relief is short-lived. When I kissed her, the alcohol on my breath wasn't the only thing I tasted. She's been drinking too, and it wasn't beer. It wasn't even tequila. It was bourbon. Tara doesn't drink whiskey.

I can't wrap my head around Jared's crash. Why would Cole say she was dead if she wasn't? There wasn't a scratch on her body. If she had been on that bike when he wrecked, she would have been hurt. She would have been killed.

She's not, and after I find her, I will pray and thank God for her. I have to find her first, though. She left in her car, so she might be alive now, but she could easily wreck and kill herself if she's drunk.

If really isn't the case and I know it. I tasted her, after all and now my guts are even more knotted.

I grab my keys and head toward the door when it opens, and my roommates fly inside. I have to grab the railing at the bottom of the staircase so I don't lose my balance from the sudden movement around me.

"God, man. It wasn't her! Tara. The chick that was killed wasn't her!" Mason is talking ninety to nothing.

"Great. See ya." My equilibrium returns, but when I walk past them, Matt grabs me by the arm.

"Great?" Matt asks, annoyed. "That's all you have to say?" I don't have time to explain that I already know Tara is alive. I need to find her now. I shouldn't have let her leave.

Tara's father walks inside the door as I shrug out of Matt's hold.

"Where's my daughter?" His face mirrors the one I had not long ago. His world ended tonight as well, I see. So that's what it takes to get Jacob Evans's attention. She had to die for him to show emotion toward his daughter. A little too late if you ask me.

"I'm going to find her." He's blocking my path when I come to the door.

"You knew?" Mason asks me, bewildered. I nod, but I don't go into any details.

"Shawn, the smell of booze is pouring off you. You're not driving anywhere right now. I lost my son because of an idiot drunk driver; I won't let it happen to someone else's son or daughter. Let's go. You'll ride, and I'll drive."

He doesn't look like he's in any shape to drive, but I don't say that. He has a point that I can't refute.

"Fine." I brush past him, heading toward his Mercedes SUV. The door is unlocked, and I get inside. Jacob joins me after a minute.

"What happened tonight? Your goddamn roommates won't say shit." I turn to look at Tara's dad only to be taken aback by what I find. I've never heard Jacob speak like that. "Speak, Shawn. I need someone to explain why I had to come identify a body that I was told was my daughter's."

Fuck. I'm not over being told Tara was dead, but I really hadn't given any thought to other people feeling similar things I had before I laid eyes on her alive and breathing.

"I messed up. I don't need to hear it from you right now about how I'm not good enough for Tara. Okay?" I turn away, looking out the window.

"No, not okay. I've been through Hell tonight. The same Hell I went through less than six months ago. This has nothing to do with you being good enough or not good enough for my daughter. We can have that discussion later. Now, tell me where do you think she went?"

"My parents' house would be my first guess."

"That's a forty-five-minute drive. Plenty of time to tell me what happened, and I do mean everything, Shawn." And here I thought my father was the only man that could make me feel like a five-year-old in trouble.

I breathe in, pulling in a long and jagged stream of air before forcing it back out. I don't know what to say to him. I don't want to admit to him—or anyone—the kind of pain I caused her tonight.

During the drive, I do what I do best, tell more lies. I don't tell him jack shit, really. Only that we had a fight that caused her to leave. She left with Jared, but that's all I know because I didn't see her actually leave with him. That part was the truth.

CHAPTER THIRTY-FIVE
TARALYNN

My finger hesitates over the round button I've been staring at for at least five minutes: the doorbell. It's late, or extremely early, depending on how you look at it. I shouldn't be here, but I don't know where else to go. I can't go to my parents' house.

I press the button. I don't want to be alone, which is why I didn't just go to a hotel. I shouldn't have driven from Oxford to Tupelo after the amount of alcohol I drank tonight. I'm lucky I didn't get pulled over or cause a wreck on the way. My ass would've been thrown in jail for driving while intoxicated. Very intoxicated.

But the truth is, I need Pam. It's wrong, in a way. She's Shawn's mother, not mine, but Pam has always been there when I've needed a shoulder to cry on, bandage my cuts, and teach me how to cook. Shawn cut me deep tonight. He stabbed the knife into my chest and ruptured my heart. He didn't just break my heart; he shattered me into so many pieces that it's likely I'll never be whole again.

The light from the foyer comes on. Seconds later, I hear the alarm being disabled, and the door opens. Bill is in a pair of plaid pajama pants and a navy T-shirt with the Ole Miss logo across the chest.

"Taralynn, what's wrong?" His brown eyes scan my face. Bill might as well be an older, un-inked version of Shawn. I want to burst into tears at the sight.

As if he knows I'm about to turn the waterworks on, Bill reaches for my wrist, takes it gently with his soft hand, and pulls me through the door and into his fatherly arms.

"Sweetheart?" It's a question. He's asking me to explain.

"Pam?" I request through my cracked vocals.

"Honey, I'm right here." I go to move out of Bill's hug, but I don't get far. He cups my face and looks into my eyes with concern.

"I'll give you over to my wife, but first I need you to answer something for me." I nod my head in agreement. "Are you physically injured?" I shake my head, telling him no even though I feel as though I am. "My boys?" Again, I shake my head from side to side. Bill comes off tough when it comes to Shane and Shawn, but I know he loves them hard.

Bill releases my face but grabs both of my wrists, not allowing me to move from in front of him. "Darling, will you go make all of us some coffee?" He doesn't turn to face Pam when he asks her this. Bill continues looking into my eyes. I feel as though I want to run up to my room and bury my head under the covers. He's always been able to look at you in a way that tells you you're in deep shit. I've seen it with Shawn a lot, and on occasion his brother, but never me. This is a first for me.

"Sure, I'll have it ready in a few minutes." Pam leaves. I don't see because I'm still looking up at Bill. My eyes are frozen, locked with his.

Once Pam is gone, his eyebrows scrunch together.

"How much have you had to drink tonight? I can smell the whiskey on your breath, Taralynn." He's mad, like super mad. I can tell just by the look in his eyes. There is concern, but there is also disappointment.

"I-I" Hell, what am I going to say? The truth is probably best in this circumstance. I've never felt the need to embellish a lie with

Bill or Pam. They've already accepted me for me. I don't have to be someone else or act a certain way when I'm in their house. I can be me. I'm comfortable just being me around them.

"I'm going to take the stutter as meaning too much to be driving. What in God's name were you thinking? You know, or you should know, I would get up at any time of the night to come get you should you need it." Damn, he really is disappointed. This is different from the way I disappoint my parents. This feels worse, so much worse. "Here's what you're going to do. Go upstairs, put on something else, pajamas, anything but what you're wearing now." Crap, I didn't think about the super-short dress I wore for Shawn's birthday. A dress that did not pay off the way I had hoped. "Then I want you to come back down and tell us what's wrong."

"Yes, sir." My voice is weak. Bill releases my wrists, and I head toward the stairs. I don't take but a step or two before Bill adds on to his demands.

"If you ever get behind the wheel of a vehicle after you've drunk too much alcohol again—" I don't turn to look at him. I can't. "You won't be able to sit for a week." I nod my head so he knows I heard him. Apparently being an adult is not a factor here.

I race up the stairs. Once I'm behind the closed door of the guest bedroom that I've often wished truly was my own, I pull the dress over my head and toss the material onto the bed. I kick out of my heels and walk over to the dresser. My favorite pajamas are still here. I forgot them when I stayed here during Christmas. I put them on over my bra and panties, then slip on a pair of flip-flops. Afterward I head out of the bedroom and down the stairs, finding both Bill and Pam sitting in the living room. Looks of concern mar both of their expressions.

What do I even tell them? Their son and I broke up, so I came to get sympathy from his parents. That sounds pathetic.

I walk over to the couch and sit next to Pam. Bill is seated in a recliner a few feet away from us.

"It's just how you like it. A little bit of sugar with a whole lot of creamer." I smile, not full on, but I know she's trying to ease me into telling them what's going on.

I pick up the small ceramic cup and bring it to my lips. I doubt the coffee is too hot. Considering the amount of cream I like, I know it won't burn my tongue. I gulp the liquid down until the cup is almost empty. I don't savor the flavor by sipping when it comes to coffee. I drink it like it's going out of style.

"Talk to us, Taralynn. What happened tonight that has you this upset?" Bill sips from his mug, then places it on the table and fixes his attention on me.

Going with honesty, I tell them a lot of what happened tonight. I leave out the part about Shawn cheating in the bar bathroom with that skank Holly. They don't need to know those kinds of details. I mainly focus on my heartache and end up letting it slip that I'm in love with their son. They allow me to talk for a long time and with them just listening, it's helping. They aren't offering suggestions on how to get over him, but talking about it is removing a some of the weight.

When I'm done, I'm lying with my head in Pam's lap while she's running her hands through my hair. It's calming, soothing, and I think I could actually fall asleep. I'm exhausted. Then again, it is some time in the early morning hours when I'm used to being asleep at this time.

"Honey, would you like more coffee?"

"No, I'm okay." A lingering question that I sometimes wonder about crosses my mind. "Why do you call me 'honey'? You've always done it, and you've never referred to anyone else as 'honey'."

Pam laughs. "Well, I guess you have Shawn to thank for that. The first day he met you, he said your blonde hair reminded him of honeysuckles. After that, every time I saw you, that's what I thought about."

Huh. He's never told me that. Of course that was years ago; he probably doesn't remember.

I'm about to sit up and ask them if I can sleep upstairs tonight when a car's lights flash through the window in the living room. It catches Bill's attention too. He stands and then walks to the door.

It strikes me as strange when he grabs his keys from a table near the door and shoves them into his pocket before he opens the door.

"She's in there with Pam." He nods his head behind him then his palm flies up. "You and I are going for a drive."

"Not until I see Tara." Shawn's voice makes me shoot up from Pam's lap. I see him standing in the door, but his dad won't allow him inside. Shawn looks toward me, and when our eyes lock, tears pool in my eyes.

"Later. First, you and I are going for a drive to talk." Bill pushes Shawn backward. That's when I see my dad walk through the door.

What's he doing here? And with Shawn, that doesn't add up.

"Daddy?" I stand from my seated position on the couch. Looking at my dad, I wait for him to explain why he is here. Did Bill or Pam call him while I was changing? No way. They wouldn't. What would be the point?

When he walks closer, I take in his disheveled suit and worry forms in the pit of my stomach. His tie is missing, and a few buttons from his white shirt are unbuttoned. His jacket is a wrinkled mess. Even his hair is all jacked up, like he's been running his hands through it all night. His eyes shock me the most. They're glossy and bloodshot, like . . .

"Dad, what's wrong?" I can see he's been crying, and he looks like he might be close to doing it again. This cannot be good.

When he stops in front of me, he pulls me to his chest and wraps his arms around me, squeezing so tight it's tough to inhale or even exhale. I feel his body physically relax after a long minute of him holding onto me.

"Jacob?" Pam's voice is also etched with the same concern that fills me.

My dad pulls back but doesn't fully release me. His hands go to my face, where he cups my cheeks.

"Tonight, I thought I lost you too." A tear falls from his eye, but I can't process what he means. Lost me? Lost me how? Pam beats me to my question.

"Jacob, what do you mean?"

He glances in her direction, and then his eyes come back to mine. That's when he lays everything out. Jared crashed his motorcycle, and a girl ended up being killed in the crash. Everyone thought that girl was me until my dad showed up to identify the body that was someone else's daughter. Jared was badly hurt and is still unconscious, so he couldn't tell anyone the identity of the woman.

Other things from tonight are becoming clearer. Shawn thought I was dead. That's why he trashed my room . . . and then when he saw me was so shocked and overwhelmed that he wouldn't let me go. I almost feel bad for kneeing him in the balls now. Almost. The jackass still severed my heart from my body.

Jared. Oh, my heart goes out to him. And a woman died tonight. It could have been me. Jared asked me to stay with him. I couldn't. I couldn't use him as a crutch or as anything to ease the heart Shawn smashed. I wanted to be alone, so I had Jared take me to Mac's. I don't know where he went after leaving me.

"Oh, my God, Jacob. I can't imagine what you went through tonight. Shawn and the boys either." Pam's eyes drop to the ground as if she's in thought. She's probably thinking about Shawn.

He thought I was dead continues to boom inside my head.

"I'm going to leave you two alone." Pam goes to leave, but my dad reaches out and stops her, wrapping his hand around her wrist. They look at each other. It's almost like they are having a silent conversation, which is weird until he speaks and confuses me more.

"I'm going to tell her." His eyes come back to mine for a moment then he turns back to Pam. "Do you have any pictures?" Pam nods, and I'm stuck wondering what's going on.

"Jacob, I'm not sure tonight is the best time to do that."

"Pamela, please, I have to get this out. I have to tell her. It's clawing at me." He shakes his head. "I never should have kept it from her to begin with, and tonight"—he sucks in a large gulp of air—"tonight I thought I'd never have the chance to tell her about . . ." He doesn't finish.

"I'll get them." She walks off, but before she does the look in her eyes has me worried.

"Dad?"

"Sit down, Taralynn." He lets go of me for the first time since grabbing onto me when he arrived half an hour ago.

I sit, and he settles down next to me on the couch. I'm turned, facing him as he leans all the way against the back of the soft material.

"I told myself the night you were born that I'd tell you the truth one day. I guess that day is today."

"Tell me what?" He's scaring me. Does he realize how freaked out what he just said has made me? I don't know what to expect. I feel like he's about to drop a bomb on me. I don't know how much more I can handle tonight.

Pam re-enters the room. She's holding a picture frame. It's turned so the only thing I see is the back. She hands it to my dad and leaves again. When I look back at my dad, he's staring at the photo inside the frame. There is a look of longing in his eyes that causes my heart to hurt. His eyes are filled with what I think is sadness and pain, but I don't know why. I don't know who's in the photo, so I ask.

"Who's the picture of?" He doesn't answer, but he does start to talk.

"When Katherine and I married, she got pregnant with Trent almost immediately after the wedding. I wasn't upset about your brother being born, but I would have rather it happened a few years down the road. I'd just started working for a law firm. I wasn't even a partner yet. I was at the bottom of the totem pole, and I was worried I wouldn't be able to afford my now growing family. Katherine was enough work and a drain on my wallet as it was, but then you add a baby to the mix. Eventually, I let my worries and stress play a factor in distancing myself from my wife more and more. I worked more. I had to if I ever wanted a partnership." His fingers brush over the frame briefly before he continues on.

"A few years after Trent's birth, I had an affair with my secretary, and it wasn't just a one-time thing. It continued for four years, and then she called it off when I wouldn't leave Katherine. It's not that I loved Katherine. I didn't anymore. I realized when I started cheating I had never been in love with my wife. But I had a son. I loved my son more than anything, and that's what kept me married to a woman I didn't want to be with. The woman I had fallen in love with, who should have been my forever, didn't understand that. She begged, and that ended up becoming her obsession for a while. Eventually it started fights between us. I couldn't leave my family, and she didn't understand why I'd stay if I truly loved her like I claimed." He chokes up on the last part. I'm still trying to wrap my mind around my father cheating on my mother. It's not something I've ever thought about, but looking back, I've never seen them so much as kiss one another.

"Why are you telling me this?" I ask.

"Just hear me out, sweetheart." He looks at me, waiting for an answer. I nod telling him to go on. "The other woman ended our relationship one night out of the blue. She said she finally understood why I couldn't leave my child. Then she told me she never wanted to see me again, and that I should forget all about her, like that was possible. I was in shock at first, and I did leave her that night, thinking she'd come to her senses in a day or two, take me back, and we would figure us out and work around my marriage. I was a fool. Her resignation was sitting on my desk when I walked in my office the next morning. She must have moved out of her apartment the same night I left, because she was gone when I went back. She had her phone number changed too, so I had no way of contacting her. It was seven months later before I saw those beautiful dark blue eyes again." He looks down at the picture, then lifts his head and turns his gaze toward me. "But they weren't hers any longer. They were yours."

A tear falls from his eye at the same time he flips the photo around to face me. I stare down, and it's like looking at myself in the mirror, but I know it isn't me in the picture. The picture is old. Older than I think I've been alive.

"The night you were born, I held you in my arms after only two minutes of finding out you. When you opened your eyes, I saw your mother again, and every time I've looked at you since, I see so much of her in you. How can I not? Except for the dark complexion you got from me, you look just like her."

"I don't understand. What are you saying?"

"This is Lynn." He raises the photo. "Your real mom."

What do I say to all this? First I have my heart shattered, then I find out my whole life has been a big fat lie—all within a few hours of each other. This is too much to deal with.

"Why are you just now telling me this? Why have I called someone else Mother my entire life?" It makes sense now. She hates me because I'm not hers. I never had a chance in hell of gaining her approval, let alone her love. "Why isn't she in my life?" I take the photo frame from him only to face it toward him. "Why am I not calling her Mom?"

Where is she? So many questions are running through my brain at once that I can't catch up. My heart is pounding so hard in my chest that I'm sure it's going to burst through my chest.

"She's dead." It's like glass shattering, only it's not glass; it's me. You can pick up glass and toss it in the trash, then buy something new. How does that work for a person's soul? How do I fix this?

My father continues speaking, and I hear every word, but it's like I'm hearing him from a distance. My mother, my real mother, took her own life a few hours after I was born. She never got over him. She was weak; he thinks he made her so weak that she couldn't deal with a life without him in it if he wasn't with her.

"Pam and Lynn were best friends. She called me the night you were born after Lynn committed suicide. I didn't learn that until after I met you. Your mom left me a note asking me to take care of you because she couldn't, and you deserved more than she could give. With the note was the paperwork for your birth certificate. Lynn had named you Tara Michelle Evans. I added the Lynn onto Tara before I submitted the papers. Michelle is Pam's middle name. I know you know that, but you are actually named after her. Pam even tried to persuade me to let her adopt you, but I wouldn't —I couldn't. You were my daughter. No one was going to raise you but me, so when I saw the spot for the mother's name was blank on the birth certificate, I made a decision. I named Katherine as your mother."

Oh, my God. Someone tell me he is making this stuff up. This can't be real. This can't be my reality.

"I'm sorry, Taralynn. At the time, I thought I had made the right choice. Looking back . . . looking back, I wish I had done so many things differently. When I see the way you look at Shawn, it scares the shit out of me."

I look up, leaving my thoughts for a moment. "What do you mean? What does any of this have to do with Shawn and me?"

"You've liked him for so long, and only him, Taralynn. You've never wanted to date other guys. It's not that I necessarily hate that, but I know deep down it's because you only want Shawn. And if you can't have him, you can't bring yourself to settle for another. That was Lynn. Our love was one of a kind, but when I wouldn't give her all of me, it broke her. She didn't want to live her life if I wasn't a part of it. She took her life because of me. I can't let that happen to you. I won't let him do to my daughter what I did to your mother."

He thinks I'm *that* weak?

Dammit, I'm not.

"Dad, no one has that much power over me. I'd never do that to myself." I shake my head. "You don't have to worry, though. Shawn and I are over." I have so many emotions coming at me right now that I don't know one from the other.

"Taralynn, look at what happened tonight. You and he had a fight, and you're so damn broken up over it. I saw that when I walked in the door. He does have that much power over you."

"A fight? We didn't have a fight. He ripped my heart out. He broke up with me and not in a 'let's call this over and done with' kind of way. No, he could have sliced me with a knife, and it would have hurt less. Shawn and I didn't have a fight. He . . ." I can't bring myself to tell my father what Shawn actually did. It's not that it's any of his business. Hell, after what I've just learned from him, I can't begin to wrap my head around any of it. Why would he keep something like that from me?

"He what?" His tone is angry, like he knows what I didn't say.

"He . . . nothing. Forget about it. I can't do this with you."

"Sweetheart, I can see the broken woman sitting next to me. Please talk to me. Let me fix it."

"Fix it? Really, Dad? There is no fixing it." I throw my hands up. "I can't deal with any more of this. I'm so tired. If you think I'm that weak, then there isn't anything I can say at this point that will convince you. I want to go to bed."

I need to be placed in a coma. I can't tell him that, though. The way he's looking at me right now might get me committed to the psychiatric hospital against my own will.

I have to try something else.

"Daddy, please take me home. I'm exhausted. We can talk tomorrow." If I'm still there when he wakes up. I'm not so sure I want to talk to him ever again after learning everything he's been keeping from me for over twenty-two years. He's the real reason she hates me.

Can I even blame her?

CHAPTER THIRTY-SIX

SHAWN

"Dad, let me in the house."

What's his fucking problem? Me, obviously by the look in his eyes, but I don't exactly care at the moment either. I need to get to Tara. I need to see her, feel her, hold her, and talk to her. I'm desperate. Can he not see that? I thought I lost her forever just a short time ago. I need her right now.

"This isn't up for discussion. Get into the car, Shawn."

"Dad," I plead when really I want to barrel through him, and anyone else, to get to her.

"Now," he seethes through clenched teeth.

I get inside his car. Not because I want to, but because with the look he's throwing me, I'm certain he'll kick my ass and then put me in the car himself if I don't do what I'm told. I'd deserve it, but that doesn't make it any easier to comply.

"Where are we going?" I cross my arms since I might as well act like a child if he's going to treat me like one.

"To a goddamn diner," he yells. "You reek of alcohol too."

"Did you just say GD?" My father does not cuss often. He certainly doesn't take the Lord's name in vain.

"Now's not the time to piss me off even more, son."

We drive in silence the rest of the way until he pulls into an all-night diner downtown.

When we take our seats, a waitress is at our table before my ass hits the cracked plastic of the booth.

"Can I get you boys something?" she asks, in an overly sweet voice for this time of the morning.

I pick up the menu in front of me but soon realize I won't be ordering off it.

"Two coffees, please, and he'll have eggs over medium with lots of bacon and toast." So I guess I really am a five year old again and my daddy is ordering for me. Just fucking fantastic.

The coffee arrives a minute later, but Dad hasn't breathed a word. He's just staring. His expression is blank, so I can't read him. With nothing to say from my side, I take a sip of scalding hot coffee.

"You can start speaking at any time now," he finally says.

What the fuck? He's the one that dragged me here, not the other way around.

"If I knew what you wanted me to say, I'd say it so I could get back to my girlfriend."

"You sure you have a girlfriend?"

I refuse to answer that. Instead, I cluck my tongue and look out the open blinds to the empty parking lot.

I refuse to believe I can't get Tara back. I love her, and I know she loves me. It's just a matter of convincing her, and I'll do whatever it takes to win her back.

"Tell me what happened tonight. Well, last night. Tell me your side of it, Shawn." He picks up his mug, takes a sip, eyeing me as he waits. I down the rest of my black coffee before I tell him everything I couldn't tell Jacob an hour ago.

He's going to hate me. I would.

Through two more cups of coffee and a plate of food, I tell my dad everything. I don't leave anything out. I lay it all on the table, from when I started pulling away from Tara after overhearing Jared confess his love for her, deciding she shouldn't be with me, and how I had planned on breaking up with her. I tell him about Holly screwing up that damn plan, making it much worse than it should have been. How I didn't come clean, letting Tara believe everything that bitch said. Then I choke up, almost losing it again, when I tell him how I thought she was dead for several hours. How it felt like my heart stopped beating and then exploded inside my chest.

When I finish, I feel raw. It feels like it happened all over again, and reliving that shit is taking years off my life. Honestly, I'm not sure how I'm still breathing. There was a point when I wanted to die too.

I'm not near as strong as I once thought I was.

"Why would you think for a second you don't deserve her love?"

"I don't know." It sounds stupid now. "I'm not a doctor, like you and Mom or Shane. I'm not a lawyer like her dad. I don't fit into that world."

"For the love of God, Shawn, are you serious? Your mother and I couldn't be any prouder of the man you're becoming if we tried. We never wanted or expected you to be someone you aren't. You're you, and you're doing something you love. How many people get to go to work and actually enjoy what they do? Not many do, son. Your job doesn't define the man you are. What's on the inside does, and how you show the ones you love and care about do."

"I know that, logically, but I don't want her to ever have any regrets. I want her to have the world. I want Tara to be as happy as possible."

He laughs. Why he's fucking laughing, I'm not sure. I just poured my goddamn heart out, and my father laughs.

"That's love, Shawn. When someone else's happiness and wants come before your own, that's love. When you find that kind of love, you grab on and don't let go."

"So how do I fix something I set out to destroy?"

"I don't have an answer for that, but my suggestion is to tell her the truth and then beg her for forgiveness. If by some chance she does forgive you, don't screw it up again."

I need her. I have to fix this.

"Can we get out of here? I need to see Tara."

"Sure. I'm still in my pajamas and don't have a wallet. You'll have to pay for all this." He stands and walks out the door, leaving me with the check.

———

IT'S HALF past three in the morning when my dad drops me off at the curb in front of Tara's parents' house. My mom sent me a text when we were on the way home telling me she left with Jacob, so I asked my dad to bring me here.

I knock on the front door, not knowing what to expect but praying she's at least willing to see me.

When the door opens, Jacob is standing there with what looks to be a glass of whiskey in his hand. I get that tonight must have been hard on him too. Trent was killed only a few months back, and then to think your daughter died too . . .

That has to be rough, but I don't exactly have a hell of a lot of sympathy for a man that has never shown her an ounce of what my parents have with me.

Telling him this probably wouldn't be smart, though. He is, after all, standing between me getting to her.

"I need to see her, Jacob. Please let me come in." I'll beg if that's what it takes. I'll do anything to get to her.

"You failed to tell me you broke her heart."

"I said I messed up, didn't I? Let me in so I can try to fix what I screwed up." He stares, not uttering a word. I feel like he's analyzing me and I don't like it, so I suck it up and beg. "Please,

Jacob."

He takes a step back, but before I enter, he says, "Don't come into my house if you're not in love with my daughter." I step inside, confirming my feelings for her, but I don't say them to him.

"She deserves to hear me say those words before I confess them to someone else."

"She's been through a lot tonight, Shawn. Remember that when you talk to her." He closes the door and then walks to his closed office door. I turn, heading in the opposite direction toward the stairs.

When I reach the top and come to Tara's bedroom door, I don't knock. I'm too afraid if she knows it's me standing on the other side, she'll tell me to leave. So instead, I turn the knob and push the door open. When I'm inside, I push it closed as quietly as I can and stand there. I watch her. She's lying on the bed, on her side with her back turned toward me. I think she's asleep, but then she speaks.

"Dad, please leave me alone for the rest of the night. I don't want to hear any more."

I walk forward and drop to my knees when I reach the side of her bed. Placing my elbows on the mattress, I entwine my fingers like I'm praying.

"It's me." Her breathing stops as her body goes still. "I just need you to listen to me. Hear me out, and then if you want me to leave, I will."

I want so badly to reach out and touch her, but I don't and I won't until she gives me permission.

Tara doesn't speak, but her body moves slowly as she starts to breathe again.

"I fucked up, baby. I know I did. Last week, I overheard your conversation with Jared when he told you he loved you, and it messed my head up. I started to believe I didn't deserve you like he said. I also heard you tell him you loved me, and that scared me. I started thinking about my parents and what they have together. Deep down, it's what I want too, but what they have seems so unattainable. Impossible. They're perfect. Their love is perfect. I don't know how to give you that kind of love." I break for a beat, needing to breathe.

"I love you." She stills once again. "I'm not just saying it. I do love you, Tara. I'm in love with you. No matter what you're thinking right now, please believe I love you. I've loved you longer than I realized, and I can love you better than anyone else ever could. That's a promise, baby. I messed up, and shit, I can't take back what I said, but it was a lie. All of it was a lie. I let doubt inside my head, and instead of being stronger than it, I gave in and lied to you, Tara. I didn't cheat on you. I would never cheat on you. I swear to you, I'm telling you the truth."

I'm physically spent, but I have to finish this. I don't know how it'll end. I'm praying it doesn't end.

"Did your dad tell you about Jared?" I hate bringing him up. I hate that someone else said the words she should have only ever heard from me and me alone, but I need to know if she knows about his wreck and the other girl being killed before I go on any further.

"Yes." The pain and struggle in her voice forces me to close my eyes. I hate that I've caused every ounce of that pain. She deserves better, but if she gives me another chance, I'll make damn sure I'm *that* better of a man for her.

"I thought that woman was you. Everyone did. There is nothing I can say to describe the agony I felt when Cole told me you were dead. I died inside. I wanted to actually die. Please forgive me."

She doesn't say a single word for at least a solid minute.

"Shawn, I can't process another thing tonight. I heard you, and I listened like you asked me to, but I can't forgive you right this minute. I probably won't be able to tomorrow either. I'm tired. I'm beyond exhausted. I want to sleep. I want to forget today happened. I want to forget my life happened." Her voice cracks on the last sentence as a sob breaks free.

My hands fall to the mattress. I fist the covers, trying to purge everything I feel inside through the material in my hands and so I don't reach out for her until she says I can.

"I don't want to be alone right now. I thought I did when I came in here, but it's all so much worse when I'm by myself. Will you get in the bed and stay?"

She doesn't have to ask twice. I kick my boots off, and I'm behind her over the covers within seconds of her asking me to stay.

"Go to sleep, baby." I pull her into my arms and wrap myself around her. At this point, I'll take any bone she throws. This is a pretty big one in my book.

I close my own eyes, and I'm out within seconds.

CHAPTER THIRTY-SEVEN
TARALYNN

I wake to the sound of yelling. It's loud and coming from somewhere in the house. When I open my eyes, I realize where I am. The events of last night come back like a flash of lightning, quick and unexpected.

I'm warm. My body feels like it's wrapped in a cocoon. I'm hot, and I know why too. I'd know the feeling of his body any day. Shawn's still here in my bed with me.

I ache all over and need more sleep, but the voice starts again. It's my mother's voice, and she's the one yelling.

Mother. But she isn't my mother, now is she?

If I hadn't seen the photograph of the other woman, my real mother, I don't know that I would have believed my dad's story. It's the next day, okay, really it's only a few hours after he told me, but I have no clue how to process all that yet.

Shawn's arms tighten around my middle.

"Do they argue like that often?" He doesn't sound like himself. His voice is scratchy.

His words filter back in too. All of them, especially the ones he said before I fell asleep. He loves me. The sucky thing is, I believe him. It sucks because I'm still upset, and now I'm livid. His lies ripped me to shreds. How do I forget them? How do I forgive him?

I don't know how.

"No. I've never heard them yell like that." Katherine is still the one doing the yelling. I haven't heard my dad, but from what she's saying, it's clear he's the one taking the brunt of her wrath. "She's not my mother."

Saying it out loud feels freeing. I don't know why. Shouldn't I feel a loss? Then again, you have to have something to lose it. I never had her, not really. I just didn't know that until however many hours ago it was that my dad told me.

"What do you mean?" He turns me so my back is flat on the mattress. He still looks almost as bad as he did when I walked into my bedroom in Oxford.

"I'm the product of an affair my dad had. Only my real mom couldn't deal with not having him completely, so she killed herself, and I've been made to believe the evil bitch downstairs was my mother this whole time. Makes sense why she hates me so much, huh?"

"Holy shit, are you serious?"

"Oh, yeah. That was sprung on me last night on top of everything else that happened."

"Why would he choose last night to tell you that? Fuck, Tara, I'm sorry." His head falls against the top of my forehead.

"I don't see there being a good time to tell me something like that, Shawn. Waiting . . . prolonging it would only serve to make me even madder at him than I already am."

"I didn't tell him details, so he probably didn't know how bad last night was for you."

"I can't deal with that right now. I need to get down there and see what's going on." I toss the covers off my legs and push away from him. Something in the back of my head that doesn't like it when I do that. Deep down, I want to stay in his arms and never leave his warmth. But that's not the real world, though, and doing so would not fix any of my problems.

I'm still dressed in pajamas I put on when I got to Pam and Bill's house. This will have to do; I don't have any clothes here.

Shawn follows me down the stairs. The voices are coming from the kitchen, so I head in that direction.

"You need to back off, Katherine." My father's tone is full of venom. "I've had a bad night. I thought I lost her."

"I wish you would have. Then you'd know what it feels like."

"You don't think I know what it feels like? Trent was my son too. I lost him the same as you did. I loved our son. And last night, I thought I lost the only other person in this God-awful world that means a damn to me, so you need to walk away and leave me alone."

"It should have been Taralynn, not Trent. Not my son. He didn't deserve to die, but that useless garbage taking up other people's air shouldn't exist. You should have never brought her into this family."

Wow. That stings like a hard slap to the face.

I stop at the entrance to the kitchen. Shawn grabs me before I realize what's happening. He pushes forward, entering the kitchen. That's when I see the look in my dad's eyes: pure unadulterated hate. And it's directed at his wife. The moment he goes for her is the moment shock takes hold of me. He intends to hurt her, but Shawn reaches him before he's can lay a hand on her, thank God.

"Jacob, no." Shawn shoves his shoulder into his chest and locks his arms around him as he pushes forward, forcing my dad's body backward. "She isn't worth it, man."

She turns, her face screwed up as she eyes me from head to toe.

"You ruined my family. You ruined my life. I hope you're happy."

"Do not talk to my daughter like that. Shawn, release me." He tries to shove him away, but Shawn's hold tightens. "I'm not going to touch her."

With those words, Shawn lets him go. My dad straightens his suit. The same one I'm pretty sure he was wearing early this morning before I went to my bedroom.

"I want a divorce," my Dad announces.

She turns so quickly that her hair whips around, hitting her in her face. Then I see her expression harden into the evil visage she usually holds for only me.

"You think it'll be that easy to walk away from me, darling husband? I don't think so. You want out of this marriage? It's going to cost you every dime you have."

Then she walks away.

"Daddy, are you okay?" He doesn't look okay.

"I've been better, sweetheart. Come here." I hesitate for a second. I'm not over what he's done to me. By keeping the knowledge of my real mother hidden from me, he's caused more pain and confusion than I know what to do with. He's lied to me all my life. He's made *me* a lie, like nothing I knew was real or true. And I guess it wasn't.

"I can't." I shake my head. I can't walk into his arms as if this never happened. I can't say that I'm not mad. I don't know what I'm feeling. I have so many emotions that I can't decipher between them.

His eyes close. It pains him that I won't walk toward him. When he opens his eyes, he nods his understanding, then directs his attention toward Shawn. "Take her home, please."

"I'd like to, but I don't exactly have transportation."

"Taralynn's car is parked outside." He digs into his pocket and pulls out a set of keys. "Your parents brought it over a few hours ago." My dad looks back at me. "You still look tired, sweetheart. Go home and get some rest."

Without saying another word, I turn and follow Shawn outside to my car, toward the passenger side. I'm too exhausted, mentally and physically, to drive home. When I get inside, I buckle and recline the seat. I don't want to talk. I want to sleep. I'll deal with him later—much later.

Not being able to help himself, Shawn slips his hand into mine, entwining our fingers. I look down at them for a second. I can't deny that his touch feels good. It feels right, but he shut me out, so I'll shut him out too. I pull my hand out of his and close my eyes without looking at him. I want to shut out the rest of the world too.

THE SOUND of a car door slamming wakes me. When I open my eyes, I see my car is parked in the driveway at Shawn's house, and I'm alone—or so I thought. The passenger side door opens, and when I turn, Shawn is leaning down and reaching for me. I allow him to pull me out of the car, but once I'm on solid ground, I push him back.

He looks just as exhausted as I feel, but that's his problem. If he wants to sleep, he has a bed in the house just like I do. I probably need a shower, but there is no way I can stand long enough to take one. I'll do good getting up the stairs to my bed.

"Tara, please let me—"

"Stop. I got it, Shawn." I walk past him, and he dramatically sighs in frustration.

We both walk inside; I kick off the flip-flops I took from Pam and Bill's last night and leave them on the floor. The house is quiet, but it's still early in the morning. Before I make it to the steps in front of me, I look into the living room and see bodies on the couch, so I detour and head there instead.

Matt is asleep in the recliner with a blanket over him. Mason and Samantha are wrapped up in one another on the couch. If I wasn't so exhausted, I'd raise an eyebrow at this. I suspected they were doing the nasty, but cuddling, I would not have figured.

"Taralynn." My eyes slide back toward my best friend. He throws the blanket off, jumps out of the chair and crushes me to his chest within seconds. "Fucking hell. I've called your phone all night."

"Matt," I whisper, not knowing what to say next.

"Oh, my God. You're here. You're actually here." I look over to see Samantha untangling herself from Mason's limbs. My eyes move past her eyes to his dark brown ones. There is relief swirling in his irises before he stands, steps to me, and yanks me from Matt's embrace.

He hugs me for at least a solid minute without speaking. I can feel his heart beating rapidly inside his chest, but eventually it slows to a normal rhythm as he pulls back. Cupping my face, he says, "Do you have any idea how good is it to see this beautiful face?" Mason pulls my forehead to his lips, where he places a long soft kiss on me.

He steps away, looking at me, then his facial expression changes seconds before his right fist connects with Shawn's jaw. No one, not even Shawn, saw it coming. He goes down hard but lands on his butt and has to throw his hand out to catch himself from bashing his head into the floor.

They look at each other. We all look at each other for a moment.

Shawn's eyes flare right before he jumps to his feet. I slip between them, placing my palms on the center of their chests.

I look at Shawn first.

"Don't."

Then I rotate my head to the other side to look at Mason.

"Feel better?"

"No. He deserves worse." Mason's eyes are locked with Shawn's. Only Mason looks like he wants to murder his best friend. Given what I told him and my friends last night at the club, I have no idea what they know or don't know. I get the feeling they still think Shawn cheated on me like I told them.

"Chill for a minute, Mase. Everyone just freakin' chill out." I drop my arms but continue standing between them. "I've had a long night, and frankly, I'm not up for recounting what happened or what lies were spewed out of people's mouths." I train my eyes on Shawn. "I'm going to get in bed now. I'll leave you to fill them in on the truth, okay?" He nods. "Without anyone else getting hit."

He huffs, his nostrils fairing, but finally he nods his agreement.

Beast is lying on the end of the couch. I step backward and go around Mason to grab the overly large cat. He's fluffy and warm. I need fluffy and warm. With him in my hands, I head up to my bedroom.

When I'm behind closed doors, I dump the cat on my bed and then sit my purse on my dresser. That's when I take in the wreckage from last night. This wasn't a good idea. Retrieving my cell phone, I scoop the cat back up and leave the mess behind.

No way can I sleep in that room with it looking like it had been ransacked. My belongings are scattered everywhere, and broken glass glitters among the mess.

I walk into Shawn's room, leaving mine behind. Why couldn't he destroy his stuff?

No, his things are neat and clean because I cleaned his room yesterday morning.

I set Beast on his bed and sit down on the mattress. With my cell phone in my hand, I turn it back on. Once the screen loads, tons of dings and chimes sing out, telling me I have text messages and voice messages. I ignore them and locate Jared's number. He doesn't answer when I call. I'm not sure if that's because he doesn't want to speak to me or because he's still unconscious.

Next, I call Cole. I need to know Jared is okay. Luckily, he answers on the third ring.

"Speak to me. I need to hear your voice, T," he begs in a tired, throaty tone that doesn't sound like the Cole I know.

"Hey," I whisper. Beast crawls onto my lap, so I start to stroke his fur.

"I need more than a hey, doll. Shit, I thought you were . . ."

"Apparently, you and everyone else."

"Yeah, because I told them it was you. I feel like shit for that, by the way." Remorse pours through the connection, and I can almost picture him on the other side of the call.

"It's okay. I know you wouldn't have done it if you didn't believe it, Cole. Don't beat yourself up over it." I could hear it in his voice. He's torn up over it. "How's Jared?"

"Alive." He pauses for a moment. "He's still unconscious, but that's because the doctors are keeping him that way until they finish running tests."

"Do you know when that will be?" I want to see for myself that he's okay.

"No. But I'm here now, and when I find out I'll let you know." The sound of a door closing causes me to look up, seeing Shawn standing against the door.

"Okay. I have to go. Talk to you soon."

I hang up the phone and lay it on the bed beside me. Beast jumps down and walks toward Shawn. He steps over him as he nears the bed where I'm sitting. Shawn's eyes have this cautious look about them, like he's expecting me to evaporate.

If only I were so lucky.

He falls to his knees, and I watch him slowly break down right in front of me.

"I don't know what to say, Tara, and I don't know what not to say. I don't want to push you to talk to me and end up pushing you away, but I also don't want to sit back and give you space and have the same thing happen. I love you, and I want to fix us." He stretches his arms out on the mattress, pushing them along my sides as his head falls into my lap.

I run my hand through his hair. The silky strands are soft as I glide my fingers back and forth. I'd be lying if I said I didn't want him to experience some of the hurt he caused me, but I can also look at him and see he may have experienced something far worse.

If I'd thought for only a minute that he was gone and I'd never see him again, I can't begin to imagine the hurt that I would have been feeling. Losing my brother was hard enough. Losing the man I'm in love with . . . I don't want to even go there in my head.

I can't just forgive him either, at least not in this moment. But I also know that making him pay by distancing myself from him will hurt me the same as it'll hurt him. I don't want any more pain. I want the wounds to start healing. How can I begin that if I'm keeping us in limbo, or even worse, let him think we're over?

"I want that more than you know, but fixing us can't happen overnight. I have to be able to trust you again. I want to trust you again. How do I know you won't do it again when you so easily threw us down the drain, Shawn?"

"I can't promise I won't make mistakes, Tara. I know I will, but there's no way in Hell I'd put us through this again." My heart believes him, but my head tells me to take this slow. "Do you still love me?"

"You aren't a switch. I can't just turn you off when I want to. Yes, I love you. That's real, and it's not going away." I take a big breath. "We can't fix what was broken, but I'd be willing to take things slow and start over."

His shoulders sag in relief.

"Okay. I can work with that, baby."

"Then can we go to sleep, please?"

"Yeah, I just need to call Natalie and have all my appointments canceled. I couldn't go in today if I wanted to. I'm in no condition to work."

EPILOGUE - PART 1
TARALYNN

8 MONTHS LATER

A new year. A new beginning. But when so much has happened, when your life, your heart, and your mind have all been through a blender, how do you mend them?

One day at a time, that is how. You wake up each morning and tell yourself you've got this. When you want something, you go for it until you've exhausted every possibility of trying to obtain it. If you don't end up with it, then it wasn't meant to be yours.

That's become my life's motto.

Shawn and I have worked hard to get to where we are today. We aren't perfect, but I don't expect us to ever meet perfection. Relationships are hard work, but what we have is beautiful. It took him months to earn my trust, but he did. I know he's still waiting for the other shoe to drop, though, and that scares me—it's like he doesn't trust himself. He's going to mess up. I'm going to mess up. But if we do this together and have each other's back, I know we'll be fine. He has to believe that somewhere inside himself first.

My relationship with my dad has taken a one-eighty, and for

that, I'm happy. I hate that he's going through a nasty divorce with Katherine, but you wouldn't know that talking to him. He's happy now too. He moved out of the house I grew up in. That saddens me a little because I have so many memories of Trent there that I'll never get to see again. He's living in a high-class apartment in downtown Tupelo, close to his office. He seems to like it. We have lunch once a week.

Through my dad and Pam, I'm learning a lot about my real mom. I get sad when I think about her, though. I hate that she was so weak that she did that to herself. Pam loved her. Every time she talks about my mom, I can tell it in her voice, and I know she misses her. It was strange at first when I realized how much I looked like her. I've seen more pictures, and I look a lot like her.

I haven't forgiven my dad completely for keeping something that huge from me, but I'm getting there. I know I will forgive and forget. I have to, if I want to move past it—and I do.

I continue to worry about Jared. He woke up a few days after his motorcycle accident. Physically, he wasn't injured too badly and only stayed in the hospital a few days after waking. He didn't attend our college graduation a few weeks later, and no one, not even Cole, has seen him in months. I think the fact that the woman involved in the wreck died is hitting him hard. I wish he would talk to someone about it and deal with the tragedy. I've tried calling him, but last month his number was disconnected.

Kylie ended up moving to Orlando much sooner than she originally planned. She submitted a letter to the director of the residency programs, telling him about her situation and asking to transfer. She was approved, and Mason tells me she's doing okay. I'm not sure if I buy that. Kylie won't talk to anyone about my brother at all. She's closed herself off to it, and that can't be good. Not only that, but there is a noticeable change in her. She used to be so outgoing, an extrovert, a beautiful social butterfly, but now she might as well be the opposite of her former self.

Shane did the same thing, but he didn't transfer to Florida.

Instead, he was able to transfer to a hospital in Memphis, where he'll finish out his last year of residency before starting his fellowship in Pediatric Cardiology. He moved to Tennessee within a few weeks of Kylie moving to Florida. All was great until . . .

"With that faraway look you have going on, I take it Matt finally told you."

I look up to see my boyfriend standing just inside the door to our bedroom, staring at me. From the looks of it, I'd say he has just returned from a vigorous workout at the gym. Shawn is sweaty from head to toe. Deliciously so, and damn if it isn't making me smile.

I didn't hear him walk in, much less close the door and remove his clothes. I glance in the direction of his discarded clothes and then back toward Shawn before raising an eyebrow. He knows damn well I can't stand any type of mess. Clothes not put in their proper place might as well equal chaos in my world.

"I hope you're planning on picking that up." He smirks as he saunters my way where I sit on the edge of our bed. Well, it's really his bed. When we decided to take the leap and combine rooms, Shawn had to have his Tempur-Pedic, saying it is like sleeping on a cloud in heaven. I couldn't disagree with him on that, so mine got moved into his old room.

He dips in front of me to plant a salty kiss on my lips. My eyes flutter closed, as they always do when his mouth is pressed against any part of my body. I can't help it; it's a reflex. Shawn's touch is my own piece of heaven, and I will savor every second I'm given with him. He grabs my boobs, but I swat his pawing hand away from my breasts. Shawn is a freakin' groper and a half. In other words, he's a boob man, not that I complain a lot. It pays off to my benefit more often than not, but I suddenly recall what he said a few minutes ago.

"What did you mean when you said Matt finally told me? Told me what?"

His eyes grow round, like he's been caught doing something he shouldn't have.

"Umm, nothing. Going to shower, babe."

"I don't think so." I grasp him by his biceps, wrapping my fingers around tightly, telling him he isn't going anywhere just yet. "Spill it, Braden."

"Shit." He pulls backward causing me to lose my grip. "You're going to have to ask him that."

"So he's keeping something from me, you know what it is, and won't tell me? Am I hearing you correctly?"

"Don't get pissed at me. It's not my place to tell you. It's his. It's ticking me off that the motherfucker hasn't grown the balls to spit it out yet. Why don't you do both of yourselves a favor and go downstairs and make him spill the beans?"

"I think I will. You shower—and hurry it up, because I don't plan on wasting a Saturday that you don't have to go into work." Shawn's lips turn up into a self-assured smirk.

"Are you trying to tell me my girl needs some of this dick?" He grabs his junk that's practically eye level with me. "I thought I gave you enough of it last night to sustain you."

I don't think I'll ever get enough sex to sate my need for the man standing in front of me. I don't dare speak that, though. Shawn doesn't need any more arrogance in that department.

"Just go shower already." I stand. Apparently my best friend has been keeping something from me, and I aim to find out what that something is. Matt and I have finally fallen back into the friendship we had in high school, so it's bothering me to know he's not telling me something.

Shawn turns, walking toward the master bath without another word. I exit the room seconds later.

After I make it down the stairs, I hear conversation coming from the living room. I start there, finding Matt and Mason yelling at the TV screen. Rolling my head, I see it's a college football game. Since it's January, it has to be a recording of a game that has already aired. Knowing they can pause and rewind, I walk over to them and stand directly in front of the television, demanding their attention. My eyes lock on Matt.

"What secret are you keeping from me?"

"What?" Matt's eyes practically bug out as he turns to look at me. "Shawn fucking told you, didn't he?" His shock turns to anger.

"He let it slip, thinking you'd already told me. But he didn't actually tell me what you're hiding from me." When he doesn't speak, I huff out a breath of air in frustration. "Well?"

"I was offered a job." He sits against the sofa, leaning his head back. This isn't making a bit of sense. This's great news. Matt's been freelancing editing jobs since we graduated.

"So what gives? Why are you keeping that from me? This is awesome, Matt! Don't you know I'd be happy for you? Ecstatic, even."

"It's in California."

Say what? Okay, I don't mean to, but I know my happy face just fell flat on the floor, and he knows it too.

"This is why I haven't told you. I didn't know how to tell you I'm leaving Mississippi."

"So you accepted the offer, then?"

"Yes. It's Lockhart Publishing. I couldn't turn it down, Taralynn."

Shit. Even I know that's an amazing opportunity. "So when do you leave? Oh, my God! You're moving away from me." Yes, as I asked him the question, it hit me like a freight train. He's leaving, and I won't be able to drive over when I want my Matty time.

"Nine days."

"What?! You can't be serious. They only gave you a little over a week to pack and move across the country?" This is too soon. He can't leave. I want to be selfish and tell him he can continue to freelance and do great. I won't, though. Fact is, I'm not selfish like that. No matter how much I want to stomp my feet and be.

"They gave me forty-five days, actually." I'm going to kill him. The bastard can leave tomorrow.

"You've known for—" I don't get to finish my sentence because there is a knock on the front door. Matt is saved by the knock, so to speak, because I was seconds away from smacking him a few times. Instead, I pivot and walk the short distance from the living room to the front door in the foyer.

When I open it, a very pregnant brunette is standing in front of me.

"Can I help you?" I ask politely, even though moments ago I was feeling anything but polite.

"Is Shawn home?" Something about the way she says his name has an alarm going off inside my head. I don't like her. I've only ever experienced an instant feeling like this once, with one person, and that was Holly. "His truck is in the driveway, so I figured he was home." She smiles a little, but it looks forced.

"He is," I tell her. "He's in the shower at the moment. Would you like to come inside and wait for him?"

"Yes, please." Her reply is too excited, but I take a step back, opening the door fully open to allow her to enter.

"You can go through that entrance and wait." I point to the living room where Matt and Mason are. I can see their faces from where I'm standing. They both look alarmed too. "He should be down shortly."

I close the door and follow her, stopping at the entrance. I prop my body against the frame as she walks to the couch and takes a seat on the opposite side of Mason.

"Who are you?" It's Mason that asks her the question. He's never one to wait for answers. If he wants to know something, he asks.

"Tiffany." Sounds like a stripper name if you ask me.

That was so judgmental and not like me at all. Still, there is a vibe I'm getting from this woman that I don't like.

"How do you know Shawn?" Again, Mason with his twenty questions. I hope she's prepared to talk until Shawn makes an appearance. Mason doesn't shut up.

368   N. E. HENDERSON

"We met a few months back. I work at Vivid Theatre." Stripper she is then. Maybe I wasn't so judgmental after all since I called it straight out. That doesn't explain what she wants with my man. Yes, my man! Shawn just became a possession to me. He's mine. I'm his. We've been through a lot of crap to get to where we are.

"And you're here to see him why?" Mason's tone turns hard. He's protective of me. Loyal to Shawn, no doubt, but I know exactly where I fit in Mason's heart.

"Well, I should really tell him, but it's going to get out eventually." She turns to look me directly in the eyes. "I'm carrying his baby. He should know, after all, and I want my baby's father in his life." Oh, if this bitch weren't pregnant, I would have jumped on top of her.

I don't react, though. The cat claws stay sheathed. For now. She obviously wanted a reaction out of me. That's the reason she looked at me the way she did.

"I don't know who the fuck you think you are, but that baby isn't his." I'd like to say it was me that made that blunt statement, but it wasn't. Again, it was Mason taking up for his best friend, his brother from another mother, so to speak.

"I have no reason to lie, and I'm very willing to do a paternity test to prove he is." Again the cunt turns to direct her words at me. Shawn's language has been having more of an effect on me lately than I'd like to admit. *The "c" word, Taralynn?* At least I didn't verbalize it. Thinking it is bad enough.

"Taralynn." Mason says my name with caution. I still haven't spoken a word since she sat down, and I don't intend to. I know exactly what I need to do, and I'm not about to waste time because Shawn is liable to make an appearance at any second.

I turn away from my two friends and the trash I let walk into my home minutes ago, grab my keys hanging next to the door and then I walk out.

"Taralynn, wait," is the last thing I hear from Matt before the door shuts, and I race to my car with a plan forming in my mind.

EPILOGUE - PART 2

SHAWN

When I come out of the bathroom, I'm hoping Tara will be naked in our bed, but that dream dies when I see she isn't even in the room. The bed is perfectly made the same way it was fifteen minutes ago.

I quickly throw on a pair of jeans, one of my company T-shirts I once again had redesigned recently, and a pair of socks, followed by my boots. If she wanted to be sexed, she should have gotten her sweet, beautiful ass back up here. Too bad for her. Now she will have to wait, because I plan on having a few hours of fun outside of the house with my friends today.

Matt is leaving in less than two weeks. Tara is going to need a distraction because my woman deals with shit too much as it is, so the four of us are going to play disc golf at a local park. It'll be fun. We haven't played in forever, and it'll give her and Matt some time together for memories to pile up.

It's not a bad thing that he'll be based in Los Angeles. It'll give us more reasons to make trips out west. Chance and I have become pretty good friends in the past year since I became the owner of my own tattoo studio. He's offered a lot of great advice. The place has done a one-eighty in a short time.

I hate that Tara isn't there daily anymore, but Natalie was a good hire. She keeps everyone in line and our schedules full. She filled our vacancies. We now have seven full-time artists in the studio. She hired a piercer who is equally as talented as he is a tattoo artist. His name is Danny. He and his wife, Carly, moved here a few months ago. Carly is also a tattoo artist, and her talent is breathtaking. Tara still does payroll and all the accounting for the business, but she mainly does it from home since Natalie took over as the manager a few months ago.

I head out of the bedroom door and jog down the stairs, landing in the foyer in seconds. I'm immediately alarmed when I hear Mason's voice booming. He's shouting.

"You're a lying bitch is what you are." Mason is angry, that much is clear. It takes a lot to set him off.

"What's going on?" Three bodies turn to face me. Matt is gripping Mason by the arm. Mason, whose face is blazing, has his fist balled at his sides. And then there is a chick that doesn't look the least bit familiar. Then again, my motto hasn't exactly changed where they're concerned. Women are still a dime a dozen.

What has changed is me, because of Tara. She's the one that's special. The one that has and will always have my attention captured. No other will ever hold a candle to my girl, the love of my life. My dumb ass wasted so much time fighting my feelings for her. I understand why, but I also know deep down they aren't logical. I keep trying to tell myself that every day. Maybe one of these days, I'll start to believe it.

Speaking of Tara, I don't see her, but I can't worry about that now. Mason looks like he wants to rip this woman apart.

"This bitch came in here saying she's pregnant with your kid."

It takes me at least ten full seconds to comprehend what he said. I look down to see the woman is indeed toting a calf, but I can guaran-fucking-tee you it isn't mine. I haven't slept with another woman since the night I first hooked up with Tara. I still have a hard time believing she and I have been together for a year. I don't count all that other bullshit when we weren't officially dating or when I had a short circuit in my brain last year and damn near cost us our future.

Tara is the only woman I want to be with. I don't miss the one-night stands. Those days are over, and I'm not the least bit sorry to see them go. No more does a quick fuck get me the release I seek. If I'm honest with myself, even then, it wasn't satisfying; it took shutting my eyes and picturing the woman I really wanted in order to get off.

"I don't know who the hell you are." I look her in the eyes, training mine on her hard. It doesn't take but a second or two for her smug smile to disappear and be replaced with what looks like a bit of fear. "I've never laid eyes on you, much less touched or fucked you."

"Look—" Her voice is drawn out and maybe even shaky, but I don't give her an inch, nor do I let her get another word out of her lying mouth.

"You came into my house. Lied to my friends. What the fuck did you hope to accomp—" I stop mid-sentence.

Tara.

Her not being here suddenly has my chest tightening like there's a rope squeezing my heart. Where is she? She didn't know what I had planned, but she was well aware the only reason I took today off was so we could spend time together.

I turn to look at my friends.

"Where's Tara?" I ask, fearing the worst. Did this bitch get to her, spewing her lies to my girl, and if so, did Tara believe her? I won't lose her again. I can't go through that again. Eight months ago, I almost lost her for good. I was stupid for doubting I was what she wanted and needed.

"She took off." Matt confirms my thoughts.

"And you both let her leave?" She can't possibly think I'd cheat on her. There is nothing or no one worth losing the person I can't live without over.

I turn back toward the nuisance taking up oxygen in my living room. "Get the fuck out of my house. Make sure I never see you again." When she doesn't make any attempt to leave, I force my point by taking a large step closer to her. "If I need to remove you from my house, don't think I won't."

I'll never touch this woman, but she doesn't know that. I'm okay with using my large build to my advantage.

"Whatever." She walks around me, heading for the front door. Good. The sooner she's out of my sight, the sooner I can focus on finding Tara and fixing this mess. "I've completed the task I was hired to do anyway."

"What does that mean?" It's Mason who demands an answer. Normally I'd care, but I don't know where my girlfriend is or what's going through her head. My priority is Tara.

The cunt turns back around to face us before walking out the door. "Seems your friend there"—she points her finger at me—"pissed off the wrong woman. She did tell me to relay a message. Something about regrets being such a bitch."

Holly Torres.

"Elaborate." Mason's tone is furious, as though it were him this woman came in and shelled out lies about.

"A few weeks ago, an uppity blonde, looking more like white trash than even me, came into the club with her bitch of a friend. Being this far along, I can't dance, so I was their server. I don't remember the blonde's name. Mandy. I do remember she called her dark-haired friend that, though. They offered me cash, a grand, to pay your girlfriend a visit and convince her I got knocked up by you, handsome."

By the mention of a club and dancing, I don't think it's a stretch to say this chick is or used to be a stripper.

Perfect.

Fucking perfect.

My girlfriend is off somewhere, thinking God knows what.

Probably that I haven't changed. That I'm still the same man that used to fuck anything easy in a skirt.

I'm not that man anymore.

I hate that I ever was that person.

I've got to find her.

"Get out of my house." Without giving another ounce of my time to her, I pull out my cell phone from the pocket of my jeans. Finding Tara won't be hard as long as her cell phone isn't shut off.

Unlocking my screen, I scroll until I find the app that will show me her location. This isn't stalking or creepy, I assure you. Tara has the same capabilities as I do. We both know each other's phone ID and password.

Within seconds, the GPS within the app locates her, giving a small amount of relief to my chest.

I recognize the location instantly. She's at the tattoo studio. Why, I don't know, but I'm not sticking around, and I don't call her either. I need to see her face to face. A part of me is afraid that if I call, she won't answer.

I grab my keys, and I'm out the door. My friends don't stop me, and I don't ask them to come with.

Typically, the drive to work takes close to fifteen minutes. I make it to Wicked Ink in less than ten. Her car is parked outside. That's good, I hope. I pull the truck to an abrupt stop, slamming the gear into park before hopping out and running inside.

I won't let anyone cost us our happiness. I fought tooth and nail to get her back. It didn't happen overnight. Tara didn't let me back in that easily. And not all the way until recently.

When I showed up at Jacob and Katherine's house, I got her to listen to me, and was lucky she believed me. But that didn't get us back together. I had to work my ass off to get back into her good graces, to get back to her trusting me again. She was hesitant with us for months. We've only recently gotten back to the relaxed easiness we had before I messed up.

I will not let another lie ruin us. We're more than lies, and we're damn sure stronger than them.

When I walk in, I scan the room, looking for her. Everyone turns, and I notice they are eyeing me strangely.

Shit, that can't be good.

Finally, I spot her, but when my eyes land on her, I suck in air in a long pull.

No.

She's lying on Adam's table, on her stomach with her hair pulled up, baring the back of her neck. That tells me exactly what's going on. Knowing she's letting someone else ink her has a tightness constricting around my heart that hurts like a motherfucker.

I don't want her being tattooed by anyone but me.

This isn't making sense, but I speak before I realize words are coming out of my mouth. "Stop, Adam. Get your hands off her." My words boom across the large room.

He complies. His hands shoot into the air in a surrender motion as he stands up, followed by his feet retreating backward. That's when I notice he didn't have a tattoo gun in his hands. I've either gotten here just in time or just too late.

I stalk in their direction as Tara takes a sitting position. Her face is flustered, but she hasn't been crying. She looks angry. Her eyes are trained on me, but I'm lost. I don't know what to say or do. Up until this point, my goal was getting to her. I never thought about what I'd say when I found her.

"Tara, baby . . . what . . . no." My words are soft and broken, not even making a complete sentence. I come to stand in front of her.

"Shawn." She says my name, but I feel numb. My eyes shut and then snap back open. I'm going to kill Adam.

"Whoa, man." He must realize my intent when I open my lids and stare directly at him. "Look, dude—" I cut him off.

"The best thing you can do right now is not breathe in my direction. What the fuck, Adam?"

"Shawn." Tara calls out my name again, but with more bite. I look back at her as she hops off the table. "Come with me." When I don't move, she grabs my arm and yanks on me to follow her. I still don't budge. "Now!"

I can murder him later.

I follow Tara. Her hair hangs down her back, covering what I do not want to look at. Is this her way of getting back at me for something I didn't even do? I can't see another man's work on her body. I can't.

When we walk inside, I close the door. Tara walks a little further inside but doesn't make any moves to turn around to face me.

"Tara, I didn't sleep with that woman. That kid isn't—"

"Stop, Shawn." No, I can't. I have to make her believe me once again.

"No, you have to believe that I wouldn't screw this up again and I wouldn't do that to you." I wouldn't. She's everything I've ever wanted, and every day I learn she's even more than I knew I needed.

"Fine! You won't shut up and listen to me, then look for yourself." She lifts her hair, gathering the strands into a makeshift ponytail and moving them away from her neck. I don't want to look, but she wants me to see it, so I focus my eyes on that spot.

I step closer to get a better look. That's when I see it isn't yet a tattoo. The ink on her neck is from a transfer. It's not permanent.

Now that that fact has sunk in, I'm breathing a little easier. That's when I take in the design, only to lose the breath I just took. Am I seeing this correctly?

"Your silence is killing me, Shawn."

I can't speak. I step another foot closer until I'm directly behind Tara, my eyes inches away from what may be the most beautiful thing I've ever seen. Not just that, but damn, seeing my name on her skin is turning me on.

The design is mine. I drew it a few weeks ago. It's an infinity symbol in black ink, and its design has the same elements as the paint splashes across my back. The writing wasn't part of the original work. Inside the symbol is my name: Shawn is edged in on the left and Braden on the right. The words around the symbol read, My forever begins with him and will continue, never ending.

"You're still not saying anything."

"Is that supposed to be paint or blood dripping from my name?" Inside the infinity symbol, there are drops of what looks more like blood dripping than paint.

She releases her hair. The strands fall, covering the place where she will soon have my name permanently inked on her body. She wants my name on her. That's fucking unreal.

She turns, facing me.

"Blood. Cool, right?" Her smile warms my insides. "I stole the idea from Eve." I don't know what that means, and right now, I don't care.

"Does this mean we're okay?" Surely she wouldn't be doing this if she believed the stripper.

"Shawn, there could always be people waiting to tear us apart. Others who, for whatever reason, don't want to see us happy. They don't matter, and they can't bring down something as solid as we have. Trust this. Trust me, and trust yourself. We can do this, be us, and be together, but we can only do it if we are in it together with all we have inside us. No one has the power to break us except us." She pauses, bringing her lips up to reach mine. She presses against me lightly before pulling back. "Are you with me?"

Trust myself, she says.

Easier said than done, but what choice do I have? I love her. I want this. I want her and I want there to always be an 'us.'

"Yeah, Tara, I'm with you, baby. Forever." I designed that

infinity symbol with her in mind. I had planned on inking it on myself.

"Then marry me."

My body goes solid. "I'm sorry. What was that?"

"I'm done, Shawn. I'm done being that girl who doesn't speak up, who doesn't go after or fight for what she wants. I want you, and I want us, forever. If you aren't in this with me, if you think there will ever come a time when you'll tire of me, then end us now." She pauses, taking a big breath. Her words are full of confidence, but I can still see the small amount of self-doubt she still carries. She'll get there, though, just like I will. We'll get there together. "End us now, or go all in and marry me."

"Shouldn't I be the one proposing?"

"Were you going to ask me today?" She arches an eyebrow.

"No."

"Well, I have, and now I'd like an answer."

"Yes, Tara, I'll marry you." I pull her into my body, needing to be as close to her as possible. I wrap my arms around her back and lower my head to kiss her.

A damn girl asked me to marry her.

Never in my wildest dreams would I have pictured that happening. This is perfect, though. This is our perfect and I wouldn't trade it for the world. Tara is my perfect and my forever.

Thank you for reading.

I hope you enjoyed the story. You'll get more of Shawn and Tara in MORE THAN MEMORIES when you read Shane and Whitney's story—which is out now.

ALSO BY N. E. HENDERSON

SILENT SERIES:

Nick and Shannon's Duet

SILENT NO MORE

SILENT GUILT

MORE THAN SERIES:

Can be read as a standalone but not recommended

MORE THAN LIES

MORE THAN MEMORIES

DIRTY JUSTICE TRILOGY:

DIRTY BLUE

DIRTY WAR

DIRTY SIN

THE NEW AMERICAN MAFIA:

Must be read in order for the complete story

BAD PRINCESS

DARK PRINCE

DEVIANT KNIGHT

STANDALONE BOOKS:

HAVE MERCY

ACKNOWLEDGMENTS

Readers, thank you so much for reading my stories. Without you, I wouldn't be able to do something I enjoy so much. I love meeting and hearing from all you and I love reading your honest reviews. Thank you.

Mo, thank you for re-editing and helping to make this book what it is now and ready for audio.

Charisse, you pushed and pushed me some more. I'm pretty sure at one point you even threatened me. THANK YOU. I'd probably still be sitting at 15k in words if it weren't for you. I'm so glad we met and became such great friends. My days aren't complete without our texts.

Tee Tate, thank you for all the tattoo world insight. I appreciate the help and advice.

Selena, thank you so much for giving me advice on one of the tattoo scenes.

Bloggers, thank you for all that you do everyday. Without you, a lot of writers wouldn't be able to reach the readers they do. Thank you.

ABOUT THE AUTHOR

N. E. Henderson is the author of sexy, contemporary romance. When she isn't writing, you can find her reading or in her Maverick, playing in the dirt. This is Nancy's third book.

This is Nancy's third book.

For more information:
www.nehenderson.com
nancy@nehenderson.com
tiktok.com/@authornehenderson
instagram.com/nehenderson
facebook.com/authornehenderson

Made in the USA
Las Vegas, NV
31 December 2022

64528467R00226